Elixir

Cancer ~~Can~~ Has Been Beaten

A conspiracy will cease to exist when everyone knows the secret...but letting it out can be murder

PATRICK A. PIPOLI

ELIXIR

For further information see:

www.elixirmakesUwonder.com

ISBN 978-0-615-20516-8

This Book is dedicated to my Mom.

She has always been sure that I could move mountains. Well I can't, but she's given me the confidence to try my best.

Acknowledgements

This page generally means very little to anyone except those whose names appear on it. But it's a necessary page none-the-less. A project such as this usually involves many wonderful, supportive, and patient friends and family, without whose constant encouragement and support, the author would seldom reach his full potential of story telling. I would guess in many cases, the words might never be put to paper. I would like to acknowledge those people and briefly mention their part in helping this writer materialize a story, which has rolled around in my head for over 23 years.

First and foremost I must thank my family who listened patiently as I rambled off page after page of writing and edits, many times hearing a certain paragraph over and over again until I had it just right. Thanks to my lovely wife Concetta, my intuitive and eloquent daughter Vanessa and my wonderful son David, who was instrumental in helping me, create the book cover for Elixir. My Mom, who constantly encouraged me to just keep going even when I thought there was nothing left. She filled me with the confidence to write another page. Our foster son, A.J., who came to us near the end of the project, but shared my enthusiasm as if he were here during the entire journey.

Our dear and special friends, Kirk and Deborah Tedrow, who over dinner two years ago, first heard of my aspiration to write this book. They were a tremendous source of encouragement and were solely responsible for me undertaking Elixir in the first place.

Warren, who read the first eleven pages, confirming that I had a great story to tell and a unique way of telling it. Helle, who listened patiently as I reached and achieved each milestone.

Tina read every page as it was being written, many days re-reading what I'd written just the day before and sharing with me her valued opinion.

I would like to mention my wonderful editor from Two Brothers Press, Ronald L. Donaghe. With hundreds of editors on the Internet I somehow managed to find the most caring, honest, and genuinely sincere Company and individual my first time through.

Thank you Ron, Lewis, and the entire staff from Two Brothers Press.

Geri Taeckens is a gifted lady, who without the advantage of sight saw more than I did while editing my work with the persistent goal of helping me make my project better.

Gerri and Jane, who listened as I shared what was next, day after day after day.

Chris Gerwing, who unwittingly helped me create one of my main characters, and Frank Kowalski, who introduced me to some basic story telling techniques.

The many friends who helped with everything from proof reading, to spreading the word about my project.

Lastly, Cameron McKenzie, self-proclaimed greatest guy in the world, who helped me put the finishing touches on this book and guided me to market. Thank you Cameron, for your kindness and generosity.

These people collectively and individually helped me to craft this novel and to each and every one I say thank you.

Patrick A. Pipoli

To Dale/Maggy
So happy we
still see you two!
Thanks for the
support, enjoy!
Patrick A. Pipoli

Prologue

As the doors slowly opened, his pupils instinctively dilated to adjust to the dimly lit car park. He stepped out of the elevator into the vacant parking garage. It was full of shadows. The only sound this late were his footfalls ricocheting between the concrete floor and the low-slung ceiling. He walked into an empty section toward his isolated car. Rising up out of the floor every thirty feet were reinforced concrete columns. Collectively, they supported the next level of the circular high-rise parking lot. Passing the last of the large pillars, he unconsciously jammed a hand into his pocket, feeling for the car keys.

They were almost within his grasp when a powerful arm encircled his neck from behind. At the same time, an equally crushing hand clamped a soft damp cloth over his nose and mouth. Choking, gasping for air, he could smell the reeking chemical fumes as he was practically lifted off his feet. He slowly sank into a deep, unwilling slumber.

He awoke dazed and afraid. As the fog slipped away, confusion flooded in. *What...what's going on here, where am I...Jesus, where am I?* He blinked several times to clear his vision. Suddenly he grasped the shocking reality. He was blindfolded. He sat shivering, bound to a chair. A thin film of sweat sheathed his naked torso and legs. The pounding in his head, from what he assumed must be chloroform, kept pace with his racing heart.

In the dark silence, even the smallest of sounds echoed through the damp, stale air. His clouded mind raced to discern which noises around him were those born of fear and which were real.

A dank musty smell assaulted his nostrils. He heard a distinctive dripping sound. Something was scurrying in the dark.

He felt the sting of the salty sweat as it slowly trickled down his bare arms. His chafed wrists burned where zip-ties cut into his flesh. He twisted, struggling for freedom. Realizing his ankles were securely bound to the chair, he knew his attempts to escape were futile. Even so, he struggled more.

He understood that he'd been abducted and it didn't make any sense. *This has to be a mistake*, he thought. *Somebody's making a terrible mistake!*

"You've got the wrong guy," he said aloud into the darkness. "Whoever you are, you've snatched the wrong guy." He had no idea where he was or how long he'd been in this place. "*Why is this happening to me? I'm sorry, I don't know what I did, but whatever it is, I'm SORRRRRYYY!*

LET ME OUT OF HERE! HELLO, IS ANYBODY HERE? HELP, HEEEELLLLPPP!" he shouted into the darkness. Startled by a new sound, he cried out again, "Is somebody here? Please ANSWER ME!"

Ting…Ting…Ting.

Ting…Ting…Ting.

"What's that noise? What are you doing? ANSWER ME, PLEASE!"

His mind struggled to recognize what it was. The sound was like the slow hum of a tuning fork after a quick snap against a metal surface. Under different circumstances, it would have been nearly melodic.

"Talk to me, PLEASE. There's been a horrible mistake, a VERY BIG MISTAKE." Silence. Then louder, more urgent than before, the eerie single note played again TING…TING…TING.

Then he heard something else, something familiar. So recognizable in fact, that he could *feel* the hair rising on the back of his neck. His subconscious mind tried to deny it. His conscious mind could not. The sound he heard was breathing. Acidic bile rose in his throat, as he fully comprehended the circumstance. The fiend orchestrating his abduction was so close, so very close, that he could hear him breathing. Logic had abandoned him as irrepressible fear rolled in like a flash flood, dominating his senses. Something cold touched his cheek. He pulled back as far as his constraints would allow.

"WHAT, WHATS THAT? WHAT ARE YOU DOING?" he screamed out in anguish. No response came from his silent, unseen captor.

The cold thing slowly traced a line from the edge of the blindfold down to his unshaven chin with a light, even pressure. Terrified, he recoiled a few more inches. The object moved with him. He tried desperately to identify the trickle that traveled steadily down his face. Almost instantly his panic-stricken mind unraveled the puzzle and his body jerked involuntarily. His trembling lips pulled back, contorting his face into a twisted mask as he emitted a ghastly, savage cry. The blood, converging with tears and mucus, formed the first of many droplets. The cool itch ended at his chin. They fell soundlessly onto his briefs.

He felt no pain, yet knew he'd been cut. Horrified he continued to jerk and shake as his bladder released its contents. The undeniable stench of fear rose from the amber colored piss as it flowed hot, soaking his underwear and running down his bare legs.

The shadows awakened as the silhouette stirred. Dark pitiless eyes bore down on the quivering man. The dim light glinted off the razor sharp knife. A living nightmare had just begun.

Part One

Chapter 1

Dr. Edwards can feel himself shuffle toward the podium. The enormous auditorium is pitch black except for the intense spotlights that nearly blind him. He raises his arm to block out the powerful light. Through splayed fingers, he sees hundreds of faceless people sitting in the audience. Robotically they slap their hands together. The applause, deafening.

His short, slender frame is cloaked in a ridiculously oversized suit. Confused, he looks down to see his fingers barely poking out of the sleeves. Stopping, he positions himself behind the mike, staring blankly at it. The enthusiastic clapping is replaced with dead silence. Suddenly a woman's voice startles him out of his trance.

"Blake Edwards, what a good boy you are Blakey. I'm so proud of you!"

Squinting out the bright light, he glances in the direction of the soothing voice. There, standing right next to him is his mother, smiling warmly. Bewildered, he gapes open-mouthed. Momentarily he is lost. Haltingly he speaks the words.

"Mom...Mummy? Is it really you?" he said doubtfully.

His mother died two days after his 40th birthday. That was eight years ago. He reaches out to embrace her. Like a fog, she fades as his hands swipe the empty air. Suddenly the bright lights grow fainter. His world is now black. He tries to catch his breath, but the wind in his face is too powerful.

'I can't breathe. I can't see, I CAN'T BREATHE!' His mind screams. Then he hears them. The screams aren't just in his head, they're everywhere. People are screaming. Someone beside him is shrieking. Slowly he peels his eyes open. There it is. He sees the steel tracks of the roller coaster being consumed in front of him. He looks down; his hands, tightly wrapped around the chrome bar are white-knuckled. Again, the squealing comes from every direction, then the laughter as the roller coaster flies toward the bottom of the hill, his body pressed into the seat.

Looking to his right he sees Francine, her lips peeled back, exposing her white, even teeth. She laughs as the car descends, banking, turning, steadily slowing as the magnetic brakes are applied.

As they lose speed, he hears the fluttering sounds before he sees the demon thing. The caped outline surrounds an abyss of blackness inside the shrouded hood. It's here, here again. Material flapping like wings, tattered from its many flights, the demon swoops down. It rips Francine from the car. As quickly as it appeared, it is gone, vanishing into the night.

"FRANCINE...FRANNNNNYYY!"

He blinks and he's in a room. His hands once again are white-knuckled, this time wrapped around the chrome bar of a bed rail. Francine lies in a hospital bed, her full, smiling face, drawn, falls into itself. The skin is tautly stretched over her cheekbones. A few thin tuffs of transparent white hair jut from her head. Tubes grow out of her like tentacles.

"Help me, BLAKE. HELP ME PLEASE!" she cries.

His eyes drop. He sees past the blanket, past the hospital gown. The demon is there, within her. It eats away at her insides, slowly looking up. Faceless, it feasts on her, taunting him. As she wails, it continues to devour her, ravenous, frenzied. He reaches inside of her, groping wildly at the demon. He's got it, it slips away, finding another secret place within her. It feeds voraciously. Blake's mouth opens as he tries to shriek. No sound comes.

*****

He sits bolt upright. The light flooding into his bedroom causes a momentary affront to his sensitive eyes, blinding him. He fumbles for his glasses on the nightstand. The blurred vision clears as he slips them on.

His rapid breathing is labored as he looks wildly around the sparsely furnished bedroom. Spotting his highboy and the red, embroidered curtains, his reality is established, his location confirmed. He takes a quick moment to shake the nightmare. This one was bad, but it wasn't the worst of them. They came, never the same, but always the same.

Blake looked at the bedside clock. Without thinking, his feet hit the floor and moved him toward the shower.

Dammit, I'm going to be late.

Earlier that morning, as Blake slept, still caught in the nightmare, another conflict ensued. The sun battled for control of the day. Eventually, the wind slowly pushed the clouds away as the beaming rays of light emerged victorious. It was to be a sunny spring day in Dallas, Texas.

Blake stepped out of the shower. Directly in front of him was an emaciated figure glancing back at him from the mirror, replicating his every move. He looked closer at his reflection, shaking his head. He toweled off a spot in the middle of the mirror as the condensation trickled down the glass. He was disturbed by his appearance. *Got to take better care of myself, start eating more,* he thought. *Getting too damn scrawny.*

He continued drying off his small, five-foot, six-inch frame. His ribs strained against the taut skin covering them. Stepping on the scale, he reached for his thick, black-framed glasses to see where the numbers would stop today. The dial barely made it to 139 and then froze. With a sigh, he stepped off.

'I was a 141 just a few days ago,' he thought. *'Better grab a bagel on the way into the lab.'*

Blake carelessly dropped the towel on the floor, stepping over several others as he made his way back to the bedroom. Entering, his eyes fix on the bedside clock just as the minute indicator flips to 7:47 A.M.

Pulling up his loose-fitting trousers, he cinched the belt at the last available hole. His morning ritual continued as he ran a brush through his hair. He noticed the gray that had started at his temples a few months before and was now invading the rest of his head. *Get a haircut soon...when I have time*, he thought casually. He never had time, never made time for such things.

While buttoning his wrinkled shirt, he entered the kitchen. Like most things that had fallen out of date, in its day it was considered the ultimate in modern décor. A few years before her death, Francine had remodeled the kitchen, replacing all the appliances. The most popular color just out had been avocado. That was in 1971, a decade earlier. Fixing the knot on his tie, Blake could barely make out the stove hidden under the pile of old newspapers. The clutter was all over the place. He shook his head as he passed the table; it too was buried under papers and stacks of files. *I've got to get some help around here,* he thought for the millionth time.

The sink was half-full of dishes, and the mess added to the disorder everywhere he looked.

He'd come close to getting a cleaning woman many times, but it always came back to Francine. He knew she would not like someone else in her kitchen. She wouldn't like it at all.

Francine had been gone for just about five years, but somehow, every day she seemed to make an appearance. The recurring nightmares were the worst. They usually began as a happy step back in time, fun and exciting. Her smiling face, always laughing. They ended with the reality that was their unwelcome beginning.

He'd had a real breakthrough. His experiments coupled with undying persistence were paying off. Soon he would be able to reveal his findings, but not quite yet.

The chaotic home was in direct contrast to his life, his real life, which was the work he performed for Novatek Pharmaceutical.

Blake was the head of a research team whose mandate was the '*Study, discovery, and development of new marketable products.*'

He was considered one of the foremost experts in cancer and stem cell research in the United States. Blake was also credited with breaking a variety of academic records set at Harvard University during his tenure. At thirty-five, he was published. His work could be found printed in medical journals worldwide. His theories, combined with his experimentation methods, had long since taken him out of the mainstream. His unique approach attracted the attention of his employer.

Novatek was the second largest company of its kind in the world. Their only rival was Wilkinson Pharmaceutical, and the gap was steadily closing. He was a member of an elite network of doctors, researchers, and scientists, all carefully chosen for their gifted minds.

His team didn't have to worry about passing the acceptable guidelines of the F.D.A., animal rights groups or a conservative American society. These explorers were given relatively few financial or bureaucratic restrictions. Novatek was an institution functioning without conscience, an unemotional machine driven by results. Novatek defined *results* as 'a desirable or beneficial consequence, outcome, or effect.' Blake knew that in plain English it meant find the answers, make the profits. Although profits were not his motivation, the objective was the same. He too, wanted answers.

Leaving the house with his satchel in one hand, he fumbled for his front-door key with the other. Exiting backward, he pulled the door closed with the inserted key.

"Morning, Dr. Edwards!" a young voice rang out.

Startled, he spun around in time to see Joey, the paperboy. He had just tossed his morning paper into the overgrown grass.

"Good morning, Joey. Hey, would you mind cutting my lawn when you get a chance, please?"

"Sure Dr. Edwards, no problem. I can do it tonight after school. Gotta go. I'm going to be late," the young boy shouted as he pedaled off.

He smiled as the youngster quickly disappeared down the street.

As Blake passed the overstuffed mailbox, he stopped briefly, grabbing the contents. He slid into the car, tossing the bundle on the passenger seat. Starting the engine, he glanced over at his mail. Without giving it a second thought, he backed the car out of the driveway and began the familiar commute to the lab.

Blake worked in a huge compound of sterile, imposing structures. There were a total of twenty-five octagon shaped buildings situated on eighteen acres of concrete and asphalt. The octagonal design was not coincidental nor was it the fulfillment of an architectural vision. It was specifically chosen so that those entering the separate laboratories would be out their neighbors' field of vision. A four-foot ornamental wrought iron section was securely fastened to a five-foot high solid brick wall. It encompassed the entire compound. The razor wire interlaced through the top of the fence looked surprisingly natural. The ten-foot-high barrier was almost impenetrable.

Discreetly tucked away within this barricade were the research laboratories, only accessible to those whose clandestine presence was allowed. Concealed in domed covers were security cameras.

The watchful, secret eyes could be found in the halls, labs and the exterior of all buildings in the compound. Officially, the facility was called Novatek Pharmaceutical Laboratory Center, simply referred to by most as the institute. The goal at Novatek was privacy. Most every employee remained unknown to each other. Each laboratory had a team, which consisted of the supervisor, their research assistants, and a data manager. Team leaders would set out the labs agenda, assigning specific projects to their staff.

The Institute was merely a means to an end for Blake. It was the perfect place to conquer the demon that haunted his dreams. He was simply left to his own devices barring a monthly mandatory report to his cryptic sponsors. The lone stipulation to his free ride was Novatek's total exclusivity on results. Individual recognition was non-existent. Each laboratory's discoveries would lead to the eventual marketing of any new products. Blake had access to the best equipment, an endless supply of live animals and any materials required for his work.

Such anonymity was a small price to pay. Blake's real goal was defeating the disease that had taken the only person he'd ever loved. So intense was his desire, some days he felt his very sanity would slip away if he failed. On other days, he believed it had. For the last two years, the disease had taken the form of an entity in his nightmares. It had become his faceless demon.

Still, the ongoing objective was to produce results. Ultimately, it was the reason he supported what he considered the mundane and inconsequential findings of his staff. The unspoken condition, freedom to work on his private experiment, was obvious. His team was required to turn out conventional, marketable product.

Speeding down North Shore Boulevard towards the research lab, Blake turned on the car's radio. Today was April 5th 1981 and the telecaster barked out new details regarding the recent assassination attempt.

"*President Ronald Reagan was shot on March 30th. Forensic reports confirm a long-nosed .22 caliber bullet was fired from the pistol and ricocheted off the President's limousine. It entered Reagan's chest under his left arm. The bullet was the exploding type, but did not explode. The main threat to Reagan's life was from blood loss and a collapsed lung,*" the announcer's voice concluded.

The news had been buzzing about the president and his would-be assassin for days. While Blake did not have strong political affirmations, he admired Reagan's charismatic demeanor. Like many, Blake was won over by his sincere fatherly concern about the country and all Americans. After listening to the newscast long enough to discern that the president was recovering nicely, he switched off the radio.

His morning routine began as he pondered the unusual findings of his experiments. *What I've been seeing for months is so amazing, it can't be wrong, could it? Could I be wrong? Have I screwed up my calculations? God, am I going crazy?* Blake's thoughts came in a flurry.

He'd been retracing his footsteps, reviewing his notes, checking, constantly re-checking his findings for months.

The notes aren't wrong. I see what I see.

This was his usual morning ritual on the drive to Novatek—re-evaluation, followed by doubt, closing with self-reassurance.

The data was momentarily forgotten. Replacing it were thoughts of the predictable recognition he'd receive when his nemesis was finally beaten.

The results all pointed to the same conclusion. Conquering the demon would immortalize him. He knew that his name would be up there with the great ones. Alexander Fleming, who discovered penicillin… Dr. Jonas Salk, who was in the history books for the polio vaccination. *Why not, why not… Dr. Blake Edwards? What I have is as big as penicillin. I'll be famous,* he thought sheepishly.

Blake's fantasy came to a screeching halt as he focused on *why* he had to be right. Why he couldn't be mistaken.

He recalled how Fran's hospital bed had been moved to their home… she was resting when he had come to check on her. As he'd looked down at his wife, her clouded eyes had opened, staring up at him. That was when she'd asked him, begged him to do the impossible.

"*Blake, do you love me?*" Fran asked weakly.

"With all my heart, darling."

"Blake..."

His mind screeched to a halt, the memory too painful.

Blake was certain he could not afford an error. He had seen doctors, researchers and scientists 'blackballed' in the scientific community. Even after an innocent slip-up or miscalculation, the future experimental results as well as the actual findings would attract undue scrutiny. Almost always, the funding stopped. Blake's research had to be perfect.

Because his search had to continue, he could not function efficiently under any negative shadow, real or implied. He became extremely cautious with any milestone he reached, fanatical about sharing the outcome. He was so careful, in fact, that he would not disclose his own discoveries to his staff. He personally performed all the necessary checks on his experiments. Absolutely everything leaving the lab required his personal seal of approval. Once Blake was convinced it would fly, it was then turned over to Dr. Evan Sinclair, the next cog of the machine for inspection at Novatek.

Blake worked steadily throughout the day, searching for a flaw in his research, repeating the experiments over and over, just like he had for months. Over the past several weeks it was difficult to conceal his growing excitement, to hold fast, to not reveal anything to anyone. He wanted to tell somebody what he'd been working on so diligently, so secretively for years. He hadn't shared it with anybody, not even Rose.

*****

The day ended much as it had begun. Blake arrived home late and exhausted. Dusk had turned to darkness during his drive. He'd forgotten about Joey's promise earlier that morning to cut his lawn. As he exited the car, he caught a whiff of the freshly cut grass and smiled. Slipping the key into the lock of his front door, he made a mental note to stuff five dollars into an envelope and hang it off the mailbox. This was the standard method of payment arranged long before, between the doctor and the young lad.

Blake sat in the brown nauga-hyde lazy-boy chair, reviewing the days' notes. In his lap were crumbs from the crackers he'd eaten for dinner. By this time of the evening, most people would be settling in front of their televisions, winding down and relaxing. Blake's TV served as another surface upon which to set things. It hadn't been turned on in years. Passing it, on his way to bed, he tossed the folder on the 26" RCA wood console. It was time to rest. He wanted to be fresh tomorrow.

His thoughts turned back to Francine as he drifted off, sleep claiming his conscious mind.

Once again, he relived the nightmare, the one that haunted him most often. This time he was standing in the living room beside Francine. The tears were running out of her tired sunken eyes.

"If you loved me you would help me."

"I can't Franny, I just can't," he sobbed.

It was there again, and again it taunted him. The demon was inside her, consuming her organs. He reaches out…got it, he almost has it this time, but like always, it slips away from his grasp.

"Love me, Blake, kill me PLEASE. Make it stop."

He stands beside her bed, the syringe filled with adrenaline, a single drop rolls down the side of the needle. She smiles up at him.

"Thank you, sweetheart, I'll ALWAYS be with you."

"I promise, Fran, I will never give up trying to find a way to stop this from happening to anyone else."

His warm tears fall on her smiling face as he injects the overdose of adrenaline into the I.V.

Her back arches as her heart races, the monitor bleeps 150, 220, 280. Then…a straight line, the intermittent beeps are replaced with a single monotonous tone. She slumps back on the bed. Blake stands over her with the empty syringe in his hand, tears flowing freely down his face.

No one ever questioned Francine Edward's death. Her heart weakened by the disease had simply given out. At least that's what the official report had said. His sleeping face contorted as his unconscious mind vividly replayed the events of his wife's last night on earth, the night he murdered her.

Chapter 2

The alarm clock screeched. The silence shattered by the annoying racket interrupted her peaceful slumber. Rose rolled over, moaning lightly, the dream abandoning her as the noise invaded her conscious mind. Hers were not visions of demons or death, but of making love to the man she'd desired for over three years. Rose hit the button, abruptly ending the droning racket, as she basked in the fading memory of her mirage.

"*I need you Rose, I want you*," her mystical lover had said. He pulled her face to his, her lips opened to meet his pressing kiss. Her heart hastened as warmth enveloped her. She loved him. She wanted him. The kiss broke as they frantically raced to undress each other. She looked deeply into his eyes, *"I love you, Blake."* The scene evaporated like a fine mist, the only remnant lingering, the upturned corners of her mouth.

Unbeknownst to her, Blake too was in the final throws of his own nocturnal illusion, but the scenes playing out on the landscape of his mind were of a much different nature.

Rose's fantasies often revolved around Blake Edwards, of being with him and taking care of him.

In an effort to fully wake up, Rose squinted and stretched her arms behind her head, forcing the stiffness from her limbs. She let off a high-pitched squeal from her pursed lips as her toes poked out from under the covers. She peeled back the down filled comforter and bounced out of bed. The too-large flannel pajamas were decorated with a smattering of teddy bear prints. Rose had the type of body that made even these pajamas surprisingly sexy on her curvaceous figure. As she danced her way to the washroom, Rose squatted, dropping her bottom on the toilet. After a pee, she brushed her teeth and went back to make up the bed. Careful to arrange the throw pillows and stuffed animals, she began her morning ritual of getting ready.

Her home was the total opposite of Blake's. The dominant colors in Rose's house were soft pink and peach. Everything was frilly, neat, and precise. It looked like a grown-up dollhouse. Rose loved it. In contrast to her achievements as a PhD competing in a fast-paced world, her environment suggested something entirely different. It hinted that maybe an insecure little girl lingered just beneath the confident exterior.

*****

Rose arrived at Novatek ten minutes early Thursday morning. As she pulled up to the security gate, Bill, the day guard, smiled as he exited the small booth, clipboard in hand. He recognized Rose and had no need to view her Novatek photo Identification.

"Good Morning, Miss Frechette."

"Morning, Bill," she said scribbling her name on the sign-in sheet.

"Have a good day," he replied, raising the gate.

"Thanks, you too, Bill," she said, returning the pleasantry as she pulled away.

All vehicles were the property of Novatek. They were on loan to the staff as long as their employment was maintained.

Staff members shopped for their desired automobiles, submitting a pre-approved application form to the team leader. The next day the car they requested would be sitting in their assigned parking spot. Rose wheeled in her BMW.

She'd sensed Blake had been quietly excited about his work, mumbling to himself for weeks while he conducted his experiments.

Rose had not left work the previous night until well after 7 P.M., much later than usual. She had suspected for some time that Blake might be on to something big. She'd hung around after the others had left, hoping he would tell her what was making him so anxious. He hadn't shared a thing.

Rose had been Blake's top research assistant for three years. She had come to know her supervisor well and, despite his flaws, had fallen in love with him.

Often he would set her to task on a project while he worked independently of the team on something else. There was an unmistakable veil of secrecy surrounding his research. Blake would suddenly stop what he was doing when Rose or Marc, the other member of the team, approached his work area. He would then abruptly ask, "What can I do for you? Is there something you need?" or some similar version of a dismissive question.

Despite his almost rude behavior, Rose and the junior researcher had come to tolerate Blake's unconventional ways. Rose never let his occasional curt responses bother her. She was too enamored with him to get offended. She assumed the junior researcher accepted it as normal, because he, too, was rather eccentric.

Rose was a very attractive woman. She was five feet, three inches tall and a bit self-conscious because her short stature emphasized her full-size bust. Her fiery red hair gently framed her soft, glowing face, nearly perfect except for a little hook-shaped scar just under her chin. An easy smile gave her a much younger appearance than her thirty-six years. Despite having just the right bait, she'd never really set the trap, staying unattached. Over the years, suitors had tried unsuccessfully to win her.

She loved science, research, and experimentation. While in university, Rose enjoyed spending most of her free time in the lab. While her friends were socializing, she was content to work.

When men came sniffing around, she was determined not to fall into the relationship game. Rose never had a terrible or heartbreaking experience—nothing personal upon which to base such a cynical outlook on love, yet she had. Then, along came Blake. He was a brilliant, driven man. Rose knew his wife had died several years before she started at Novatek. Rumor had it he still loved his wife and therefore never dated. He simply existed for work. Everything in his life involved his self-proclaimed mission.

Rose admired his unfaltering commitment to the research, the development of medications and remedies. In her eyes, Blake was uncompromisingly selfless.

The whole tangled web of love, devotion and commitment, the mania she avoided her whole life came flooding in when she met him. Rose felt he *needed* a woman.

As she went about her morning duties, she removed bacterial samples from a refrigeration unit. She tried to imagine what Blake could have found so fascinating to make him ignore the entire staff and their research.

Usually he was bustling around the lab, elbowing his way into the microscopes and looking at the current slides. He would then check the files assigned to them, asking a variety of questions. But the last few months had been different. He seemed engrossed in his notes, checking, and then scrutinizing his findings.

His glasses were constantly perched on his forehead as he bent over examining the slides in his high-powered electron microscope. Rose knew she'd be made privy to his current experiment, all in good time. He had always confided in her, eventually. There were times he'd held back. He would seldom discuss a new pill, remedy, spray, or anything else Novatek could manufacture. He'd told her in the past that he didn't want to deal with the F.D.A. red tape process, at least not until he was very sure it would be approved.

A few months earlier, she asked Blake to join her for a bite to eat after work. At dinner, they became engrossed in a conversation discussing the work and their employer.

"Blake, this is our function, our mandate isn't it? We take common viruses, bacteria, diseased tissue, and search for a cure. At the very least, we come up with a product that alleviates some of the discomfort caused by the condition. Look at what our little team has accomplished Blake. We have successfully produced everything from birth control pills to antihistamines. We're all looking for the same thing, aren't we?"

"Rose, how can someone so intelligent be so naïve? Do you really think we're supposed to find 'cures'?" he argued. "I know you feel our work here is dignified, and I do respect your noble approach, Rose, I really do. Relieve a symptom, improve the quality of life for the common man. I know it's what you want to do. But have you ever considered that the pharmaceutical industry is not really interested in reducing world pain or finding those magic bullets? What if the only real motivation of our employers is just to increase profits and stock value?"

"Of course I am aware of that possibility," she replied. "But along the way I still feel that we can do some good and help people feel better. We can reduce suffering. It's our responsibility to find those remedies."

"It's true, Rose, we can do all those things. But unless the discovery is monumental, the *cure so large* that it couldn't be ignored, I'm afraid it would be disregarded."

Rose stared disbelievingly at him. "I know you think the pharmaceutical companies are more interested in treating diseases than curing them Blake, but why?"

"Well Rose, one could only guess the millions of dollars lost with the antidote to the common cold. Think of those *'over the counter snake oils'* that seldom offer much relief. Now imagine all the money lost if a simple pill were created eliminating a cold in one day." Blake stared off into the distance as he spoke. "One cure alone could threaten stock prices by 20%. Novatek recognized the cost long ago. Treat the symptoms, not the disease. I'm afraid there's no money in cures," he said, more to himself than to her.

Leaning in closer Rose said, "Blake, how can you be so cynical? We are given all the tools necessary to heal. Our only limitation is in our ability, or lack of it, to find the answers," her voice quivering, near tears.

"Think about it, Rose, Dentists…sixty bucks for an extraction, then zero. No future revenue derived from that tooth. Ahhh, but keep that tooth alive and it could produce a steady stream of revenue. There would be cleanings, fillings, in time, root canals, or crowns. The dental profession realized that simple fact thirty years ago. I'm afraid the pharmaceutical industry also follow the same philosophy these days."

"So why do you do it, Blake? Why do you work so relentlessly for the industry that you think doesn't want us to succeed?"

A self-assured smile spread across his face and he said, "Because Rose, if it's big enough, so revolutionary, even they can't ignore it. And I have dedicated my life to finding one single miracle."

Listening to him intently, Rose found herself unable to resist him. His perseverance, the passion he had for his work and his brilliant mind were all aphrodisiacs to her. The wine had given her the necessary courage. She saw an opportunity to seduce him. A little voice inside told her now could be a perfect time. Staring dreamily into his eyes, she suspected he too felt the attraction. *He has to know the chemistry between us is real,* she thought shamelessly. She took the chance.

"Blake would you like to come back to my place for a nightcap?" she'd asked, trying to sound nonchalant.

Blake hesitantly looked at his watch.

"Ahhh, well, ummm…it's almost nine o'clock. I think it may be a little late for a visit. Morning comes quickly."

"Oh yeah… sure, well maybe another time," she said, awkwardly hiding her disappointment.

*Dear lord! I don't know how to pick up a man. I guess shoptalk for hours...well definitely not the way, s*he thought. Fumbling with the napkin in her lap, she desperately tried to hide the humiliation his quick response had triggered. Her expression slipped from a wine-induced picture of seduction, to a crushed look, immediately. Knowing that Blake saw her expression change, she felt a sudden flash of heat and her cheeks reddened even more. *Oh god this is what a hot flash must feel like*. The notion brought a smile back to her face and her color quickly returned to normal. *I will figure out a way to win your heart Blake Edwards,* she silently vowed.

Chapter 3

Eric Brunner sat in the comfortable chair, with a leg hooked over his knee. His heel bounced nervously as he waited to be called. He was 6'2" tall, lean, and well muscled. Eric's chiseled Arian features accented the piercing blue eyes, and long, blonde hair added the finishing touch. When he walked into a room, people stopped, many stared. By most standards, the man was beautiful.

A light sheen of sweat began to appear on Eric's forehead and he noticed a slight increase in his heart rate. The sudden perspiration wasn't a case of nerves resulting from the dental appointment, nor was it the lack of air conditioning that caused the warm air to hang motionless in the waiting area. The wave of anxiety was a result of his wandering mind, and the memories conjured up whenever he visited this place.

"*Eric, we owe our lives to America,*" his grandmother would often tell him when he was a child.

When Hitler began the Nazi movement, his grandfather had been arrested, eventually perishing in a death camp. His grandmother had managed to flee Germany with her only daughter. They'd found refuge in America. She had repeatedly recounted the stories of the camps and her many near-brushes with death. "*Eric, our debt, your debt to this country can never be repaid. If you ever have a chance to do something great for America, embrace it, and you make me happy.*"

During his last year of college, Eric had met Bruce Vargo. It was a chance meeting, just luck, a friend of a friend sort of thing. He found later that the introduction was not so much by chance as it was by design. Bruce was his answer.

Eric remembered everything as if it were yesterday. It always came back when he'd see his dentist, Dr. Sharon Sturgeon. He'd felt a comfortable warmth whenever he saw her. She reminded him so much of Jane. Those memories induced a flutter of emotion. They were some of the happiest times of his life, as well as some of the darkest. They never came in any specific order, just a shuffle of recollections. Today his memory conjured up a discussion he'd had at the campus pub, with Bruce Vargo. The conversation revolved around the Patronums.

"I want in, Bruce. It's my calling, I've felt it my whole life. This is right for me, everything about it is right," he'd said earnestly. "I won't let you down."

The reminiscence faded as a child's shrill cries emanated from an unseen procedure room.

I should find a new dentist, he thought, as he flipped through the reading material in the waiting room. He'd considered it many times, but always rationalized staying with her. At some point, he'd realized he kept coming back to her because she *did* remind him of Jane.

"Eric, she's ready for you," the young assistant announced.

He casually tossed down the unread magazine and followed the girl down a hallway. He walked into the exam room where Dr. Sturgeon stood smiling. "Good Morning Eric," she said, looking away from an X-ray that was illuminated on its stand.

"Hi Sharon," he replied. A genuine smile crossed his face as he sat in the dental chair.

"So, It's a crown today," she said, holding the X-ray.

"Yes, ma'am, you said I needed it!"

"Alright Eric, just make yourself comfortable and we'll get started in a few minutes," she said. Once Eric was settled, she clipped the splash bib around his neck and then exited the room.

Lying back, he closed his eyes. Eric was an expert in several types of pain control. His favorite was dissociation: moving the sense of self outside the body. He began the technique by filling his mind with memories of a lost love, and how he'd become a Patronum…

It hadn't started off as an argument, but had quickly turned into one, as Eric tried to explain. The memory, years old, seemed like it was yesterday. He was sitting across from her at the two-chair kitchen bar in her off-campus apartment.

"Jane, you don't understand. I was meant to do this."

"Eric come on, a secret society? People who make decisions about what's good for us? Good for America? Get real. That's no different than the government. At least the government is accountable to some degree," she shouted.

"They do more than that. Every consideration is made for the people, for the country. The Patronums *do not* base their actions on personal gain or political advancement. Nobody even knows of the work they do. Baby, I really need your support. I need you to *understand* if we're ever going to have a future together."

He desperately wanted her to recognize the value of their work, for he'd broken the cardinal rule of the Patronums. He had disclosed their very existence.

Eric was in love with her. She was bright, vivacious, and beautiful. He'd wanted to marry her, have a family with her.

In college, their relationship became serious. After performing the flirting and dating rituals, they made a pledge to one another. It seemed fitting that the pact occurred in the afterglow of an impassioned lovemaking session. Resting on Eric's shoulder, she found herself enjoying one of life's perfect moments. "Let's have no lies, no secrets in our life, not ever," she said. "If we are going to be serious, together forever, we can't hold back anything. Eric you're my best friend and I want to be yours. Okay?" Together the two young lovers had agreed.

Eric had seen no flaw in that approach, not until he told her of the secret society. What he had failed to mention that day was the fact that he was already a Patronum. Suddenly, the memory was interrupted as Sharon's voice rang out.

"How are we doing, Eric, everything okay?" she asked.

"Uh ha," he managed, giving her the thumbs up.

He'd been sitting in the chair for almost an hour, his mouth stretched open with a dental dam. Dr. Sturgeon's face was less than a foot away. "Uh Ha" was the best he could do.

Looking into Sharon's big brown eyes, as she worked, he could have been staring into Jane's. With the mask on, all he could see was her deep dark pools and silky chestnut locks. They were so much like Jane's…her face shimmered, suddenly it *was his former lover's face,* and he was back at the apartment…

"Honey, think about it, please," he'd begged. "The Patronums is an organization that takes into account every aspect of American life, wealth, world position. Not just for the *now*, but for the *future*, our children's future." He was frantic.

"They don't have the weight of 'this term or the next election' clouding their judgment, swaying their decisions."

He explained that theirs was a secretive fraternity, which did not involve itself with initiation rites, secret handshakes, or passwords. The Patronums operated in cells, independent of each other, their tentacles reaching into all levels of society. Their numbers included the obvious, the powerful and wealthy. Conversely, it also touched the less obvious professionals such as schoolteachers, bus drivers, construction personnel, the everyday man or woman. Those displaying extreme patriotism, combined with ability could be inducted into the secret society.

In his initial excitement, he had told Jane everything. He'd been faithful to their promise not to keep secrets from one another. Eric explained the word Patronum was the Greek word meaning "Protectors." Their mandate was very simple. The goal was the preservation and the advancement of the American way of life, although in their quest, the Patronums would never risk jeopardizing America's status as the world's largest super-power.

No individual member could decide what the ideal path of "protection" was. There was no set political alliance or agenda. As the economic and social climates changed, so did the direction of the Patronums.

"You're kidding, right, Eric? This is worse than communism," she said, jumping to her feet and starting to pace. Recalling the scene, Eric could feel the tension heighten as she walked frantically back and forth in the confines of the small apartment. The whole thing had taken on a more hysterical air. His eyes pleaded for her acceptance as he unfolded the details of the secret society. Her stride became frenzied, and his hope turned to panic. His plan to attain a greater closeness with his lover was turning into something beyond his control. Bruce's warning during his initiation to the cloaked fraternity surged to the forefront of his mind. *"Remember Eric, consideration for membership into the brotherhood is not taken lightly. All members have to be invited and educated in the way of the Patronums by their mentor. It is my duty to find, select, and indoctrinate new members. Once a candidate becomes a member, I become responsible for your allegiance for life."*

A chill ran up his spine as he envisioned Bruce's eyes boring into him. The gravity of the moment became clear when Bruce finally spoke his next words.

"Becoming associated with the Patronums has one other extremely unique twist, Eric. Disloyalty on any level, results in an untimely and always fatal accident. Confirming involvement with or even acknowledging the existence of the Patronums has the same outcome. Deliberately, and without exception, your mentor, who is me, would suffer the same fate. Eric, WE DO NOT EXIST. Our organization can never be discussed with anyone who is not in the brotherhood. Do you understand?"

"Of course Bruce, of course I do."

He'd not been faithful to the promise made to Bruce that day.

*****

Eric could not help but notice the proximity of her semi-intimate position as she pressed gently into him while she worked. He recognized her flirtatious smile and breathy voice as a typical response to his endearing charm. Eric was quite aware that he could be alluring and knew how to use his good looks and charisma to his advantage, controlling situations with women. On occasion, even members of the same sex became enamored of him. It was something he made appear so natural, so hypnotic, always polite and familiar. He'd never refer to *her* as Dr. Sturgeon. Eric always made a point of using her first name, as a friend would.

His charismatic and crafty attributes are what first attracted his Patronum mentor, Bruce Vargo. Eric soon became an exemplary candidate for membership into the group. When he had met Bruce twelve years earlier, he knew he had been impressed with his natural instinctive aptitude. Bruce would not have been impressed with his naiveté where his lover was concerned.

As Sharon worked, his mind insisted on reliving the scene in the apartment that night. He recalled Jane ranting and raving as she prowled the room like a caged animal.

"ERIC, this can't be real. If it is, you need to tell someone, the authorities, the FBI, or C.I.A. SOMEONE! IF YOU don't I will!"

Oh MY GOD! What have I done? He thought. Reasoning with her wasn't working. He knew that by exposing the Patronums he had placed Bruce Vargo and himself in grave danger. Simply by breaking the first rule, he had confirmed their very existence. He was in love with Jane. His mind raced. He'd panicked.

Sharon's voice disconnected his step back in time.

"Okay, bite down, please. How does it feel, Eric?"

"Great, perfect actually." He clenched once again to see if his teeth meshed properly.

After an inspection of his molar, Sharon saw his bite was perfect. The assistant handed her the apparatus for taking the final impression. Minutes later, she was finished.

She stretched an arm across Eric's chest and the other encircled his neck as she removed the bib. She pressed her breast against his shoulder as she fumbled with the clasp, her face only inches from his. She was so near, he spotted the goosebumps and her downy arm hair standing on end. He detected her shiver as she brushed against him. Despite his efforts, Eric could not suppress the small grin from spreading across his lips. He enjoyed the attention, her resemblance to Jane. It was the flashbacks that troubled him.

"Well, we're all done here for now, Eric. Do you have any questions?" she asked, trying to remain professional.

"No, as usual I trust you have done a wonderful job, thanks a million. Ahhh, that feels better," Eric said as he sprang from the chair, casually stretching.

"Don't forget to book your next appointment on the way out."

"I won't, thanks so much, Sharon," he replied, touching her arm as he spoke. He turned as he left, winking, flashing his winning smile.

As he rounded the corner of the procedure room, he stopped to look at his watch. He was still within earshot when Sharon's assistant blurted out, "God, that man is so sexy!"

"You think?" Sharon replied, her husky voice laced with a lewd overtone.

Eric smiled to himself as he eavesdropped, then continued toward the reception area to book his next visit.

He wondered how '*sexy*' the assistant would have thought he was if she knew he'd been the Patronums head assassin for twelve years. Or if Sharon would still get that flushed look every time she brushed against him if she'd realized the things those hands had done, or the memories she induced. Memories of the first woman he'd ever loved…the first of many he had killed.

Chapter 4

Exiting the dental centre, Eric was struck with the brilliance of the Dallas sun as it moved steadily towards high noon. He raised a hand to his brow in an effort to shade his eyes, wishing he'd grabbed his sunglasses when he ran out of the house earlier. The other hand found its way to the knot on his tie. The unrelenting sun had him perspiring for the second time this morning. So preoccupied was he, adjusting to the sudden brightness and heat, that he didn't notice Bruce pull up about a hundred feet past him.

By the late '70's most manufacturers had sized down in the name of fuel economy, the exception being the luxury carmakers whose designers' equated size with wealth and decadence. Driving a Lincoln Continental Mark V, Bruce pulled the huge 20-foot long coupe up to the curb. After a minute, he saw that Eric was just standing there.

Isn't that something, I can't believe he didn't see me, he thought a bit surprised. Vargo pushed down hard on the horn and began waving. Eric turned toward the resounding blast and waved back. He walked over to the flagship car, opened the passenger door, and slid in.

Bruce's resonating voice instantly shredded the melancholy veil, which had begun to drape over Eric. It was the unwelcome result of his conjured memories.

"Good lord boy, are you going to tell me you couldn't see *this* car pulling up?"

Eric responded with a small, embarrassed grin.

"Well, can you talk or are you going to drool all over the place?" Bruce said.

"I didn't get any freezing," Eric replied with a shrug.

"Damn, you fancy yourself one tough customer don't you?" Bruce said in a sarcastic tone as they both chuckled.

"Word's down from the Committee, you have an assignment," Bruce said. Casually, he reached behind him, fumbling to find a brown manila envelope on the back seat. He handed it to Eric.

Eric knew the job could be as simple as some detective work, background checks, or surveillance. On the other hand, it could also mean planning and orchestrating someone's last day on earth. He was never sure.

Judging by the thickness of the package, he assumed there were multiple individuals. Occasionally the set-up took weeks, sometimes even months. He'd spend countless hours studying the backgrounds, habits, and routines of the principals enclosed.

"So, Bruce, when are you going to give me a heads-up on this one?" Eric said, weighing the package in his hand while lifting his eyebrows questioningly.

Bruce glanced over as he expertly maneuvered the massive vehicle through traffic. The look he had on his face was a cross between a frown and a smirk.

"Everything you need is in there," he replied, trying to sound stern. After all these years, Eric had no difficulty reading his mentor and easily interpreting the message on Bruce's face. Eric loved ribbing him. He knew Bruce would never speak aloud about a mission. Everything necessary would be contained in the envelope. An individual's family history, affiliations, medical records, and even social activities would be detailed. The files would be complete, so much so that if elimination were ordered, there'd be a vast choice of how the intended would die. An overdose, mugging, car accident, or a chemically induce heart attack. An assassin's list was endless.

It would be up to Eric to decide how the chosen would meet his fate. Once the Committee had marked someone for termination, his or her demise was inevitable. The only real issue was how the death would appear. It had to fit neatly into one of two categories, natural or accidental.

He was comfortable with his choice to act in this capacity for the Patronums. Eric knew if a name had made this file, then in some way, no matter how obscure, they were an imminent threat to America.

"Bruce, I have a question for you."

"Shoot. If I can answer it I will."

"Were *we* involved with the assassination attempt on Reagan?"

he said, once again playing with his mentor's head. Bruce was always so serious.

"You know better than that. If *we* were, I would never tell you. And if we were, he'd be dead."

"What makes you think *we* would have succeeded?" he asked fishing for answers.

Taking the bait, Bruce responded, "Because I would have had my best on the mission." Bruce winked as he tilted his head in Eric's direction.

The two shared a special bond, much deeper than a mentor and protégé. On occasion, each felt it was more like a father-son connection.

Eric didn't need to know how these or any of the people whose names had made his list, could affect the future of America. When he gave himself to the Patronums, he gave them everything, including his soul, free will, and if necessary, even his life. Sometimes the threat to the vast majority was evident to Eric, but many times, it remained a mystery.

Eric's days were filled with a regular job like anyone else. When not in the service of the Patronums, he was a Central Intelligence Agency field operative, referred to as a *suit* for the C.I.A. As a fully trained field agent, he was extremely proficient on all levels. His recruitment into the Patronums had come before his choice of career. The fact was, he hadn't actually chosen his profession. Bruce chose it for him.

In many cases, when a young recruit was selected, their mentor would decide where they would be most useful. Acceptance to the appropriate learning facility, money, and all that was necessary would be provided to ensure the ultimate outcome. If a student needed coaching, an instructor would receive a similar envelope. The details contained in the tutor's would be very different from Eric's, the areas of difficulty clearly outlined and all information necessary to help the new apprentice would also be included. Many had found themselves in their professions as a result of the secret society. Politicians, doctors, lawyers, as well as mechanics, policemen, and many others were in their vocation, courtesy of the Patronums. Professions would be chosen based on aptitude, intelligence, and need.

Eric's I.Q. was in the mid 160's making him exceptional, useful in a multitude of areas. But it was his combined qualities that had made him the perfect choice as a C.I.A. operative. He was a rare commodity, a logical idealist with an unfaltering loyalty. Even his superiors at the agency, non-Patronums, recognized his charismatic personality. That, combined with his good looks, seemed to mesmerize all he met. Men wanted to befriend him, women wanted to seduce him. Very fit, he easily endured the physical demands of a field agent.

As they turned off the freeway, Eric's muscles involuntarily relaxed. He was always surprised how quickly life seemed to slow down when the speed limit dropped from seventy-five miles per hour to thirty. They weaved through several streets in the three-year-old development known as Linden Wood.

The land developers had set the benchmark, now the city enforced it. No building permit could be pulled for Linden Wood unless the proposed home was between 2,000 and 2,500 square feet, two stories, with an attached garage. The builders had developed four sets of house plans that fit the bill. The floor plans differed slightly, but the exteriors were almost identical. The advantage was that the homes could be erected quicker and cheaper. The disadvantage to the neighborhood was that the homes did not display individual style or uniqueness.

"Well son, there you go," Bruce said as he pulled up in front of the two-storey contemporary house. Even though he owned what many referred to as a *"copy house,"* Eric loved it. Some days he felt it was the only thing about his life that was normal.

"Thanks, Bruce, I appreciate the lift."

He knew the point of the ride was the file, but nonetheless he enjoyed spending time with Bruce regardless of the reason.

"Not a problem." Bruce responded with a nod.

"Thanks again." With the envelope in hand, Eric shot Bruce a parting glance as he exited the car.

Once inside, Eric walked down the long hall to the rear of the large home and his office. A *criminal profiler* might have found much of his environment fitting for his personality type. His home was extremely precise. Everything in it served a specific purpose.

Furniture was arranged perfectly, natural daylight was utilized and taken into account, right down to the amount of reflective glare on the television screen. Even the candles were arranged so that in the event of a power outage, every room in the house would be illuminated quickly and evenly.

These habits were just part of his exacting nature, and were never implemented with much forethought. The eyebrow of a profiler might also be raised at the subliminal nature of the artwork. It was simple, bright and repetitive. More than half of his paintings were of flowers, fruit and fields. The rest were of mother and child and not just paintings. Of course, there were the paintings, but also ornamental plates and statues. Even his calendar depicted a different mother and child scene for each month of the year. Eric assumed his attraction to them was based on the good maternal relationship he had with his own mother. A psychologist may have uncovered the deep-seated admiration he had for his grandmother. Her remarkable strength and determination ensured the survival of her bloodline, and consequently, his very existence. Indirectly, she'd molded everything Eric had become. The bright, simplistic flowers and other images were just a subconscious reach for a simpler life.

Sitting comfortably in his plain office chair, he laid the manila envelope down on the uncluttered desk and turned on the reading lamp. The uncomplicated ritual began as he opened the file. An hour later, papers were neatly spread over the surface of the desk. Each principal became a separate intricate component of the overall assignment. This mission could be a challenge. The marks were four lawyers. They were well-respected members of the community and all were very high profile. The gentlemen in question also happened to be senior partners in the same law firm in New York. He was given a week to complete the operation. It was not specified in a dossier, but he knew their demise must be beyond reproach.

As Eric read the file he noted that one of the partners, Joseph Poole, was Gerry Hanover's attorney. Hanover, a wealthy steel magnate was also a Patronum. Chatting baseball once with Bruce Vargo, it had come up that Hanover was a New York Yankees nut. The fact that the steel industrialist was the owner of an executive box at Yankee Stadium had also been mentioned.

"All for one and one for all," Eric said aloud, as he dialed the private number. The phone rang twice before a voice brought the ear-piece to life.

"Good afternoon. Gerry Hanover here"

"Gerry, Eric Brunner."

"Hi, Eric," he replied, after a slight pause.

Eric detected the immediate tension in Gerry's voice. He involuntarily rolled his eyes, while shaking his head.

On a physical level, he was quite aware of the affect he had on people when they first met him. Just as recognizable was the anxiety fellow Patronums displayed when he phoned. After all, Eric was the grim reaper, and he was calling on *them*.

"Hello, Gerry. Sorry to bother you, but I need a favor."

"Sure…sure Eric, anything, what can I do for you?"

Great, he just jumped from a three to a nine on the scared shitless meter, Eric thought sadly. Unlike some who might enjoy such power, he hated having that effect on his fellow Patronums, or anyone for that matter. Eric preferred the art of manipulation through personality, charisma, and desire. He wanted people to *want* to do things for him of their own accord. In person and behind the scenes, it was easily accomplished; however, high-ranking Patronums were quite aware of his area of expertise.

"I'm sorry to have to ask but I need your box for next Wednesday," Eric said into the receiver.

After a brief pause, Gerry answered. "I take it you're referring to my stadium box."

"That's right, Gerry, sorry but it's business."

"I understand, of course, the box is yours."

"Thanks, I apologize for any inconvenience. Now here's what I need…" Eric carefully spelled out what he was to do next.

*****

"Dammit," Gerry murmured as he slammed down the handset. "Biggest game of the year and that son-of-a-bitch wants my stadium box!" he yelled furiously in his empty office, the fear of the Patronums head assassin now forgotten.

Gerry knew the match between the Yankees and Dodgers was going to be critical and possibly the last. And regardless if it wasn't the ultimate battle, an ardent Yankees fan like him hated missing any game.

"Carol, I need you to take a letter," he barked into the intercom.

"Yes sir, I'll be right in." she nervously responded.

Minutes later with the secretary seated across from him, Gerry dictated the letter precisely as Eric had instructed.

*****

Eric's next phone call was to Emilio Escobar, a dedicated Patronum for over twenty years. He was a professional driver and explosives specialist trained exclusively within the realms of the secret organization. His day job was as a New York hack. Cruising a taxi around one the largest cities in the world kept his driving skills honed. Bruce Vargo had used him many times and had introduced the two years ago. Emilio had no military or industrial background that could be flushed out, tying him to an accident. Eric liked that fact; it kept things cleaner, safer.

As the day stretched into nightfall, Eric continued making phone calls as he set a plan into motion. Satisfied that his operation had gathered the necessary momentum, he proceeded to the neat, well-organized kitchen. Opening his fridge he scoured the offerings. He considered the previous evening's leftover pork chop but it looked too bland and uninviting.

Eric's last phone call of the day was to his favorite pizza joint, Poppa Jo-Jo's. By 10 P.M., he was sleeping soundly.

*****

"Mornin', I have a registered delivery for Joseph Poole," the bike courier said. The switchboard buzzed before she could respond, and the stern-looking receptionist instantly pointed to the ceiling with her index finger.

"Good morning, you've reached the law offices of McCarthy, Lomax, Rousseau and Poole, how may I direct your call?" she asked the disembodied voice at the other end of the phone. "Yes, I'll connect you now, one moment please."

"Damn, that's quite a mouthful," the courier joked, reaching into his backpack.

"Yes, now what can I do for you?" she replied dismissively, glancing briefly, then returning her vigilant gaze back to the switchboard.

"Right, like I said, I have a registered letter here for Joseph Poole. I need him to sign for it personally."

She stared back at the messenger as she spoke into the switchboard headset. "Mr. Poole, a delivery for you at the front desk. It requires a signature. One moment, sir, I'll check."

“Who is it from, please?" she asked returning her attention to the young man.

Holding the mail up he announced, "Gerry Hanover."

She parroted the name into the small foam ball that floated just beyond her chin.

"Mr. Poole will be right out, please take a seat."

The courier sat on a red-leather couch and admired the large, curved wall of one-inch-thick glass behind the receptionist. A variety of wild animals and outdoor scenes were cleverly etched into it. Within a couple of minutes, a tall, thin man in his mid-thirties emerged from behind the picturesque glass partition. The sand-blasted image of a polar bear appeared to be swatting at his head as he rounded the corner.

The lawyer walked toward the young man announcing, “I'm Joseph Poole”

Standing up, the courier walked toward the lanky attorney.

"Good Morning Mr. Poole, this is for you and I'll need to see some identification, sir," he said holding up the letter.

Poole reached into his back pocket and fished out his wallet, then produced a New York driver's license. Placing it on the circular piece of granite that served as the reception desk, he reached for the envelope. As the courier documented the credentials, Poole took a quick look at the correspondence. Immediately, his brow furrowed as he spied the bold red letters below his name: 'URGENT'.

A moment later, he was sitting at his thirty-eight-thousand-dollar bird's-eye maple desk, staring anxiously at the envelope that lay atop of the oversized surface. Gerry Hanover was the firm's largest single client and the young attorney had made partner based solely on his account.

The desk he cherished was a personal gift from the senior partners when he'd convinced the steel tycoon that this was the firm for him. In the six years he'd been Gerry Hanover's attorney, he had never received an unannounced registered communication. Joseph Poole had a pre-disposition for over-thinking. It made him an excellent lawyer, but a personal wreck. At thirty-six years old, Joe had already acquired a long list of ailments. Besides his premature baldness, his personal disorders incorporated everything from acid reflux and ulcers, to irritable bowel syndrome. Because the account was so lucrative, he was unnerved by anything out of the ordinary. Joe timidly opened the envelope, sure it contained a letter of dismissal from the five-million-dollar-a-year client.

After reading the correspondence, he called an emergency meeting. An hour later, the other three senior partners, Sean McCarthy, Bill Lomax, and Frank Rousseau were gathered around the large mahogany boardroom table.

Gruff and impatient, Sean McCarthy, the firm's patriarch, was also the eldest member at sixty-seven years old. He didn't appreciate being snapped out of his routine in the middle of the morning. He was the first to speak. "So what the hell's the big '*emergency*' that couldn't wait until tomorrow's bloody meeting, Joe? Hell's bells lad, we just wrapped up a damn sit-down two hours ago," he said, referring to the routine morning session. "Why the heck couldn't you mention whatever was so darned important then?" Finishing, he banged his cane on the floor, emphasizing his irritation.

Bill Lomax, handsome at fifty-three and the office playboy, perked up next. With just slightly more diplomacy, he posed a similar question. "Ya, Joe, you said it was urgent, so let's get to it. Not sure why this couldn't wait until tomorrow. I've an appointment this morning out of the office." Lomax loved to refer to every activity outside of the office as an 'appointment.' Whether it was a rendezvous with his secretary or a round of golf, he was 'out on an appointment.' Today it would be an 11:45 tee-off.

"Sorry to bother all of you fellows," Joe said using a solemn voice, "but this morning I received a registered letter from Gerry Hanover." Immediately he had everyone's undivided attention. Earlier, he had prepared for the meeting by photocopying the letter. He'd actually copied it three times, sealing it in three separate envelopes, each marked 'URGENT'. Walking around the boardroom table, he delivered these personally to each of his partners.

He wanted to share with his colleagues a taste of the apprehension he'd felt just an hour before.

With all the reverence he could muster, Joe solemnly said, "Gentleman, please open the dispatch."

Each of the partners ripped at the envelopes placed before them. Frank Rousseau, the next youngest lawyer in the firm at forty-three years old, did not have the game face of the two more seasoned solicitors. Having just purchased a sprawling home for his young family, he, too, seemed nervous that this could be the deathblow from their largest cash cow. They all studied the letter and shared looks of utter confusion.

McCarthy's Irish ire quickly surfaced as he blurted out, "Is this supposed to be a fookin' joke boy?"

Joseph Poole's face sported a huge grin as he basked in the moment. Poole silently laughed as he recalled the words on the page. The note said,

Dear Joseph,

In recognition of the exemplary representation my company receives from you and your law firm, I would like to invite you and the senior partners as my personal guests to next week's Yankees- Dodgers game. I extend to you the exclusive use of my private executive box. I will send a car for all of you on game day. I would like to discuss a rather large acquisition I am contemplating after the game. My secretary will call to confirm.

Sincerely, Gerry Hanover.

"No Sean, this is no joke. *My* client wants *us* to be his guests at the most coveted sporting event in the world!" Joe was a huge Yankees fan and had tickets to the game. They simply didn't compare.

"Jesus, Joe, you had me crappin' my pants!" Frank exclaimed. "I thought he was canning us. With the new house and the mortgage…well ya know…wow!"

The fact that he'd recently taken out a 1.9 million dollar mortgage with monthly payments of $13,941 for the next thirty years was the reason his heart was still racing.

Bill Lomax was irritated, and unexpectedly said, "Joseph, was it necessary to make such a big, stinking deal out of the invitation?" Instantly composing himself he added, "Yes, well Joe, please send my regrets. I have an appointment next Wednesday and won't be able to make the game." Glancing around at his colleagues he was sure no one suspected that Wednesdays were his "*sleep-with-the-secretary,'* standing appointment.

Sean McCarthy's gnarled hand was firmly wrapped around the 18kt. gold handle of his cane. Loudly clearing his throat as he rose to his feet, he addressed Lomax.

"No, you'll be there, Bill. We'll all be there. I personally can't stand the game. Stupidest thing I ever saw. Grown men running after a ball, grabbing their crotches and slapping each others asses', so, you'll be there, understand? Hanover is this firm's lifeblood. Just be thankful he doesn't enjoy cock fighting, or we'd all be going there instead," he snarled.

Bill reluctantly nodded. With that, the old man limped toward the boardroom door. As an afterthought, he stopped and looked at Joe.

"Next time, laddie, save the theatrics for the wife, okay?"

Joe's retort was a smug grin. He was pleased that he'd shared just a little of the stress he alone suffered with this particular account. A sharp pain in his gut told him it was time to take some Imodium.

Joseph Poole spent the next week floating on a cloud. Not only did the firm's biggest client single him out for an accolade, he would be hovering over the Yankee-Dodger game in an executive box, eating lobster. Life was truly good.

*****

The week passed quickly and game-day finally arrived. At the morning meeting, Joseph could hardly contain his excitement. It was contagious.

"Well, boys, are we ready to watch THE YANKEES KICK SOME LOS ANGELES DODGER'S ASS!" he barked out.

Everyone at the boardroom table smiled; even old Sean McCarthy couldn't suppress a grin.

"I actually can't wait," Frank Rousseau said. "This will be a blast!"

I bet it will be. This is a long overdue outing for ya Frankie, and you're welcome, my pleasure, Joe thought comically. He suspected Frank's mortgage payments were taking a toll on his finances. Socially, Frank and his wife had almost fallen off the map.

"I just hope we get a piece of whatever it is that Hanover's planning to do," Bill Lomax said. He was referring to the possible acquisition mentioned in the letter.

Joe watched the clock's hands slowly slide from one hour to the next as he waited for the workday to end and the game excitement to arrive. Finally, at five o'clock, all four men were crowded into the elevator. Stopping on every floor from the fourteenth down, the crowds prepare to navigate their way home.

When they walked out of the high-rise office building, the day was picture-perfect as the sun beamed down and a light breeze kept the heat at bay.

"Damn, almost a shame to be inside a box on a day like this," Frank said, taking a deep breath.

"Yeah, you won't be saying that when you have a perfect view of George Frazier, striking out those Dodgers, come-on, swing, badda-badda-badda..."

"Mr. Poole?" The fellow saying his name was short, very short.

Wow, this guy can't be more than five-four, five-five. Wonder if he's Mexican or Puerto Rican, Joe thought as he acknowledged the dark-skinned man. "Yes, I'm Joe Poole, and these are my associates."

"Sirs, very pleased to meet you all. My name is Emilio Escobar. Gentlemen, if you would follow me."

He walked toward the black limousine parked in front of the building next to the curb and effortlessly swung the back door open.

"Please watch your heads," he warned as they climbed into the vehicle.

Bill Lomax was the last to crawl in. Joe was bouncing around the car like a kid, yammering non-stop about how the Yankees were going to take the Pennant tonight.

Slowly, Emilio pulled away from the curb and effortlessly eased into the steady stream of traffic.

They were going to be early. The game didn't start until eight o'clock. The subway would have taken forty minutes, but in the limo, they'd be an hour just getting on the freeway.

"Frank, Bill, Sean…how about a whiskey, guys?" Joe asked as he held the bottle of Jameson’s next to his beaming face.

Sean grinned. The Irishman in him could never turn down a Jameson’s whiskey, not the first one anyway.

"Yes, boys, let's have a few, but keep yer heads about cha, lads. Don’t forget, there’ll be business going on after the game."

Joseph Poole poured. Four successful, happy men lifted their glasses in unison. Joe proposed a toast.

"Here's to the NEW YORK YANKEES bringing the Pennant home TONIGHT!" he shouted. A round of ‘here-heres’ and the sound of four clanging glasses followed the toast.

Emilio smiled as he eyed them in the rear view mirror.

*****

At five thirty the morning after the sixth World Series game, Eric Brunner rolled out of bed. First stop was the bathroom for a pee, then to the kitchen to put on a pot of coffee. While it was brewing, Eric showered and brushed his teeth. Twenty minutes later, he sat with a steaming cup in one hand and the morning newspaper in the other.

"Well I'll be damned! The Dodgers won it," he whistled through his teeth as he read the headlines on page one.

"Los Angeles Dodgers cruise to a 9-2 victory over the New York Yankees and another World Series title!"

On page 2, there was another headline.

"Four of New York's finest, True Yankee Fans perish in fatal automobile accident"

The article revealed that four well-known lawyers had died in a horrific car wreck. "Through a miracle of God," it said, the limousine driver luckily escaped the fiery twisted metal with just minor injuries.

Eric smiled. He was glad Emilio had gotten out virtually unscathed. He was a loyal soldier who would be useful again someday.

Chapter 5

"Well friends, looks like we're gettin' our comeuppance today! Ya'all know the ribbin' we've been givin' our neighbors to the south 'bout all that gorgeous sunshine up here in Dallas? Yes-sir-ree folks, here comes the rain! Steady light rain showers are expected throughout the day with a 20% chance of thunder-showers tonight..."

The radio announcer's voice trailed off as Rose walked from the bathroom into the front living room. Pulling back the elegant white drapes, she visually confirmed what she'd already suspected. The weatherman's forecast had missed the mark…again.

"Light-rain-showers my eye," she murmured as she spotted the droplets exploding, bouncing off the hood of her beamer. The up-to-the-minute weather information had her back in the walk-in closet, substituting her earlier choice with a new outfit. A moment later, the jade-colored skirt and flowered blouse were back on the hanger. Now lying on the bed was a pair of black dress pants and a burgundy blouse. Considering that Rose and her co-workers wore lab coats, she still 'dressed to impress'.

Forty minutes later, Rose was bending over, stretching to reach the umbrella that had rolled off the passenger seat and onto the floor. It was a bit tricky exiting the mid-sized car while opening the umbrella quickly enough to keep her hair from getting wet.

The door to the lab was only a short distance from where she parked. There were exactly thirteen parking spots in front of the fortified steel door of the octagon building. The center one was larger than the six on either side and served as the loading zone.

The peculiar structure had no windows other than a ribbon of heavily tinted glass. The panes circled the parameter of the building thirty feet above the ground. They appeared hinged at the bottom, sharply jutting out at a forty-five degree angle. The odd stretch of glass added an architectural flavor to the otherwise bland design. On bright days, beams of light reflected downward, elusively touching those who dared to be near enough.

Rose was well aware of the predicament facing the pharmaceutical companies. They needed the scientists to create the remedies, which in turn spelled huge profits. Novatek protected its secrets like a dog guarding its bowl. When formulas were stolen, invariably the culprit was usually the scientist who'd created it in the first place. And therein lay the conundrum. Security was tight, and someone was always watching. Rose glanced up at the band of opaque glass surrounding the building, her skin breaking out in goose bumps as she envisioned unseen eyes.

Entering the institute, she slipped her bar-coded security pass into the slot, just above the handle. Instantly the electric lock made the familiar 'CHU-CLUNK.' The sound indicated she had five seconds to close her umbrella and open the door before the lock would re-set. Once inside, she dropped her umbrella in the large shallow bin and cautiously approached the scanner. After nearly three years, the harmless-looking gadget still made her nervous.

When she first started at Novatek, Blake thoroughly briefed her on the procedure.

"Rose, these things detect anything from metal objects to radio activity. They record your image along with all your possessions. Every entrance has one. Be careful what you wear or carry in your purse. Damn thing goes off even if it detects a large belt buckle or a clump of keys. Trust me, you don't want that to happen. If it does, don't move. There's an armed response by security within seconds." He paused a moment, his face blushing as he cautioned her about the consequence of tripping the device.

"If security shows up, they perform an immediate strip-search in the small rooms right next to the system. There are no exceptions. Sorry," he said almost apologetically.

"Thanks for the heads up, Blake, I'll be careful," she recalled saying.

Less than a week later the warning was forgotten, lost in the flurry of new surroundings. Daydreaming, she proceeded through the sensor, the ear-piercing siren screaming.

"DAMN!" she blurted. Rose jumped as her heart leapt into race mode. Just as Blake had forewarned, the guards appeared out of nowhere. Rose vowed never to be caught in that predicament again. The humiliation of the shakedown was embarrassing.

She pushed aside the vivid memory as she looked warily at the paddles. As she had for the last three years, she held her breath while passing through the security checkpoint. Seconds later, she exhaled a familiar sigh of relief at the welcome silence. Arriving a half hour early she casually proceeded down the wide corridor toward the laboratory. The click-clack-click of her heels on the high-gloss granite floor echoed through the deserted hallway. Rose stood in front of the lab a half minute later and once again used her security pass to unlock the solid steel door.

"Hi, Miss Rose," Henry chirped brightly, as she entered the lab.

"Good Morning, Henry," she responded, smiling.

Henry was the Institute's animal handler, responsible for cleaning the cages as well as the disposal of carcasses. His duties also included the delivery of the replacement animals used in testing.

Henry was usually in by six and most often gone before the team arrived, although occasionally, on some mornings he could be found still sanitizing the last of the cages. Rose suspected he had a small crush on her, hanging around until she showed up. Henry often stayed long enough to talk about the weather, his car, or even the animals.

He was what most people referred to as "*simple*." With the extreme measures taken for security, Rose suspected Henry was chosen for the position *because* he was a bit slow.

He could go from lab to lab looking after the animals without Novatek being concerned about the theft of trade secrets or files. *Poor Henry wouldn't know the difference between a placebo and the next miracle cure*, she correctly surmised. Henry was a harmless fellow and Rose had a soft spot for him.

"So how's work going, Miss Rose?"

"Aw, you know, Henry, same as always."

"Yeah, me too. Sure has been nice out lately, hasn't it?"

"Yes, I'm glad spring has finally brought some warm weather."

"Me too. I hate the cold."

She knew he hated the cold. It was his opening line every time she'd talked to him throughout the winter.

Gathering up his sterilized container with a few mice carcasses, he began making his way toward the windowless lab door.

"Well, you have a really nice day, Miss Rose. Don't work too hard!"

"Thank you, Henry, and don't YOU work too hard either." *He's such a sweet man*, Rose thought as he pulled the door shut.

With the familiar sound of the resetting tumblers, Rose put her hands on her hips and looked around. She surveyed the room where she spent more than half her waking hours, and tried to decide how to best use the next twenty minutes of quiet.

One side of the scientific workspace was lined with a continuous surface of stainless steel. It was fifty feet long and ended at the wall outside the lounge. Every five feet there was an electron microscope securely bolted to the counter. In front of each microscope was an ergonomic swivel barstool. The lighting was perfect, soft enough to avoid eyestrain, bright enough to see easily. No expense was spared to ensure that the researchers would never become drained due to the work environment. There were even rumors that oxygen was pumped in through the ventilation systems to ensure 'vigilance'.

Rose turned, taking in the refrigeration units, animal cages, and lockers on the opposite wall. There was also a large shelving area for the storage of all required materials. She moved toward the middle of the oversized room where a work centre with several desks was located. Each desk had a partitioned enclosure surrounding it. The design was conceived not with privacy in mind, but with an uninterrupted work environment being the objective.

With her hands still firmly planted on her hips, Rose glanced toward the back of the large space where the lunchroom was located. In the lounge were several vending machines that offered a variety of beverages and food. Everything was set up in such a way so the doctors and researchers never had to leave the laboratory during the workday.

A mischievous smile crossed Rose's lips as she thought about the moon pie back there with her name on it. She seldom indulged, and only when she was alone. "Ah, what the heck, I haven't had one in a long time," she said aloud, wandering toward the beckoning marshmallow treat.

So clever were their mysterious employers, that even cash was not necessary. The bar coded security card she used to unlock the doors also worked the vending equipment. Just a swipe of the card after she pushed the buttons marked A-6 and the coiled wire holding back her treat made a half turn. The tasty morsel slid down to the collection area as the purchase was simultaneously registered to her bar code. Rose's next paycheck would show the snack had been deducted along with any other goodies she bought.

After her small indulgence, Rose began gathering the previous day's notes and experiment results. She then placed them neatly on Vanessa's open workstation.

Vanessa Hargrave was the only member of the team who did not have a doctorate or any other degree in research. Although not a scientist, her job was challenging nonetheless. She was responsible for deciphering the various chicken-scratches of the doctors, then typing, cataloguing, and filing the results.

Rose was still puttering around the lab getting ready for the day when Marc Andrews, the third and final member of the research team, entered the laboratory.

"Hey, sexy, how are we this morning?" Marc boldly inquired, as he peeled off his blue jean jacket.

"I'm not sure how 'we' are, but I'm fine," Rose said, keeping her tone light. Marc stopped abruptly. Following his gaze, Rose knew what he was staring at. Feeling exposed, she couldn't resist the urge to pull her lab coat over her breasts.

"Ohhh, I bet you're *real fine*," he responded with a sexual innuendo.

Oh, you're such a jerk, she thought, rolling her eyes.

Marc smirked, tilting his head while comically batting his eyes as he walked past her toward the lockers.

Rose found his comments and actions unprofessional and

disrespectful. On several levels, she didn't care much for Marc. In her opinion, he was a *very* odd person. One minute his boyish charm would disarm her, the next his comments would have her blushing like a schoolgirl. Oftentimes he was gregarious and cheerful, over-confident and forward. Then there were periods when he was dark or gloomy, his eyes often avoiding direct contact. She suspected he was a near-genius with a bit of neurosis thrown in for good measure.

As he slipped on his lab coat, he walked toward Rose who was perched high on her chair, trying to look busy.

"Hey, where's ole 'flakey Blakey' this morning? Not like *him* to be late," he asked.

"Why do you have to be such an ass?" she snapped, her annoyance surfacing.

"Uh ha, a little sensitive this morning, Miss Frechette?"

"Do you make an effort to be obnoxious or is it a gift?"

"It's just a gift, no effort at all," he replied smugly.

God, he's so irritating sometimes. I wish Blake would just fire him, she thought, feeling exasperated. *Jerk's got me all worked up and it's not even nine o'clock.*

Marc came to a halt just beside her. *Why does he get under my skin so?* she thought flinching at his close proximity.

"Ah come on, don't be so uptight. How 'bout some sugar, sugar? Let's just kiss and make up," he said. Leaning closer, his puckered lips jutted outward, as he made exaggerated kissing sounds.

Rose instinctively pulled back looking appalled. Suddenly, Marc appeared embarrassed at the severity of her unspoken rejection.

The problem was this tall, lean, bad boy was a brilliant biochemist hand-picked by Dr. Edwards. Ultimately, she had no choice but to tolerate his juvenile behavior.

Yeah, well he's been a lot more careful about pulling his crap in front of Blake, she thought gratefully, recalling an 'episode' two months prior…

It had all begun when she'd arrived at work early that particular morning. She'd greeted Blake warmly, but as usual, he seemed pre-occupied and headed toward the lounge or bathroom, she wasn't sure.

Rose stopped at the lockers and slipped on her lab coat. Just then, Marc walked in. He made his way to the changing area, positioning himself so that her path to the lab's work section was blocked.

"Hey Red, how's it hanging?" Marc said, leaning against the locker directly in front of her.

"Look Marc, I don't have time to 'chat', I need to get to work."

"Relax, I'm not going to bite." He moved in a bit closer.

Though Rose knew Marc was harmless, she suddenly felt annoyed by his foolishness. *What if Blake sees him and thinks I'm okay with his flirting?* she thought irritably. Nervous warmth surrounded her and she felt uncomfortably hemmed in.

"Marc, PLEASE stop bothering ME!" she blurted, and forcibly pushing her way passed him, stumbling, she fell. Blake had barely caught her, reaching the changing room unnoticed during the brief exchange. Instantly, all three co-workers had a look of surprise on their faces. An awkward silence hung in the air. After helping Rose regain her footing, Dr. Edward's broke the silence.

"Marc, perhaps I'm not keeping you busy enough if you have time for such tom foolery. Or maybe you're not happy here at the lab or on my team. So how about it Marc?" he asked impatiently, expecting an immediate answer. When Marc did not instantly reply, Blake prompted him once more. "So, Marc?"

It was clear to Rose by the pinched look on Marc's face that he was more embarrassed than concerned over Blake's annoyance.

"Hey Doc, I'm cool, sorry Rose, I was just playing around," he said sheepishly.

"Yes, well Marc, we don't 'just play around' here. Please refrain from this type of behavior in the future," Blake said sternly.

Marc did not reply. He was either retreating into himself, like he often did or simply sulking; Rose couldn't tell which.

"Do you understand?" Blake repeated.

"Yeah, sure, Doc," he said as he quietly scurried away. Passing Rose, Marc didn't notice her glowing cheeks. Fanciful thoughts of Blake were racing through her head. *My knight in shining armor has just rescued me,* she fantasized adoringly.

So now, whenever Blake was around, Marc was quite cautious.

Rose snapped her thoughts back to the present moment as she watched Marc stroll toward his newly-claimed station. Though Rose hadn't asked why he'd moved, she quickly deduced he wanted to be closer to where Vanessa worked.

A few moments passed and Marc grabbed a bundle of notes as he approached her. Rose looked up and as his eye caught hers, he grinned. With his bruised ego fully recovered, he began sparring again.

"Hey, Red, did you happen to notice Edwards was *mondo bizzaro* yesterday? He was all jittery, just babbling to himself, like he was having a bad acid trip or something," Marc quipped.

Jesus, that's not even a word... 'MONDO BIZZARO,' Rose thought, *'and an acid trip... oh brother!'* It wasn't long after she began working with Marc that she suspected *he* was a recreational drug user.

"Blake would no more take acid than anything produced here at Novatek," she retorted defensively.

She knew of Blake's medication phobia. He would not take a pill or even a cough remedy. He felt the body was designed to fight most every bacterium. Blake thought overusing prescription drugs reduced the effectiveness when a serious virus took hold. He once said to her that only in an extreme emergency would he personally medicate. Blake's work at Novatek seemed a paradox.

"Yes, ma'am," Marc articulated, "he was pretty antsy, in fact, has been for months, but yesterday, he was a total retard."

Frustrated, she clenched her fists. *Dammit don't let him get to you like this*, she scolded herself, clamping her mouth shut so as not to blurt out anything she might regret. Rose was sure he was calling Blake names to get even more of a rise out of her. Though the comment infuriated her, what it really did was re-affirm her belief. Marc was a very, very strange man.

Each workstation had frosted glass partitions on either side of the microscope. There was six feet between the privacy barriers in which to work. The distance separating the dividers made it easier for her to feel hidden. *I wish Blake would get here. I wouldn't have to put up with Marc then*, she thought, leaning forward just a bit more.

The notion had barely formed itself when, like an answer to a prayer, she heard the welcome sounds of the electronic tumblers. A half second later the large door swung open. With his head bent forward, swinging the weathered satchel, Dr. Edwards entered.

"Morning," he said, to no one in particular as he proceeded toward his station. He never broke stride when he came into a room. An onlooker might think that he was in a foot race. Even in the grocery store, his gait was the same, although today, he *was* on a mission.

"Good morning!" Rose said, grateful for his arrival. She hoped Marc would finally shut up.

"Hey, what's up, Doc?" Marc exclaimed.

Oh brother, can't he come up with a new line, she thought. He'd been greeting Blake with the same corny "Bug's Bunny" axiom for nearly two years. Blake was either oblivious or just didn't care.

"Yes, good morning", he replied, walking straight to his station and to work. Apparently, he had no time for pleasantries or fretting a small thing like Marc's warped sense of humor.

After turning on the overhead light and sliding his satchel under the workstation, Blake walked over to the lockers. In one fluid movement, he put his sweater on the hook while grabbing a lab coat. Slipping it on, he made his way to the cages. Rose instantly perked up when she saw him walking toward the animals. Passing a cabinet, he paused long enough to take out a syringe.

He stopped at the cage marked '*Lucy',* which housed his latest experimental mouse. It was a common practice for the researchers to name their animals. The mouse wiggled in his hand as he proficiently extracted a small amount of blood. He gently placed the squirming test subject back into it's small haven, and immediately proceeded to his station. Rose's eyes never left Blake for a second, as she watched him with his furry little friend.

Her heightened interest had begun one day a few months ago. Everyone had left to go home that particular evening and Rose had just finished tidying up her desk, when she approached Blake. He was staring off into space as he ran his index finger down the white mouse's back.

"Cute little guy, isn't he?" she remarked in an effort to make small talk.

"Oh, she's a girl," he said almost dreamily.

"Really? Well what's her name?"

"This is Lucy. Possibly the most important little mouse in the world, aren't you girl?" Blake was talking more to the rodent than he was to Rose. He seemed barely aware of her presence. "You're my little accomplice, aren't you Lucy? The results you and I are getting could be the answer to a very big problem, couldn't it?" he asked rhetorically. He stared for a moment into its tiny black eyes, the pointy nose wriggling as the hairless tail whipped lightly on the back of his hand.

"What's that, Blake? What experiments are you conducting on our little friend here?" Rose asked curiously.

Snapping out of his momentary trance, he replied, "Ah… Oh… nothing, nothing at all Rose, I was just daydreaming." He quickly returned the animal to its cage and bolted toward the lockers. Rose wouldn't have thought much of it, except for one simple fact. Experimental mice didn't seem to be around as long as this one had. It really hadn't occurred to her until that very moment, but she'd noticed the name on the cage for months.

So now, every time he retrieved *Lucy*, it seemed to raise her curiosity. Shaking the memory, she watched as he returned to his station. He pulled a fresh slide from the box beside the partition. Depositing a drop of Lucy's blood on the clear sterile glass, he positioned it on his prized microscope.

Blake had previously mentioned to Rose how much he loved his new Video-enhanced contrast microscope. It revealed cellular structure and macromolecular complexes invisible to the naked eye or film. What made it even more special was the fact that it was not available to the public. Once again Novatek had come through with the best money could buy. Sliding his glasses to his brow, he leaned forward looking into the eyepiece.

No one really noticed Vanessa's tardiness until the lock sounded and she rushed in looking flustered. "Sorry I'm late, Dr. Edwards," she said, bustling to her oversized cubicle.

"Pardon me?" Blake responded absently.

"Sorry I'm late, Doctor. I slept in," she answered sheepishly.

"Oh, not a problem, it's fine," he replied dismissively.

Vanessa definitely stood out among her colleagues at the lab. At twenty-nine years old, she was an absolute beauty. Her proficiency as a lab administrator was the only attribute that allowed her to fit in. When Rose first met her, she wondered if her background was in modeling or acting. Rose thought Vanessa would find the deciphering, typing and filing unglamorous. Rose had guessed she wouldn't last a month. She had underestimated Vanessa's tenacity.

Quietly approaching Blake's work area Rose asked, "So what's the order of the day, Doctor? Do you need some help?"

"Uh...no thank you, Rose," Dr. Edwards said, jumping a little, her voice apparently startling him.

"I'm fine here, just carry on with what I assigned you last week, or see if Marc could use a hand."

Glancing toward Marc, she noticed he was standing in Vanessa's booth. Caught off guard by Blake's abrupt dismissal, Rose could feel her cheeks redden as she moved in the direction of her other co-workers. Walking toward them, she couldn't help overhearing the exchange.

"Vanessa, plans tonight?" Marc whispered.

"Uh, no, not really."

"Do you want to grab a drink?"

"Hmm, sure, why not," Vanessa replied with a shrug.

As Rose entered the stall, Marc left, winking as he passed.

For the life of me, I can't figure out what that girl sees in him, she thought.

"Vanessa, is there anything I can help you with?" she asked awkwardly.

"No, I'm fine here," she replied curiously. Rose had never really offered to help before. "Rose, I do have a question for you though. Have you noticed that Dr. Edwards is really obsessed with his work lately?" she whispered, motioning in Blake's direction.

"I don't know. Do you think he is Vanessa?" Rose probed. Because of her feelings for Blake, she didn't really trust her own judgment. She'd become more than a bit oversensitive.

"Yeah, I do actually. He's even been keeping all his own files in order. It's almost like he's trying to hide his results," Vanessa said warily.

"Oh, I don't think that's the case, Vanessa. The doctor gets, 'cold feet' with some of his experiments, I guess, for lack of a better term. He just likes to play his cards close to the vest until he's sure of what he's got," she offered in an equally hushed voice.

"Well whatever, he really acts strange sometimes. But on another note, I'm sure *you've* noticed Marc's playful flirting lately, haven't you?" she queried.

"No, I haven't," Rose lied. "Has he been bothering you?"

"Heck, no! Marc is quite exciting, and honestly," lowering her voice even more, she added, "I think he's very cute too. You know Rose, we should grab dinner or something some time, just get away from work and have a girls' night out!"

"That'd be great, let's do it soon," Rose agreed eagerly. "I'd better get to work," she smirked as she exited the area.

*****

Vanessa tapped a pen as she sat at her desk, carefully analyzing each of her co-workers. Scrutinizing the staff had recently become routine.

Blake, she decided long ago, was more interested in microbes than people, much too difficult to melt. If a hot little number like Rose gushing over him all day didn't raise his eyebrow…well who was she? Then of course, there was Rose. She was a sweet, sincere gal, that under different circumstances would have made a wonderful girlfriend, confidant, or maybe more.

She looked over toward Marc. He spied her glancing in his general direction and smiled. It was more of a lecherous smirk than a smile. Although this was business, Vanessa became aroused and suddenly felt flushed. She had already been on several dates with him. Her approach was to focus on the weakest link and probe. She had decided the weakest link here was Marc. Vanessa believed he might shed some light on Blake's mysterious experiments. She had tried unsuccessfully to 'be of help' to Edwards with his organizing. He was adamant about taking care of his own files and notes, removing them from the building every night. This made her unethical superiors very interested in what he was working on.

If any of them had known the real reason for her late arrival, her stolen glances at Dr. Edwards's notes might have made sense. Vanessa was late because she had a pre-arranged meeting with Michael, her surreptitious contact. As a spy for Wilkinson Pharmaceutical, Novatek's only real competitor, her objective was to report any large breakthroughs. So far, there had been nothing new to pass on to Wilkinson, at least not anything Vanessa wanted them to know. A strange turn of events had begun to take place. Although she kept her eye on Dr. Edwards, Vanessa had more than her eye on Marc.

Chapter 6

An evening chill hung over Dallas as Bruce Vargo drove down Congress Street toward the meeting. With no real plans for the following day, he contemplated whether to spend the night. Beside him on the seat was a packed overnight bag, just in case. A few drinks, a cigar, and a couple games of pool might be just what he needed.

The Patronum headquarters was a large, fully restored structure, originally built as an elite private social club. The red brick building itself was a masterpiece, crowned with high, arched windows and matching nine-foot doorways. Building aesthetics being one thing, and functionality another, Joseph Augustus Rodenham, an ingenious architect had envisioned both. Samuel L. Jacobs, founder of the cattleman's association wanted to make a bold statement, and in 1876 had hired Rodenham to make his dream a reality. Two years later the construction of the richly appointed building began.

Jacobs was a genuine cowboy carving his fortune from the lucrative cattle business in the 1850's. During the latter part of the century, cattle ranching was a measure of a man's true grit in Texas, and in northwestern California, it was gold. Each phenomenon had produced its fair share of wealthy men. Fortunes made in the gold rush were often a result of tenacity, hard work, and pure luck.

Samuel Jacobs had been bigger than life. He had a zest common to men in the west, but was reluctant to take a chance with Lady Luck and the California gold fever. Over three-hundred-thousand prospectors showed up in less than five years and he knew they all needed to eat. With a dedication to hard work and a head for business, Jacobs was a millionaire by his thirtieth birthday. He felt every American had a God-given right to reap fortunes and inherit the earth. Jacobs believed those who were smart and willing to work hard were entitled to the spoils. He had an equal enthusiasm when it came to enjoying life. Within four years of engaging Joseph Rodenham, the private cattleman's club was completed. The club provided a wonderful business opportunity, as well as a way to socialize. But only with his fellow Americans, and only those who had ripped their fortunes from the raw wilderness.

That's how it appeared on the outside. Many of the locals quietly ridiculed the name of the exclusive club. Jacobs had decided to call it 'True Phantoms.' The extravagant six-story building was designed to accommodate the traveling families of the rich cattle barons of that time.

Samuel Jacobs made many daring and amazing strides in his seventy-three years on earth, but this was to be his legacy. No one would ever know how his ideals and prophecies would come to affect a nation or the world a century later.

So began an era of concealment with Jacobs as its father. The first secret was brilliantly embedded in the name of his fortress. There was certainly no reason for anyone to play a game of anagrams, the mixing of existing letters to create new words. Had someone been so inclined with the words 'True Phantoms,' they'd have discovered those letters would create over five-hundred different words, one of which spelled *'The Patronums'*.

*****

The Patronums' headquarters were located just three short miles from the infamous Texas School Book Depository. It was the very location in which Lee Harvey Oswald was *assumed* to have inflicted the fatal wounds ending the life of President John F. Kennedy. There were still surviving Patronums who knew exactly how and why the charismatic president had been eliminated.

Proceeding down the ramp to the underground parking, Bruce Vargo opened the window of his car. As he came to a stop, he placed his thumb on the biometric identifier. Seconds later, his fingerprint was verified. The steel door creaked as it rolled up, allowing entrance to the underground complex.

"Hello, sir," the valet said, opening the driver's door.

"Hi, Harold. Park it in the back, please. I plan to stay the night," he said.

The Patronums Committee meetings' had been Wednesday evenings, and had never changed in over a hundred years.

As the elevator rose, Bruce tried to determine if the helicopter he heard on the roof was landing or taking off.

The fading whop, whop, whop, of the blades confirmed that it was in fact, leaving. Stepping out of the elevator, he was greeted by the concierge.

"Good evening, Mr. Vargo. Ah, I assume you will be our guest this evening, sir."

"Yes, Francis thank you," he said. Passing him the small overnight bag, Bruce proceeded to the large round table in the meeting room.

The building was fully staffed with suites available for any member of the committee who wished to spend the night. Less elaborate rooms were provided for their personal drivers and bodyguards. The recently renovated structure was equipped with the most modern technology available.

"Hi, Bruce, how are you tonight?" Victor asked.

"A bit tired actually, Victor. You?"

"I'm feeling good. The Doc's handling tonight's little get-together, you know," he said matter-of-factly.

"Yeah, I know. I wonder what's up."

Several gentlemen were already seated as more strolled in. The Committee was made up of fifteen highly educated men. All were considered brilliant. Most happened to be very wealthy as well. Often the meetings consisted primarily of cognac, savored with the finest cigars. Others dealt with very serious issues.

On the first Wednesday of each month, there was a vote on continued servitude between the Committee constituents. If advancing age or personal issues affected judgment, that name would inevitably come up. If it did more than eight times in a vote, the member was unceremoniously asked to leave. It was all a matter of the ultimate goal. Not often, but on occasion, the exiting associate left the Committee with animosity. Such was the case with Ian Mackenzie the year before.

His Scottish stubborn streak had come with an equally bad temper. That particular evening had clearly demonstrated that his clarity of thought was now jeopardized by the onset of dementia. Old man Mackenzie had risen to his feet after the announcement that it was to be his last meeting.

"Goddammit, I've served this committee for over twenty-eight years! I'll be damned if I'm going to be kicked out like this!" the eighty-four year old screamed.

"Ian, calm down. You're not being '*kicked out*,' You're simply being asked to '*step down*.' It's time for you to sit back, let others take care of business," Victor told him.

The rest of the committee looked warily at Ian. When it came to retirement, the term 'asked to step down' was used loosely. It was not a request. It was the law of the Patronums. Exiting members were well aware that bitterness could translate into a question of loyalty. That question was very dangerous.

"I don't give a damn what you want to call it. This is my chair. Has been and will be until the day I die!" Ian shouted as he plopped back into his seat.

"Fine, Ian. We'll discuss it again next week." They would not. "Unless there is any new business, let's adjourn to the lounge for a cognac," Victor had invited casually.

Ian Mackenzie died of a massive heart attack later that same night. The coroner's report stated that the cause of death was 'natural.' There was nothing natural about the white powder that had been slipped into his drink earlier in the evening. Such was the fate of a member who did not embrace the Committee's decision to relinquish his seat.

As part of a large network, each committee delegate represented the 'voice' of his particular cell. All communications were between each individual Patronum and his mentor. The mentor would in turn report to *his* mentor, thus ensuring anonymity amongst Patronums. This chain would eventually lead to the upper echelons of the ruling fifteen.

Committee members were selected based on their area of expertise, combined with the overall ability to manage their particular cluster of confederates.

Victor Kaplan was a retired Supreme Court judge. His branch dealt exclusively with all legal matters. Unlike Ian, Victor's clarity was never in question, even though he was eighty-one years old. He was head of the network consisting of everyone from court stenographers to judges. Anything in the legal arena that concerned the Patronums made its way up through the various mentors until it reached him. A variety of resolutions would be considered, ending in a vote taken as to the appropriate course of action.

Every cell dealt with any situation where freedom from disorder was maintained through an established authority. The ultimate authority was always the Committee.

"Are you staying tonight, Bruce?" Victor asked his old friend.

"Actually, I am, Vic. You?"

"If you are up to a game or two, I imagine I will."

Victor was referring to the billiard room, were the two would often play, discussing old times or current affairs.

"Depending on how late it goes tonight, I wouldn't object to whooping you at some pool," Bruce said light-heartedly.

"So, like I was saying, it's Doc Emerson's meeting tonight." Victor repeated.

"Right. So have you heard any rumors?" Bruce asked.

"No, very hush-hush," Vic replied as they both found their seats. The committee members were all shuffling to their chairs.

The fifteen cells of the Patronums were separated into factions. They included government, military, science and energy, even foreign affairs. Bruce Vargo's was intelligence and security.

When all were present, Victor Kaplan called everyone to order. After the murmur of whispers died down, the floor was turned over to Dr. Emerson, head of the medical sector.

"Fellow Patronums, I have been given some preliminary information I feel should be brought to the attention of this committee. Initial reports will be handed out to each of you."

As he spoke, the documents were distributed to the members.

"Based on the information we've received, I'm calling upon the security division immediately. Bruce, we'll require full surveillance on the principals involved until confirmation of the report can be obtained."

Bruce Vargo looked at the doctor and nodded once, indicating he understood the request.

"Information will be forwarded to you about the individuals involved so your department can begin a work-up on them. Verification of the dossier will be conducted by my people."

Bruce knew all efforts would revolve around researching the validity of the documents received. The information contained in the brief stemmed from a Patronum employed at the Novatek Pharmaceutical Corporation. Dr. Evan Sinclair was a virtual unknown at this level. From the look on his colleague's face, Bruce realized the intelligence Sinclair had passed to his mentor would have had to catch the attention of every link in the chain to make its way into Dr. Emerson's hands.

"Gentleman, if this report proves to be valid, we will require immediate action from all departments. The potential impact to the United States as well as the world could be enormous. As usual, it remains our duty to determine if this will have a positive or negative impact."

If Emerson's team could verify Evan Sinclair's report, a flurry of activity would be set in motion. The committee leaders whose cells dealt with government and finance would be called upon to determine the potential outcome.

Once each cog of the well-oiled machine completed their assignments, the total of all results would be made available to every associate of the Committee. When each and every question was answered satisfactorily, a secret vote would be taken. The outcome of the vote would decide whether the results would be made public or simply withheld, hidden away and stored for future considerations.

It was protocol that the first page of any brief identified the subject, whether an organization or an individual.

Page two contained a synopsis of the complete report, less the technical information that followed in subsequent pages. The concise summary, regardless of the reader's expertise, would clearly explain why the Patronums might consider involvement.

"Gentleman, please refer to page one."

All Committee members picked up the folders placed in front of them. When they opened the report there was only one name in large bold type: ***DR. BLAKE EDWARDS***.

Chapter 7

"Ohhh, SHUT the hell up," Dr. Evan Sinclair murmured, his voiced laced with embellished sarcasm. The barrage of incessant horns echoed from behind, startling him out of his momentary trance. The rubber squealed as his new red corvette shot away from the intersection. The car didn't suit the balding, pudgy man.

Despite his thirty-nine years, the thick glasses that partially hid the full, round face, made him look like a youngster behind the wheel. The crowning touch to the whole picture was his stature. Evan used to joke in college that he was 'height challenged,' barely standing five foot six.

Although he was in fact a young man, Evan had earned the professional credentials of someone twice his age. In his repertoire of accomplishments, he had achieved a doctorate in medical science, health science and a masters degree in biochemistry.

"It's green for god's sake! *Not the right shade* for you, lady?" he shouted. Pressing down on his horn, he set into motion a collective symphony of sedition from the impatient souls in his rear-view mirror. With short-lived satisfaction, he smirked.

Twenty minutes later, he was entering his office at Novatek. Dr. Sinclair peered at the newest pile of files sitting on his desk. He wondered how a man of his stature could be stuck in here, an eight by ten windowless cubbyhole. He'd moved to Dallas with large expectations, craving acknowledgment as well as financial rewards. The latter was best fulfilled here, at the pharmaceutical level. Recognition and credit appeared to be reserved for others.

He felt drained from the episode at the kitchen table earlier that morning. *Dammit, I'm just not in the mood,* he thought plopping into his armless office chair. He swiveled toward the keyboard of his typewriter and stared at it sitting there, daring him to draft his next report. It was going to be a long day.

At breakfast, his wife Audrey had rehashed the same long-standing argument. It started with his working late. It migrated to the fact that he seemed to have no time or energy for her or the kids. The quarrel was an old one, but still he hated how it dampened his spirits.

I wish she'd fight like other wives, maybe after dinner when the kids are in bed. At least then, I'd be able to digest the whole thing along with my roast and potatoes, he thought.

The bickering at the Sinclair home always took place first thing in the morning. Evan would leave for work burdened with the fight, frustrated that he'd missed the chance to get even. Often the clever comebacks didn't pop into his head for a few hours. By the time they came, he'd be at his desk, just as he was now. His eyes glazed as he stared blankly at the typewriter, not seeing it at all, the memory of the spat all too fresh in his mind.

"Damn it, Audrey, do you think this house pays for itself? Dance lessons for Katie, Jimmy's music lessons? Your bloody new car, do you think this is all free?" Evan exclaimed. With a broad wave of his arm, he attempted to signify their lifestyle.

"I have to work. SOMETIMES I HAVE TO WORK LATE!" he yelled.

"Yes, I understand you have to work! I know that you provide for us all, but we haven't gone to a movie, dinner, or even made love in months," she retaliated.

"For crying out loud, Audrey, I'm tired at night."

"You make *choices* Evan, *choices*. You have a wife and two kids and you go out and buy yourself a two-seater sports car? What kind of message is that? How am I supposed to respond to *that?*"

"Oh, for chrissake Audrey! With the hours I put in and all the work I do, don't you think I deserve a little something too? That car has been a dream of mine since I was a *kid!"*

"The last time we acted like a family was at Christmas for God's sake. Evan, do you call this a marriage? Things had better change around here very soon, or one day, the kids and I will be gone," she snapped, exasperated.

Audrey stormed out of the oversized kitchen and disappeared up the oak staircase, officially ending the fight.

He felt relieved as she vanished. He was out of excuses. *She's right, this is no marriage,* he thought glumly.

Of course, Evan knew the work was real, to a point. He regularly put in about fifty hours a week.

His task was to carefully examine all data supporting the findings of the researchers in laboratory's one through four at Novatek. In his review, if he found no flaw in the written data it was then forwarded to the 'Final Development Department'. That branch merely followed in the footsteps of the scientists, duplicating the experiments. Obviously, theirs was a much simpler task. After mimicking the experiments and assuming the same results, the next step was FDA approval and the paper flurry that came with it.

Evan often read data that claimed breakthroughs and proposed remedies in a wide range of areas. They could be pills for depression, high cholesterol, or bacterial infections. If he found something didn't make sense, it was returned to the respective laboratory for further clarification. If everything checked out, off it went to Final Development.

Evan stared at the accumulation of neatly stacked papers and folders on his large oak desk. The office was a collection of file cabinets that covered almost every square foot.

Scrutinizing the complex documents that came into his small workplace often created a mountain of files. He somehow managed to make the area look incredibly well organized. It was clear Evan Sinclair was a very meticulous, very busy man. Despite his best efforts, he never seemed to catch up with the constant demands of his work.

He considered the true source of his troubles, and not for the first time since Audrey's discontent had begun surfacing.

The real problem here isn't work or money. The real problem here is Loretta, he thought feeling out of control.

Loretta's three-thousand-dollar monthly allowance along with her two-bedroom penthouse suite was putting a dent in more than his marriage. He was slowly going broke.

With his eyes bulged and still fixed on the unseen typewriter, the same question assaulted his mind for the hundredth time.

How the hell did I let myself get in so deep with her?

"Yeah, well that's no mystery, *it's the sex*," he muttered under his breath.

Recalling vivid images of the intimate times he had with Loretta, he knew his wife could never engage in the carnal favors he enjoyed with this woman. He had decided that even discussing those types of relations with Audrey would be embarrassing for them both. In his mind, he often thought of Loretta as his wet dream.

Evan's conquests in his college days were mainly limited to academic degrees. The social aspect of campus life had eluded him entirely. Often it was by choice; most often the choice resulted from a lack of self-confidence with women. The constant insecurities he'd felt resulted in his eye avoiding the ladies. For all intents and purposes, it was deliberately stuck in the lens of a microscope. He spent countless hours reading endless chapters of science, biology and medical journals. All free time was exhausted in the on-campus library.

He had met Audrey at church. Mutual loneliness was their largest single bond. She was shy, quite pretty, but in a simple way. Her interests were not in science or his work. She dreamed of children, a house, the dutiful husband and provider. For the most part, she couldn't understand a thing he was talking about when he discussed his latest victory.

Evan took his responsibility at Novatek seriously. In lieu of the recognition he longed for, he imagined himself as the proverbial guardian. When he caught flaws on the proposed medications at this level, Novatek would save large expense. The anticipated work would not make it to 'Final Development' until the errors were corrected. When that happened, he was elated and felt his position served an important purpose. Audrey couldn't have cared less. She just wanted to stay home with her husband, her children and enjoy a family life.

Evan had declared his love for her on their first date, hoping for sex. Audrey had given him the sex on their first date, hoping for love.

They were in their late twenties when they met and both felt a sense of urgency to make it work.

In an alcohol-induced moment of honesty, they'd confided to each other their genuine reasons for engaging one another.

Evan admitted to Audrey that women just didn't come on to him like she did. Based on that she *had* to be the one. As an afterthought to the admission, he remembered to add that he was of course in love with her. Audrey's rationale, quite simply, was that it was the right time for her to wed. Those were not the ingredients most people considered a solid foundation for a marriage, but the Sinclairs had managed to make it work rather well. Of course, that was until Loretta Benton walked into his life looking for employment.

Evan continued to stare mindlessly as he recalled Loretta's version of how she came to be at his office searching for a job.

The headhunting bureau had informed Miss Benton that she didn't have the qualifications to earn an interview with Novatek. She felt that her *'friendly demeanor'* at the placement agency had scored her the meeting with Dr. Sinclair. Evan guessed it was more likely the revealing top she was wearing when she arrived in his office, after leaving the agency that fateful day. He couldn't help but notice that the blouse stretched tightly across her chest. After all, he had to inspect the security pass, which was pinned to thin material. It didn't take Evan long to realize that she possessed none of the skills required for the position, unable to even type. Loretta flirted the entire time she sat in his small office.

"Dr. Sinclair, it would be a great honor to work alongside such a brilliant man," she gushed. "Exactly what do *you* do, sir?"

"Well, Miss Benton, here at Novatek, I have a great deal of responsibility. All data comes directly to this office. It must be reviewed, translated, and then verified for accuracy."

Even the mere memory of what she'd said next during the interview made him feel flush as the blood-rush reddened his cheeks… just like they were that day.

"*WOW*, that is such fascinating work, doctor, it's just so *amazing*. I would really *love* to work with you."

Evan basked in the accolades she bestowed upon him. A sense of responsibility prevailed, although his resolve had been weakened. As she rattled on, he reluctantly accepted the simple truth. *Like it or not this cupcake will just add to my troubles. How the hell can I concentrate with those in my face?* he thought as he stared at her breasts. Evan remembered how hard he'd struggled to regain his composure.

"I'm sorry, Miss Benton. Unfortunately you do not have the necessary training for this position," he told her, mustering up what little tenacity he had left.

Loretta's eyes immediately welled up with tears. "I understand, Dr. Sinclair. I was just hoping..." her voice trailed off in a dejected whimper.

Reaching for the Kleenex box on his credenza, he felt uneasy.

"I'm terribly sorry, Miss Benton, I wish there was something I could do," he apologized, offering her a tissue.

Out of nowhere and with lightning speed Loretta seemed to pull herself together.

"Well, Dr. Sinclair, maybe you could think of another department in this huge place that could use someone with my experience," she implored, dabbing her eyes.

Evan, caught off guard, began wracking his brain.

Jesus, where could she work? She has no skills. He came up blank.

"Miss Benton, off hand I can't honestly think of anything, although Novatek *is* a very large company. I would have to cross-reference the inter-office directory and I could also check for any recent postings. If you would like to call tomorrow, I might have some information for you."

In retrospect, he recognized that it was at this exact moment that Loretta had moved in for the kill.

"Evan, it *is* okay if I call you *Evan,* isn't it?"

"Ah, yes...uh, sure...no problem," he stammered shyly.

"Instead of calling tomorrow, could we meet tonight? There's a lounge over on Tilley Avenue. You've probably seen the place. It's called Tilley's," she giggled.

"Ahhh yes, I know the spot, aha, Tilley's, over there on Tilley Avenue, right." Evan had no idea where the bar was, or for that matter where the street was either.

"Say around seven-ish?" Loretta cooed.

"Ahhh sure, that would be perfect," he heard himself reply.

"Great, I'll see you then," she said amorously.

Loretta leisurely rose from her chair. As she stood, her breasts seemed larger than when she'd entered the room, her back more arched, and her neck elongated as she seductively meandered toward the door. Loretta stopped, purposefully turned, winked and smiled. His heart skipped a beat. Minutes after she was gone, he began to contemplate the can of worms he was about to open. *Damn, seven o'clock isn't good at all. Five would've been better. Jesus, what am I going to say to Audrey?* His head was spinning and his emotions mixed. On the one hand he was excited at the prospect of going for drinks with this bombshell. On the other, guilt began to creep over him like a cold wet blanket. *What am I doing?* he asked himself. *I'm really not doing anything wrong, just trying to help the poor girl find a job...* Evan shook his head. *Crazy thinking. What am I, delusional? That woman couldn't get a job* at *Novatek sweeping floors.*

Evan continued to struggle for an hour as he read a file. Guilty thoughts kept popping up, but in the end, he knew he'd lost the battle with his conscience and would rendezvous with the seductress as planned. Halfway through their first evening together, Loretta's trap had been baited and sprung. More than Evan's ego had been manipulated. She didn't get a job at Novatek that night, but with Evan Sinclair as her new benefactor, she didn't need one.

That was the beginning of the deceit, lies and unexplained late nights. Loretta's only real gift was a body built for sex, partnered with the willingness to use it. After a short time, he'd figured out that the potential of a plush lifestyle was her driving motivation. Loretta was unstoppable.

Finally, Evan blinked his eyes. As he pulled his gaze from the lone typewriter on his desk, he became acutely aware of the present. With the hypnotic spell now broken, he still felt the full weight of his troublesome burden. As moisture bathed his strained eyes, he tried to shake the miserable feeling.

Abandoning his depressing thoughts, he became fully animated, and picked up the file in front of him.

"Well," he said, "what do we have here?"

Evan opened the file and began reading aloud,

Rose Frechette, File Number B12D35fGG09; April 29th 1981. Product description: Vaginal Cream

Condition for suggested treatment: yeast infection.

Cause of Condition; Vaginal yeast infections caused by Candida alb cans, normally present in… *Blah, Blah, Blah… god these reports can be so boring,* Evan silently grumbled.

Without exception, the results coming out of Edwards's lab were always complete and ready to kick upstairs. Evan was going to miss out on that little job-satisfaction rush. He accepted that this review would be an exercise in futility. But regardless, he read every report in spite of their origin.

Ah geez, sometimes I really hate this job, he brooded.

His thoughts kept returning to the fight with Audrey and the situation in which he now found himself. He was painfully aware that all too soon he would have to make a difficult decision. He would have to choose. Fix his marriage or leave his family in the name of lust. It seemed like it should have been an easy choice. Audrey was, of course, the perfect wife, and he *did love the kids* and was already missing the fun he'd had with them before this all began. Except the things Loretta did made it very complicated. At least in Evan's mind.

Pondering the possibilities, he halfheartedly admitted several realities. Number one, if he hooked up with Loretta permanently, the sex would never be the same once she had him. Number two, she would rape him financially and so would Audrey. Evan rubbed his forehead as the beginning of a migraine began to take hold.

Chapter 8

Henry's mood was bright as he climbed out of his beat-up, old Nova, and was excited about the plans he had for the evening. He walked up the rotting wooden steps that led to the small porch. The one and a half storey wartime home was in desperate need of repair. A coat of paint would have concealed some of the decay, but a general refurbishing was long overdue. Extensive renovations were not in his meager budget. Ironically, Henry worked for a pharmaceutical company and the biggest single draw on his paycheck was his mother's medications.

"Hi Ma, I'm home!"

As the wooden screen door banged shut, he could hear his mother's cheerless voice echo down from the upstairs bedroom.

"Well, it's about time, Henry. I've been alone all day."

He ascended the creaky stairs and there it was, the familiar knot in his stomach. He wasn't articulate enough to label it as '*guilt.*' The upset feeling was just there whenever she spoke to him in her caustic tone.

He rounded the corner, stepping into his mother's room. There, propped up with pillows, Agnes Miller was watching the twenty-one inch black and white television. Suddenly, Bob Barker shouted out, "Rod, who's the next contestant on the PRICE IS RIGHT!" Lying on top of the blankets, still in her housecoat, the hawk-faced woman glared straight ahead.

"Ma, why aren't you dressed? I thought Noreen was coming by to take you shopping," he asked.

"She called me this morning, claimed her arthritis kept her up half the night. Poor woman sounded like she was exhausted." An accusatory look flashed across her withered face as she said in a hushed voice, "I'll bet it's from all the pills she takes."

This was not going to be a good time to tell *Mother* he had made plans tonight with Jennifer. He tried to time his outings with his girlfriend on days when his mother would be occupied. A day out with Noreen meant she would drift off early, not expecting his constant presence. Even a trip to her doctor would give him a break.

Henry stared at the etched lines in his mother's face, each one a testament to a life fraught with bitterness and hostility. He tensed. *Ma's going to be hard to talk to now. I wish I didn't still live here*, he thought grimly. He'd just turned forty-six.

When Henry was five years old, his father had walked out on the young family. Agnes was devastated. She was a hard woman to live with, always antagonistic, managing to fill most days with an unending string of complaints.

During an argument, his young father, frustrated with her razor sharp tongue, blurted out, "I can't take YOU or the STUPID KID anymore!" Later that night he left the house and never returned. In her mind she laid the full blame of her husband's sudden abandonment on the young boy. As he grew older, she shared the sentiment…often.

Being a nice-looking woman in the mid 1940's offered plenty of opportunities for new beginnings. World War Two had just ended and there was an abundance of returning young soldiers eager to get on with life back home. Granted, Henry was a simple child, but loveable nonetheless. It was Agnes who scared the young men away, not the boy. She was a malcontent that would never change and flaunted her bitchiness like a badge of honor. When Henry's father left she was twenty-three and an attractive young woman. By her thirtieth birthday, the wretched look of discontent had carved itself permanently on her face. She never again felt the warm touch of a lover, could never tempt someone to share her life. She also failed miserably at finding a father for her young son.

While Agnes aged, she became more dependent on her only child. Everything in her arsenal of manipulation was used to control him. She often reminded him that, if he were just a little brighter, his father would not have walked out on them. It served as the single reason she needed to justify her dependence on him.

It had all been working for years. He felt responsible for his mother. Alone, he bore the guilt for his father's abrupt departure. She always managed to make him feel simple-minded.

"You don't have the sense God gave a June bug."

"Do you know what a simpleton is? It's you, boy."

"You're just like your father. He was stupid too."

The barrage was endless and anything could set her off.

He would often sit in his bedroom, repeating, *"I'm a stupid boy, I'm a stupid boy."* He was still saying those words well into his thirties.

One day, after a harsher than usual scathing from his mother, he'd gone out for a walk. Jamming his hands into his pockets, he kicked at the gravel on the sidewalk with his well-worn sneakers. Stumbling along he mumbled under his breath.

"What's the matter, Henry?" a pleasant voice echoed.

Henry looked up, and saw Mr. Johnson. He owned the neighborhood groceteria and was sitting in a tattered chair just outside his storefront.

"Ahhh hi, Mr. Johnson, nothing I guess," Henry murmured.

"Why the long face, boy?" he asked, his tone sincere.

"I don't know Mr. Johnson, I guess I just wish I wasn't so stupid, so darn stupid," Henry blurted out.

"Son, you're not stupid." The old man's voice softened more.

"Yes I am. I'm very stupid, can't even add numbers or anything." The full-grown man-child was near tears as he spoke.

"Can't add numbers? Well that's not stupid, son," he said gently, hearing the despair in the young man's voice. "It's a matter of being *uneducated.* Did ya finish high school?"

"No, I had to quit. Got a job to help out my Mom."

Raising the young boy as a single mother with only an eighth grade education herself left little choice. As soon as Henry could get a job, Agnes had pulled him out of school. He never finished the sixth grade.

"Well, there you go, boy, get yourself into one of those night schools. They teach arithmetic, reading…all those things."

Consequently, Henry embarked on a journey for his GED, which had eluded him since he was a boy. Seven years later he achieved his dream of being a high school graduate. Henry didn't feel stupid when he received his diploma.

Agnes did not attend his graduation ceremony. She couldn't bear his happiness, or the threat of his looming independence.

Three great things came of his persistence. An enormous sense of pride accompanied with a bit of well-earned self-confidence, a driver's license, and his position at Novatek as the animal handler.

He was still working up the nerve to break the news to his mom when her disagreeable voice broke the silence.

"You go get the crib board out. I'll come downstairs to play a few games of cribbage tonight. Later on we'll watch Johnny Carson," his mother cawed.

Henry shoved his hands in his pockets, his eyes dropped to the ground and he bit his bottom lip. He felt like he was six again and afraid to face her. Summoning his courage, he squirmed as he spoke the words.

"Ma, I'm going to the movies with Jenny tonight."

"You know I can't stand that tramp. Why don't you stay home with me and we'll watch Johnny."

"Ma, I promised Jenny I would pick her up by 7:30. We can play a little cribbage until then and I'll fix you something to eat," he offered.

"No, that's fine, you go to the picture show with your whore. Just leave your poor mother. I'll fix my own food. I don't need you to watch Johnny with me either, just get out."

As the knot in his stomach tightened, Henry wished that every time his mother spoke it didn't make him feel so lousy. Two years earlier it would have been enough to make him stay home. Henry understood why she tried to make him feel bad, and he knew that his mom was doing it on purpose. He knew it was true, because Jennifer had told him so, and she was smart.

She, too, was a dropout and like Henry attended classes at night. Recently he told her why they couldn't spend more time together. Jennifer could not hold back any longer, and shared her feelings about Agnes.

"Henry, I know you love your mom, but you have to realize she doesn't want you to be with me. She's thinking that if we are together, there would be nobody to take care of her," she said.

"Well Jenny, me and you could take care of Ma, couldn't we?"

"Your mom would be happier if I wasn't around. You're all hers and I think she'd like to keep it that way."

"Do you really think Ma doesn't want me and you to be together?" he asked innocently.

"No Henry, I don't think she wants that at all."

She looked at his childlike expression. It was a mixture of confusion, admiration and sadness. She couldn't help but hug him gently.

"Jenny, you know one of the thousand reasons I really, really love you is because you're so smart," he said sheepishly.

His reminiscence shattered as Agnes coughed the phlegm from her throat. Henry lowered his head as he recognized that here he was, dealing with his Mother once again. *I might as well go. Ma's gonna be mad now, no matter what,* Henry thought.

"Okay, Ma, you have a good night, I'll check in on you when I get home," he assured her.

"Don't trouble yourself Henry. You don't have the time for me now, don't bother with me when you get home," Agnes chided.

"Okay Ma," he said, reaching over to hug her.

She stiffened at his touch, turning her bird-like face away when he tried to give her a kiss on the cheek.

"Love ya, Ma."

"If you really loved your mother, you'd stay here to play cribbage with me, and then we could watch Johnny Carson," she crowed one last time, in a final attempt to impose some measure of guilt.

Relieved that the confrontation had come to an end, he was already thinking about where to take Jenny for dinner.

He left the room without slowing or turning to look back.

Walking down the creaky stairs, he didn't notice the smile that had unconsciously slipped onto his face. Henry's mood brightened steadily as he distanced himself from the house—and his mother.

*****

As he drove the fifteen minutes to Jennifer's apartment all he could do was think about her and the different things they talked about. Though Jennifer was somewhat brighter than Henry, he thought she was brilliant and looked up to her. Early on in her young life, she was forced to become street smart.

Not long ago she had told Henry of a secret, one she'd kept all of her life. It began when they were talking about receiving their GED'S and being high school graduates.

"One reason I worked so hard to get my diploma was so that I could get a good job. The other reason was so I could at least see what it was like to be a kid in school," she said solemnly.

She began her story by telling Henry about Jake. He was the man her mother had started dating when she was a little girl. He moved in with the small family before she was in first grade. Henry had difficulty grasping what Jennifer meant when she got to the part about Jake's inappropriate touching when she was only seven years old.

"By the time I was eight, Jake was forcing me to touch him, *there,*" she'd explained haltingly, as she pointed.

Henry cringed, and couldn't look at her. The whole explanation embarrassed and frightened him.

"Why would a grown-up do bad things like that Jenny? Make a little girl do something that awful?" he asked incredulously.

"I don't know Henry, some people are just born bad I guess," Jennifer responded, nearly as confused.

"Sometimes at night when I would lay in bed, I could hear them, the footsteps in the hallway of the trailer we lived in. I knew when it was my mom because the floor never squeaked when she came. I think she walked too fast and wasn't heavy enough to make the squeaking noises. But when someone walked slow and then stopped and then came again, the floor creaked. I always knew when it was Jake who was coming to my room. That was the worst sound I remember when I was a kid, the floor creaking."

She stopped talking for a moment and Henry timidly looked in her direction, and saw her eyes glazed and moist.

"When I heard that noise it was like the same feeling you get when you hear finger-nails scratching on a black board. When I was still eight the monster stopped. I pretended it was just a horrible nightmare. For a long time I made myself believe it was just a very bad dream. But it wasn't. It was all real, and it happened to me."

"Jenny I don't want to hear this, it's too scary, and it makes me sad to see you crying. How could that man do all those awful things to you? Please don't tell me anymore."

His brow wrinkled and he had begun wringing his hands sometime during the telling.

"Henry it's important we know everything about each other, even the *bad stuff*," she said, reassuringly.

Torn between not wanting to hear about her horrible childhood and wanting to please her, he lifted his face towards her and said, "Okay Jenny, go ahead and tell me anything you think I should know about what happened to you."

"When I turned ten, my mother said she was giving me a daddy for my birthday, Mom showed me…."

"Well, that was a good thing, right? Your mom was getting a new dad for you," he asked skeptically.

"No, Henry, that was not a good thing, because the dad she was talking about was Jake," she said patiently. "Like I was saying, Mom showed me the ring that Jake gave her and told me they already got married. My mom said I had to call him *Dad*," she shivered.

She continued telling Henry about the attempted rape when she was fifteen and how she fought back.

"I hit him. I hit Jake hard with a steel lamp in my room." Glancing over, Jenny decided not to describe the actual injuries after spotting the distressed look on Henry's pasty face. She didn't tell him how her mother had rushed in and saw *daddy* on his knees, the blood running down each side of his neck. She also omitted the part where Mom didn't believe her claim that it was a sexual attack.

"After everything happened, a policeman came and I told him what Jake had tried to do."

"Then they took him straight to jail and didn't let him hurt you anymore, right?"

"I guess back in 1960, even the police didn't want to believe people could do something that horrible to a kid. They told me I must have made a mistake about what Jake wanted," Jenny said, trying not to sound as depressed as she felt sharing the painful memory.

"The next day, I left. For a week I slept in the park and lived on the street. Then I got my job washing dishes at the Pangs."

She noticed Henry's squirming the entire time she was describing her early youth. Grabbing both his hands in hers, she looked at him. He again avoided eye contact.

"Henry, look at me please," she said softly. Slowly lifting his head, she stared directly into his eyes.

"I needed to tell you that Henry. My childhood and the abuse I went through growing up is the whole reason why I trust you and why I love you so, so much. I fell in love with you that day in the pet store," she said sincerely.

He smiled shyly recalling the first time they'd met.

"Yeah Jenny, that was the luckiest day of my whole life when we ran out of mice. I was so happy that Dr. Edwards asked me to go find a place that sold mice that time," he said, happy to talk about anything other than her abusive childhood.

"I know, Henry, it was the luckiest day of my life too!" Jenny warmly responded. "Can you believe it was almost four years ago? When I saw you, sitting there, talking to the puppies, I just knew then you were such a kind man, that I had to meet you."

"Aw Jenny, you know I love the puppies," he said as his cheeks flushed.

"Do you remember what you said to me when I asked, *'Can I help you, sir?'*" she re-counted in a mock voice.

Henry's face reddened even more. Jenny giggled as she repeated his words from their first meeting. "You said, *'Aw, I'm no SIR, I'm just Henry.'* I fell in love with you right then and there, Mr. Miller. It's what they call, *love at first sight."*

"I know, I know, Jenny I just get so darned embarrassed when you tell that story." he said bashfully.

"You were so quiet Henry, lucky I asked you to go out, or we'd never got to be together," she said absently.

Henry was getting so self-conscious, he felt as awkward as he had with the conversation about her childhood.

"Jenny, do you think we could stop talking about all this stuff now?" he asked innocently.

"Oh sure. I just can't help it. You know, *YOU* are the love of my life," she said adoringly.

Then they talked of marriage. Initially, Henry became so flustered he could barely stand it. Jennifer had gently brought him along. Looking into her eyes as she lightly smoothed his collar out, he said. "Jenny, you know I want to marry you. But I just can't. Who would take care of my mom?" he asked naively.

"Henry, I would never make you do anything you didn't want to do. I know what that's like," Jennifer said looking away from him. He blushed, and she waited patiently.

As her apartment block came into view, the memories slipped away.

Pulling into a parking spot Henry carefully maneuvered the trusty old Nova into place. Approaching the building, he chuckled, thinking of the joke he was about to play.

Using his key, he entered the apartment. Hearing the door close Jennifer set down her hairbrush as she exited the bedroom.

"You're early!" she said, a bit surprised.

The date was originally set for an hour later. Henry had mentioned he would have to cook for Agnes, before they could grab a movie.

"Yeah, I thought maybe we could go out for some supper," he said mysteriously.

"Oh, that would be great! So how was your mom today?"

"She's good," he said, glancing away as he spoke. "Jenny, I don't want to talk about my mom. Let's just have fun, okay?"

"Sure, sure Henry," she answered. Jennifer gently kissed him and he responded in kind.

I'm getting stronger, thanks to Jenny, I'm gonna marry her, he thought as he squeezed her tight, *I'll move in here someday soon.*

"I was thinking I would take you out for Chinese food tonight," he said releasing her, a wide grin spreading across his face. "How about Pang's?"

Mr. and Mrs. Pang owned the restaurant where Jennifer first worked when she left home. The Pang's liked her and had given her a small room to live in. Jennifer told Henry that when she worked there, she was allowed to eat as much of the left over food as she wanted. Jennifer came to love the Pangs, still visiting them at least once a week. Their kindness had prevented her from suffering a life on the street, or something worse. Still, just the smell of Chinese food, could make her woozy.

"Henry!" she said, teasingly. He smirked, and in no time both were giggling at his suggestion.

The two ended up deciding to have a burger at Al's Place on the same block as the Orpheum Theatre; it would be quick and easy. A short time later both were gaping at the big screen, clutching each other's hand, as Harrison Ford desperately tried to outrun the giant boulder in *Raiders of the Lost Ark.*

Later that evening they arrived back at Jennifer's small apartment chattering excitedly about the adventurous film. Soon it would be time for Henry to get back home. Without warning, Henry stopped speaking and hugged her closely.

He whispered into her soft clean hair, "Do you know why I love you so darned, darned much Jenny?"

She tried to pull back and see his face. Henry held on tight.

"Yes I know, because I am so smart, ha ha," she answered shyly.

"Yeah, but not just that Jenny. It's 'cause you never make me feel stupid or useless or bad."

His warm tears were wet on her cheek. His body hitched as a quiet sob slipped from her child-like man. She gently stroked his hair and rocked him, whispering, "I love you too Henry, I love you too."

Chapter 9

“I’ll have coffee, rye toast, and a soft boiled egg, please,” Blake announced.

The pencil scratched out a code that only the cook could decipher and the request was acknowledged with a nod. The name- tag read ‘June,’ and was pinned to the collar of the woman moving her head up and down. June was what most would call a career waitress. She was somewhere in her fifties, stern-looking and pressed into a white uniform which had fit nicely at one time. Her scowl made it obvious that she wished she were elsewhere.

After jotting down Blake’s order she looked at Rose, her pencil hovering over the pad. June tilted her head back and raised her eyebrows, indicating that she was ready.

“I’ll have a western omelet, small orange juice, and coffee with two creams, please,” Rose said.

The waitress again nodded confirming she got it all. Their eyes followed her as she walked away from the table. Just beyond her, the cook, visible through an opening in the wall, was bustling over the steaming grill. A bar style counter sported the many regulars who were perched atop the shiny metallic trimmed stools. On the opposite wall was a line of booths with high wooden backs. They offered a certain amount of privacy at the expense of comfort. The Formica tabletops were carefully arranged between the counter and the booths.

The greasy spoon was alive with chatter. They waited over ten minutes for a seat. An old man nursing a cup of tea finally left one of the tables, surrounded by four heavy chrome chairs.

Occasionally, Blake and Rose would share a cup of coffee or a non-romantic dinner to mark their small successes. The discovery of a new antibiotic, a birth control pill, or maybe even an acne cream, were cause for celebration. Usually, all minor discoveries were discussed at the lab. If there was to be an informal dinner or coffee outing, it was always the result of Rose’s prompting.

This time it was different. It was only yesterday, just before five when Rose saw Blake approaching her. She was thrilled when he invited her to join him for breakfast. Rose accepted his offer, resisting the urge to question the unusual proposal. She suspected he might want to share some breakthrough in his current series of experiments. She wished it were something more personal. Rose smiled as she whimsically pondered the possibilities. It was obvious that whatever he wanted to discuss he didn't want to do it at the lab. And therein lay the glimmer of hope, that it could be something more personal.

"Oh, don't be so high school, its just eggs and toast silly," she joked to herself aloud as she drove home.

In bed last night she thought, *maybe, just maybe Blake's starting to realize how I feel about him. He knows how good we'd be together...tomorrow we'll talk.* She flipped over from her side onto her back. She laced her fingers and rested her hands on her tummy. The moon was full and she could see her bedroom clearly. Looking down she realized she couldn't see her hands, her chest obstructing the view. Suddenly, she jumped out of bed, and flicked on the light. Her eyes adjusted quickly as she stood in front of the dresser mirror and lifted first the left, then the right braless, flannel covered breast. Cocking her head to the side she said "maybe they're too huge? I wonder if his wife's boobs were this big? What if he doesn't like big boobs?" Then she smirked, remembering an affair in college, when she'd allowed herself a short fling with a biology professor, named Dr. Jerry Longo.

"Do you think my boobs are too big Jerry?" she'd asked, doing the same hefting and lowering in the mirror that day.

As he walked up from behind, admiring her perfect body, he wrapped his arms around her waist. The charismatic professor rested his head on her shoulder. Speaking directly to her mirrored reflection, he smiled broadly and said, "Young darling, we're men, there is no such thing as boobs that are too big."

Recalling the silly banter from that night so very long ago she grinned. "Yeah, he'll be fine with them," she said aloud, dropping them simultaneously. Giggling at her juvenile crush, she literally jumped back into bed. A while later, drifting off, Rose prayed she would find the courage to share her feelings with Blake. When she awoke in the morning, her nerve was gone. She resolved to see what it was he had to say first. Now was the moment.

"Well, Blake, what's with all the mystery?" Rose asked.

For a few seconds both watched as June-the-waitress pushed the slips into the short-order carousel, and with a quick spin, landed the breakfast requests in the hands of the man with the spatula. Blake returned his attention back to his breakfast companion.

"Rose, I'm convinced I've stumbled across a huge finding." Blake's inability to keep the shoptalk at work sent Rose's spirits plummeting. Seeing the look on his face, a feeling of defeat crawled into her stomach and for a moment just sat there.

Dammit it's always about work isn't it? Doesn't he know there is more to life than work? she fumed.

"Rose, are you listening to me?" The impatience in his voice brought her out of her momentary trance.

"Yes, yes of course I am Blake, what have you found?"

Rose let all romantic inclinations fall from her mind. He was more excited than she'd seen him in a long time. Pushing her desires aside, she granted him all her professional attention.

"You've known for a while that I've been dabbling with a variety of research projects which I haven't been reporting to Novatek," he stated matter-of-factly.

"Yes, Blake, I'm aware of that."

Shocked, she lied, assuming that *all* experiments were being reported to their employer. She had no idea that the research he'd been engrossed in for so long was not being disclosed. However, appearing more intuitive to his idiosyncrasies than she actually was, Rose hoped it might draw Blake closer.

"Actually I've been working on this particular research off and on for about four years. At first, just when I could find the time. Lately, it has been all-consuming," he admitted.

"We've all noticed, Blake. I'm sensitive to the fact that you like to be left alone when you're in the investigative stage of a process, so I've kept my distance at the lab. Of course, Marc and Vanessa have been preoccupied with their own thing. Those two haven't really noticed much of anything lately."

She meant for these words to suggest that Marc and Vanessa were less than ambitious where work was concerned. The inference went right over Blake's head.

"Yes, I want to thank you for your discretion, also for taking up the slack at the lab. Marc's been a great help as well."

God, the man is blind at times! She thought, annoyed, resisting the impulse to roll her eyes.

"I would like you to look at my findings. I've been testing and retesting for months now. I believe I've come to an undisputable conclusion."

Rose recognized the flustered look on Blake's face and found it sweet but a bit comical. He appeared tense with his browed wrinkled, but not angry, calm, but agitated all at the same time. She could almost see the gears in his head turning and braced to keep up.

She knew that he was excited and predicted that he might be referring to scientifically complex information and formulas a mile a minute. *He is so eager, poor boy doesn't know where to start,* she mused.

"Rose how familiar are you with the exhaustive research being conducted around the introduction of bacterium to reduce or inhibit the rapid growth of cancerous cells?"

"Not overly," she replied honestly.

"The research has met with failure, or at best some very limited results."

Rose wondered if Blake was about to say grace as she watched him lean forward. His fingers were laced together as he stretched his interlocked hands out on the table in front of him. Blake was so focused he'd not seen the waitress's arrival. The place was a zoo and she was the only one working the floor. She stood beside him, balancing the tableware and holding the handle of the coffee pot ready to pour refills. Impatiently June announced the arrival of breakfast with a curt, *"Here ya go."*

Rose saw Blake flinch at the sound of the server's voice, and at the same time noticed the annoyed look on his face.

The waitresses' unexpected return to the table also prompted him to sit up straight, his hands pulled back and resting at his sides. Suddenly at attention, he looked like someone caught in the middle of saying something inappropriate. With breakfast in front of them, neither felt the urge to eat.

Rose could tell he was ready to share the information, and suspected Blake was as anxious to disclose it as she was to hear it. The waitress receded as quickly as she'd appeared. Once she was out of earshot, he seemed to refocus.

"I started a series of experiments with an array of viruses," Blake began. "Months after trying a multitude of known bacterium, my experiments met with the same results as the others. After carefully analyzing the data, I could find nothing, nothing at all.

Sitting wide-eyed Rose patiently waited for the punch line. So far, this was not very revealing.

"It was really staring me right in the face," Blake went on. "All of the failed attempts, my experiments as well as those of other researchers, shared one commonality."

Recounting his story so passionately, Rose found herself fascinated.

"The common link between the previous failures was the introduction of only one virus at a time to the infected cells. When I finally recognized the connection, I immediately began combining different viruses. Then I introduced them to the cancerous cells. The results were dismal, the side effects numerous. Feeling defeated I was on the verge of abandoning this methodology. I actually did ignore it for months at a time, but the principles of the approach kept drawing me back."

"So, you're saying you were unsuccessful? It didn't work?"

"Right, it didn't work, not until I added a mild carcinoma to a formula of viruses. I found that by combining six different bacilli, the sixth being the cancerous component, that the interaction was beyond belief. Their fusion was giving me the most positive results I've ever seen. The introduction of the cancer virus pooled with the other five actually produced a new disease. This mutated pathogen had what appeared to be a cannibalistic effect on the malignant tumors," he excitedly divulged.

She watched as he stopped just long enough to gulp down his water.

"I don't understand, what do you mean by *cannibalistic?*" she asked, a bit puzzled.

The clamor of the busy coffee shop was inaudible to them both. So engrossed in the story, neither heard the sound of a crashing plate or the words that followed from the cursing waitress.

"Not only did the formula stop the reproduction of the cells, but it actually fed on those that were present. It also fed on the *existing tumor*, until it was gone. Rose, this new microorganism virtually feeds on the cancer. It searches it out as a source of nutrition, consuming it until it's gone. The virus has an incredible survival instinct and even attacks pre-cancerous cells for nutrition. When all sources of nourishment are exhausted, the bug simply exits the host through the elimination process. At first, I was skeptical. Cancerous cells have a way of mutating, re-inventing themselves. Even though I was getting positive results initially, I was prepared for the transmutation, I really was."

He stopped mid-sentence, Rose's gaze following his hand as he reached again, this time for the sweating glass of water in front of her.

As he drained the glass, she imagined him back at the lab. She pictured him with his eye pressed against the microscope studying the virus he'd just described. As quickly as she had zoned out, the sound of his voice instantly brought her back.

"I was waiting for the cancerous cells to reconstruct, to fight off the virus. Rose, it didn't happen, it just didn't happen."

Rose jumped as he quickly reached across the table, grabbing her arm hard, "I can barely believe this is true Rose. The new microorganism consumed the malignant cells at such a rapid rate, I don't think they had time to evolve or mutate."

Seeing movement from the corner of her eye, Rose looked up and noticed the restaurant was more than half empty. Neither had touched breakfast. Just then June-the-waitress appeared at the table, she ripped their bill from her pad. "Are we all finished here folks?" she asked, motioning to the untouched plates.

"Yes, thank you, maybe just a fresh cup of coffee please," Rose said.

"Sure, just be a minute," she answered, scooping up the plates while discretely positioning the bill beside Blake.

After she left, Rose finally spoke up.

"You're saying this new disease exterminates cancer cells? You *do* realize what you are asking me to believe here, don't you? Cancer has killed millions, probably hundreds of millions worldwide since it was first recognized over a thousand years ago," she said disbelievingly.

He leaned forward whispering, "Rose, when you see this under the 'scope, you'll find it hard to believe too. For months I thought my findings might be flawed. When it became evident they were not, I began looking for other problems. I haven't found any."

Blake lifted his cup to take a swallow of coffee. Rose wondered how he could drink it cold, and assumed he was parched from all the talking. She thought the excitement might have jangled his nerves; she knew hers were. After what seemed like an eternity of silence, he continued.

"Side effects are minimal, like a bad case of the flu, with a complete recovery in seven to ten days. I then began introducing the microorganism to a multitude of various cancers," Blake continued. "First skin cancer, then brain cancer, lung, and breast cancer. The results are all the same. This virus is like a little '*Pac Man'* eating it's way through all the malignant cells."

Rose was astonished, and felt embarrassed for thinking about romance while listening to his remarkable claims. Blake was brilliant, but he was also an overworked eccentric.

"Blake, you have to run tests confirming that the tumors don't come back. We have to research the long-term effects of the introduction of this miracle recipe and its reaction on human subjects. This sounds remarkable, but it's a long way from being more than just an experiment," she declared.

"I discovered the formula months ago. All I've been doing since is running tests, validating and re-checking. Rose, that is what I do, all day, every day at the Lab. You remember my test mouse, Lucy? I have injected her with every cancer virus known to man. Once the tumors begin to grow, I then inject her with the serum. I've been killing and curing Lucy for eight months."

Stunned, Rose could not think of what to say. Her eyes widened as Blake looked around to see if someone might be eavesdropping.

"I'm sorry but this seems—well honestly, this is unbelievable," she finally said.

"I know. I know it's hard to believe, but it's true. Soon you'll see for yourself. I've told no one else, and I am swearing you to secrecy, Rose, do you understand?"

Feeling dumfounded with Blake's possible discovery and thrilled with his confidence in her, Rose tried to think of what to say next. Finally she spoke. "Uh, yes, yes of course, I understand," she stammered.

"I've actually named the formula. I'm calling it ELIXIR," he said sheepishly.

Rose couldn't put her finger on the why of it, but knew that was the moment, the very moment that she truly accepted every word he said as fact. She knew Blake would never come forward, not even to her, unless he was absolutely certain about his results. Still, she needed to ask, to confirm what she already accepted.

"Blake, are you saying what I think you're saying?"

Both stopped talking as June-the-waitress brought two fresh coffees. Without fanfare she set them on the table and silently retreated. Blake reached for the steaming cup, taking in its rich aroma, before indulging in a sip. It was the first time Rose saw him relaxed since they sat down. Leaning back in the heavy chrome seat he smiled as he looked directly into her eyes and whispered, "Yes, Rose, I think I am."

Chapter 10

"Hellොoo, Evan are you even listening to me?" Loretta bawled.

Evan Sinclair wasn't paying attention to her. He was laying comfortably with his arm under his head on the king sized bed, trying to relax.

Loretta Benson's interview at Novatek six months earlier had been a success. Dr. Sinclair's occasional conjugal visit was a good trade for the extravagant lifestyle she loved.

Loretta assumed she was being ignored and her tenacity instantly surfaced. She stomped towards the bed with her hands firmly planted on her hips. Like a mother about to scold her child, she leaned forward and barked, "Well? Are you?"

"Yes, of course I'm listening," he lied. His mind had drifted to far more important things while Loretta prattled on. Dr. Blake Edward's apparent discovery was dominating his every thought the past few days, and even now, it was creeping in.

"Don't ignore me when I'm talking to you!" she demanded. Evan exhaled heavily. He'd arranged this little rendezvous with Loretta as a break. His objective was to actually *stop* thinking about Edwards's breakthrough, for a couple of hours. It wasn't working. Formulas, numbers, the whole damn report, was still invading his conscious mind. And then of course, there was Loretta.

"Well, how about it? Is it a problem?" she challenged.

Not long ago he truly enjoyed the melodious ring of Loretta's voice. Lately it sounded a lot more like the high-pitched squeal of a stuck pig.

"Sorry dear, what did you say?" he asked, bracing for an ambush. Loretta's mounting brashness was more evident each day.

"Evan, what I said was, I *need* two hundred dollars before you go," she repeated.

Her demand ripped his thoughts from the Edwards report. Irritated with his current reality, he snapped back at her. "*WHAT THE HELL Loretta,* today is only the 12th, where is the money I gave you TWELVE DAYS AGO? Tell me you haven't gone through three thousand dollars already!" he retorted.

It was more money than he gave his wife, Audrey, to run their entire household, yet she managed. She paid the mortgage, all household expenses and the car payments. Loretta didn't pay a bill, not even the rent.

"*Sweetie*, I really need the money," her tone softened. She crawled onto the bed beside him and with the nail of her index finger, began drawing an imaginary doodle on his bare chest. "I've been shopping for some nice clothes. You know I like to look sexy for you, darling," she offered seductively.

Slightly shaking his head, Evan rolled his eyes. Both gestures went unnoticed as Loretta rested her head on his chest.

They hadn't gone out in public for months. Although he loved the risqué low cut tops, short skirts, and spiked high heels, Loretta drew attention, a great deal of attention from both genders. Men fantasized about being with her and women despised her. The scrutiny did not lend itself to keeping his infidelity discreet.

Staring at the ceiling above her bed, he recalled the night they both felt like Italian…

Three months ago they'd been dining at Alfredo's, a quiet, out-of-the-way restaurant renowned for its Italian cuisine. Suddenly, without warning, someone was tapping him on the shoulder. Startled by the unexpected contact he turned to see Jonathan Aiello hovering over him.

"Dr. Sinclair, how are you?" Aiello's voice rang with simulated formality as he thrust an open hand towards him. Evan felt the color drain from his face and his body went rigid as he shook hands. The previous year he and Audrey were volunteers on the parents' council at Trillium Court, the kids' school. It was there he met Jonathan and Susan Aiello.

"Jonathan, wha…what are you do…doing here?" he stammered.

"I'm here with my wife. You remember, Susan? It's our anniversary," he said pointing to the other end of the restaurant. Evan instinctively glanced in the direction Jonathan indicated. There, he saw Susan sitting, gawking as she gave him a cursory wave. Feigning a half smile, he tilted his head in a 'hello' gesture.

Returning his attention to his own table, Evan couldn't help but notice Jonathan staring. Gawking at Loretta's heaving chest, his eyes bulged like a hungry breast-fed baby. Evan grinned impishly, hoping Susan had caught the lascivious look. Still the anxiety he felt had the blood rushing back to his face as quickly as it had drained. It was getting very warm.

"So Evan, how are Audrey and the kids?" Not waiting for a response, he added smugly, "And please, introduce me to your friend." Evan felt his shirt sticking to his torso.

"Oh, Audrey's fine, everybody's great actually. Jonathan, I would like you to meet Loretta, my new assistant."

Actually, I really don't want you or anyone else that we know meeting her, he thought nervously.

"Very nice to make your acquaintance, Loretta."

Moving around the table, Jonathan extended his hand and, grasping hers, he bowed at the waist. His mock etiquette allowed him a better vantage point and once again Evan saw Jonathan ogle Loretta's ample cleavage. *Why don't you just jump right in asshole*, Evan mused. Jonathan's face came within inches of her chest, as he bent over.

"Ah-ha, nice to meet you, too," she replied robotically. Evan felt the sweat beading on his forehead. He wiped it before Jonathan could notice.

"Isn't that lovely, taking your assistant out for dinner. Well, Evan, please give Audrey and the children our best."

"Sure, Jonathan. It was nice seeing you." It was not. "And please tell Susan, a very happy anniversary, to you both." *I hope you divorce and rot in hell,* Evan thought maliciously.

"I will. Nice meeting you, Loretta."

She responded with a disinterested nod.

Within minutes of returning to his table, Jonathan was engaged in solemn conversation with his wife. Evan was convinced he knew the subject matter of their intense dialogue. "Sanctimonious pricks," he cursed quietly. "Loretta, let's get going."

They had finished their meal, but the *Chateau Sainte-Marie*, which sat chilling in the ice bucket, was almost full.

Oblivious to the humiliation Evan was feeling, Loretta swirled the wine in her glass. "I'm not ready to go yet, we've hardly touched the *Chateau*," she griped.

Forcing a smile, he rose and pushed the words through clenched teeth. "Loretta, we are leaving now. Please put the glass down."

She hesitated another full half minute, plainly demonstrating her displeasure at being forced to leave. Loretta made her point by methodically raising the wine glass to her lips and slowly draining it while glaring over the rim at Evan.

She was fuming and he couldn't have cared less about her sensitivities. She was the other woman and subject to certain indignities; it was the price paid for sleeping with a married man.

Considering the discomfort the good doctor had experienced, Alfredo's would be their last public appearance together.

As far as Loretta's contrived story about "looking *sexy* for him," he knew *that* was pure nonsense. He had suspected for some time that his mistress was, in fact, cheating on *him*. Most probably with some young stud who could tolerate her infidelity. It would be a small price to pay for fine dining and nights on the town. All extravagances shared with her and possibly others were courtesy of Evan Sinclair. Whoever he was would likely be getting the same sexual favors, without the financial obligations.

All of it was beginning to sink in. Evan's marriage had become a casualty of his trysts. The price was too high.

Ah what the hell, tonight's already bought and paid for, he thought wickedly. As Loretta's slow twirling fingernail made its way down to his groin, Evan became aroused.

The sex was a pawn, expertly plied as the bargaining chip. He knew she would ask again for the money. If he found the courage to deny her, the anticipated erotic treat would be quickly withdrawn. She was losing her grip on him a little at a time, but most definitely not tonight.

Erotically finessing him as he'd predicated, she cooed once again, "Sweetie, can I have the money?"

"I guess so," he replied weakly, his resolve fading.

Two hours after giving into the extortion, he was speeding homeward. The illuminated dashboard clock glowed brightly. It was almost five past midnight and he still had fifteen minutes to drive before he'd arrive at his suburban home. Soon Evan would be facing his contemptuous wife. Audrey would stay awake long enough to give him one of her looks. It was her new ritual before slinking off to the guest room. The choice of beds was also new. She'd been sleeping there the past few weeks as her suspicions grew.

At that moment he wasn't thinking about Audrey's uncertainties, nor was he thinking about the prize Loretta had energetically bestowed on him for handing over more cash. Evan's mind was clear and focused, re-running the compilation of data he'd been consuming for days. He was certain he'd be burning the midnight oil, analyzing the statistics he'd brought home. The data was from laboratory two, Dr. Edward's report.

In the ominous glow of the dashboard light, a twisted grin appeared on his face. An added benefit to working late that evening suddenly occurred to him. It would serve as a testament to Audrey just how hard he labored. So hard in fact, there was no choice but to bring work home with him.

Three days prior, Dr. Blake Edwards personally delivered to him the four hundred seventy-eight pages of documentation. In itself, that was enough to make the dossier worthy of his immediate attention. Edwards did something else though. After handing over the eight separate file folders, Evan noticed him make an odd gesture. Though a common practice for most, he couldn't recall ever seeing it so freely displayed by this particular scientist. Evan was instantly aware that the material in his hands was something to pay attention to when he saw Blake Edwards *smile*.

Chapter 11

As thick fingers wrapped around the ornate brass handle and pulled, the eight-foot heavy oak door swung easily inward. The short, portly frame of Dr. Gregory Emerson looked dwarfed as he stood in the large opening. He hesitated for a moment, taking in the ambiance brought on by the fresh, spring bloom. The well-manicured yard could almost take his breath away at this time of year. He loved how new life was cropping up everywhere he looked. Taking a deep breath he could smell the lilac trees even though the buds were just beginning to emerge. Soon they would make a full, proud debut. Gregory, after his brief pause of wonderment, bent down and picked up his evening paper.

With the newspaper in hand, he was walking toward his favorite chair when the ringing telephone sliced through the serene moment.

"Hello," he said with a slight edge to his voice.

"Hello, Gregory, Dan here. I hate to bother you, but I need your opinion on a project I'm working on."

Daniel was the doctor's right hand man in matters concerning the Patronums. The call meant a significant issue had come up through the ranks of his division. There would be no exchange of information over the vulnerable phone line.

"Well hi, Dan, great to hear your voice," he said, his tone nonchalant. "Sure, when would you like to meet?"

"I realize that it's short notice, but say in an hour or so?"

Gregory's heart skipped a beat, the sudden release of adrenalin shooting into his tired seventy-four year-old body.

He'd found life felt quite empty after he'd lost his wife, May. He now lived for the Patronums, Wednesday meetings, and the chance to feel the excitement of a call to duty. The lack of forewarning suggested urgency, adding to the thrill.

"No problem at all. Where would you like to meet, my boy?"

"I was thinking the playground,"

The term '*playground*' was a code for the research station that was part of his team's branch. He would be contacted only if his cell received and carefully examined any incoming medical data. If it was determined that such a circumstance existed, it would require Gregory's personal review. As a result, if the matter were of an urgent nature, the Committee would be notified. As the intel was passed from mentor to mentor in an upward spiral, each one would examine it thoroughly. This procedure ensured that the information was worthy to be bumped up to the next level. Once it reached the highest echelons of the Patronums, it would necessitate a meticulous review by the Committee. The last hurdle was always the head of the specific sector. In this case, the buck stopped with Dr. Gregory Emerson.

"The playground it is. I look forward to catching up with you, Dan. I'll see you in an hour."

"Thanks, see you soon."

Gregory hesitated momentarily while organizing his thoughts, then replaced the receiver in its cradle. Passing the dining room table, he casually tossed down the unread newspaper. He was no longer interested in the recent Dallas news.

The doctor was in the midst of mulling over what the emergency might be, when Fredrick's voice cracked the silence.

"Sir, dinner will be served in five minutes," he announced. Startled, Gregory's overworked heart once again skipped a beat.

"JESUS, FREDRICK, you gave me a start. Bloody hell man, don't sneak up on me like that!" he barked.

"Very sorry, sir. Will you be taking dinner in the sitting room, this evening?"

"I'll be skipping dinner tonight. Bring the car around in fifteen minutes. We're going to the playground," he said, still shaken.

"As you please, sir," Fredrick obediently replied.

*****

Frederick's familiarity and past experience told him the old man would be excited, anxious to get underway. The car should be out front in ten minutes, or sooner. He next informed the cook to put dinner on hold, in case the doctor was hungry upon their return.

Fredrick quickly changed, then preceded to the garage. He pulled the car out and stood dutifully near the rear door of the Cadillac. He had been with the Emersons a long time, a very long time indeed.

Approaching sixty, Frederick could still break the neck of a man half his age, if a situation called for such drastic measures. Not only was he the driver, consummate butler, and general houseboy, but he was also the bodyguard.

Prior to being assigned to Dr. Emerson, Fredrick was well trained in the art of espionage and security. Instinctively, he could spot seemingly harmless events that signified a possible threat. In thirty years of service, his unique skills had never been required. However, still training two hours daily, his body and his senses were as sharp as ever.

Fredrick had never married, giving himself totally to the Patronums, and to the Emersons. He'd been a young man, not quite thirty, when he came to them. May Emerson was only a few years older and a very handsome woman. With Gregory's demanding hospital schedule and the duties he performed as a Patronum, she was often left alone. As the years passed, 'left alone' turned to 'lonely' and she'd become closer, much closer with the family bodyguard. Fredrick had given more of himself to May than was appropriate.

*****

On a number of occasions, Gregory believed he'd spied shared glances between them. He was never quite sure if the effortless familiarity was real or imagined.

Fredrick had always maintained a proper and respectful demeanor in the presence of both the Emersons. Still, Gregory wondered. Choosing never to confront either of them, May left this world with her secret. When she died, his melancholy manner confirmed the doctor's suspicions. Fredrick mourned privately for months. Somehow the loss of a shared love brought the two men closer. Gregory forgave his bodyguard's unnamed trespasses with as much articulation as he'd employed acknowledging the suspected affair. He had simply said nothing.

They arrived at the playground exactly forty-five minutes after Gregory had set the phone down at the house. The *playground* from the outside was nothing more than a huge Quonset building. For all intents and purposes it appeared to be a cold-storage unit. Inside, the structure took on an entirely different look and feel. The floors were all a high-gloss, concrete finish with dozens of desks aligned down the centre. Carefully arranged along each wall was a perimeter of workstations. Ironically, it was similar in layout and design to the Novatek labs, although unlike the laboratories at Novatek, the workstations were self-contained units surrounded by sound proofed solid walls. Here the objective was not a steady, undisturbed working environment, but a *private* work area. The facility could house as many as one hundred researchers and medical personnel at any given time.

Dan was there as expected. The two proceeded to a large cluttered office inside the research station. Dan briefed Dr. Emerson for almost an hour before they re-entered the common area on the floor. Together with Fredrick, the three walked toward a workstation. Dozens of cell members were bustling about, all apparently intent on their particular assignments. No formalities or greetings were exchanged with the doctor as he entered. Most did not realize who he was. Fredrick stood several feet from him, always close, but never in the way.

Doctor Emerson's glasses were perched on the end of his nose as he peered into the microscope.

"This is remarkable, simply remarkable. The odds of finding this combination…" his voice trailed off ending in a whisper.

He straightened as he stared at Dan. Then, as if to confirm what he had just seen, he tilted his head once more. His eyes again gazed at the magnified images.

"These results are confirmed?" Gregory asked.

Dan responded with a silent nod. All three returned to the office where the briefing took place moments before. This time, an energized Dr. Emerson lead the way.

"Daniel, this is amazing. Time is going to be of the utmost importance here. How long have we had this?"

He responded uneasily, "too long, Doctor. We intercepted it six days ago. We've been working on authentication twenty-four hours a day since. I wanted to make certain the findings were more than a wild goose chase, before involving you sir."

Gregory winced. There would be pressure on the committee to analyze the probabilities, the overall affect of a discovery this significant. Time would be required to determine how best to use the information. Nonetheless the secret organization was a well-oiled machine. They would analyze the data as quickly as possible, but timing would still be crucial.

"How long before all the statistics are pulled together for a report to the committee?" Gregory asked.

"General synopsis can be ready within twelve hours. A comprehensive detailed report will take twenty-four hours," Dan responded uncomfortably, shifting his weight from one foot to the other.

Dr. Emerson should have been informed of the situation days ago. He understood that Daniel would have wanted to be certain about the information before involving him. No doubt his right hand man didn't expect the results to be as indisputable as the team had found them. There was no point in criticizing Daniel's decision, to withhold what turned out to be the facts.

Today's Monday, I'll have enough time to do a complete review. I'll just add finishing touches to the report before Wednesday, Gregory pondered.

His mind, when called into service, was as sharp as the day he'd graduated from Harvard University fifty years before. He already predicted the largest single challenge facing the committee. Until a decision was made and a direction chosen by the leaders of the Patronums, controlled containment would be the objective. Dan, having this information for nearly a week, would have a better handle on the current situation.

"Daniel, has our team managed to gather any basic facts regarding the principals involved? We'll need some particulars for the Intelligence cell."

Although security was not the responsibility of the individual factions, it was standard procedure to supply some fundamental background of those involved.

"Yes, sir. Based on Novatek procedure and our point of interception, we are positive we have one-hundred per-cent containment so far. All new research goes to a review department. We have a man in there, which intercepted the initial dossier at the first level. The team leader who submitted it doesn't expect a full review for thirty days. That scientist is Dr. Blake Edwards. We have a brief profile on him, sir."

Gregory instantly recognized the name. He had read several of Blake's theories over the years. Based on the published works, he'd formed the opinion long ago that the doctor was a genius. The present findings confirmed his assumption.

"Edwards is a widower and lives alone with no social affiliations. According to our man on the inside, Dr. Evan Sinclair, Edwards initially keeps his findings very close to the cuff," Dan said.

Gregory was mesmerized by the discovery. Again he gave Dan's lapse in vigilance only a cursory reflection and then dismissed it. Life had taught him the value of remaining calm over 'spilt milk'. Easily grasping the details, the doctor was mentally dissecting the technical information of the discovery.

"Good, very good. I need the preliminary findings to review. I also require the names of all principals before Wednesday."

Daniel handed over a thick manila envelope with what sounded like a true sigh of relief.

"I anticipated your request, sir, this is the entire file," he said. Raising an eyebrow Dan added, "Sir, Edwards is calling his serum, *Elixir.*"

Dr. Emerson was not surprised at Daniel's welcomed efficiency. Taking the package, he grinned whilst musing over the name.

"Elixir. How very appropriate." The doctor's tired eyes widened with curiosity as he asked, "Daniel do you know the precise meaning of the word *elixir*?"

"Umm well, sir. I *believe* it means mixture or formula."

"Close son, very close. But that's not the entire meaning. Webster's definition includes the words '*cure or remedy*'. Edwards has appropriately named his formula, *the cure*."

Chapter 12

He turned the key in the lock slowly, soundlessly. Once opened, he gently pushed the door inward, stepping to the right. Silently, a count of three, then he was inside, his gun drawn and ready. The motion sensor detected the stirring. Light suddenly flooded the neat hallway, signifying his was the first movement in the foyer of the home. Although hard-wired, the unsophisticated warning system could not be completely trusted. A determined intruder might simply bypass it on the main electrical panel, but the simple device, combined with the burglar alarm was enough to comfort him.

Satisfied there were no unexpected trespassers occupying his home, he holstered the gun. Sequentially he punched in the numeric code on the digital keypad, disarming the wireless security system. Extreme caution without justification had become his credo. Eric Brunner's semi-ritualistic homecoming was complete. On most days he entered his residence just like anyone else would, but never when he was on assignment. During those times he was extremely cautious and very alert. Like a cat, he was the hunter; always prepared.

Eric carelessly tossed the file containing the details of his latest job on the small kitchen table. After a quick survey of the fridge's contents, he went with a beer. As Eric leaned against the counter, he took a long hard draw on the can.

Staring at the wall clock he watched the second hand approach the twelve as it marked seven o'clock exactly. His glance shifted toward the envelope. It had arrived; his moment, a moment of silence, before viewing the contents. Once it was opened, lives would change, some might end.

After he settled comfortably in his office, Eric removed the dossier, carefully scanning the documents. Each file's first page displayed a photo, a physical description along with all pertinent facts. Address, phone number, place of employment, and more. On the second piece of paper neatly typed were his orders. Each individual's file was laced with details. Those he would examine later, one at a time, making notes as he reviewed the information. First, he scrutinized the face of each person, then the name. Next,

Eric read the details of the actual mission and without thinking, exhaled with a sigh. At the moment, this was going to be an easy one. Six people in total, six lucky folks, for now. All the job called for was surveillance. Some phone taps, and the strategic placement of listening devices. He would set his staff to the task first thing in the morning.

On no level did Eric actually enjoy his job. He just knew that it was essential to the Patronums, and ultimately, to all Americans. Tonight, he would study the files. In the event that an addendum was made to the job, thorough knowledge of the principals would be essential.

The crisp knock on the door startled him, and Eric looked toward the clock; 9:46 P.M. Almost three hours had flown by since he ripped opened the envelope. He quickly gathered the scattered documents.

"Be right there," he yelled, "just give me a minute."

Damn, forgot about Monique, he thought. As engrossed in the files as he was, the prearranged visit had completely slipped his mind. Eric didn't know he'd be reviewing information tonight, when he was lying next to her in bed this morning. Considering the send-off she'd given him before work, the late-night invitation had seemed quite appropriate.

Even though he was sure he knew who was on the other side of the door, he approached it cautiously. For the second time that evening, he stood off to the side with gun in hand.

"Hello, who is it?" he said through the closed door.

The sultry voice, slightly muffled, sarcastically responded, "Hmmm, whom were you expecting?"

Eric grinned and holstered his weapon.

"Monique, it's you, what a lovely surprise," he said as he swung the door open, adding his own brand of sarcasm.

Even the way she was leaning against the open entrance suggested sensuality. Not feigned or staged, but rather an erotic grace that seemingly came very naturally to her and often eluded other women.

Like her demeanor and poise, her features were defined and elegant. Eric stared admiringly at her slight, nearly six-foot-tall frame. Her blue-black hair cascaded down her shoulders and to the middle of her back. The high cheekbones accented her huge dark brown eyes. Above Monique's pronounced collarbones, was a graceful elongated neck, which ended just below a perfect smile. There was a modest, unassuming confidence about her. She was the image of a top runway model. In his eyes, she was simply amazing.

Eric had bedded many beautiful women over the years, but Monique was different. She didn't attempt to impress him or influence him with her charms. Many of her predecessors had tried using their sexuality, eager to win his heart. She had actually turned him down not once, but twice when he first asked her out for coffee. He'd initially met her during an investigation with the CIA as a field agent. His primary function for the CIA was to obtain information about foreign governments, corporations and individuals. He would then report his findings to the various branches of the government.

Monique owned a small but exclusive employment agency. The local political factions often used her firm to find temps. Often her services were called upon during the holidays, maternity leaves or when a permanent replacement was required.

When they first met, Eric had been investigating a suspect with alleged terrorist ties. A young middle eastern woman had been under surveillance by the CIA. She applied to Monique's company specifically requesting placement at the State Senate in nearby Austin, Texas. When a more promising opening became available, the applicant had remained insistent; only a position in the administration was acceptable.

Monique was eventually questioned about the suspicious character, who had since been taken into custody by the CIA.

Arriving at the *LaFountaine Temporary Service Agency* that day, Eric didn't expect to be so enamored of her.

"Miss LaFountaine, did you not find it odd that Azar Yazdi was so adamant about aquiring a position in the State Senate? Particularly when other equally desirable positions became available?" he asked in an official monotone voice. His pen hovered above a blank page in the note pad awaiting her response.

Seated at her desk, she just stared at him. The corners of her mouth turned slightly upward, her chin resting comfortably in her hand.

When it became evident she was not going to answer without further prodding, he'd obliged.

"Miss Lafontaine?"

"Yes, Agent Brunner."

"Did you understand the question?"

"Of course I did, Agent Brunner."

"Ahh…okay then. Any thoughts that you would like to share?"

"Well, I have no idea what would motivate Miss Yazdi to want a placement at the Senate versus McNally's Animal Clinic, or any other place for that matter. In the past we've had a lot of young ladies, whom I suspect were really searching for a husband. Possibly Miss Yazdi was looking for a potential partner with a bright political future," she said as she smiled innocently, adding, "or perhaps just a new bed mate, I really don't know, Agent Brunner."

Her last comment completely knocked him off balance. Clumsily he responded, "Hmmm interesting. Anything else to add, Miss Lafontaine?"

"Just one thing Mr. Agent Man. Call me Monique."

After the interview he couldn't stop thinking about her. Eric made up an excuse to see her within the week. Shortly after arriving at her office, he confessed that the visit had been unofficial.

"Monique, would you like to join me for a coffee after work?" he asked.

"Thank you, Agent Brunner, but no," she replied politely.

Eric was not going to be so easily deterred. "Please call me Eric. Alright how about a drink then? Or perhaps dinner?"

Laughing, she looked up at him standing in front of her simple desk. "Agent Bru....Eric, are you trying to bribe me with a better offer? A drink...maybe dinner? You're cute, thank you, but no. I'm really busy for the next few weeks, but thanks anyway."

He had left her small office a little surprised. He couldn't remember the last time he'd been turned down.

As the weeks slipped by, he often thought of her dignified self assurance. It excited him, and was actually driving him crazy. On his third attempt, she finally agreed to a coffee. Coffee led to dinner, dinner led to more. Eventually she became a regular visitor.

Eric knew he should cut her loose. Usually he dated the same woman no longer than three months. It seemed that was around the time things began to get complicated. Being full time at the CIA and constantly on call for the Patronums often raised too many questions. He'd been seeing her for six months.

Stepping casually into the hallway, Monique sauntered past Eric as she entered the large living room. She began removing her jacket as she walked. Smiling provocatively, her gait slowed as she looked toward him. Just out of reach, she stopped and turned. Without a word she dropped her jacket to the floor, then began seductively unbuttoning her blouse. Never taking her eyes off Eric's, she had him locked in a trance. On the last button, she turned on her heel resuming her dreamy walk toward the bathroom. By the time Monique disappeared into the washroom she was naked. A moment later, the shower was running.

Grinning, he followed the watery serenade, removing his shirt and tie as he went. Her perfect form was visible through the frosted glass of the shower door as he entered the bathroom.

Monique tilted her head back and the cascading water ran down her smooth, olive skin. He could just make out her exquisite body through the glass before it became enveloped in steam. Impatiently, he unbuckled his belt, letting his trousers drop, then pulled off his briefs. Just as seductively, he too slipped into the mist-filled shower with Monique. As they embraced in a lovers' tangle, their flawless bodies became one with each other. The touch of her skin, combined with the warmth of the water soon dissolved the details of his mission and they faded from his mind.

Chapter 13

"Vanessa, do you feel like grabbing a movie?" Rose asked. This was the first time Rose had ever suggested going to the show after a work day. In the past they'd grabbed a few meals together. Some casual chitchat about their colleagues and the lab had been the extent of the socializing. Last time out, it was Vanessa who had mentioned taking in a movie sometime.

Blake left the lab a few minutes earlier with a handful of files. A moment later, Marc smiled, announcing that he was "going to drain the vein," as he inserted his card in the electronic lock. Vanessa thought he was childish, but couldn't suppress a grin nevertheless. Rose approached the cubicle just as Vanessa was translating Marc's most recent notes.

"Sure. Do you have a movie in mind?" Vanessa responded.

"Well, *The Final Conflict* just came out. It's the last in the '*Omen Series*.' I loved the first two. I'd like to see it, but not alone. Too scary!" Rose said. She added an obvious feigned shiver to emphasize the point and both women chuckled.

Vanessa hadn't been getting anywhere with Marc. Not where information was concerned anyway. She actually didn't care for horror films, but really needed to get an idea about Blake's current research. *This just might work out,* she thought slyly.

"How about I pick you up at eight?" Rose asked.

"Yeah, eight would be great." The girls again giggled, this time at the unintentional quip.

Ready to call it a day, Vanessa tidied up her desk. *I wish Marc would've asked me to the movies,* she thought absently, stuffing papers into a file folder. He was distant, distracted, acting stranger than usual. Vanessa didn't think he suspected anything, but couldn't be sure. When she'd asked him what he thought Blake was working on, his only comment was about the doctor's unusual behavior. She too noticed Blake was more outgoing lately, in fact, telling her just the day before how nice she looked. He had never been so cordial before and it took her by surprise. Vanessa liked Blake's brighter disposition and thought it might be the result of positive findings in whatever he was working on. Marc, on the other hand, had said he found the 'new' Blake's pleasant, jovial mood strange and ominous. Vanessa found *his* version, bizarre and slightly twisted.

Saying her goodbyes and finalizing the rendezvous with Rose, she left the compound. With a couple of hours to kill, she casually drove until she spotted her favorite drive-through. Pulling up to the speaker, she waited. A few seconds later the friendly female voice boomed, "Good afternoon and welcome to Daisy-Mays, home of the freshest burgers in Texas."

After Vanessa placed her order, the faceless yet cheery voice said, "that'll be six nineteen. Please drive up to the next window. Thank you!"

Pulling out of the parking lot, she regretted not asking Rose out for dinner before the movie. "No reason why we couldn't have grabbed a bite together," she said aloud. Just then, Queen began singing *another one bites the dust* on the car's radio, and she started tapping the steering wheel to the beat. In no time she was loudly singing the lyrics and as the radio blared she drove home. The *Daisy burger deluxe* was in a paper bag on the passenger seat.

Two hours later Vanessa was standing out in front of her apartment block when Rose pulled up.

"So, Rose, have you noticed that Dr. Edwards has been in a great mood lately?" Vanessa asked, just minutes into their drive to the theatre.

"I have, as a matter of fact. I've got to say I personally love it, makes work a little less dreary, don't you think?"

"Absolutely. Boy, he's sure been busy lately. Must be something top secret. He hasn't let me check his notes or files in months."

"Honestly, I have no idea. You know how Blake is, he doesn't share much of his research until he's sure it's going to be bumped to the next level," Rose said evasively.

The cat and mouse banter continued for fifteen minutes as they parked the car, then stood in line for popcorn and drinks.

Damn. This is going nowhere. Now I'm stuck sitting through a lousy horror flick, Vanessa thought as they weaved through the theatre looking for just the right seats.

She resolved to make it a social evening and enjoy the company. The movie was worse than she'd suspected, very disappointing, bordering on stupid at times. Even Rose regretted suggesting it, apologizing as they left the theater.

"Don't be silly, Rose. It had its moments. I'm just not a fan of horror flicks. If they're too scary I get nightmares."

"Why didn't you say something? We could have gone to another show," Rose said, blushing. "I thought it would be nice for us just to spend some time outside the lab."

"Relax, Rose, the movie was fine! The good news is, it wasn't TOO scary," Vanessa said. *I might as well buddy up with her,* she thought as she studied Rose's profile. *She'll tell me what I need...when she knows what's going on.*

Exiting the Elm Street Movie Palace, Rose asked, "Would you like to grab a quick drink? The traffic coming out of the parking lot will be crazy at least a half hour. It'll be my treat, to make up for the movie choice," she added sheepishly.

"Tell you what, if you promise *not* to mention the movie again, I'm in."

Smiling, Rose nodded.

Casually strolling in the humid Dallas air, they slipped into a lounge called "Dukes." Vanessa relaxed, enjoying the rest of the evening; however, where Blake's work was concerned, she was still no further ahead in uncovering his cloaked experiment.

Two hours later Vanessa was home changing into a nightie, and ready to hit the sack. She climbed into bed, grateful to be slipping between the cool, inviting sheets. Exhausted, sleep quickly overtook her as she unconsciously jumped from dream to dream. The last one was so vivid she could actually hear the sirens in her mind.

She woke in a fit of coughing. Instinctively, she drew a breath to replenish the void in her lungs. The pain in her throat was excruciating. It felt as if she was swallowing broken shards of glass. She opened her eyes, but it was impossible to see the end of her bed in the smoke laden room. Even in her sluggish state of mind, the word "fire" screamed in her head.

Vanessa lived in a three-story walk-up. She had chosen the third floor to reduce the chance of being burglarized. The possibility of a fire had not occurred to her then. She knew that being close to the floor was her only chance of escaping the oxygen-depleted room before it swallowed her up; she needed air.

She gingerly tested the floor next to the bed with a few quick taps of her foot. Satisfied that the blaze had not ravaged it yet, she dropped down onto her stomach. Although the linoleum was hot to the touch, the space was cooler, the smoke less dense than the air choking her when she first awoke. She crawled towards the door on her stomach. As she approached, flames flickered at the closed exit to her room. It took all her will power to resist giving into the panic that threatened to take control of her entire being. She started rising up to her knees. With each inch she ascended, she could feel the heat's power intensifying. Quickly she dropped back to her stomach.

Calm down. The window, get to the window, she thought frantically. Making a hundred eighty-degree turn, she crawled toward the opening. Her hand bumped into something.

"The nightstand, I'm almost there," she gasped.

Even at floor level, the blackish mixture of gases and suspended carbons was beginning to bury her as its veil fell quickly downward. She felt the wall's flat vertical rise. She could hear the door crackling, burning as the flames hungrily consumed it. She caught a flash of yellow through the swirling cloud of black smoke. Vanessa took a deep breath of the poisonous air, as she stood fully erect in front of her only escape. She felt the pliable screen netting. She pushed it with both hands, the screen fluttered silently to the ground below. Desperately, she thrust her head forward to snatch a mouthful of the cool night air.

Someone below screeched, "UP THERE, LOOK OVER THERE IT'S A WOMAN!"

Vanessa heard a jumble of voices and for the first time became aware that the street was alive with activity. Two fire trucks with ladders extended were on the other side of the flaming inferno. Several police cars, along with more emergency vehicles were scattered below, all with their lights twirling. The street was a kaleidoscope of color.

She felt the intensity of the heat on the back of her legs and buttocks. *God, I can't wait. I've got to jump,* she thought hysterically. Several firefighters were running with a rolled up tube, positioning themselves just below her window. The emergency team scrambled as they dropped their cargo. Skillfully, they unrolled the inflatable jumper pad. With no time to fill the device with air, rescuers and onlookers alike took up positions around the parachute material. Before it was completely off the ground one of the firefighters looked up in Vanessa's direction. "JUMP MISS, JUMP, WE'LL CATCH YOU!" he shouted.

Within seconds, others were prompting her to jump as well. Spotting the flames shooting out of the windows on either side of her, Vanessa climbed up. Carefully positioning herself on the narrow window ledge, she clutched the sides of the opening for balance, her legs dangling thirty feet above the ground. With her eyes squeezed shut, she fell three stories into the yielding parachute fabric. Landing with a thump, she was gently lowered to the ground. The nearest firefighter helped Vanessa to her feet as she cleared herself from the rescue apparatus.

"Are you alright, Miss?"

Coughing, she took a long, hard breath.

"Yes, I think so."

"Miss, someone will be here in a second to check you out."

He trotted off. Pulling his mask back down over his face, he assumed a position on a nearby fire hose, the surge of pressurized water continuing to beat back the flames.

An ambulance attendant rushed over to Vanessa, placing an oxygen mask over her nose and mouth. As he took her from the crowd of onlookers, several asked her if she was okay. Others commented on how lucky she was. She overheard one woman mention that there were people who'd died. Their lifeless bodies had been pulled out and were covered on the lawn. The paramedic had Vanessa lie down in the back of the ambulance while another medical technician visually examined her for injury. The large, black, female attendant removed the oxygen mask.

"What's your name honey?"

"Vanessa," she whispered.

The questions came in a flurry.

"Have you been burned?"

"No, I don't think so."

"Do you have any pain or numbness?"

Vanessa moved her hands over her body, feeling no strange sensations or pain, she again responded, "No, I don't think so."

"I am going to check your throat. Can you open wide? Say Ahhh, please." With a small penlight in one hand and a tongue depressor in the other, she carefully inspected Vanessa's breathing passage.

"You're lucky. There doesn't seem to be any burned tissue in your throat. I'm going to put this mask back on you. Just take deep breaths and try to relax. Another ambulance will be here soon to take you in for a thorough examination. Glad you made it out sweetie," the woman added sincerely. She jumped off the back of the ambulance, retreating around the corner. Vanessa rested her head on the small, hard pillow. Less than ten minutes before, she was resting comfortably in her own bed. In a split second she fast-forwarded the horrifying experience in her mind. It was so improbable, it all felt like a terrible nightmare. But here she was, staring up at the ceiling of an ambulance, and the cool oxygen was steadily hissing into her mask. It had all really happened.

Recalling the comment made by the woman about the dead bodies, the reality of the moment came crashing down.

My God, I could have died. I COULD HAVE BURNED TO DEATH! Overwhelmed with emotion, she began sobbing into the silicone mask. Only one word came to mind...*Novatek.*

*****

An insistent pounding awakened Marc. Only after a minute did he realize it wasn't his imagination. Somebody actually had the nerve to be hammering on his door at this hour.

"I'm coming, I'm coming. Just hold on for crissake." He looked at the clock as he passed the stove, 4:39 A.M. "This had better be important," he shouted at the bolted and secured entrance to his home.

“Who the hell is it?” he snapped as he reached the triple locked doorway. From the other side he heard a small, frightened voice answer, “It‘s me… Vanessa.”

Immediately he softened. He began unbolting the three locks, then the two chain latches. As he swung the door inward, she stood motionless in the hall, clad in green hospital scrubs.

“Jesus, Vanessa, are you okay?” he asked worriedly.

Standing there, unable to answer, her chin began to quiver as she fell into his arms weeping.

“Okay, okay, Ness. Just tell me what happened.”

Marc suddenly felt awkward. *I’m no knight in shining armor,* he thought. His experience with distraught women was less than adequate, as was his patience. It was obvious his co-worker and newly acquired bed partner was overwrought. Not knowing what to do, he simply pulled her into the apartment.

It was 5:20 A.M. before he got the full story of how her apartment block, along with all of her personal belongings, had been destroyed.

“Wow, you are one lucky gal,” he said, wincing as he spoke.

Realizing sex was out of the question, he decided sticking around this morning would be uncomfortable, senseless actually. He wouldn’t know what to do to console her anyway.

“Vanessa, I’m going into work. I’ll explain to Edwards what happened. You just get some sleep and take whatever you need.” Then it occurred to him, *Ahhh geez, she’s got no clothes, no wallet, and no credit cards.*

She wouldn't even be able to get into her bank account until all her IDs were replaced. A feeling of unexpected anxiety overwhelmed him.

“Ahhh, I’ll loan you whatever cash you need until you get squared away.” Then another thought came to mind. “Vanessa, by any chance do you have fire insurance?” She nodded.

“Oh my god! That’s great, excellent, good for you!” he replied, a bit too enthusiastically. Distraught, Vanessa didn’t notice.

Marc brightened as he realized the full aftermath of the situation. *I'm gonna get full points for this. No muss, no fuss. No inconvenience at all. Tomorrow she'll be in a motel with cash from the insurance company. She'll be all squared away and I'll be the hero.*

Feeling incredibly relieved, his generosity took flight. "I've got about three hundred bucks here for some clothes and cab fare. Take my credit card until your insurance company fixes you up. Go get anything you need, baby," he beamed.

Marc retreated to the bedroom, scouring his bureau for cash. Retrieving the gold visa from his wallet he re-entered the living room where Vanessa was sitting on the couch. He gave her the cash and credit card. Her eyes welled up again.

"Thanks, Marc. I really appreciate this," she said, her reservoir of tears spilling from the corners of her eyes.

"Hey, what are friends for? No problem. Just make yourself at home. Get some rest. You know where the bedroom is." He couldn't resist the sexual implication.

"I'm going to take a shower. I'll look in on you before I take off," he announced jubilantly.

*****

As Marc weaved his way through traffic, his closing thought on Vanessa's ordeal was how the *fickle finger of fate* had intervened on her behalf. It was not her destiny to die in that fire. Almost heartlessly he put her ordeal out of his mind.

He recounted the last few weeks at the facility. Blake had been weird, really weird. He'd been overly friendly, smiling, and even chatty. In the two years that Marc had been employed there, Blake had never asked him what he did outside of the lab, not once. Suddenly, he seemed to have an extreme interest in everybody who worked there.

Friggin spooky if you ask me. Edwards couldn't give a shit about what any of us do, except when we're there. Something's up, something big, that's for damn sure. Marc swung the mustang into his parking spot at the lab.

*****

Vanessa lay awake, staring at the unfamiliar ceiling of Marc's bedroom, thinking about her close call.

Could it have been Novatek...could they know that I'm working for Wilkinson? Would they really try to kill me? God, I'm so tired...being paranoid. They wouldn't kill somebody for stealing secrets, would they? Suddenly she jumped out of bed. A half hour later she was sitting in the back of a taxi. Her hair was still damp from the quick shower. Swimming in Marc's oversized sweatshirt and jeans, she had run an errand, a very urgent errand. Before noon, she was again in Marc's apartment. Inside his bedroom she casually tossed the shopping bag containing two new outfits on a chair and slipped back into bed. She drifted off in a fitful sleep. Images of flames and burned corpses crowded her dreams. She'd never know that Novatek was *not aware* of her spying. Another fact Vanessa would be spared was that, had they known, an accident *would* have been arranged. One she would not have survived.

Chapter 14

Thomas Phoenix raced towards the hospital, his young wife Loren, huddled on the seat next to him. She was in labor and about to have a baby.

"What a break," Thomas said. Sirens screamed as he fell in behind the mammoth truck that weaved effortlessly through the traffic. The brightly colored red and chromed fire engine was speeding to an out of control inferno. Even as they drove, a reporter was receiving a tip. The story was about the blaze that had engulfed a three-story walk-up. He'd have the report on paper in time for the morning edition.

"Breathe, Darling, remember your breathing techniques," the father-to-be prompted.

Through pursed lips, she exhaled three short bursts.

"Thomas, can't you drive any faster? Ahhh…"

Holding her breath she leaned forward pressing on her abdomen as another contraction gripped her. Looking over at his wife, he winced at her contorted expression.

He felt helpless. The young Dallas District Attorney was not accustomed to feeling powerless. Thomas was proud of the fact that he could command most situations in which he found himself, but this, this was totally out of his control. He knew it was a possibility, but like most never thought it would happen to him. Who would have expected his pregnant, young wife to go into labor a month earlier than the due date? Neither of them had really been prepared when she awoke, crying, just a few short hours before. When it became obvious the pain wasn't going to pass, he'd dialed their obstetrician, Dr. David Hunter.

"David, it's Thomas Phoenix. I'm sorry to be calling so late," his voice sounded anxious. "Loren's having contractions. They're really coming fast."

"That's alright, Thomas. When did they start?"

"A couple of hours ago. First five minutes apart, then closer. The last few have been less than two minutes."

Suddenly, Loren moaned again, then she began to cry. Rushing to her side, he dropped the receiver on the floor beside the nightstand. His eyes followed her gaze. The burgundy bedspread was now a darker red between her legs.

When the contractions had awakened them an hour earlier, Loren thought it might just be cramps. Thomas brought her a few extra pillows and propped her up in bed. Neither wanted to get up, assuming that the discomfort would pass. It hadn't.

"Something's wrong, David," Thomas's voice was filled with panic. "She's wet between her legs. I think she's bleeding!"

"Relax, Thomas, just relax. Check for blood, but I'm sure her water just broke," the obstetrician said calmly.

With a sense of relief, Thomas touched the bedspread. Looking down at his dampened fingers, he confirmed the fluid was indeed clear.

"Loren, are you okay?"

"I've soaked the bed," she whimpered, "I think my water broke."

"David, you're right. What should I do now?"

"Well, that baby wants to come out, Thomas. Just keep Loren calm and relaxed, everything will be fine. I'll meet you both at the hospital. Drive safely, but you should go now."

Thomas hung up and went directly to the closet to pack an overnight bag.

"Loren, honey, tell me what to grab here."

"Just get me a fresh nighgoww…" her sentence went unfinished as another contraction stole her breath away.

Loren continued doing what they had practiced for weeks in Lamaze class. After a minute of quick rhythmic breathing, she completed her request.

"I need some fresh clothes. I'm soaked."

He fumbled in her night drawer looking for a flannel nightgown. The first items he came across were the some of the more risqué nightwear that had gotten them into this predicament in the first place. She had been more amorous than usual for months prior to getting pregnant.

Thomas had wanted to start a family. However, with his eye on a seat in the state senate, he'd felt this was not the best time. Loren, on the other hand, wanted a baby the first year of their marriage. He'd been able to put her off—for the last five years. He had suspected her newfound interest in sexy lingerie and the miscalculated cycle had not been entirely coincidental.

"This one okay?" He turned toward Loren holding up a knee length flannel nightshirt for her approval. Another contraction had taken hold of her. Nervous at how quickly they were coming, in a quiet voice he said, "Honey, I'll help you change and then we'll go. I'll bring the overnight bag to the hospital later."

Loren nodded, her eyes welled up as tears spilled down her cheeks. "It hurts," she cried in a small voice.

"I know, I know sweetie. Let's just get you down there." *I feel so useless*, he thought.

"Thomas, noth…nothing's going to happen to our baby, is it?" she implored in the same unsure voice.

"No, honey, of course not. The baby is going to be just fine," he replied reassuringly.

She smiled, simply believing him. They would get through this together. He knew that she considered him her protector, her hero. Again he'd felt an overwhelming wave of vulnerability.

Now, barreling down the freeway, the overhead sign DALLAS GENERAL HOSPITAL NEXT EXIT was illuminated by his headlights.

Taking the off ramp much faster than the recommended forty miles per hour, he looked over at her. "We're almost there sweetheart, just a few more minutes."

He loved Loren more than anything and would have gladly taken her pain. All he could do at the moment, however, was drive as quickly as possible to the hospital.

"Okay, honey, we're here."

The car screeched to a halt right in front of the automatic sliding doors. They had made it to the Dallas General Hospital in record time. He'd done his best and smiled, knowing an ambulance would have been no quicker. He saw the attendant making his way toward them with a wheelchair. Thomas jumped out of the car and hurried to the passenger side. He offered his wife a hand to exit.

"Phoenix?" the tall, gangly man asked.

"Yes, that's right. Loren Phoenix," he anxiously replied.

"I'm to take you straight to the fifth floor. Dr. Hunter is ready for you," he said as both men helped Loren into the wheelchair. "The doctor told me to take your car keys, someone will move your vehicle for you."

Thomas handed the young man his car keys and relaxed for the first time in hours.

This was not his area of competence. He was content to give the responsibility over to those who could take care of his wife and unborn child. As they exited the elevator, the doctor was there to greet them.

"They called up from downstairs and said you had arrived. I'll take it from here, Mike," he said to the attendant. The obstetrician assumed the position behind the wheelchair, pushing her towards the labor room.

"Loren how are you doing?"

"I'm okay Dr. Hunter. Is my baby going to be all right? Is this normal? I'm not due for another month and two days," she said in a rush, before the next contraction came.

"Quite normal Loren. I'm sure your baby will be fine. He's just in a hurry to meet his new parents, I suppose," he said, winking at Thomas as they walked.

It was the first time since Loren's cries had awakened them that Thomas thought about his budding power. He was proud of his position and status in the community. He was pretty sure Dr. Hunter didn't give his personal home number to all his expectant mothers. He also doubted the invitation to 'call day or night for any reason,' was extended to every patient. He knew for certain medical personnel didn't valet park arriving cars. This treatment was reserved for the elite.

As the doctor wheeled Loren into the labor gallery, she grasped her husband's hand. Looking up, she smiled at him.

"We are going to have our baby," she said.

As he looked down into her radiant face, he felt his own eyes water. "Yes, sweetheart, it looks like we are," he responded, his voice cracking with emotion. He loved Loren with all his heart, but at that moment, Thomas loved her even more.

Seven hours had actually passed since their arrival. To Thomas it seemed like his wife had been having contractions forever. The labor nurse was measuring Loren's cervix periodically. After the last measurement, she left to summon the doctor. Minutes later, Dr. Hunter entered, announcing that Loren was fully dilated. She was quickly moved to the delivery room.

After the nurse had strategically attached the monitor pads to Loren, Dr. Hunter gave the only remaining instruction.

"Loren, during each contraction I need you to push, okay?"

"Yeah, I want to pusssh….oh Jesus… here…it…cooooomes," she managed. Her face was sweaty and beet-red.

Thomas was stunned. The next fifteen minutes was a flurry of grunts, groans, and cursing. Every one emanated from Loren's sweet lips. All he could do was hold her hand and mimic the doctor's words of encouragement.

The doctor gave her a final urging. "Push Loren, we're almost there, on three a good hard push. One, two, three, PUSH!"

Teeth clenched, sitting almost upright, she squeezed her husband's hand with amazing strength. She emitted a hair-raising scream through her almost-closed mouth. Exhausted, she collapsed. The doctor held the new life in his hands. With a smile, he said to them both, "Congratulations, it's a boy."

The nurse quickly took the newborn over to the table, gently placing him under the warmth of the heat lamps. She carefully wrapped the baby in a blanket as the doctor prepared to deliver the placenta. Thomas was amazed. Never had he expected this feeling of pure exhilaration. He turned to Loren, who was lying still with her eyes closed. "I love you, sweetheart. We have a boy, honey. He's beautiful."

"Doctor, we have a drop in pressure," the nurse monitoring the machine announced. "63 over 47… 58 over 42… 51… over 33." The medical team began to scramble as Loren's blood pressure descended at an alarming rate. The doctor peeled back Loren's eyelid. With a penlight, he examined her pupillary response. One of the nurses softly put her hand on Thomas's back, gently escorting him out of the birthing room.

"David, what's wrong, what's the matter? DAVID WHAT THE HELL'S GOING ON!" he hollered.

"Sir, calm down, please let the doctor examine her," the nurse said empathetically.

"What's going on here?" he repeated as he stumbled through the big double doors. Thomas was frightened. It was another unfamiliar emotion. The nurse directed him to a chair in the abandoned waiting room.

"The doctor will come out and talk to you as soon as he knows something, sir. Please try to relax." In a flash, she retreated back down the hall. As she disappeared into the room that held his precious family, the invisible ceiling speakers bellowed.

"*Code Blue, Code Blue, crash cart, Fifth floor.*"

An overwhelming sense of dread enveloped him. He slumped in the chair. He buried his head in his hands. Slowly he began to rock back and forth.

Nothing's wrong. Everything's going to be just fine. Nothing's wrong, nothing's wrong. He mumbled the words over and over, as if the repeating would make it so.

Time lost meaning. He had no idea how much had passed. Thomas heard footsteps from far away. They grew closer. He peered through his fingers and saw the contorted face of Dr. Hunter moving towards him.

He felt the doctor lightly place a hand on his shoulder. The voice sounded strange as David began to speak.

"Thomas, the baby's fine. We are going to keep him a few days, for observation."

*****

He was back at the apartment. As the birds sang their melodious song outside the open bedroom window, Thomas looked like he'd been hypnotized. His vacant stare was fixed on the empty overnight bag. He replayed David's words…

"Brain embolism, a thin blood vessel...pressure from the pushing...probable cause of rupture...undetectable, she never felt a thing...I'm so sorry for your loss, Thomas."

The explanation had come ninety minutes earlier. The doctor's words pummeled his brain. He felt totally numb. He could not speak. He'd never experienced such loss. He sat motionless, devoid of hope. In the clouded recesses of his mind, the memory of the baby's birth fluttered. First like a flickering candle, then burning brightly, giving faith that somehow he would go on. Soberly he asked to see his son. Looking at his tiny face, he uttered the child's name, "Carl, Carl Phoenix."

His eyes were glazed, still locked on the overnight bag. It would never be packed, never be needed. The reality of the past two hours overwhelmed him. His knees buckled and he collapsed to the floor. His body surrendered to the anguish that suddenly overpowered him as he shuddered with uncontrollable sobs.

Chapter 15

"In conclusion gentleman, there is absolutely no doubt that the results are irrefutable." The fourteen members of the committee were draped in silence. Nobody sitting at the round table moved. The only sound that emanated from the collective group was an even, quiet breathing. The words still hung in the air, permeating the thoughts of all those who were present.

Dr. Gregory Emerson had just completed delivering his summation of the report. His team had generated the summary based on Dr. Blake Edward's findings. In the past, situations had been presented which, at first glance, appeared to be amazing. Subsequently, after all necessary analysis was completed, '*amazing*' proved to be unremarkable. Such was not the case this time. *Elixir* was confirmed, on all levels. The discovery was monumental.

"Gentleman, the floor is open," Gregory announced.

Murmured voices buzzed around the table as members shared their immediate thoughts. Sam Elliot, head of science was the first to speak.

"Well, from a scientific point of view only, this is a miraculous event. Quite frankly, the unearthing, to coin a phrase, must have been like finding a needle in a haystack. I am quite sure the end result was accidental. With that said," Elliot paused momentarily, ensuring he had everyone's undivided attention—the room was hushed, as he continued, "Who among us has concerns about the release of this information, without an intense examination at ALL levels?" Most hands ascended simultaneously. Sam Elliott nodded in stern affirmation as he dropped back into his leather bound seat.

The next to speak was the head of government, Gerald Fitzpatrick. "The first thought that occurs to me is the global ramifications of this *Elixir*. Will we be required to surrender this finding to other countries? From a humanitarian point of view, most third world countries will be unable to afford the vaccination once the pharmaceutical sector has set a price point. Pressure from foreign governments, many of them allies to the United States, will be enormous," he said solemnly.

Dr. Emerson felt compelled to respond. "Gerald, that is a very interesting question and we trust your cell, in conjunction with foreign affairs, will generate an answer by early next week for this committee."

Fitzpatrick glanced toward the head of the foreign affairs, and in concurrence, they both nodded their affirmation as he retook his seat.

Walter Byres would prove to be the member with the largest single undertaking regarding Elixir. Mr. Byres was the head of finance. He didn't really seem to fit the role of a number-cruncher, not from a physical standpoint anyway. He looked more like a well-aged screen actor with a generous head of distinguished salt-and-pepper hair. Although not a real look-a-like, his presence could be easily compared to President Ronald Reagan, Clarke Gable, or Cary Grant. He was sharp, handsome, and very well-liked.

As Walter stood to address the assembly, an unsuspecting onlooker might guess he was accepting a lifetime achievement award from the Screen Actors' Guild. His clear, rich voice possessed a soothing resonance as he spoke.

"Gentleman, my branch will have a complete report on the overall financial impact, whether positive or negative on the country as a whole. In order to investigate all implications and provide the most accurate data, we will need at least one full week. Our department will require immediate cooperation from any team called upon, day or night. Findings from all cells should be directed to my department immediately, ensuring a timely response. When verification of data is confirmed, the statistics will be incorporated into our figures."

Confirmatory nods came from every member, with a few "here, heres." As Walter Byres took his seat, he stopped midway, once again standing to his full six-foot-three-inch stature. "I assume arrangements have been made for the containment regarding all aspects of Elixir?"

Bruce Vargo, head of security, rose like a tall oak. At sixty-three years of age, he still possessed the body of a very powerful man. Towering over six feet five inches, time had not yet begun its callous attack on his anatomy.

"Fellow Patronums," his powerful voice boomed, like an ancient warrior addressing his troops before battle, "all necessary precautions have been taken to ensure the suppression of this sensitive information. However, it is imperative that this committee completes its assessment as swiftly as possible. Something of this magnitude is like a grass-fire, one minute contained, and the next completely out of hand. The gateway for control over the destiny of Elixir is open, but rest assured, gentleman, it closes a bit every day." Vargo had, in fact, been given a list of the principals. The classified files had then been delivered to Eric Brunner. So far, there were no leaks.

"The information was intercepted exactly eight days ago. We have approximately twenty-two days to act. After the twenty-second day, the original research team must be notified as to the outcome of the evaluation. If there is to be a dispute regarding the results, the report will be sent back to the research team for revision and further scrutiny. Our boy Edwards will be getting anxious soon. He knows he has a winner. He wrote the book on this stuff. We'll contain it as long as possible, but depending on this committee's decision, concealment of Elixir may not be necessary. On the other hand, it may be imperative. Understand, Gentleman, many lives rest in your capable hands." The giant man resumed his seat.

An open discussion ensued with all aspects of Elixir's overall affect on the United States. Questions, as well as suggestions of areas to be examined were brought to the floor.

"How many people are employed fighting the disease?"

"How many die annually?"

"How will a cure affect the thinning of the herd?"

"What's the average age of victims?"

"How many millions are spent and then injected into the economy via the pharmaceutical company supplying pain killers, chemotherapy, etc.?"

"Medicare, pensions, social security implications?"

Suggestions of areas to be reviewed were endless. All seemed valid in the eyes of the committee members.

Dr. Emerson occupied the stage at the end of the evening, and brought the meeting to a close.

"If there are no more questions, my friends, we have work to do."

Those with the most important roles were quick to leave. Phone calls had to be made. Cells had to be activated immediately.

Dr. Emerson's mind was conflicted about the actual implications of Elixir, aware that his team's work was not over yet. Walter Byres would need statistics from the medical cell. Emerson had an uncomfortable feeling that the facts provided would not favor Elixir or Dr. Blake Edwards.

Chapter 16

Vanessa was nervous and had slept poorly. Her harrowing experience, less than forty-eight hours behind her, was still fresh enough to make her mind swirl with the precariousness of life, especially hers. The excitement of being a 'pharmaceutical mole' was quickly losing its allure. She was scared.

Walking the familiar corridor to the lab, she wondered what reaction lay behind the big solid door? She braced for a moment before sliding her card through the lock. She entered the lab. As the door opened, she was almost knocked over with a frantic but heartfelt hug. Rose stood at arms length looking into her face.

"God, we're all so happy that you're okay," she said, squeezing her shoulders.

The deceitful façade was taxing, particularly just then. *I'm nothing more than a traitor,* Vanessa thought pulling away from the sincere embrace. She was touched by the gesture, but worried that her undercover status had somehow been compromised. *I'm just being paranoid* she thought.

"It was terrible. When Marc explained to us what had happened, we were all very upset. Thank God you're alright," Rose said, her voice strained with emotion.

"I really appreciate everyone's concern, thank you. The whole thing was terrifying, but it was over so fast—it's just a blur now."

Vanessa found the guilt becoming difficult to hide, and the entire conversation regarding the fire was begging to overwhelm her.

"I really feel awful about the people who didn't get out." Vanessa said, referring to the newspaper story about a retired couple that had been overcome by smoke before they could escape.

"You know, sweetie, Blake said you could take the rest of the week off, to get your things in order," Rose said.

"Yes, Marc told me. Yesterday I did as much as I could, but for now, I just want to get back to work," she replied.

"Well Vanessa, if there is anything you need, don't hesitate to ask, okay?"

"Thanks, that really means a lot to me." In an effort to change the subject, she added, "Rose, where's Dr. Edwards this morning?"

It was after nine and Blake had not arrived at the lab.

"I haven't seen him yet. It's not like him to be late, but he *has* been working long hours for weeks. Maybe it just caught up with him today."

Vanessa shrugged and moved toward her work area. She stared at the files strewn carelessly about. *Geez I was only off for one day. This place is a bloody mess,* she thought. It seemed everyone had just dropped their papers in no particular order on the desk. Marc popped his head around the corner of her cubicle. "Hey, how are you? Everything okay today?" he asked.

"Yes, Marc, I'm fine. You?"

"Great, good. Yep, I'm great too. OK, gotta get back at it, talk to you later," he said as he quickly disappeared.

If not for Marc's very odd behavior, she wouldn't have been as nervous about her situation. Since the fire a few nights ago he had been acting very edgy. Last night he'd spurned her advances at his apartment. After tossing and turning for a half hour, he'd moved to the couch. He left the bedroom with a pillow under his arm saying he wasn't used to sleeping with anyone. When she awoke, Marc was gone. Vanessa resolved to arrange a hotel suite after work. Staring at a clear spot on her desk, she recalled the last thirty-six hours…

When Marc left the apartment the previous morning right after she had told him of the fire, Vanessa had jumped out of bed. Finding some of Marc's clothes, she'd showered and was in a cab within the hour heading directly to the *Daily Dallas News*. Once inside the lobby she walked toward the 'classified' section. This wasn't her first visit here. With no one in line, she approached the counter.

"Good morning, how can I help you?"

"I would like to place an ad," Vanessa responded.

“Certainly, your name please?” the young girl asked. Her fingers suspended over the keyboard of the electric typewriter were set to whirl it into action.

“Vanessa Hargrave,” she replied matter-of-factly.

The typewriter ball spun to life and the clack-clack-clacking was over in an instant.

“Address, please?”

Vanessa hesitated, realizing she didn’t have a home anymore. Rather than explaining the fire, she gave her still smoldering address.

”17815 Kinver Avenue, Suite 303.”

Again, a sudden burst from the typewriter.

“What section ma’am?” she asked.

“Wanted,” Vanessa replied.

“Alright, go ahead please.”

Vanessa geared up for the explanation she always offered after saying the words.

"WANTED: First class ticket to Mars."

Once again, the young girl’s fingers expertly danced across the keys of the electrically operated keyboard. When her mind caught up, they stopped.

“Pardon me ma’am?” she asked, with a not-so-sure-look.

“That’s right, it should read, ‘WANTED first class ticket to Mars.’ It’s just a little game I play with my boyfriend when we’ve had a fight and it’s my fault.” Lowering her voice she leaned over the counter and said, “He’s constantly accusing me of being from another planet. I run the ad, we laugh, and all is forgiven.”

“Oh, I see, that’s kind of cute. I thought I was hearing things,” she said with a chuckle. A moment later the order was finished. With the secret message placed, Vanessa proceeded to the cashier window and paid.

The purpose was to arrange a covert rendezvous with Michael, her contact at Wilkinson, Novatek’s only rival in the pharmaceutical world. The coded ad was always the same and guaranteed a meeting.

After leaving the newspaper office she made several stops for some clothing. Vanessa returned to Marc's apartment by eleven. Exhausted, she'd dropped into the empty bed and was out like a light. Even as she slept, the classified was being typeset and prepared for the next morning's early edition.

At 5:20 P.M. the following day, she entered *The Velvet Glove,* ten minutes early. Michael was there, sitting in the dimly-lit lounge. Vanessa proceeded to the private booth that he regularly occupied when they met.

The bar was a discrete place, frequented by many businessmen after work. They were usually sitting in one of the secluded areas with a female who most often was not a wife. It would have been a cynical speculation to assume the establishment had been built with just that in mind. An isolated rendezvous spot where drinks at six bucks apiece was considered a bargain. Six dollars would be a good deal for those who wanted to meet under an ambiguous veil of transgression. This was a safe, public place. There was no actual evidence of any infidelity, or intention of such a motive. A drink here was not exactly like inviting your secretary to a hotel, although many meetings that started here, ended there.

It was certainly not the case with Michael. Vanessa often thought him an odd choice as an undercover spy for Wilkinson. At six foot seven inches tall and barely a hundred sixty-five pounds, he was rail thin. His wispy brown hair barely covered his boney cranium. If his tall, frail look weren't enough to etch him into one's memory, his eyes definitely were. The sockets were unusually deep-set, forming dark shadows, and the absence of reflection from his pupils gave him a sinister look. The meager skin stretched over every part of his skeletal figure. Even his hands seemed to be oversized for the amount of flesh and membrane allotted. When Vanessa saw Michael, he reminded her of Lurch, the butler. He was the character who'd played the faithful servant on the 1960's television classic, *The Addams Family.*

"Look, Michael, I'm scared. I'm sure Novatek is onto me. I think they may have had something to do with the fire at my apartment. Whatever Edwards is working on is big, very big." Lowering her voice, she could barely speak the words, “Michael, I’m pretty sure Novatek tried to have me killed.”

The gaunt man lifted his six-dollar Tom Collins slowly to his lips and took a drink.

She wasn’t sure if it was the shadowy booth they occupied, or the tunnels his eyes shone from, but at that moment they seemed to glow. Without warning goose bumps sprang to life on her body. They started on her calves and prickled all the way to the tip of her head. She shivered, remembering the childhood fable; someone had just walked on her grave.

Leisurely reaching into the breast pocket of his extra-large jacket, he removed a letter-sized envelope.

“Miss Hargrave, our employers share your misgivings. They secured a copy of the investigating fire marshal's report.” His head tilted slightly forward and he’d looked up through his bushy eyebrows. She could barely see them, yet she felt his spooky eyes burrowing into her from their bottomless pit.

God, he creeps me out, she thought.

“The fire was a result of faulty wiring,” he said handing her the report. “Our employer also feared for your safety,” he added as an afterthought. Scouring the paperwork, it hadn’t occurred to her to ask just *how* they’d obtained the private details so quickly.

“I don’t really care, Michael. I’ve had it. I'm out,” she said tossing down the document.

He moved so quickly, she barely saw him reach into his oversized jacket for the second time. His boney fingers slowly fished out a thick brown envelope. Placing it methodically on the table in front of them, he leisurely pushed it toward her.

“They predicted you might need an incentive. We want to know what Edwards is working on, Miss Hargrave.”

Vanessa took it. Looking inside, she cursed under her breath. “How much is here?” she hissed.

“Twenty-five thousand,” he said with a lewd expression.

Twenty-five thousand bucks is a year’s salary, and a fresh start, she thought reluctantly. After only a moment’s consideration, she said, “Fine, I’ll stay long enough to find out what he’s up to. But regardless of what it is, when I find out, I’m through. Understand?”

“We have no problem with those conditions, Miss Hargrave.”

That was yesterday in the Velvet Glove. Today, she had to contend with the filing on her desk. She'd resolved to turn up the heat. *To hell with being overly cautious, I want out of this whole ugly business.*

*****

In another part of the Institute, Blake Edwards entered the small, organized office of Evan Sinclair. "Dr. Sinclair, I’m just wondering how you’re doing with my data?”

“Good Morning, Dr. Edwards. Please come in.”

The invitation was unnecessary. By taking one step past the doorway, Blake was already in the cramped space. Since the only chair present was stacked high with unread files, he simply leaned on the corner of the desk. With a small grin, he posed the question again.

“So, have you formed any opinion on my findings, Doctor?”

Evan fidgeted for a moment. Eric Brunner had briefed him on the importance of containment regarding Edwards’ breakthrough and the possibility of a call. “Evan, be prepared for Dr. Edwards' next visit. He’s not likely to wait the thirty days before he starts poking around. My guess is, he’ll want to know how the review is going long before the thirtieth day.”

Evan didn’t expect to see Blake for at least another week. Tapping his pencil on an opened folder, he tried to mask his nervousness with feigned irritation.

“Dr. Edwards, look around here. I’m only one man. I have thirty days in which to file a report to you. I only received the data from you a week ago,” he snapped.

“Actually, Sinclair, it’s been twelve days.” Blake retorted, the impatience evident in his voice.

Brunner’s words were ringing in Sinclair's head. “Evan, it’s imperative to keep Blake Edwards calm. He’s likely to be disappointed when you tell him it's going to take more time. Don't do anything to aggravate the situation or *him.* If you do, he might try to go public, or worse, have his findings reviewed by an outside agency. You do understand we can't have that."

Thinking of Brunner's warning, Evan said, "Blake, I'm sorry. I've been having some personal difficulties with the wife. Plus, I'm just swamped. I'll finish the review I'm currently working on, then analyze your data." He chose his words carefully and delivered them apologetically. "Actually, there are two files in front of yours, but I'll skip them. I promise you one thing, I'll have a fully detailed review along with my recommendation before the thirty days. Fair enough?" he asked. He felt he was doing a good job at pacifying him.

Blake could barely contain his anger.

"Dr. Sinclair, Are you saying you haven't even started reviewing the information? I believe Novatek would be VERY, VERY INTERESTED IN THIS DATA. Not to mention, VERY UPSET that it's COLLECTING DUST HERE ON YOUR DESK," he shouted.

Eric Brunner's words of warning faded, as Evan's own temper began to rise.

"I'm sure they would be, but I have *rules,* Dr. Edwards. I'm quite aware you researchers ALL feel exactly the same about your potential discoveries. That is precisely the reason that Novatek established the thirty-day regulation. All reports typed, back in your lab in THIRTY DAYS." Evan said. A triumphant smiled started to form on his face as he caught himself. "I mean, I'm sorry to have to put it to you like this, but it's really the best I can do," he explained. The only thing he was *really* sorry about was that he couldn't share the self-satisfaction he felt at having spouted off his true feelings. "Doctor, I'll do my best to speed it up. I should be able to give you an indication of my findings by the 25th or 26th day," he said calmly.

Blake stomped off without responding. As the door slammed, Evan could hear the shouting as Dr. Edwards proceeded down the hallway toward his own lab. Evan was sure one of the muffled rants was something along the line of *goddamned idiot.* He fumbled for the aspirins in the top drawer of his desk. Once he found them, he slammed the drawer closed. Lately he'd felt powerless to control the events in his life.

*****

The tumblers in the lab's electronic lock moved and as usual, all eyes shifted toward the door. Though Vanessa and the others guessed who it was, they gawked anyway. As Blake entered the lab, it was obvious that he was in a bad mood. The look on his face showed his frustration. His brow wrinkled, and the corners of his mouth turned down. His jaw muscles flinched involuntarily.

Vanessa glanced toward Marc just in time to see him bury his face in a file. Rose looked perplexed. Vanessa felt her pulse increase. Something was up and she was on guard for any opportunity that would get her closer to Edwards' secrets.

"Good morning, Doctor," Rose offered.

Blake tried to be cordial, but pleasantries seemed to be elusive this morning. With a cursory nod, he looked at her and simply said, "Rose."

Approaching Vanessa's work area, he stopped briefly. Without thinking, her body became rigid, her mind raced irrationally. *Oh MY God, He knows about Wilkinson…HE KNOWS!!*

"I was sorry to hear about your mishap. Glad to see you're okay," he said blandly. He continued on his way without waiting for a response. Marc, he ignored completely.

"Thank you, Dr. Edwards," she called after him. A welcome wave of relief spread over her as her tensed muscles relaxed.

Vanessa saw the confused look cross Rose's face. It was obvious something had happened to upset the doctor. She expected that Rose would try to find out what it was. Vanessa got into position directly across from Edwards' station, hoping to overhear something. Standing in front of a large file cabinet, she busied herself with what appeared to be filing. Within moments Rose wandered over to his station. Vanessa strained to hear whatever she could.

"Blake, is everything all right?" she asked quietly.

"Yes, Rose, fine."

"Well you just seem so upset this morning."

"It's Sinclair. That moron hasn't even opened my file," he said in a hushed voice. "I got the definite impression the fool thinks I'm after the cash carrot they dangle here," he muttered looking at Rose.

Blake was referring to the incentive bonus Novatek had incorporated several years before. It could produce a small windfall when data was bumped upstairs. Ultimately, it was a profit-sharing inducement for products after they hit the shelves. Many team leaders would be anxiously awaiting the extra dividend when the first stage of the process was complete. It was common knowledge that the fringe benefit could be thousands of dollars. Blake's small share would result in millions.

"I have a good mind to go to Sinclair's superiors. Trouble is, with all the security around here, I really don't know who his supervisor would be."

"I know it's hard to be patient, Blake, but you'll have your answer in three weeks. Then it will be months of testing before it ever goes to the next stage. There will be testing required on humans to see how we react to…" Suddenly Blake squeezed Rose's arm, shushing her, as he noticed Vanessa.

In her fervor to eavesdrop, Vanessa had stopped filing. Actually she had stopped moving entirely, for fear of missing some of the whispered conversation. With the abrupt pause in chat, Vanessa turned to see both Rose and Blake staring blankly at her. *Dammit, busted*, she thought as she grabbed a file and closed the drawer. She averted their gaze while walking back to her desk. *Damn, he'll be on the lookout now.*

Rose glanced back at him and then realized what was going through his head. "Blake, relax, Vanessa was just doing some filing. You're becoming too obsessed over Elixir," she said.

Blake looked exasperated at the prospect of being spied on.

*****

Meanwhile Evan was dealing with his own frustrations. "Mr. Brunner, this is Dr. Evan Sinclair at Novatek."

"How are you this morning, Doctor?" Eric responded.

Evan was nervous. Although recruited long ago into the Patronums, he had never been called upon before. Given his lack of experience in such matters and his recent poor judgment in his personal affairs, he was afraid of screwing up.

"Well, Mr. Brunner," he said, sweating, "we have a problem. Edwards was down here first thing this morning, and he was very upset. I did as you instructed and tried to get him to calm down, but I'm not sure how well it worked."

"Alright, Evan, just relax. Now tell me word for word what Edwards said."

Over the next twenty minutes Evan recounted to the best of his recollection the exact details of the conversation. He did, of course, omit the parts he contributed that may have added to Dr. Edwards overall frustration.

*****

From her desk area, Vanessa saw they were again engrossed in a hushed conversation, and once more she strained to hear. Moving about the lab, Vanessa casually walked by them. Each time she did, both stopped speaking. On her final pass, Blake tossed her an irritated glance. Frustrated, she retreated to her desk.

Rose again continued on with what she was saying. "Blake, like I was mentioning earlier, Elixir has to be clinically tested on humans to see how the tissue and our bodies react."

"Rose, I've already conducted tests in four human subjects and the results are irrefutable. They are all cured, one hundred per cent, with no side effects. No indication they ever had the disease and no trace of Elixir in their systems," he said in a barely audible tone.

With her mouth agape, she stared at Blake. As unfeasible as it seemed, she comprehended that he'd accomplished what no one else could over the last hundred years. The enormity of the achievement suddenly overwhelmed her and her eyes began to well. The tears ran freely, spilling down her cheeks. Blake, about to say something else, turned toward her.

"Rose, for God's sake, get a hold of yourself," he scolded her in a muffled voice. "Until this is made public, you're the only one who knows. I'd like to keep it that way." He looked away from her and glanced in Vanessa's direction.

Sensing the gaze, she raised her head, just as Blake looked back toward Rose. Vanessa was surprised at the sudden flash of anger she felt seeing Rose wipe tears from her face. It appeared that Edwards had said something to make her cry. *You jerk,* she snapped under her breath. The soft spot she had developed for Rose was growing. Vanessa instinctively glanced toward Marc, and saw that the exchange hadn't slipped past him either. He was looking in their general direction with a twisted grin on his face. She was sure it was the result of the tearful scene, and his insensitivity saddened her.

*****

"I'm sorry, Doctor," Rose apologized, after regaining her composure.

"That's fine. But please, in the future show some self-control. There seem to be prying eyes here," he said quietly, gesturing with his head toward Vanessa.

"Yes, don't worry, I will." Getting so close to Blake that he could feel her hot, moist breath on his ear, she formed the words for the first time, "You've actually done it, haven't you? You've really discovered a cure for cancer."

Turning his head, their noses almost touching, he looked into her eyes and whispered, "Yes, I have."

Chapter 17

The soft lights of the well-used lounge made it difficult to appreciate the nostalgic look of the establishment. The artwork, for the most part, was of '50's and '60's celebrities. The portraits of the movie stars were primarily in black and white. The colorless tones of the characterizations, along with the hairstyles, helped to mark the generation they represented. Intermittently, a collection of colorful, hand-painted scenes effectively reflected the bygone era as well. One such scene portrayed a gas jockey with a gleaming white smile. He made it appear that filling the 1957 Bel Air convertible with gasoline was his happiest experience. Another lively canvas brought to life the canopied parking lot of a drive-in restaurant. Waitresses on roller skates and special food trays that hooked onto half opened windows had enticed many of that generation.

Marc stared fleetingly at the depiction of a simpler time. He sat with Vanessa in the darkened room at an overworked oak table. Scratched into the varnish was an assortment of messages, many of the authors, now senior citizens.

"So, what do you make of it?" he asked, stirring his drink.

"Really, Marc, you're thinking way too much about Dr. Edwards. You know he's a bit eccentric," she responded.

"A bit eccentric," he mimicked sarcastically. "The guy is friggin' bizarre. The way he constantly mumbles to himself, ignoring everything in the lab for months. Then out of the blue he's everybody's best buddy. I'm telling you, Vanessa, something really weird is going on."

She agreed, but was getting nowhere nearer to finding out what it was. Marc was completely hopeless when it came to getting any real clues regarding Blake's research. All he had done was talk incessantly for weeks about Edwards' odd behavior. Lately, Vanessa was finding Marc's incoherent ramblings quite irritating, not to mention boring.

Jesus, I wish he would shut up about Edwards. I just want to forget the whole thing tonight.

Vanessa had no idea Marc was slipping into his own bizarre mind. It was an avoidance technique he had mastered long ago when things really bothered him.

Her initial attraction to the boyish charm and bad boy demeanor was fading fast. Marc was paranoid, and his carefree attitude was just a pretense to help mask his suspicious nature. His almost psychotic fixation regarding Blake's change in routine was getting her no closer to completing her final mission. The more he spoke, the clearer *that* was becoming.

"Marc, let's go back to my hotel suite. We can forget about work for a few hours. I'm sure we could come up with something better to talk about. What do you say?" she asked invitingly.

He'd been staring intently at the melting ice cubes in his cocktail. Engrossed in the change of state from solid to liquid, Vanessa's voice was barely audible.

"Huh?" he murmured, not looking up from the sweating glass.

"I said I'm tired and was thinking of heading back to the hotel," Vanessa responded, her voice tainted with frustration.

"Yeah, sure, see ya tomorrow," Marc replied absently.

It was clear he didn't entirely comprehend her meaning or notice her sudden change in mood.

Vanessa promptly stood, mimicking his send-off with a curt, "Yeah, see ya tomorrow."

Exiting the small establishment, she resolved to cut off any further romantic involvement with Marc. *God, what a waste of time. And I was actually falling for the loser.*

She had suspected Marc, like many others in her past, would have flaws. Vanessa was realistic enough to accept the simple fact that nobody was perfect. Over the years she had been reminded of it time and again. *Jesus, what do I expect? Look at me, pharmaceutical espionage. My life's a mess,* she thought sadly. But an eccentric was a personality type she had no desire to be involved with. They were far too unpredictable, their actions almost never made sense to anyone but themselves.

As she hailed a cab, Vanessa suddenly felt a sense of loss. Here already, the end of yet another failed relationship had arrived. Her life seemed meaningless as tears began to flow from her beautiful brown eyes. Quickly regaining her composure, she entered the yellow cab, informing the driver of her temporary address. "Downtown Holiday Inn, please."

*****

Marc hardly noticed the lively gum-smacking waitress with a large round tray resting on her hip.

"Can I get'cha another?" she asked dutifully.

Without breaking his intensive gaze or looking up from his glass, Marc dully responded, "Yeah, sure."

With a loud snap of her gum, she confirmed the order, "Jack and coke, right?"

Marc simply nodded. He could've been a guy whose wife walked out, whose dog had been run over, or maybe a poor schmuck just fired from his job. That was the look of hopelessness he wore. An ominous feeling steadily crept over him regarding Edwards' complete turn about at work. *It's not good. I don't know why, but it's not good. I feel it,* he thought obsessively. He'd been trying to put his finger on it, but just couldn't. An irrational cloud of gloominess had cloaked him for weeks. Marc trusted his instincts, feeling he possessed a sixth sense about such things. He tried to rationalize this intense sensation of dread. At first he was sure it was just anxiety about the possibility of being reassigned to some "go-get-em-tiger" type. He'd also worried about getting stuck with some jerk of a boss who would be chasing Novatek bonuses. Marc quickly dismissed the idea. He had a hunch there'd be larger repercussions from Edwards' current course of research. An illogical fear had taken hold of him and he couldn't seem to shake it.

The perky waitress snapped the drink down on the table with a bang, startling him out of his self-induced, hypnotic trance.

"That'll be two fifty, please."

Marc withdrew his wallet from the back pocket of his jeans, randomly pulling out a ten-dollar bill.

"Keep the change," he said, handing over the cash.

"Wow, thanks a lot!" the waitress said cheerfully. Smiling, she moved through the bar, searching out her next drink order.

Marc looked up for the first time since Vanessa's sudden departure and finally comprehended that she was gone. *Wonder when she took off?* he thought without real concern.

*****

Vanessa, still feeling melancholy, was flipping channels on the TV in her large hotel suite. After a few minutes she turned off the television, stretched out on the luxurious bed and impulsively, picked up the phone and dialed.

"Hello," the voice whispered sleepily.

Looking at her watch, she saw the time was 11:21 P.M.

"Hi, Rose. It's Vanessa Hargrave. Geez, I'm sorry, I woke you. We can talk tomorrow," she said apologetically.

"Don't be silly, Vanessa," Rose replied, clearing the sleep from her voice. "I was just dozing on the couch. Is everything alright Hun?"

"Yeah, I guess so," she responded hesitantly.

Jesus, why am I calling her? She doesn't even like Marc.

"Vanessa, what's wrong?" Rose asked worriedly.

She felt her eyes moisten slightly as she spoke. "Oh, it's just Marc. I guess I'm concerned about him." *I'm worried about my whole goddamned life. I'm worried about my safety, just everything,* she thought miserably.

"Is he alright?"

"Yes, he's fine. You probably know that I've been seeing him outside the lab, socially. Nothing real serious, but I guess I was kind of hoping it might go that way."

With her head resting on the thick overstuffed pillows, she began leisurely twirling her hair. A small smile turned up the corners of her mouth as she thought, *just girlfriends, chatting. This is nice.* She knew calling Rose would make her feel better. Vanessa had no girlfriends.

"Well, Hun, I assumed you were, when you stayed at his place after the fire. What happened, sweetie?" she asked, sounding mildly curious.

"I guess it's over between us. He's just, I don't know, so strange, but I was starting to really like him. He's so wrapped up in Dr. Edwards' change around the lab. He's convinced himself it's somehow a bad thing."

"Oh, Vanessa, Marc will be fine. Dr. Edwards is working on something wonderful. Trust me. The results will be anything but bad. Marc is just a nervous man. He's a very vigilant fellow, probably feeling left out of the loop."

Vanessa sat bolt upright on her bed, the hair-twirling abandoned. *OH MY GOD... SHE KNOWS, damn, she knows what Edwards is working on,* her internal voice shouted. Romance instantly abandoned, she instinctively began the cat and mouse play of acquiring the secrets Wilkinson paid her for. Her mind automatically plotted the best way to extract the information she sought. *Keep her open, use the Marc thing.*

"I guess, Rose, but I can't take a guy like him. He just gets so down in the dumps. I never know what will set him off. I think it's over. He probably won't even notice."

"Don't be so hasty, Hun. I'm sure it'll all work out very soon and Marc will be his old self before you know it," she said.

“Rose, what's Dr. Edwards' been working on that's convinced you that Marc will change?” *That's it girlfriend, keep talking.*

After a slight pause, Rose responded, "Just trust me. I'm sure Marc will be fine,” she said, her tone changing from concerned to guarded.

Not wanting to raise any suspicion, Vanessa abandoned her line of questioning. She found her Achilles heel. Rose was the weak link. There was always tomorrow.

"Well, thanks. I'm sorry to even bother you with this, but I was feeling blue. I needed to talk with someone. None of my friends have even met Marc." *I really don't have any friends,* Vanessa thought sadly.

"It's no bother at all. Call me anytime to chat.”

Oh, I will, you can bet on it.

“Like I said, just wait and see how things pan out before making any definite decisions." Rose said in a reassuring tone.

"I will. And thanks. You have a good night Rose. I’m sorry I woke you."

"No problem, Sweetie, just get some rest. I'll see you at the lab tomorrow."

"Night, Rose, and thanks again."

"Good night, Vanessa."

Replacing the receiver in its cradle Vanessa flopped down on the soft pillows. *What a stroke of luck. I thought Marc was a dead end. Turns out he's going to be the link I need after all.*

*****

Finishing his drink, Marc slowly stood up. He proceeded to the exit of the tavern, passing the waitress as he left.

"Thanks again, Hun. Come back soon," she said, winking.

He produced a half smile, nodding as he walked out in a cloud of despair. Standing by the curb he looked for a cab to hail when he felt the first of the raindrops. A moment later the skies opened and the rain began to pound down. A clap of thunder officially marked the event. Marc saw a yellow cab and waved, indicating he was looking for a lift. It flew passed without even slowing, covering him in a fine mist. *I won't be sleeping at all tonight,* he thought miserably as he pulled up his collar.

Chapter 18

"My God," Byres whispered softly as he reviewed the preliminary report his team had prepared. The past three days had taken a toll on the Patronums' committee-leader of finance. Walter Byres looked haggard and exhausted.

"I had no idea the numbers would be so large," he said to his assistant, Joanne.

"I know, it's hard to believe isn't it?" the stout woman replied. She was almost sixty years old. With her short thick frame and round pudgy face, she looked like a woman who was more adept at knitting or baking. No one would have suspected she was actually *'the right hand man'* of the secret society's head of the financial cell.

Walter's team was meticulously coordinating the statistics he requested. The information received from Dr. Emerson's medical brief had been carefully integrated. The figures were incredible. Even at this early stage, it was becoming apparent the economic and financial impact on the United States could be devastating.

"Joanne, would you please get me Emerson's report again?" as if reading the results once more would alter what was inevitably becoming a reality. She retreated to her outer sanctuary where the vast amounts of data were neatly catalogued. In less than a minute Joanne returned with the crucial report.

"Thank you," he said as he stared at the Emerson brief. Walter Byres leaned forward as he turned the first page, reading the report for the umpteenth time.

Synopsis Report on Cancer Victims

- **Newly diagnosed cases of cancer in the United States per day: 2650.**
- **Average life expectancy after first diagnosis: less than 5 years.**
- **Ages of newly diagnosed cases: 75% over sixty years of age.**

- **Average normal life expectancy for Men: 70 years**
- **Average normal life expectancy for Women: 77.4 years**
- **Cancer deaths per year in the US: 630,000**
- **Current number of Americans with cancer: 3,900,000**

His cell had worked diligently, converting the information into numbers. Those figures were spelling out the financial impact Elixir would have on the U.S. Rubbing his brow, Walter shook his head as he once again read the numbers. They were indeed staggering.

Walter had received Dr. Emerson's brief three days prior. He'd immediately set his network into action. The information his team needed in order to assemble an "Impact Statement" was flooding his mind immediately after reading the Emerson report. Just seventy-two hours before, he'd begun by dictating his orders to Joanne.

"Jo, we're going to need several specifics right away to get a handle on this."

Her stubby fingers were wrapped around the pencil, ready to take shorthand notes the instant Walter spoke.

"First, I want to know approximately how many of the casualties are senior citizens. Then I want their economic status, along with average educational background of those afflicted. Next, I need the number of jobs created in battling this disease. I also want an estimate of how many will be re-employable if Elixir becomes public. I require as broad a scope as possible with 'best estimates' of overall socio-economic impacts. The report needs to be comprehensive, everybody who provides in any way for the victims of the disease. I want to know how many researchers, doctors, nurses, orderlies, hospital kitchen and laundry staff. How many manufactures are out there making things for these people? How many beds, tongue depressors, syringes or anything. Heck, I even want included in the estimate paid canvassers for donations, charity organizations, graphic artists making brochures and even the cost of stamps spent on mailers. Rental and tax incomes for offices, fuel used to go to work to treat these people. Put the cell to work Jo, I don't want any stone left unturned. I want to know about every job, income, and dollar created by this disease."

A bead of sweat had rolled down her large face as Joanne's eyes widened, rapidly scrawling her coded script. Suddenly she stopped and looked directly at her mentor.

"I've never considered all the people who might actually benefit directly or indirectly from this illness, have you?"

"Quite honestly? Never even crossed my mind until the meeting and Emerson's report." Walter responded frankly.

"You do realize the extent of this request, don't you? Our people will be working around the clock. I'm afraid they may only be able to scratch the surface," she said.

With an exasperated sigh, Walter concurred. "I know, Joanne, I know. That's exactly what I'm afraid of." Once again, she poised her pencil for the flurry of words that would be written on the pad.

Taking another deep breath Walter continued, "Also, average social security income, effects on defined pension plans, Medicaid payments covering seniors with cancer. I would like totals of the typical injection of money into the economy by those trying to survive the sickness."

A new train of thought suddenly occurred to Walter as he dictated his instructions to Joanne.

"Contact Dr. Emerson. I will need approximated adjustments to average life expectancy for both genders. Assuming cancer deaths no longer existed, people would on average live longer."

Walter spoke uninterrupted for the next thirty minutes. His mind reeled, aware that the numbers were going against Elixir becoming public. *This is the greatest medical discovery in a hundred years. Dollars will decide whether it's ever made public,* he thought sadly.

He suddenly felt old. His shoulders sagged under the weight of what he and his colleagues were about to do. Playing God was wearisome.

He had dictated the orders to Joanne a few days before. The finance cell had been working day and night since, following the investigation he had set out for them. As Joanne had predicted, the task was enormous. Not all of the intelligence required was readily available, and some of it took days to trickle in. The network of people was far-reaching, There were hundreds involved at various levels. Only the most senior Patronums were aware of why the information was being gathered. The rest just did their jobs.

"The information is still coming in from all departments sir. I'm pulling it together as I receive it," Joanne said.

Armed with her fastidious work ethic, Walter had never questioned Joanne's thoroughness in their thirty-year working relationship. He was confident she would be carefully checking the steady stream of updates. Once scrutinized for validity, she'd type a preliminary draft for his personal analysis.

The mounting data made him aware that security should be stepped up to the next level. He placed a call.

"Bruce, Walter here," he said into the phone, "It's time we caught up a bit. I'd like to meet for a drink."

"Hi Walt, sure, where would you like to get together?"

"Why don't you come by my office? We'll leave from here."

The immediacy of the meeting as well as the tone of Walter's voice made it clear that this was of an urgent nature.

"Sounds good, I'll see you shortly," Bruce said.

*****

After only one ring, the phone was picked up. "Hello."

"Hi Eric, Vargo here. Walter called inviting me out for a drink. I thought you might like to join us."

"Sure, when and where?"

"We'll be heading out from his office. You know, to make things easier, I'll just swing by and pick you up."

"Yeah sure, that'd be great." Of course, Eric had no idea where Walter's office was.

"See you in, say, a half hour?"

"I'll be waiting."

He did not know who Walter was, but assumed he was involved with the recent assignment. They'd played these coded phone games for years, and although not much was said, Eric deduced several things from the call. First, *Walter* would have no idea that he would be joining them. Otherwise, Bruce would have said, '*WE*' thought you might like to join us, instead of '*I*'. It stood to reason that if there were questions about the mission he was currently on, usual protocol would take longer. Updates to the operation would be easier to facilitate face to face. All security personal had been prepared that *time* may suddenly become a vital factor.

Eric began gathering his notes along with all the files. He would bring everything he had on the assignment, just in case.

An hour later, he was shaking hands with a distinguished gentleman who was simply introduced as Walter.

"I'm pleased to meet you, sir."

"As am I, Eric. Please have a seat."

He settled into one of four overstuffed chairs surrounding a beautifully handcrafted coffee table. The large, uncluttered desk was at the far end of the room. Behind it, glass stretched twelve feet from the floor to the oak-covered ceiling, the window reaching from one side of the room to the other. The view from the fifteenth storey office was magnificent, and overlooked Town Lake. The outside walls were lined with dark oak shelves, stocked with hundreds of hardcovered books.

"As you are aware, Bruce, we are in the middle of this investigation. It has become obvious that containment of all those involved must be at the highest level. It seems the integrity, as well as the confidentiality of all information must be maintained, for now anyway," Walter said, before continuing. "Gentlemen, how confident are you that suppression has been sustained?"

Bruce knew the stakes where high on this one. The head of finance's apprehension confirmed what he previously suspected. The world might not be ready for Elixir.

"Eric, perhaps you could enlighten Walter as to the status," he said, graciously, removing himself as go between. He leaned back in his seat as his first in command took the reigns.

Eric had memorized the principals' habits, routines and phone calls. He personally reviewed all the tapes of the domestic conversations that the listening devices had picked up.

"Sir, to the best of my knowledge, containment has been maintained at one hundred percent. As far as my team can tell, we don't think that Edwards has confided in anyone yet; however, we are not entirely sure about his research assistant, Rose Frechette. She may be aware of Elixir. Recently, Edwards and Dr. Frechette were followed to a small, secluded restaurant. We could not get a man or listening device in place quickly enough to monitor the discussion. What we do know is that the conversation seemed very intense, and that neither of them touched their breakfast. We're confident there is no romantic involvement between them."

Eric held a pad, but didn't refer to his notes. He knew everything about them all.

Walter seemed perplexed at the discovery that someone else might know of Elixir. It could lead to more leaks. He then turned to Eric, "Can you give me a breakdown of the principals, along with the possibilities of the information being shared?"

Eric spent the next hour going through everyone who worked in the lab. He also spoke of acquaintances, family, even outsiders involved with the principals. He'd saved Vanessa for last and then let the bombshell drop.

"Sir, Vanessa Hargrave is a spy for the rival pharmaceutical company, Wilkinson."

Walter was visibly shaken, "Eric, what's being done about that potential leak?"

"I'm afraid we missed her. A fire, but she got out," he responded. "The situation is currently under review. At this time we are absolutely convinced she has no idea about Elixir."

Eric knew she didn't need to die, not yet anyway. He was convinced Edwards had not shared his discovery with anyone other than Rose Frechette. He was going wait for the committee to vote. It wouldn't be necessary to kill Vanessa, if Elixir was to be made public. He wasn't sure if it was her photo, or the fact that her birthday happened to fall on the same day as Jane's, his first true love, but he wanted her to have the benefit of the doubt. He also lied about the fire. Neither he, nor the Patronums had any involvement. He hoped it would be enough to stall the committee from ordering her elimination.

Bruce Vargo remained silent throughout the inquisition. The most accurate information would come from Eric.

"Well, Eric, obviously, I'm very concerned about this infiltrator, Vanessa Hargrave. It's imperative that she not be allowed to share any information regarding Elixir."

"I will be closely monitoring the situation, sir."

"Walt, if Eric says it's under control, rest assured, it is," Bruce confirmed.

Eric twisted in his chair. Had Bruce been aware of the lie regarding the fire, he knew his faith would have been shaken.

"Well, that's good enough for me. I wanted you gentleman aware that we're moving to the next level of security. Bruce, I'll be prepared for Wednesday's meeting. Please bring any information you or Mr. Brunner feel may be relevant."

Standing, he extended a hand to Bruce Vargo, indicating the meeting was over. The head of security gave a quick nod as he shook the offered hand.

"Young man, it was extremely nice to meet you. Please, keep up the good work," he said to Eric and once again reached for the ritualistic good-bye shake.

Ushering the two men out, Walter felt somewhat relieved, satisfied that only the animal handler, Henry Miller, had a spouse. With no one else romantically involved, he breathed easier. He knew that secrets never stood much of a chance in bed. With the principals having no strong ties to friends, family, or community, all they had to do was get a handle on the girl. With Vargo's confidence in young Brunner, temporary containment seemed possible.

As the heavy wood door closed behind them, Walter returned to his desk. There, neatly stacked, were file updates. They had become an almost steady flow for the past twelve hours.

He picked up the top file, opened it and read the disturbing contents. Within minutes, he was speaking into the intercom.

"Joanne?"

"Yes."

"Can you come in with your pad please?"

"Certainly. Would you like a coffee or juice?"

"Ahhh, no thank you."

He was faced with the monotonous task of assimilating the large amounts of information. Then he had to condense it, highlighting the most pertinent statistics.

As Joanne entered the inner office, she placed a glass of orange juice down on a coaster next to him.

"Walter," she said in a scolding tone motioning to the juice, "you know you have to keep your strength up."

"I know, I know, thanks." Exhaling heavily, he continued. "We're going to be working late tonight, Joanne. Could you please have dinner delivered? My treat, your choice," he said.

"Good," she replied, "I'm starving."

Walter smiled knowingly, aware that Joanne was always hungry. He could tell the way the chubby grandmother bustled out that she was pleased that the choice was hers tonight. After retreating to the outer office, she dialed her favorite Chinese restaurant, *Pang's*

Chapter 19

“Morning, Miss Frechette.”

“Good Morning, Bill,” Rose responded to the security guard.

“She’s going be another hot one today,” he said.

“Looks like it. You have yourself a good day, Bill,” she replied as the gate made its ninety degree salute. She drove passed the raised arm and into the complex.

It had been a terribly long week and she was glad it was almost over. As Rose slid her BMW into the parking spot she was surprised to see Henry just standing there. A big, goofy grin was pasted on his face. From each hand dangled a cage with a few lifeless mouse carcasses. His brown Nova was parked in the delivery area and he was leaning against the rusty old chariot.

"Hi-ya, Miss Rose. How're you doin today?" he cheerfully greeted her.

"I'm fine, Henry, you?" she said, exiting the car.

"Well, Miss Rose, I’m really, really good!" he exclaimed excitedly.

"My, aren’t you a cheery fellow this morning." She couldn't help smiling at his juvenile enthusiasm. "So, did you win the big lottery last night?" she teased.

A confused look crossed his face, as he cocked his head to one side. "Ahhh no, Miss Rose, I didn't win no lottery last night. At least I don’t *think* I did."

"I’m sorry, go on Henry. I was just teasing about the lottery."

“Oh, oh, okay. That was very funny, Miss Rose, hah, hah, hah. Well, anyway I have a girlfriend. Her name is Jenny, Jennifer if you don't know her like I do. And guess what, Miss Rose?" Not giving her an opportunity to respond, he blurted out, "We're getting married! Yep, that’s right! She asked me and I said yes sir, well, yes ma'am actually, and guess what else, Miss Rose?" Once again Henry didn't wait for her reply. "We are going to get married today right after I get off work. But I have to get all cleaned up and changed first. I figured I should have my own life and Jenny says so, too. My Ma didn't like it much at first. But then, I told her if she wanted, Jenny and me could live with her and take care of her. Jenny said she would. We could be together. So you're not going to believe it, but now my Ma said she loves Jenny, too!"

He looked like an animated cartoon character with his arms flailing as he told his happy tale. He was so excited he didn't seem to notice the cages with the dead mice swinging as he spoke.

"Well, Henry, that's the best news I've heard in a while." She leaned over, giving him a hug, then a small peck on the cheek.

"Congratulations! I'm so happy for you both." Rose said.

He stiffened at her touch; in his lifetime only Jenny and on the rare occasion, his Mom had ever hugged him.

Rose immediately sensed his discomfort and broke off the harmless embrace.

"Sorry, Henry, I guess I just got excited there for a moment."

Embarrassed, he smiled shyly. "Aw geez, it's okay, Miss Rose. I already told Jenny how nice you are. I feel bad because we can't invite you. We're having a real small wedding at the courthouse. Jenny and me can't afford anything fancy."

"Oh, Henry, don't you dare feel bad about anything today! So, how many people are going?"

"Hmm, well, there's Ma and her friend Noreen, and Jenny's friends the Pangs. They own Pang's Chinese restaurant, ya know. I guess just four. Well, I have to get goin', Miss Rose. Gotta get cleaned up and get married!"

Henry's enthusiasm charmed the hell out of her.

"Oh, I forgot to tell you, Miss Rose, Jenny is the best—and I really love her a lot, too."

"Henry, that's lovely. You have a wonderful day. When do you think you will be back to work?"

With a bewildered look, he responded innocently, "Uh, tomorrow. Okay, Bye, Miss Rose, I've gotta get going. Maybe I'll see ya in the morning!"

Rose couldn't help but smile as she went through the familiar routine of entering the lab. She could not have imagined a better start to the day.

Once the lock tumblers completed their mechanical waltz, the lab door slid open effortlessly. She was surprised to find Vanessa there standing over Blake's Microscope.

That's odd, why would she be here so early and what is she up too? Rose thought warily, Blake's cynicism, suddenly invading her mind.

"Good Morning, Vanessa. Wow, you're off to an early start this morning, what are you up to?" she said. Her tone was off.

"Oh, hi, nothing Rose." She stepped away from the microscope. "You feeling alright?" she asked, responding more to the uneasiness in her voice, than the question.

"Yes, Uh, yeah, I'm fine, just," Rose said. Stumbling, she tried to regain her composure. "So, you thinking of a change?"

"What? I don't get what you mean Rose," Vanessa hastily replied. She barely masked the apprehension in her voice.

"I mean instead of deciphering the notes, maybe you'd like to help us make em?" Rose said jokingly, sounding a little more relaxed and like herself. *God I'm so stupid. Blake's got me turning into a doubting Thomas, thinking that Vanessa could be nosey geez,* she thought, chastising herself.

Rose quickly dismissed Blake's suspicions about Vanessa. Everyone there knew the familiar sound of the electronic lock was plenty of warning that somebody was entering the lab.

If she were doing anything she shouldn't, there would've been lots of time to move away from Blake's station when she heard the lock. With that final thought, she dropped any suspicious ideas.

"Hah, hah, hah, fat chance of that, Rose. I can't understand a damn thing I'm writing about, and you expect me to make it up? I was just curious about what the heck you guys are looking at under these things all the time," she said, efficiently masking her nervousness.

"Ya know, I didn't even spot your car out there. I was too busy talking with Henry, the animal handler. Do you know him?"

"Hmmm not exactly, but yes, I've seen him in here and in the parking lot before. Every time I look at him, he stares at the ground and almost runs off. The guy's a bit creepy, isn't he?"

"Ohhh, Vanessa, no, Henry's not like that at all. He's a very harmless, and awfully nice fellow, who's just a bit slow. I'll introduce you to him sometime. On the way in I was chatting with him, and he mentioned he was getting married today." Rose smiled and shook her head, recalling the pleasant start to her day.

Just then the tumblers clicked to life again. Instinctively both women's eyes turned in the direction of the sound. Blake walked in, Rose was just inside the door, and Vanessa stood a few feet in front of his workstation. "Good morning, Dr. Edwards," they said in unison. Looking past him toward each other, it was all they could do to keep from giggling aloud. Blake hadn't noticed at all and seemed to avoid eye contact with each of them. Walking by them en route to his locker he simply said, "Ladies."

Each reacted differently to the aloof greeting. Vanessa nonsensically lifted her shoulders as he passed, and with a gaping mouth and bulging eyes, she comically raised her eyebrows.

In contrast Rose had the initial makings of a frown but forced a half-smile for Vanessa's sake.

"I'll chat with you later, Vanessa. We better get busy," she whispered, cocking her thumb in Blake's general direction.

"Sure, we'll talk later," Vanessa, smirked.

It was obvious to Rose that Blake was still upset, and she was concerned over his mood lately. It had been twenty days since he presented his report to Evan Sinclair in research. Blake had hardly spoken to any of them in a week. She was the most affected by his isolated state, deciding that today she would try to cheer him up. During the past week, she found herself thinking a lot about what was going to happen next. Part of her was overjoyed about the future prospects, but she was just a bit sad too, knowing that their little family here was going to be dissolved. It was easy for Rose to imagine how Blake's discovery would affect them all. Anyone who was associated with him would be caught in the limelight to one degree or another. A word from the 'soon to be' famous Dr. Blake Edwards would be second to none in their field. She imagined even Vanessa would benefit.

Blake approached his station from the back of the laboratory. Once he settled on his stool, she walked up to him.

“Hi Blake,” she said in a small voice. “I suppose there’s no word back yet?” she asked cautiously.

“Hello Rose. No dammit, still nothing. I can't help it, you know—” Without warning the lock began its motion and again, all eyes turn toward the door. As presumed, Marc walked in, but he looked like hell. His eyes were bloodshot, his hair was ruffled, and he was still wearing yesterday’s clothes. Blake gave the initial greeting. It was the first time he spoken to him in a week. “Good morning Marc, are you feeling alright today?”

“Yeah, sure Doc, right as rain. Just a rough night, didn’t sleep very well. But I’ll be cool," he said guardedly.

“Good, that’s good,” Blake responded, somewhat reassured.

Marc began walking toward the bank of lockers, stopping at Vanessa’s desk. He engaged her in a quiet dialogue.

Rose realized that with those two talking she would get an opportunity to privately chat with Blake. Just as she was about to jump at the chance, he began speaking first.

"This whole thing is so damn asinine," he whispered to her. "Novatek procedure! Dammit, people are dying TODAY. I can help them right now. I have a good mind to take this to someone else, the papers, or Wilkinson. By God, they wouldn't have this information sitting on the corner of some fool’s desk for weeks." Even though he was frustrated, Rose loved it; as his only trusted confidant, she welcomed every second of his rhetoric.

“You will have your just desserts Blake, very soon,” she said reassuringly.

Just then, they both glanced toward Vanessa’s desk, where she and Marc seemed to be engrossed in deep conversation. Rose assumed that they might be talking about their relationship.

“Rose, just look at this,” he said pulling out a bundle of papers from his satchel. It looked like a legal document. ”Do you recall signing one of these when you started here?”

Blake produced the copy of his confidentiality agreement that Novatek's legal minions had assembled. It was an ironclad contract leaving nothing to chance. All Novatek personnel signed the fifty-eight page contract upon hiring. It was duly notarized in triplicate, then registered at the courthouse.

After a brief glance at the first few pages, she said, "Yes, I remember signing that. You *know* that a confidentiality agreement is pretty standard with research companies, right, Blake?"

"Yes, yes of course, but look here," he said pointing manically at a paragraph. "It clearly states here I can not share any information, on any level, with anyone. According to this, if I were to get caught breaching this arrangement," his voice, barely a whisper already, was lowered further, and she guessed at several of the words, "my medical license will be immediately suspended until my case comes before the disciplinary board."

Included in the documentation were three separate precedents. Each had resulted in the permanent loss of medical licenses in the state of Texas. The harsh consequences resulted from disclosing confidential information discovered in other pharmaceutical companies.

"Rose, do you realize that I've already violated this thing by sharing the results of my experiment with *you*?" he said shaking the document. The breach was due to the fact that he had already *presented* his findings to Novatek, through Dr. Sinclair.

She felt herself become flushed at the thought of having his future in her hands. Although she knew she really didn't… it felt good nonetheless. For a fleeting moment she wasn't sure if it was the feigned power or the intimacy of the implication, but the result was the same. She was excited.

"My hands are tied, Rose. There isn't a damn thing I can do about it either. But that little weasel only has ten more days, just ten more days," he whispered through gritted teeth.

Rose smiled at Blake. Actually she beamed.

"Are you making fun of me Rose? On what level do you find this humorous?" he asked incredulously.

"Oh no, Blake, I'm not making fun of you at all." It was all she could do to refrain from kissing him right there.

"Do you realize that in ten days, your life will change forever? You'll be on your way to fame and fortune, like nothing you've ever imagined. I'm just so proud of you, Blake Edwards, and a little sad about the idea of our group here disbanding."

His expression softened and he even blushed a bit.

"Oh, Rose, yes, I want everyone to share in the success. You've been a wonderful assistant, Marc as well, both of you took so much pressure off me so that I could work unencumbered. I'll make sure you're all recognized when this comes out."

Rose basked in his glory and thought this was how the Caesars must have felt. They were all powerful, able to hand out riches, favors and life. So, too, were Dr. Blake Edwards' prospects. She knew that any association with him in the near future would be very beneficial to some people.

"I wouldn't worry about anything for the next few days Blake. Just try to use the time to organize some thoughts and responses. I think you're going to have a lot of microphones and cameras shoved in your face soon," Rose said under her breath.

She was sure Blake, in his modesty, hadn't given that possibility much consideration. Staring at him she thought, *he's had to think about it, but soon it'll all be real.* Rose was surprised by the sudden surge of anger that invaded her mind. She thought of Dr. Evan Sinclair sitting in his small, cluttered office. He was making *her* Blake, and tens of thousands wait for what they should all have now. Elixir.

*****

"Vanessa, Edwards is really freaking me out. He hasn't said a word to anyone in weeks, not even Rose, and now look at him," Marc said, pointing to Blake as he engaged Rose in hushed, animated conversation. "Tell me the guy isn't a wacko!"

"Wow, calm down, they're just talking, for god's sake."

His bloodshot eyes darted over toward Blake's hunched-over form. He squinted as he scrutinized the scene just forty feet away.

"Look at him, Vanessa. He's been like a dog protecting his bowl for months. He doesn't say anything. We don't know what the hell is going on here, nothing!"

Marc's right, but still, oh my god he's losing it, she thought.

"Oh just relax and look at this in the right perspective. Big deal! So our boss is a bit eccentric and reclusive where his work is concerned. *WHO CARES*?"

"Vanessa, this is not good, not good at all. I don't know why, but I'm telling you—I have a very bad feeling about this whole thing with Edwards."

His fixation was evident, as was the fearful overture.

"Marc, are you stoned or on something right now?" Vanessa asked suspiciously. She was beyond worrying about his sensitivities. His reaction to the question under different circumstances might have been comical. By stating the obvious he began acting even more paranoid, delusional, *and* stoned, as if someone else were there, someone invisible. He began to scour the lab with quick, short, darting glances as if an unseen voice had whispered the evident into Vanessa's ear.

At first, she suppressed a tiny smile. He virtually looked like a little boy in the process of being caught doing something, but almost instantly she saddened. The psychotic man looking for an invisible fly lighting on his nose or buzzing in his ear was the last guy she'd felt anything for in a long time. *God what's wrong with me*?

"Marc…Marc, just settle down. You're getting too freaked out about things around here. Why don't you take the day off, or if Edwards bothers you that much, just quit?" *I'm thinking of getting the hell out of here myself,* she thought, glancing toward Rose and Blake, who were still engrossed in conversation. Just then, she saw Blake take some papers from his satchel and wondered what she was missing, sitting here, talking to psycho boy.

"Quit! Do you think quitting here is going to matter? Whatever he's done would follow us, wherever we go," he predicted.

That was the final straw; now he was scaring her. "You know, Marc, you're too weird for me, why don't you just go to work? I have stuff I need to get done here, okay?" The look she shot him was halfway between disgusted and dismissive. It didn't faze him at all. His attention had already started to drift.

"Yeah, yeah, I've got shit I gotta get done here too. Nice talk, Vanessa." Staring at Blake and Rose he began walking toward his locker. Immersed in their own exchange, Marc had gone completely unnoticed by either of them.

As he left her cubicle, she stared at him. *Nice talk? He's got to be kidding,* she thought in amazement.

Vanessa was aware that the time had come for her to get out of this place as well. After a visit from the insurance broker the previous day, she was having second thoughts about Wilkinson's money and the whole damn thing. The insurance agent indicated she could receive a check within days. The offer, if uncontested, was $18,937.29. That along with the $6,200.00 in her savings account was more than enough. She could get out of Dallas and start fresh anywhere she wanted. Vanessa had actually looked at a world atlas the night before. *Canada, yeah maybe Canada. I've heard life's pretty good there and the people are supposed to be really nice.* She'd thought flipping though the book. A much simpler life is what she needed. Drifting off last night, she considered giving Wilkinson back the $25,000.00 and drafting up a letter of resignation for Novatek. Her last thoughts before sleep invaded her conscious mind had been…*I can handle it…a few more weeks…at Novatek, just a few weeks, and then I'll have Wilkinson's money too…*

But today, Marc's ramblings had sealed the deal. Two more weeks in this nut house was more than her nerves could bear. *To hell with it. I'll give my resignation next week, and arrange a meeting with Michael.* She decided to return the Wilkinson money. Reaching for a file, she smiled. *A couple more days and I'm outta this loony bin for good,* she thought.

*****

Marc stared into the eyepiece. The slide was clear, the lighting ideal, and the cells perfectly discernible, yet he saw nothing. His drug of choice was lysergic acid diethylamide or LSD, and he'd had a very bad experience last night. He was still suffering the paranoia it had induced this morning. Thankfully, the hallucinations that had become the high were all but a horrible memory today.

Recalling last night's 'trip' made him shudder. The visions were very bad. Not his usual, images of busty girls running topless down a sandy beach. And they were vivid, far too vivid…

Just before leaving the lab yesterday, he decided that he didn't want to be alone. Casually wandering toward Vanessa, he pretended to be dropping off a file.

"Hey sexy, how about a drink tonight?"

"Ummm well, Marc, I think I'll pass tonight. I have a meeting right after work with my insurance company, and I've got a lot of stuff to do. I have to start looking for an apartment, furniture, you know, all of it. Maybe another time."

"Yeah, sure, no problem. Of course you have crap to do. I'll catch you later," he said dismally.

Marc went directly home. In the end, he decided not to go out for a drink alone. At one point he caught himself mumbling aloud. That fact only served to make him more depressed. He knew Vanessa was giving him the bum's rush. *Yep, acted like a real nut-job the last couple of times we hooked up,* he recalled sadly. Feeling down, knowing that he had likely scared her off for good, he grabbed a beer from the fridge.

This sucks, nothing to do, he thought as he plopped down on his sofa. He suddenly remembered a few hits of LSD purchased some time ago. Digging out his wallet, he looked for the small round 'punch outs'. That was how LSD was sold. Circular pieces of paper, called blotters were soaked in the liquid substance. Salvia then re-activates the chemical and boom, you're stoned. He took a few of the drug-soaked blotters and spread them around his coffee table.

"Ah yeah, this is what the doctor ordered," he said aloud. He placed one piece under his tongue, returning two of the four punch-outs back to his wallet. When the one in his mouth was soggy enough, he swallowed it.

"Right on, that's right baby, yeah that's what I need. He began humming, and in no time was singing the chorus of 'Wildwood Weed.' Jim Stafford had made the catchy little tune famous in 1974. It was a song about getting high. Unable to remember anything but the chorus, the jingle became monotonous, fading after a few repetitions, the last run through, barely audible.

"Man this crap isn't doing a thing," he whispered as he ingested the second piece of paper.

Relaxing, he leaned back and thought about Vanessa, her smooth body and bright smile. He reminisced about his initial hesitation in approaching her. He grinned. *Yep, didn't take me long to get over that, did it?* he reflected. His eyes closed as he thought about her apartment fire and what it must have been like; then the drug took hold. The hallucinations began. A mental picture started to form.

Vanessa was on fire, sitting in the middle of a room burning. She didn't scream, didn't flail about or try to extinguish the flames. She just burned. As if the sight wasn't strange enough, through the hot red blaze Marc could see others burning. He couldn't make them out as he stared, watching the flames consume her. Her delicate skin becoming blistered, splitting, oozing as it twisted into a raw, bloody mass. Her face was burning, distorting, as she sat there in a hypnotic trance. Vanessa gazed straight ahead… at nothing.

The teeth had become visible as the soft, pink flesh surrounding them swelled, split and melted away. Her beautiful smile, now just a mocking, perverse snarl, the blackened lips receding from the charred enamel. So vivid were the images that he could feel the intensity of the flames in his mind. Marc heard the bloodcurdling screams he himself emitted, all in his drug induced state, all in his mind. Not a sound came from him as he curled up on the couch at home. He awoke just hours ago in a fetal position. His aching arms still wrapped around his bunched up knees. He fled the apartment seeking the sanctuary of the lab. He was afraid to be alone.

Now, looking up from his microscope he glanced in Vanessa's direction. There she sat, beautiful, vivacious and alive, working away over an unseen project. He surprised himself when he entered the lab and was able to go directly to her cubicle. Leaving his apartment earlier, he was sure seeing her would set off flashbacks of the previous night's horrors.

I'm never taking that shit again, he vowed. His eyes darted toward Rose, and then back at what he'd been doing. *Jesus, what was I doing?* Still rattled about the whole thing, he grabbed up a random file and began reading.

Chapter 20

The heat wave blanketing Dallas was rivaling records set in previous years. More than ever, the damp, sticky air diminished the joy one could feel as a result of the beautiful, clear blue skies. As the sun beat down with unrelenting might, it took a toll on the elderly and the sick.

The air conditioning in the building had been working overtime. It pushed out the cool, dry air that forced the thermometer's mercury to sit at a comfortable sixty-eight degrees.

Walter didn't know if it was the combination of the swelter and the news he had for the committee, but he could feel his heart thumping. The neatly pressed blue shirt was showing signs of perspiration as it stuck to his torso, while beads of sweat formed on his forehead. Together with Joanne, he was organizing copies of the report.

Within the hour he would be in front of the committee. He had the unenviable task of sharing with them the probable economic impact on the U.S. regarding the release of Elixir.

How many lives, American lives, will be sacrificed, to do the right thing? he asked himself. That question haunted him throughout the entire process. Another disturbing uncertainty troubled him as well. *Is this the right thing?* A reliable soldier, dedicated to causes that sometimes didn't seem to make sense, he felt weighed down. Fatigue and loyalty were his burdens just then. He would present the findings and vote with his conscience when the time came.

"I'm too old for this kind of responsibility," he said aloud.

As they trickled in, Dr. Gregory Emerson was among the first to arrive. Spotting Walter Byres at the round table as he prepared for the meeting, Gregory approached.

"Good evening, Walter. I imagine the meeting tonight will be a little disturbing," he said in a somber tone. 'You know, I must say that I'm having a very difficult time with this whole damn thing. Based on the preliminary medical report my boys came back with, I'm concerned about what your team has put together. This has been a struggle for me and I haven't had good night's sleep since this whole business began." Like Walter, the doctor, too, looked a bit disheveled.

"Yes, Gregory, I'm afraid the report will be more than a bit unsettling," he replied, offering no further information.

With the final arrivals of the committee members, the meeting of the Patronums was called to order. All eyes were turned to Walter, as he stood to address the group.

"Good evening, Gentlemen. As you are aware, my team has been working non-stop since receiving Dr. Emerson's preliminary findings regarding Elixir. My assistant, Joanne, will distribute the summary now. I would ask that you wait before opening it."

A slight nod to Joanne set her in motion as she began circulating the critical report.

Entering the inner circle of the round table she handed out the paperwork. Walters' colleagues sat as the file was set in front of each of them and waited for what was coming next.

"Gentlemen, the results of this report weigh heavily on me. Given a margin of error of not more than plus or minus five percent, I think you may find the information disturbing to you as well."

Walter paused momentarily. What he asked next was not a standard request, but given the circumstances, he felt it was justified. He would have no choice but to respect the committee's decision, whatever the outcome.

"I would like to make a motion postponing the vote on the actual report until tomorrow. Given the magnitude of the decision we must make, I think it wise to have sufficient time to consider the information you're about to evaluate."

Voices murmured around the table as the men conferred with one another. This was an unusual request indeed. Votes were always taken following the discussion. After the secret ballot, suggested lines of action would then be presented. Victor Kaplan, head of the legal cell, spoke on behalf of the committee.

"Mr. Byres, the general consensus of the group is that we are willing to bypass the formal vote until tomorrow."

"Thank you, fellow Patronums. I am sure you will agree once we review the synopsis that we should all have an opportunity to sleep on it before making this vital decision."

"Please turn to page one in your folders. We have included Dr. Emerson's original summary page regarding the number of those who are afflicted with the disease. These are the most recent statistics available and are based on the year 1979. The medical cell has also provided an estimate of those who will become infected in the future."

As everyone skimmed the information previously reviewed, Walter was convinced that they would share his surprise and frustration when they began reading the subsequent pages.

Synopsis Report on Cancer Victims

- **Newly diagnosed cases of Cancer in the United States per day: 2650.**
- **Average life expectancy after first diagnosis: less than 5 years.**
- **Ages of newly diagnosed cases: 75% over sixty years of age.**
- **Average normal life expectancy for Men: 70 years**
- **Average normal life expectancy for Women: 77.4 years**
- **Cancer Deaths per year in the US 963,000**
- **Current number of Americans with Cancer: 3,900,000.**

Walter read aloud the first page of statistics before continuing to his part of the report. Other than the rustle of turning pages, the room was deadly silent. Walter then began reading his opening summary of the two-hundred-page report.

"Financial Report in conjunction with medical findings."

"Below are the approximate numbers as well as assumptions based on Elixir being released to the public. Of course, the number of future cases of cancer would be zero.

- Cancer deaths in the United States of persons (both male and female) over sixty-three years of age are averaging 1908 per day, 365 days per year.

- Total deaths in those over age sixty-three, 693,000 per annum.

- Total deaths in those under sixty-three, 270,000 per annum.

- Impact on life expectancy of males: increased by 3.9 years.

- Impact on life expectancy of females: increased by 4.7 years.

- The financial impact to the Social Security program by the additional annual payments: These additional payments are projected based on the survival of those who would have been afflicted with cancer dying within five years. Additional payments: 9.5 billion dollars annually.

- Additional deficit to defined pension plans from public and private corporations, approximately 4.6 billion dollars per year.

- Additional Medicaid costs for surviving seniors, 2.13 billion dollars per year.

The hush in the room had become a series of low whistles and heavy sighs as the group digested the enormity of what was being presented. But the largest numbers were yet to be unveiled.

- Number of positions relating to all aspects of cancer research and care, including collateral products, 3.837 million jobs currently filled.

- Average wages of all positions $19,838 per year.

- Probability of those re-employed in other positions after the release of "Elixir", 1.912 million.

- Those unemployed or unemployable, 2.925 million.

- Social benefits paid to the unemployed in the form of unemployment and welfare, 10.364 billion dollars per annum.

- Loss of wages to the economy and tax base, 22.33 billion dollars per year.

- Dollars injected into the economy by victims of cancer during their 5-year survival rate, 2.15 billion per year.

➢ Overall negative financial impact on the United States of America per year, approximately 43.6 billion dollars the first year. Years two, three, four, and five will be adding another 2.8 million lives saved that will be entitled to additional benefits as well. By the end of year five, total cost will be 96 billion per year.

The report continued with the actual breakdowns for over two hundred pages. A pall hung over the room like an ominous shadow. Other than the head of finance, no one spoke for the next two hours. Members of the administration could be heard making a variety of surprised sighs, whistles, and grunts as Walter waded through the report page by page. After the completion of the narrative, Walter Byres was simply exhausted.

"Patronums, these are the findings of the financial cell. As stated earlier, they are accurate to within plus or minus five percent."

The information was potentially devastating to the economy, but the certain loss of human life *without* Elixir was appalling.

Walter slumped in his chair as Dr. Gregory Emerson, recognizing his drained state, took up the torch. "Mr. Byres, on behalf of this council, I would like to thank you. This administration also extends our deepest gratitude to the entire financial cell for the detailed synopsis. I think it would be an excellent decision to give everyone the night to review and consider the ramifications of our vote tomorrow. I propose we all meet at the round table by twelve o'clock noon. Those in favor?" Emerson said, raising his hand. The vote was unanimous.

"Questions?" he asked.

For the next thirty-five minutes a variety of inquiries were expressed. For the most part, the governing body accepted the numbers as fact. The meeting was finally adjourned at 9:22 P.M. Most everyone retreated to the smoking lounge where the mood was melancholy. Without exception, all indulged in a cocktail. Victor Kaplan, along with Dr. Emerson, were the only ones to corner the financial cell leader.

"Walter, you mention in the brief that our nation's current national debt is 897 billion dollars. Help me get a handle on these figures. Are you saying that with the release of Elixir we will match our current national debt within ten years?"

"Give or take a few years, yes, Victor, that's correct. The national debt *will* double in about ten years, then again in ten more."

Victor lifted the goblet of eighty-year-old cognac to his lips as he gulped down the smooth burning liquid. Shaking his head, he strolled toward the bar for another.

Dr. Gregory Emerson stood beside Walter sighing deeply, while staring straight ahead. "My God, Walter, I had a feeling the numbers would be bad, but this, this makes it all very difficult."

It seemed like the men of science were more affected by the data than the others. They were awed by the obvious genius of the man known only as Dr. Blake Edwards. Others had come to view Edwards as a national threat.

The lounge had emptied within an hour. The executives retired to their respective suites to review sections of the brief they might want clarified the following day.

Any individual would be allowed the floor prior to the secret vote in order to ask questions or expound on the information. Also, those wishing to make a statement before the vote would be recognized as well. Many read and re-read the report that night.

The next morning over breakfast, the buzz revolved around the huge number of job losses and increased life expectancy of the elderly. Even though the fact was not mentioned above a whisper, it did not go unnoticed that many who died were no longer financial contributors to the economy. Rather, the disease killed off many who'd begun to draw on the country's resources. As noon approached, they filtered into the meeting room and took their places at the round table.

Walter felt refreshed. Pure exhaustion had finally forced his mind to shut down the previous night and he had enjoyed a somewhat restful sleep. The meeting began.

"Good morning, Gentleman, I hope everyone slept well," he said, stopping briefly to clear his throat. "I would like an opportunity to address this assembly before a motion is called. The vote today is to decide whether Elixir is to be made public or is to be kept tucked away from the world." He paused for a moment to organize his thoughts. "I recognize that the financial cost to this country as well as the economic fallout would be enormous. But I find myself asking another question. Do we, the Patronums, have the right to keep this miracle cure a secret from the world? Not just from Americans, but from all of humanity. That, Gentlemen, is the question we all have to ask ourselves before we cast our ballots. Vote with your conscience, for we will all have to live with the outcome." Walter briefly glimpsed each face before taking his seat. Sometime during the last few days, Walter Byres had come to a decision. He would resign his committee seat as head of the financial branch, regardless of the vote. Next to speak was Bruce Vargo, and he looked aggravated.

"Patronums, I personally would like to thank Mr. Byres along with his team of experts. The detailed analysis of any financial consequence that our country would suffer was information essential for this committee to DO ITS DUTY."

The room erupted in an uneven round of applause, in recognition of Walters' efforts. Vargo continued in his booming voice. "With all due respect to the head of finance, we must not think of what we have the *right* to do. As Patronums, there is only one consideration. The one and only consideration we have is *our duty* to this country and our sworn directive. This disease seems to prey on the elderly, and some survive, some do not. I believe this to be a natural thinning of the herd, survival of the fittest. For thousands of years, three conditions have existed to keep our population in check. War, famine, *and disease*. It is the natural order of things. However, regardless of my own or anyone else's personal feelings, this committee is duty bound. In this case, it is imperative we vote not what our conscience suggests, but what our obligation demands."

Vargo shot a disapproving glance at Byres as he sat. Walter knew the head of security was right. He felt Vargo's statement vindicated his decision to step down. He had lost sight of the decree. No longer did he possess the strength of conviction necessary to remain a committee member of the Patronums. He wasn't alone with his doubts. Dr. Gregory Emerson shared his sense of conscience, as did several others on the executive board.

No one else felt the need to speak, as both sides of the case had been well represented.

The time of reckoning had arrived. Victor Kaplan volunteered to take the count. As the ballots were distributed to each man, Victor reaffirmed exactly what was being voted on.

"Please indicate whether or not you feel Elixir should follow its present course, making it available to the general public through Novatek Pharmaceutical. Those opposed to the release of Elixir would indicate *that* by marking the circle beside the word 'NO.' Those in favor of Elixir becoming public would so indicate by marking the circle beside the word 'YES.'"

Every electoral would make their mark alongside their selection, fold the ballot once, and insert it into the small stainless steel ballot box. The lightweight box made its way around the table rapidly and was placed in front of Victor. At the end of the count, any member had the right to review the ballots for verification.

Victor opened it, and glanced to see where it looked like things stood. As he read, Joanne was busy marking the yays and the nays. She handed the final count back to him. The vote was not even close, but it did come as a surprise to some. The verdict was, ten opposed, five in favor. Elixir would remain a secret. Several of them stared vacantly around the room. They were the ones who had voted in favor of releasing the cure.

*****

Among those with an unmistakable look of despair was Gerald Fitzpatrick. As the head of government, he had not carried out his sworn duty. He knew full well the figures would have been inflated even more if all the numbers his department produced had been submitted. Gerald's heart was heavy, the cure was within arm's reach. Only days after the initial Emerson report, his son Francis underwent a minor operation. When the doctors opened him up, they discovered that he was riddled with cancer. Francis was given three months. He would die before his 44th birthday. Gerald's weary old eyes moistened, as tears began to form. He, too, would step down a month after his son's funeral.

This was now in the hands of security and intelligence alone. The meeting continued with Bruce Vargo taking up the reins as the next move was discussed. Vargo prepared to have his team carry out their mission. There was one more secret vote that evening. It was with regard to the controlled suppression of Elixir. The vote came back once again ten-five in favor of permanent containment of the now classified information. The sentence was to seal the fate of six people forever. The meeting carried into the early evening of Thursday.

Outside people bustled about, oblivious to how their lives or the life of a loved one had been tremendously altered. The temperature soared to 101 degrees Fahrenheit.

Chapter 21

The Dallas swelter was almost unbearable as it seeped its way into the air-conditioned areas. The refrigeration units achieving maximum outputs were taxed.

Following the weighty decision of the committee, Bruce Vargo did not join his fellow committee members for a drink. He retired to his suite and just past midnight, placed a call to Eric Brunner; he picked up on the first ring.

"Sorry to be calling so late, Eric. Bruce here. I just wanted to let you know that the project you are working on has been rejected. It will be necessary to close it down." He knew Eric would understand the secret message.

"Your assignment has been fast-tracked to the final stage. We should probably meet to review the details," Bruce stated matter-of-factly.

"I understand. Do you want to meet tonight?" Eric sat up.

"No, I want you well-rested. This is a big job with a small window. We'll meet Friday at noon. Have your detailed plans in position by then, okay?" Vargo said, his tone more casual now.

The rendezvous was set. They'd meet at McNealy's, a small Irish pub on the east side of Dallas.

*****

As Eric hung up the phone, he turned and faced Monique.

"Problem?" she purred innocently.

"No, not really, just work."

"Hmm, work. Irish bars are part of your job now?"

"We're not going to start with those kinds of questions tonight, are we?" he replied, only half-jokingly.

This was the very reason Eric's relationships with women never lasted very long. There were always too many questions, too many lies, and never enough truth.

"Sweetie, it's just some undercover work," he said softly.

"I have some undercover work for you right here, mister," she responded playfully. His profession as a CIA operative had been discussed. Monique was well aware of the covert part of that business. It also doubled as a great cover. Eric had not made her aware of the Patronums or his role there. Not then; not ever. He'd never again pay the price he had with his first love.

They were in the master bedroom of Eric's house, relaxing, watching some television when Bruce's phone call came. As a result of the extreme heat they'd been lying naked on top of the covers. The shrill cry of the ringing phone had brought them out of the tranquil state. Now fully alert, Monique's innuendo tempted him as he sensually caressed her.

Eric considered getting out of bed right then and reviewing the details of the plan that he'd already pulled together. He was always prepared in the event that his assignments went to the next level. But Monique's playfulness was just what he needed. The file could wait until morning. After all, Bruce wanted him to be fresh. He smiled as he settled into her open arms. It was blissful taking in her clean, fresh scent as he buried his nose in her long, black hair. He began gently kissing her bare shoulders. That night their lovemaking was not frenzied or urgent, but careful, measured, and passionate.

Afterward, with her head resting comfortably on his shoulder, Eric listened to her steady, even breathing as she slept. He gently stroked her hair as he stared into the blackness, his mind working effortlessly, adding details to his preliminary plan. He mentally made notes of people to call and things to do. A short while later, content with the groundwork as he envisioned it, his rhythmic breathing soon matched hers as he too, fell asleep.

At 4:47 in the morning, without the aid of an alarm clock, Eric's eyes opened. Quietly, he slipped from between the satin sheets and went downstairs to shower. Monique would doze at least another hour, before her internal alarm would silently go off.

Working at the glass-topped dining table, Eric walked over to pour his third cup of java when she entered the contemporary kitchen. "Good morning, to you, *Miss* Lafontaine, you look radiant this morning." She really did.

"Good morning, Agent Brunner," she responded teasingly.

When they'd first met, she'd referred to him as Agent Brunner at the end of every sentence. It had become their private joke. He stared at her with an appreciation that almost bordered on wonderment. *How can anyone look so beautiful*? he asked himself.

As she poured a glass of orange juice she noticed Eric intently watching her. "What? Do I have something in my nose?" she joked.

He broke the gaze. "No, everything is great, just great. Would you like a cup of coffee, Hun?"

"No time, Agent-Man, but thanks," she said finishing the last of the juice.

There was an effortless ease between them, a genuine quality that existed in their realationship. It was uncommon, and for Eric, unmatched. He had no doubt that he'd fallen in love with her. They parted with a kiss. While he winked, she smirked girlishly. As she drove away, he waved, then glanced at his watch. "Time to work," he whispered as he climbed into his car.

*****

Like the rest of Dallas, Evan, too, had been suffering from the heat that morning, but knew he would be uncomfortable regardless of the temperature outside. He glanced anxiously at the file folders that sat piled high, unable to focus. Looking around his congested office he felt claustrophobic. The walls seemed to be closing in on him, but not because of the cramped space. *Edwards is going to come at me again. I know he is,* he thought nervously, staring at the untouched mountain of work. An idea suddenly occurred to him. *Blake Edwards can't trap me if I'm not here. I'll just leave. Get the hell out of Dodge*, he thought with a grin. *I'm not getting a thing done here anyway.*

Going back home was out of the question. The atmosphere there had been very negative. Audrey's mood indicator had been stuck in the 'extremely pissed off' position for weeks. There would be no hiding from the day's stresses on the home front. He decided to surprise Loretta with an early morning visit. It was the perfect sanctuary.

Evan slipped away from Novatek virtually unnoticed. Left to his own devices, he was basically unaccountable to anyone on a day-to-day basis. The only thing left for him to do was lock his office and leave. Bill, the security guard, gave him a quick nod, as he drove out of the institute. Feeling like he'd just broken out of Alcatraz, Evan smiled mischievously as he maneuvered the sleek corvette toward the downtown area of Dallas. Kim Carnes was belting out her newest single, *Bette Davis Eyes*, with her trademark raspy voice. Evan did his best to mimic the lyrics. He did so entirely out of tune.

The high-rise luxury apartment block had come into view just as he was deciding where to park. Ten minutes later he was on the elevator sailing toward the fifteenth floor. He was silently hoping that this unannounced visit was going to relieve more stress than it caused.

Arriving at the apartment door, he'd decided to surprise Loretta. Using his key, he unlocked the penthouse suite. Quietly entering the sprawling apartment, he looked toward the sunken living room. The TV was on in the front room, but there was no sign of Loretta. *Perfect, she went back to bed*, he thought lasciviously, as he slowly pushed the door closed. From the bedroom, he could hear muffled voices. He shrugged and assumed that she had the bedroom television on as well. As he approached the open door, the voice he heard was clear and masculine.

"Yes, that's right baby, make some noise."

Wha...who the hell?

"Ohhh, yes that feels so good, Phillip! Yes, yes, YESSSS. Ohhh baby, faster," a female voice squealed.

It was clearly obvious that it *wasn't* the television. Evan recognized *that* sultry voice. The familiar sounds of lovemaking did not stop him. Although he had no desire to see what was going on, something inside told him he *had* to see it.

He rounded the corner to the huge master bedroom. With the door opened he saw *Phillip*. Evan guessed the young man whose back muscles were flexed and gleaming with sweat was in his late twenties. Young, lithe *Phillip* was slithering sensuously over *his mistress*. Evan, too, was breaking a sweat, but his was a different sort.

He backed out of sight, pressing against the wall, his own emotional state rising. The situation dictated that he should be enraged. He was not. Evan experienced a sudden uncontrollable sense of utter panic. *Oh god, what have I done? I need to make things right with Audrey,* he thought frantically. It was all very, very clear. He knew that Loretta was nothing more than a paid mistress. There was no secret there. But it wasn't until he *saw* her with his own eyes that he acknowledged there was no future with her. His conscious mind assessed the risk to which he'd exposed his marriage and family. He feared the worst.

No time to argue with Loretta, but still. He popped his head around the corner for the second time and stood in the open doorway. Neither of the tangled lovers noticed the intrusion. Whether it was actually a spot of courage or indignation, Evan managed to loudly clear his throat.

As Loretta's head whipped from side to side, she caught sight of him standing in the doorway, just as he made his presence known… *Ummm Hmmm.*

"Jesus, Evan, get the hell out… ***GET OUUUUUT***!" she screamed.

Startled and embarrassed, he fled the room, running from the penthouse. He hadn't expected her to be hostile.

As he anxiously awaited the elevator's arrival, Evan was thinking clearly for the first time since happening upon the carnal scene. Without warning, his embarrassment quickly turned to outrage. *What the hell—Get out? I'll give her GET OUT, that bitch,* he thought furiously.

As he entered the elevator, a push of the button sent him spiraling downward toward the superintendent's floor. A half hour later, Evan was speeding home toward his family, with a pocket full of hope. His new dream was to have Audrey forgive him when he confessed the affair.

For a few seconds Evan thought about Blake Edwards and Novatek as he drove. At the moment, those problems seemed minor compared to his current predicament. *Is she going to push me away? Do I tell her or just pretend it never happened?* His mind reeled as he made a left onto his street. Slowly wheeling down the road, he suddenly had a new appreciation of the elegant neighborhood with the oak trees lining each side. Successful, people lived here. He pulled into the driveway. Sitting in his car, he stared at the beautiful home he owned. It was like he was seeing it all for the first time. A renewed sense of appreciation for what he had, settled over him. At the same time the threat of loss loomed like a storm cloud. Looking around, he couldn't believe he had risked it all for a little tramp like Loretta. As the sun dried the last of the morning dew, he looked at his watch. It was only 9:20. He'd left for the office just over an hour ago. He jumped out of the car armed with only a new found humility and the sincere wish that his marriage could still be saved.

*****

By noon Evan was standing in the penthouse suite again with Loretta. "Like I said, Doc, if you think you're tossing me out on the street, you better think again. What would little '*Miss Peaches and Cream'* say if I told her where you've been spending your nights the last six months?"

"Well Loretta, I don't imagine you'll get too far with *peaches or cream*. You should get busy looking for a new place to live. Maybe *Phil* has something nice for you," he added mockingly.

"Evan, are you leaving Audrey?" she fished, suspiciously.

"No, I told my wife all about you. I told her the whole sordid story. Then I begged for her forgiveness. It came easier than I thought. She just assumed you were a gold digging little whore, taking advantage of a stressed out, hard working husband and father." Smiling, he added, "I *concurred*."

Loretta fangs had just been pulled. With nothing left to fight with, she resorted to her old reliable arsenal.

"Evan, sweetie," her voice was soft, inviting. "I'm sorry about that little thing with Phillip. I just met him and I was lonely. You know you've been working a lot lately and I've hardly seen you. I missed you so much I couldn't help it. I just lost my head. Come here and let me take care of my big strong Doctor. You know I love you, Evan."

She had begun to seductively lower her bra straps during her spiel. By the last syllable her breasts were fully exposed. "Sweetie, I want to make you happy. Come here, baby." She used her best

Marylyn Monroe voice and added a pouty smile as she lowered her eyes alluringly. Evan felt weak for a second, staring at her full breasts, hearing her words. He'd even considered the possibilities momentarily. Then he recalled her whining voice, the unreasonable demands and the sexual bartering. Instantly, he recovered his willpower.

"You have twenty-six days to get out. I've given my notice and the super will be changing the locks at the end of the month. Good bye, Loretta."

She realized her final attempts were futile. Her benefactor had officially dumped her. A high-pitched squeal replaced the throaty drawl she'd employed just a heartbeat before. Pulling her bra straps back up, she spewed a series of insults.

"You are a stupid, impotent, little man. It made me sick to touch you. Do you think I enjoyed having sex with you? It was all I could do to keep from throwing up each time you came near me. I called Phillip up every time you left. I used YOUR money to buy HIS clothes, and to take him out for dinner. Remember when I was visiting my mom last month? It was HIM, we went to Miami. We laughed at YOU while we were making love. MMMM... thank you, Doctor," she said licking her lips. She began laughing hysterically and it sounded like an evil cackling. Loretta's attack became a blue streak of emasculating insults.

The bombardment had rendered him temporarily immobile. He consciously instructed his feet to move, but they were frozen to the spot. Finally, they carried him out of the penthouse and away from Loretta's droning voice. His battered ego could bear no more. He pointed the red Corvette towards his suburban home. Audrey was the most important thing in his life now, Audrey… and the Blake Edwards' file.

*****

As Rose rounded the corner to the laboratory, a look of disappointment crossed her face. Henry's rusty Nova was not in the parking lot in front of Lab 2. "Damn," she mumbled under her breath. Even though Blake's car was here, she had wanted to catch Henry. Rose was looking forward to hearing about his little wedding ceremony. His were the only smiles she was getting around work lately. She hadn't seen Henry since Wednesday and assumed everything had gone just fine. Rose decided she would make a point of getting to the Institute extra early on Monday so she could chat with him before he left.

Walking into the lab, she spotted Blake, hunched over his pad, busily jotting notes. He was humming.

"Good morning, Blake. My, we're in a chipper mood this morning," she said happily.

Barely suppressing a small grin, he peered over the top of his glasses. "Well, Rose, Monday is day twenty-five and that's when I'll be paying my ol' friend Dr. Sinclair a visit."

Her brow slightly furrowed at the suggestion. "Blake, you know you didn't handle it very well the last time you went to see him. Why don't you wait until he contacts you?"

"Rose, this time I promise to be civil. I just want to find out what his impressions are so far. He's definitely well into the data by now. It'll be a full thirty days next Saturday. He said he would have the report by the 27th or 28th day." He smiled.

She knew next Saturday was day thirty. After the report nothing around here would ever be normal again. She was fine with the prospect. Lately, *normal* had been very depressing. Rose was excited for Blake; well mostly for Blake. She blushed when she thought of her own potential notoriety on the horizon. She smiled again as thoughts of Henry and his new bride slipped in. Maybe someday soon, she too would be having a little ceremony of her own.

*****

Henry had worked fast that morning in order to get home as early as possible. By the time he arrived at Jennifer's small apartment she had breakfast on the table and fresh coffee brewed. Taking off his shoes, he noticed her baggage just inside the front door. There wasn't much.

"Jenny, is this all you want to bring over to Ma's?" he said looking at the suitcase and three shopping bags.

"It'll be enough for right now, Henry. We can bring the rest over a little at a time."

“Okay. Are you happy to be moving in with Ma and me?” he asked.

“I’m a little nervous,” she said timidly. “Your mom is scary.”

“Yeah, I know she is sometime, but Jenny, she said she loves you, too, and I think everything will be okay,” he said hopefully. The two finished breakfast without much chatter. After finishing up the dishes they drove over to his Agnes’s house.

It was the beginning of a beautiful day and the sun was quickly burning off the morning haze. Once they parked, Henry took his new bride's hand and said, “Jenny, it’ll be okay.”

Fifteen minute later, Agnes was showing her around. "Jennifer, this will be your room," she said entering the extra bedroom off the main floor. It was sparsely furnished with a single bed and a paint-chipped dresser. “I’ve emptied the bureau for your things, dear. There should be enough room in the closet. Just be sure not to mix your things with mine."

Jenny shifted from one foot to the other, clutching her suitcase with both hands as she stood helplessly in the dimly lit room. She looked pleadingly at her new husband.

"Ma, Jenny's going to sleep with me. She don't need her own bedroom," Henry said quietly.

Agnes clutched her chest, with both hands in contrived shock. She looked toward Henry, then Jennifer, and back again at her son.

"You can't sleep in the same bed. Tell him, Jennifer," Agnes wailed, her voice shaking with simulated shock and anger.

"Agnes, we’re married. Of course, we’re supposed to sleep together," Jennifer responded. She and Henry had discussed possible situations that might arise with Agnes. Both looked stunned; neither had expected any problems, not the first day anyway, and certainly not this.

"Not under my roof you won’t," Agnes maintained.

Henry stood immobilized as the two women he loved faced off.

"Agnes, where do you think we slept last night?" Jenny responded defiantly.

She was referring to the $29.95 honeymoon suite at the Ramada Inn on Church Street they'd occupied the last two nights.

"Well, Dear, *this* is NOT a motel, now is it? I'm not comfortable with those kinds of activities in my home," Agnes retaliated.

Not knowing how to do battle with such an unreasonable woman, Jenny stood looking defeated. Everyone became quiet and the self-assured look Agnes wore, indicated she sensed a win.

Henry shocked both women as he walked across the room, toward his new bride. Gently touching her arm, he looked into her eyes. "Jenny, get your things, we're going to our apartment," he said softly.

Without question or hesitation, Jenny, still holding her suitcase, managed to scoop up the other bag.

"Ma, I'm forty-six years old and married now. You can't boss me around anymore, and I don't want you to *ever* boss my wife around, either," Henry said firmly.

It was difficult to tell which of the three was most shocked and uncomfortable. He'd spoken with more conviction than any of them could imagine, himself included.

"When you're ready to accept that Jennifer is my wife, and that we both need to be treated nice, like real people, we might be back. It's going to be up to Jenny. Ma, if we do come back, we'll be sleeping together like normal married people."

Henry took hold of the remaining bags. Passing his mother, he glared boldly at her as he headed toward the front door. As their eyes locked, each wore a discernable mask. Hers was of disbelief, his—defiance. Jennifer was right behind her husband. That was the first time in his life he had stood up to Agnes. As they backed out of the driveway, he glanced at his new wife. "I'm sorry, Jenny."

"Henry I'm so proud of you. You're my protector and I love you," she said as tears rolled slowly down her cheeks.

He reached over and held his brides hand. Today he was a man. The two innocent newlyweds slowly drove to Jennifer's apartment block. They emptied the trunk and, together, walked up the stairs.

*****

Alone in her home, Agnes did not have the capacity to cry. Instead, her mood became caustic as she sat mumbling under her breath about how she wasn't going to allow any fornicating under *her* roof. She was destined to spend her last few days on earth alone, bitter to the very end.

Chapter 22

Friday.

The pub seemed oddly lit. Individual streams of sunshine sliced through the lettered front window, as the smoke-laden air hung listlessly on the unwavering sunbeams. The shards of light penetrated the deepest, hidden depths of the tavern, drastically altering the nocturnal look of the watering hole. The ultimate transition over the next ten hours would be exciting to anyone willing to observe the lively establishment come to life.

The head on the beer had not completely disappeared as he banged the empty mug down on the old, beat-up table.

"I really needed that," Bruce said, as he sang out for another.

Eric held up his hand, waving off the next mug before it was offered. He'd hardly touched the first.

He had carefully listened to his mentor as he relayed the details of the committee meeting. Always cautious regarding the fine points of a mission, the 'double talk' continued.

"I'll be able to facilitate the request, Bruce. When would you like to see this project terminated?" he asked.

"We'd like to have this matter concluded Monday or Tuesday. It's not much time, son. Can you have the site cleared by then?"

Eric considered the setup necessary to pull off the task.

"Yes, I think we should be able to finish it up by then. I can get back to you if there's any difficulty," he replied.

"Those things will kill you, ya know," Vargo joked as Eric snubbed out the Marlboro he was smoking.

"Yeah, I know. I'll be quitting Tuesday," he confirmed.

Eric only smoked prior to a hit and then never again until the next. An occasional cigarette before a mission was his only nervous habit. Since Bruce's call, he'd smoked over a package. Vanessa's deadly future had gotten to him. Last night he'd dreamt of Jane for the first time in years.

The purpose of the meeting was two-fold. There was another name added to Eric's hit list, and Bruce wanted confirmation that the deadline for completion was feasible.

Eric took the single file of the new mark. He would review it later at home and was sure he knew the name it contained.

"Well, lad, it looks like you have your work cut out for you," Bruce said seriously.

"I'm comfortable with my game plan."

He suspected that Bruce was looking for an indication that a plan was already in the works.

The specifics of the operation would not be shared, not even with his mentor. It was just one more security measure on this sort of mission, the sort that had terminal results. In the event that Bruce was picked up and questioned before, during, or after the events, he wouldn't be able to confirm or deny details.

Earlier that morning Eric's disturbing dreams had him out of bed at three. While Monique slept, he'd carefully completed a final review of the files. Sitting at the glass dining room table, he'd methodically laid out his preliminary strategy. He assembled a list of those who would be intricate participants in the final chapter of this saga. Those on the list would need to be contacted. There was no pleasure derived in preparing for the assignment. Down deep, Eric was sorry for the seven, who would have no idea what they'd done to deserve such an abrupt fate. Nonetheless, he knew the order would not have received a green light if an imminent threat to the United States weren't real.

He had worked on the final particulars until the sun peaked through the haze at six o'clock. Returning to bed, Monique stirred.

"Couldn't sleep?" she asked, slowly emerging from her sleep.

"Just working on some files."

"Ah, yes the 'undercover' work," she whispered mockingly.

She stretched the sleep from her well-rested muscles as Eric playfully tickled her waist.

"That's right, my 'undercover' work," he echoed, with a smirk as she squirmed. Unintentionally his hand brushed against her breast.

Monique's squirming slowed as every part of her body responded to him. His strong touch became a soft fondling.

Forty-five minutes later, Monique was basking in the after glow, while Eric stood in the shower. As the hot water beat down on him, he decided to make all his calls from a payphone in the south end of town. It was just another safeguard, ensuring that nothing led back to him. As he toweled off his tanned, lean frame, he stared intently at the image looking back. Eric knew his day would consist of many phone calls. Arrangements would be made for the manpower he needed in place by Monday. He'd decided Monday would be the day. He would require no more time than that, and wanted the mission to be finalized. His first call of the day would be to Evan Sinclair.

*****

At the Sinclair home things had returned to normal. Audrey's life was back in order. Evan had come to his senses. He had abandoned the brazen slut in favor of his wife and children. She was a naïve young woman when she first married but over the years had become quite shrewd. Audrey was aware of the allure her husband's position and income might hold. The most tempted, of course, would be the gold-digging sluts. They'd be willing to barter their wares in exchange for the rewards. The whores were predatory.

Audrey had held Evan quite blameless in the whole affair. She chose to focus her anger on the tramp that lured him into his infidelity and the ignoring of his family. The rationalization, of course, left her quite blameless. She assumed only minor responsibility in the events leading to his temptation.

Audrey caught the phone on the third ring.

"Good morning," she answered brightly.

"Good morning, Mrs. Sinclair. Is the doctor still at home?"

"Yes, he is. One minute please." Audrey set the receiver of the wall phone down on the counter. She followed the sound of running water. Just as she rounded the corner to the bathroom, Evan was spitting out as he set the toothbrush down on the vanity.

“Darling, someone on the phone for you,” Audrey said.

Drying his hands, he frowned. "Who is it?"

"Not sure, Hun, want me to tell them to call back?"

"No, that's okay," he said walking past her to the kitchen phone. He guessed who it might be. Immediately he felt the familiar pressure of heartburn.

"Hello, this is Dr. Sinclair."

"Good morning, Eric Brunner here. How are you today?" he asked, leaning against the glass wall of the phone booth.

"Yes, fine thank you," Evan responded nervously.

"I'd like to buy you a cup of coffee, Evan. Let's meet at Ernie's Café, on Queen Street, the 300 block. Are you familiar with it?"

"No, but I'm sure I can find it. When?"

"Can you be there in say, a half hour?"

"It depends. Do I need to stop in at Novatek for anything?" he asked. His forehead was suddenly gleaming with perspiration.

"No, it's just a coffee, Evan, so, a half hour?"

"Yes, I'll see you there, good-bye," he replied, then slowly hung up the green phone on the wall cradle. Planting both hands on the counter, he leaned forward. His chest tightened even more. Evan closed his eyes for a moment, suspecting an anxiety attack was looming off in the wings. He drew a couple of slow deep breaths and was fine, as fine as he was going to get anyway. He wiped off the slight dampness that resulted from hearing Brunner's voice. Audrey had been bustling around readying the kids for school. She was oblivious to Evans' apprehension as a result of the early morning call.

"Audrey, I have to go in a little earlier today for coffee and a meeting with a colleague. I'll see you later."

"Is everything alright, Dear?" she inquired, absently.

"Oh, yeah Hun, everything's fine."

Somehow, he knew it wasn't.

Twenty minutes later, damp with sweat, the chunky man was sitting across from Eric Brunner.

"Evan, the committee has made its decision. Nothing you need to concern yourself with other than one small detail."

He could feel all the muscles in his body tensing simultaneously, and feared he would get a cramp or just seize up completely. Instead Evan nodded and pasted a fake smile on his face.

"We don't want you to go into work today. Dr. Edwards may question your progress on the report and we don't want to put you in that position. Go back home and spend time with your lovely wife. Just take the day off and enjoy a nice long weekend. Come Monday, if Edwards questions you, you can confirm his findings. If he doesn't approach you, do nothing. Work as usual and then go home."

Evan felt his entire body relax. He was so relieved that he thought he might just pass out. He hadn't realized until then that he'd been holding his breath. Slowly exhaling, he hoped that Brunner hadn't noticed.

"The Patronums and the United States of America are indebted to you for your loyalty. You have fulfilled your duty. Everything you think you know must be expunged from your mind." With a frightful glare, Eric added, "Many good lives depend on it."

Message received loud and clear, Evan thought. He wished he'd had a moment to bask in the glow of appreciation. He was mindful of one simple truth. There could never be a hint of any mention of this whole incident. He knew if he ever breathed a word of any of this, it would most definitely be his last. He didn't dare ask Eric Brunner what Dr. Edwards' ultimate fate might be. He felt a pang of guilt, and then shuddered as he considered the possibilities.

"Do you have any concerns, Dr. Sinclair?" The question was asked rhetorically.

"No, sir, everything is very clear. Don't go into Novatek today. Monday, if Edwards approaches me, I confirm his findings; if he doesn't, I do nothing. And none of this ever happened, correct?" Evan asked apprehensively.

"That's exactly it," Eric replied as he rose and extended a hand. Leaving five dollars on the table he said goodbye and exited the restaurant.

Ten minutes later, Evan was driving down his street. He arrived just in time to see the big yellow school bus pull away from his home. Only forty-five minutes had elapsed since Brunner's early morning phone call to the Sinclair residence.

Man, I just left here, Evan thought, as he pressed the button on the remote control. Automatically, the double garage door opened.

"Hi, honey, I'm home!" he said comically, entering the house through the garage.

Audrey came out of the kitchen, drying her hands on a towel. "Evan, what's wrong?" she asked uneasily.

"Nothing Darling, I just missed you. I'm taking the day off to spend with my beautiful wife."

She melted into her husband's arms. Her eyes welled up as she smiled. All was well in the world.

*****

Another sweltering day was winding down in Dallas, Texas. The masses rushed to meet the weekend and a contrived state known as 'time off.' They'd spent the whole week frantically planning and scheming. These two days would be full of everything from household chores to leisure activities. Mondays were a welcome reprieve for many.

4:52 in the afternoon. Her workday was nearly over. Vanessa had been watching the time continually, willing it to go faster. First, she'd eye the large ivory-colored dial of the wall clock and then look toward her handbag; she'd been doing both all day.

Carrying twenty-five thousand dollars in cash is hard on the nerves, she thought, rubbing her thumb against the grainy leather of the purse.

"PSSST." She jumped, startled by Marc's sudden presence in her cubical.

"Hey, I want to talk to you. Can I buy you dinner?" he asked in a hushed voice.

"Marc, actually I have an appo…" *I don't want to go through this every few days.* "Marc… I have a date tonight with somebody…I'm sorry."

“Hmm, okay, no problem. It wasn’t important anyways,” he said awkwardly. Without another word he turned and walked out of her work area.

I hate this place. I just feel lousy all the time around here... Vanessa thought. It was five-thirty and her meeting with Michael couldn’t come fast enough. The plan was to return the cash to Wilkinson and on Monday give her notice to Novatek.

After bidding everyone a goodnight she proceeded to her car and the rendezvous at the Velvet Glove. Rose and Dr. Edwards both seemed in good spirits when she’d wished them each a nice weekend. Marc, on the other hand, had scarcely flashed her a look, while nodding his head.

As she entered the Velvet Glove the humidity had reached a new level of clamminess outside. The air-conditioned lounge was a welcome relief. Walking to the booth, she spotted Michael’s odd silhouette in the warm, back-lit glow. Not intending this to be a social call, she approached him with a stern determination. Vanessa decided not to sit.

“Michael, Dr. Edwards has bumped whatever he was working on to the next level. It’s now in *Development*. I couldn’t find out a thing. I’m quitting Novatek next week, and I’m through with Wilkinson, right now.” Somehow, she’d managed to get it all out in one burst. Nervous about his reaction, she’d wanted to present the cash-stuffed envelope while simultaneously saying her ‘goodbye, nice working with ya,’ line. She reached around the shoulder strap and tried to unzip her purse compartment. Maybe it was her nerves, maybe it was her anxiousness to get it on the table, but somehow the zipper snagged. While she briefly struggled to unleash the envelope, Michael spoke.

“Miss Hargrave, as per the agreement, our employer releases you from any further obligation.” He lifted the six-dollar drink in a mock toast. Draining the glass, he gently set it on the black lacquered table. Vanessa had stopped moving at the sound of his voice. Still frozen with one hand holding the shoulder strap, the other firmly grasping the zipper tab, she blinked. “That’s it?” she said, shrugging her shoulders as she squinted.

“That’s it, Miss Hargrave. Of course, our employer would like to retain a positive relationship with you. In the event that you find yourself working in the pharmaceutical industry again in the future, please feel free to contact me in the usual manner."

Just the thought of doing this work again gave her an instant chill, and without thinking, she shivered.

Michael stood to his full height and towered above Vanessa. She had a stunned look of disbelief. Instinctively she reached forward as he enclosed her dainty hand inside his boney mitt.

"It's been a pleasure, Miss Hargrave." A cursory handshake, an awkward bow, and the tall lanky giant vanished into the dark bowels of the lounge. She plopped onto the red velvet upholstery and slid inside the booth. Her hand again went to the zipper tab of the purse. Pulling the tab, it effortlessly slid down, allowing her instant access to the contents. It was as if fate had intervened and would not allow her to return the loot. She could barely believe what had just happened and removed the large manila envelope. Opening it, she peered inside. Whether she could actually *see* it in the darkened lounge or just *felt* it was there, she glared at the cash. *Oh God, oh my god, I get to keep it. They're letting me keep all of it!*

Stuffing the envelope back into her purse, she waved the blonde server over to the table.

"Could you bring me a Singapore sling and make it a double please?" When the attractive waitress returned, Vanessa shoved a fifty into her hand. "Keep the change, honey." A lewd smile appeared on Vanessa's face. *Ohhh yeah, I really need to get lucky tonight*, she thought wantonly.

The following morning while still in bed, Vanessa heard rustling in the kitchen. As she stretched to her full length, the sheet slid sensually down her naked body. She beamed, recalling the hazy, frantic night. With a tray in hand, the overnight guest wandered back into the room.

"It's the best I can do. I'm not sure where anything is." There was steaming coffee, two slices of toast, a clip of cream cheese and a sliced orange. Smiling, Vanessa looked up and said, "It's perfect. You *do know* exactly what I like, even when the sun's up, don't you, Amanda?" The generous tip had been a great icebreaker. Amanda slipped back into bed beside Vanessa and didn't leave all weekend.

*****

Rose's Saturday and Sunday had been rather uneventful. She whisked it away shopping for some new clothes. She wanted to be ready for the predictable future; possible interviews, photographs, and maybe even some television appearances. She treated herself to a facial and made early bedtimes a priority all weekend. Rose tried unsuccessfully to reach Vanessa for some idle chitchat. *Oh well, probably for the best, wouldn't want to let anything slip,* she thought.

*****

Marc's weekend was stress-filled, spent feeling irrationally distraught. He paced restlessly about his apartment, spending his time playing solitaire, watching TV, and drinking. That weekend, he'd not left his home, not even once.

*****

Monday.

Rose had entered the institute that morning in a particularly good mood. She came into the lab pleased to find Henry busily cleaning cages.

"Good Morning, Henry!" she sang out.

"Well, hi-ya, Miss Rose. What the heck are you doin' here so darn early?" he said, changing the shavings in a cage.

"I wanted to be sure to catch you this morning! WELL?"

Henry stopped cleaning the cage, gawking at her with the bewildered look of a child on his friendly face.

"Ahhh, '*WELL*' what, Miss Rose?" he asked, puzzled.

Rose loved Henry's simple, unpretentious innocence.

"Your wedding day, silly. How was your wedding day! Did everything go well for you and Jennifer?"

"*Oh that.* Yeah, Miss Rose, it was really nice. We all went to Pangs' Chinese Restaurant after, for supper. Jenny, she don't like Chinese food very much, but she still went, too. Do you know, Miss Rose, it was the first time I ever seen Jenny eat Chinese food.

Like I said before, she really don't like it, on account she worked there for a long, long time."

Henry prattled on for the better part of fifteen minutes and the only detail he left out was the honeymoon night. He did mention the run-in with Agnes, regarding the sleeping arrangements at her home. During that part of the story, Rose smiled. She could have sworn he was blushing.

"I'm so happy for you, Henry. Congratulations to you both. I'd love to meet Jennifer one day," she said.

"Oh sure, Miss Rose, I know she'd like to meet you, too. She told me, 'Henry if you say Miss Rose is nice then I would like to meet her someday.' That's just what she told me, Miss Rose," he announced proudly.

"Well, Henry, we'll have to arrange that soon, very soon," she confirmed. Happily she said her good-byes and casually retrieved her lab coat from her locker.

*****

Blake was leaning on the cool, tiled wall in the corridor outside Evan Sinclair's office when he arrived.

"Good morning, Dr. Sinclair," he said guardedly.

Expecting his visit, Evan felt thankful to get it over with, first thing. "Good Morning, Dr. Edwards, nice to see you," he replied.

Unlocking the office door, he invited Blake into the inner sanctuary of his small, precise world.

"Well, Dr. Sinclair, how are you doing on the report?"

Reaching over, Evan startled Blake as he grabbed his hand, quickly pumping it up and down.

"Far enough to know that you are the next reigning father of medicine, SIR. I want to be the first to congratulate you. Dr. Edwards, your findings are not only beyond imagination, they are astounding," he gushed with genuine admiration.

He felt tremendously relieved at being able to finally say all those things to Blake Edwards. In his heart, he believed them all to be true, with one small exception. He suspected Edwards would never reap the just rewards for his genius.

Blake was overwhelmed with emotion as tears began streaming down his face. So overjoyed, he almost pulled Sinclair over the desk, while simultaneously embracing him. Evan, almost seventy-five pounds heavier than Blake, was nearly pulled off his feet.

"Dr. Sinclair, you have no idea the emotional stress I've been under. Please forgive my previous outbursts. Your confirmation, well, it's—it's like an enormous weight has been lifted from my shoulders. I feel like the air is breathable again," he blurted out. He took off his glasses and wiping his face, breathed a huge sigh of relief.

After a half hour of mostly rambling he pulled himself together.

"Dr Sinclair, I feel foolish. Please forgive my impatience as well as this emotional outburst, " Blake said bashfully.

"No, please, Dr. Edwards, forgive me. I was just following the Novatek protocol on your report. Rest assured my recommendation will be upstairs by tomorrow, with full review details." Of course it would not. However, Evan wanted to give this moment to Dr. Edwards.

"Well, thank you, thank you very much. I always knew that you were a sharp cookie, Sinclair." Blake took naturally to his new status as the modern day Caesar. He would begin by forgiving the impertinent Sinclair. After the final thank you and congratulations were exchanged, he left Evan's office for the last time. Blake strolled down the hallway toward Laboratory two, his arms swinging loosely by his sides as he whistled.

*****

The quiet hum of lowered voices was inaudible as Eric sat across from Otto Muller in the Dallas Public Library.

"I don't want any suffering, no pain. I'd like them to just get drowsy and fall asleep. Otto, can it be done?"

Otto was a medical examiner and a Patronum. He was of German descent and right down to his hair and glasses, looked like Albert Einstein. Although not as brilliant, he rivaled many with similar qualifications.

"Yes, Mr. Brunner. Carbon monoxide poisoning can accomplish that." Eric was familiar with the gas known as the 'silent killer.'

"The only obstacle, sir, could be that highly trained scientists would likely recognize the symptoms," Otto explained.

"What are the symptoms?"

"Well, sir, breathing carbon monoxide in high concentrations can cause a feeling of tightness across the forehead, throbbing in temples, weariness or dizziness. After a while, more serious symptoms may develop. They can include nausea, vomiting, weakness or loss of muscular control. Exposure to very high concentrations will cause rapid collapse resulting in death within minutes."

"Okay, Otto I've got it. Is it detectable during an autopsy?" he asked in a hushed voice.

"Most definitely, sir."

"How?"

"Well you see, sir, carbon monoxide is colorless, odorless, and tasteless, making it almost impossible to detect by the victims; however, it does block the absorption of oxygen into the bloodstream from the lungs, ultimately poisoning the red blood cells so they cannot *carry* oxygen. If body tissues do not receive a constant supply, they simply stop functioning. The brain is extremely vulnerable to oxygen deprivation. But, sir, it will leave its fingerprint in the blood."

"Thank you, Otto, I understand. Please have enough carbon monoxide to produce a high concentration for a twelve-hundred-square-foot room within three minutes. You will be contacted in five hours."

Eric's challenges were few on this assignment. He had carefully planned a sequence of events. These actions would guarantee Elixir would be kept secret forever, *or* for as long as the Patronums saw fit.

*****

By noon, Blake could no longer keep still. He organized a few notes, then hollered out, "Everyone, please come here, over here please."

Rose knew the moment Blake entered the lab that Sinclair had confirmed the results. The elusive Grail was his.

She was the first to move, stationing herself right in front of Blake, her face beaming. Vanessa, anxious to find out what he was about to reveal, was close behind. Marc looked over, avoiding direct eye contact while pointing to his chest in a questioning fashion.

"Yes, Marc, please come here. I have an announcement."

Marc shuffled uneasily toward the girls. He slid in behind them, bracing for news he was sure couldn't be good.

Blake was just rehearsing for the numerous interviews he would be granting. He suspected his fate would entail becoming a public figure. It was inevitable and a bit frightening in an exhilarating way. For the next couple of hours, he spoke to his captive audience, recounting the discovery of Elixir. All three listened, dumbfounded, as the impassioned doctor recounted his minor victories and finally the main event. Even Rose, who'd heard it all before, still found it miraculous.

"I won't forget any of you. Rose and Marc, I wouldn't have had the time to do the necessary research if you two hadn't been running things here during my temporary absence."

The dread that had surrounded Marc the previous months quickly evaporated as the ramifications of the discovery sunk in. His mood swung from apprehensive to euphoric as he peered through the microscope. Marc barely believed his own eyes as he witnessed Elixir eradicating the cancerous cells in the blood sample.

"*Temporary absence?* Man, I thought you'd left the planet, Doc. You were seriously freakin' me out," Marc chided.

Although he wanted to take hours to review the data, Marc had seen enough to be convinced. "Well Doc, no matter how weird you've been lately, from what I can see, this stuff is legit." *The little geek did it. Like Dr. freaking Frankenstein in the horror films, Edwards has created life* Marc thought even as he stared at Elixir gobbling up the malignant cells.

"And Vanessa, thank you for everything you do here. No one would ever be able to decipher our work if it weren't for you."

"Dr. Edwards, I'm so happy how things all worked out for you, I guess for the world." She really had no understanding of the implications that Elixir would bring. Not in the same way as Marc and Rose did. But Vanessa was truly sincere about being happy at how things had gone. She knew Wilkinson accepted the fact that it was too late once Edwards had submitted his findings. Her job was to get the information *prior* to it becoming official. Wilkinson would then make the decision about whether or not to steal the data, or coerce a scientist to switch teams. The implication of the loss that her benefactors would suffer was just sinking in when a security guard entered the room.

"Where do you want this?" he asked pushing the dolly. On it was a large barrel of bottles sitting atop a small mountain of ice. On a tray beside the barrel were several oversized wine goblets.

"This is a little treat from Dr. Sinclair. He said you all had something to celebrate," the guard mentioned casually.

"Right here is fine," Rose said, indicating a spot in the middle of the lab.

"Enjoy," he said as he closed the laboratory doors.

Rose pulled out an ice-covered bottle, "Dom Perignon, 1969, WOW!"

The simple fact that alcohol wasn't allowed anywhere on the premises eluded them all in light of the announcement.

"Jesus, this stuff is like, two hundred bucks a bottle," Marc proclaimed as he snatched up a glass. "Come on, Doc, let's celebrate. I'll pour."

At the exact moment that Marc popped the first cork, power to all cameras was cut, even those in the parking lots. The tapes had been looped and security, watching from *their secret place,* viewed images from previous recordings. Marc quickly drank down two full glasses and then began drinking straight from the bottle. Everyone was excitedly chatting and Marc opened several more bottles. Laughing, he took one for himself and handed a bottle off to each of the others. The jubilant atmosphere gave rise to an idea.

"Doc, I'll be right back, I just need some air," he said.

"Certainly, Marc, but this is still top secret, you understand?" Blake said sternly.

"Oh yeah, Doc. I'm just going outside for a few. Get some air. Vanessa, wanna come?" he asked hopefully.

The news hadn't changed anything where Marc was concerned. In Vanessa's book, he was still a neurotic paranoid.

"No thanks, Marc. I'm going to have some more champagne," she replied, holding up her bottle.

With the security cameras disabled, no one noticed Marc dancing down the corridor and through the scanner. He activated the electronic door lock with his card as he exited the building. He waltzed out into the warm air making his way to the grassy hill, several hundred yards off the parking lot. Scurrying up the embankment, he lay in the long grass staring at the sky.

Back in the lab, Blake was finally unwinding, maybe even ready to live a little. He hadn't touched alcohol since before Franny died. It tasted simply delicious. The smoothness was incredible.

"Well ladies, I do believe I'll be drinking a lot of this stuff soon," he said, a little unsteadily. "I'm getting a bit tipsy here, I'd better nurse this one," he joked to Rose and Vanessa, holding up a half-empty bottle.

All three laughed uncontrollably. They could have been accused of giggling like kids more than actually laughing.

The girls were feeling the effects as well. Rose, without warning, reached her arms around Blake's neck and kissed him deeply.

"Blake, you're wonderful," she whispered in his ear, as she slowly pulled away.

"Rose, I love you." His reply shocked them all, himself included. He'd been so careful not to feel much of anything since Fran died.

Vanessa stood a few feet away from the couple with her mouth agape. Aware that she was gawking like a teenager, she grinned.

"Hot-damn, this stuff is good, really good. I'm drunk already," she announced, walking toward the lounge, then mumbled incoherently as she lifted the almost-empty bottle to her lips. As an after thought she added, "Rose did you just tongue the doctor?" All three burst out laughing.

Of course, none of them realized the champagne had been laced with a concentrated tranquilizer to induce a peaceful slumber. Nobody recognized the effects of the carbon monoxide as the silent killer circulated through the air ducts. Blake and Rose joined Vanessa at the back of the lab in the lounge. The three laughed and tried talking. Words became slurred and sentences were left unfinished as their focus began to slip away. They didn't feel themselves dying; it just happened.

"I'm gettin' drunk," Blake proclaimed as he yawned.

"Getting drunk? I've been drunk for—well, I'm not sure how long," Vanessa added, giggling nonsensically.

He loved me, he loves me, so tired, I'm sooooo *tired, he loves me, Mrs. Rose Edwards.* Rose's final thought had been of Blake Edwards and their wonderful future together.

Conversation stopped without warning as Rose slipped away first. She died as she'd lived the last few years, loving Blake. Blake was next. But somewhere inside his clouded, brilliant mind, he knew. His last cognizant thought was the realization that he was being murdered. Vanessa was comfortably curled up on the lounge chair. *Just close my eyes for a minute, just for a minute,* she thought. She too was oblivious that her life had simply been unceremoniously snuffed out.

*****

Marc stared at the vast sea of clear blue straight above him. Closing his eyes, he began envisioning *his* new life. It was fantastic. As he emptied the champagne bottle, he remembered what was hiding in his wallet. Abruptly sitting up he dug it out of his hip pocket.

"Ah, what the hell, it *is* a celebration," he murmured mischievously.

He pulled out one of the two blotters of the LSD left over from the other night. Placing the small piece of paper that had been soaked with the mind-altering drug on his tongue, he swallowed. Lying back down in the grass, his arm tucked comfortably behind his head, he dreamt.

His dreams were of fast cars, faster women and power. In his altered state *he* was the distinguished explorer. He had become the brazen soul who uncovered the enigma that had eluded them all for so long. Noise, sirens and commotion had somehow seeped into his dream.

Marc, slowly awoke, the clear, blue blanket was now a dusky gray ceiling above him. He was groggy, not really sure of his whereabouts. Hesitantly he rolled over as the sirens screamed, shattering his drug induced state of mind. He raised his head, looking down toward the lab, his lab. He could feel the intense heat from three hundred yards away. The entire section containing Laboratory Number Two was completely engulfed in the blue and yellow flames that rose a hundred feet into the night sky. He froze, trying to separate reality from fantasy. For a moment he thought it was just a hallucination. His head was reeling and he prayed it was all a mirage. The truth was that his face was burning, the heat was so intense.

"Oh, FUCK, I knew this was too good to be true. I knew it, I just knew it," he said staring in disbelief., still dazed and trying to work out the scene below.

Just then, Marc had a terrible sense of *déjà vu.* He suddenly thought of Vanessa's apartment fire and the horrible hallucination. The one where she'd burned and others were burning behind her. Marc almost screamed aloud, as it all became clear in his confused frame of mind.

"THIS was supposed to happen," he whispered.

During the confusion, he made his way, unnoticed, out of the compound. He simply weaved through the crowd of curious onlookers. Unobserved, he slipped past the deserted security post. Twenty minutes later, the place was sealed tight.

Marc's paranoia had kept him alive that night and was to become his new best friend, living intimately with him.

Sirens shrieked as hoses swelled, all in an effort to snuff out the raging fire. The chaotic scene also forewarned bystanders of the dangers that lurked within the compound.

*****

At that very moment, somewhere across town, Eric Brunner rang the doorbell. Almost instantly the door swung open.

"Good evening, Ma'am. My Name's Joseph Zackary. I'm with the *Newlywed Life Insurance Group.* Is your husband in? I would like to speak with you both, if I could," he said convincingly.

Jenny was deciding whether it was safe to invite the tall, attractive stranger in. Before she could respond, Henry was at the door shaking '*Joseph Zackar*y's' hand.

"Hi, come on in, Mr. Zackary." Opening the door, he moved aside. Jenny, too, stepped sideways and allowed Eric to enter.

"I'm Henry and this is my wife Jenny. What's this about?"

Eric smiled, *Charming fellow*, he thought. He wanted this to look like a simple robbery gone wrong. It would be easily accomplished with these two. Eric sensed instantly that both were very naïve to the treacherous world in which they lived. The file also indicated that both were a bit slow, so he knew this would be uncomplicated. Eric Brunner left less than sixty minutes later. As he gunned his car down the bypass toward the phone booth, he wondered if Bruce would be as easily convinced.

Just as Eric was passing the turnoff to the Lincoln tunnel, Henry sat on the sofa looking at his new wife.

"I think Mr. Zackary was right. Life insurance would be a good thing, Jenny. Just in case, like he said, *'Ya just never know if something bad is going to happen.'"*

*****

"Bruce, I interviewed them for an hour. They're harmless, no way Edwards confided in the animal handler. I made a judgment call. I don't think either one is a threat to the project. I feel retiring them would be just murder," he said persuasively.

"Son, I guess I have to trust your judgment. I won't be around forever, and someday you'll be making the decisions."

Eric knew what he was referring to. Although Bruce had never come right out and said it, he'd hinted for years that Eric would be his replacement.

Earlier that day, before visiting Henry and Jennifer, Agnes Miller had suffered a fatal heart attack. Henry would find her body a week later. She'd been the seventh file. In her presence for only minutes, Eric did not find the redeeming qualities he had in the newlyweds. A capsule of white powder was easily slipped into her tea. He'd done well. None of them had felt a thing.

*****

It would be days before the bodies were recovered from the rubble. The heat had been so intense that identification of the charred bones would be made through dental records. The Patronums searched extensively for Marc Andrews. His file was never closed, nor were his whereabouts ever discovered.

Dr. Blake Edward's epitaph could be found neatly typed on the investigating fire marshal's report.

Cause of fire: *Alcohol related, resulting in probable intoxication of two females, two males in the vicinity of highly explosive chemicals.*

Actual cause: *Undetermined.*

Suspected cause: *Accidental.*

Arson: *Ruled out.*

Casualties:

Dr. Blake Edwards, male, aged 48 years

Dr. Marc Andrews, male aged 35 years

Dr. Rose Frechette, female, aged 37 years

Vanessa Hardgrave, female, aged 29 years

The inquest had been carefully manipulated. The target had been Blake's memory, which was forever tainted with the accusations of impropriety and poor judgment. It was Eric's largest single regret regarding the mission and rightfully so; the eternal injustice to Dr. Blake Edwards was enormous.

Part Two

Chapter 23

Carl's gaze was fixed on the luminous orb as he took a long hard draw on the cigarette. The full moon starkly contrasted the jet-black night. It hung faithfully suspended by its invisible tether across the celestial background.

He flicked the half-spent cigarette off the balcony watching the sparks flutter off as it twirled the eleven stories downward. He spotted the orange, red speck scatter firefly embers as it hit the pavement below, and then, it was gone. The low steady hum of Washington D.C. seemed a million miles away, as the cool, night air filled Carl's lungs. Behind him the wooden French doors opened wide to the balcony. A light wind brushed the sheers inward toward the room, producing an eerie ghostlike shimmer.

The eight hundred square foot hotel suite was more than luxurious. It was decadent. At a thousand dollars a night it would have to be. The round, feather-soft bed was the centerpiece of the circular room. Everything was mastered to highlight it. The ceiling was domed and fifteen feet high in the middle. The walls shot straight up from a hand spun Indian carpet. Nine feet from the floor a striking black mahogany cove that trimmed the room opulently marked where the walls began a slow arc to the centre of the dome. The light fixture over the breakfast nook was a collection of elongated crystals, surrounding obscured halogen light bulbs. The continually changing symmetrical beams of light were amazing. The room was designed to replicate the domed shape of the capitol building. For those who could not deduce that simple fact from the appearance, there was always the name; it was called the *Capitol Room*. The richly appointed suite was just another perk from Congressman Edward Monroe, Sarah's neglectful spouse.

She could see Carl's flawless silhouette as the backlight of the full moon outlined him perfectly. She also spotted a stream of smoke hovering weightlessly above his head. Sarah disliked the filthy habit, but easily accepted it as part of the arrangement. The unspoken understanding was they could enjoy each other, with no expectations or demands.

Sarah Monroe was a forty-one-year-old, married woman who filled her empty nights with whatever, or whomever helped her feel alive. To risk the attention, however fleeting, of her young lover over something as trivial as smoking would be asinine. Carl made her feel desirable and sexy, his presence helped restore the self-esteem her marriage had slowly eroded. Being the wife of Edward Monroe had taken its toll. His aspirations of reaching the next rung on the legislative ladder had left her a "political widow."

The Congressman had long since taken up the habit of using discrete escort services when he traveled abroad. Sarah had suspected lately that her husband's indiscretions were no longer limited to out-of-town excursions. The telltale signs of a full-fledged affair were evident. Sarah assumed the perpetrator was someone younger, offering the freshness that a twenty-year marriage, no matter how polished, lacked. Sarah disliked the situation, but found a way to rationalize it in her own mind.

Feeling especially ignored by her husband one day, she'd gone shopping for clothes. Arriving home with an armful of bags, Sarah began unpacking her treasures.

Ahhh, I love it, this is exactly what I needed, she thought, admiring the new dress she held to her lithe frame. Her spirits were lifted, and she was happy to see her smiling reflection in the mirror. Walking into her closet, she scanned for an empty hanger. A past favorite outfit hung ignored and neglected, a dress she found so glamorous at one time that she just had to have it. For weeks Sarah had looked for occasions to wear it. Without a thought she carelessly pulled it from the hanger and dropped it into the clothesbasket. It would be donated to the local thrift store. Unpacking her parcels, she suddenly had an epiphany. Sarah stopped and looked into the wicker basket at the beautiful outfit she'd just discarded. Tears flowed as she accepted the simple truth. *She too* was being recycled. Sarah had become arm dressing for special events and dinner parties, the loyal wife, smiling brightly as Edward campaigned. Over time, she had replaced resentment with complacency.

"Come in, Darling, it's getting cold out there," Sarah said to her young lover.

"Yeah, it is a bit cool out here, ahhh, but it feels so good!" Carl said, re-entering the suite wearing nothing but a grin. Glancing over at the fiery redhead, he moved to the edge of the bed. Sitting, he gently held his hand against her cheek.

"Sarah, you are truly beautiful." He meant it.

She was two inches shorter than his six foot, one inch frame, standing at a full five feet, eleven, with the body of a woman half her age. Her creamy white skin was flawless. The impeccable contour of her jaw framed a perfectly matching set of dimples, adding to her refined beauty. Sarah's emerald green eyes were symmetrically set, her perfect nose sat atop an angelic smile. In Carl's eyes, she was a masterpiece of beauty.

"You are a refreshing young man," she said quietly as she pulled his head toward her bosom.

"Forgive me for saying so, but Edward is an idiot," he reaffirmed.

*****

Carl Phoenix had met Sarah during one of his runs. He was a courier for sensitive government dispatches. He'd been recruited by the senator, or as he liked to say, *forced* into the position. Sitting in his father's Dallas office six months prior, the onset of his new career had taken place. He recalled it vividly…

"I will cut you off, by God. I mean it, Carl, if you drop out of college without the courtesy of discussing it with me!" Thomas had barked.

"Well, Tom, I really didn't think it was any of your business, after all it is my life. I would sooner enjoy it while I'm young," Carl said. He knew calling his father by his given name would annoy him.

"Don't call me *Tom*. I'm your father, dammit! I will not have you disrespecting me. First, you ignore my wish to attend law school. I could live with that disappointment. You know damn well I hoped you'd follow in my footsteps. I spent twenty years blazing a trail for you on the Hill. But no, you chose to study medicine at MIT, reluctantly I supported that decision. Now, halfway through, you quit? Son, where is this coming from?"

Carl saw the frustration that emphasized the deep lines which time and years of stress had etched into his father's brow. He knew the senator from Texas met with few challenges as difficult as the ones he personally could create. Carl was unsure of why he did it; perhaps it was a power struggle. He knew that Thomas Phoenix's iron-will, backed with the power of his office, could produce a potent cocktail. He grinned as he watched the old man squirm.

He got a perverse pleasure from the fact that his dad's immense control stopped where he was concerned. Even as a child, he'd been stubbornly difficult. If Thomas suggested they go to the movies together, he wanted to go to the zoo. Carl had no idea why he was so belligerent, he just was. In his eyes, the mighty senator could never get it right.

Carl's therapist suggested once that perhaps it was the fact that the powerful senator could do nothing to save his young wife. Loren Phoenix had died giving birth to him. The insinuation had officially ended his therapy.

Thomas had wanted him to attend his alma mater, Harvard, to study law. Carl instantly rejected the idea, choosing medicine at MIT. Thomas was exasperated.

"Dad, I'm just not interested in medicine anymore. I don't want to waste my youth in school, staring at cadavers," he said indifferently.

"Well, son, I don't know what to say, but trust me on this one. You get back to school or you're on your own mister, and I mean it."

Carl was aware that his lifestyle would quickly devour what little savings he had set aside. He knew his father acknowledged the only real control he had over him was the huge allowance. He received a monthly check from his father for ten thousand dollars. It was a mere drop in the bucket considering that the senator had invested considerable sums, wisely, in the early boom days. Thomas had thrown himself into his work after Loren had died. He had amassed a fortune, mostly in oil. Texan's fondly referred to it as *Black Gold.*

By the conclusion of the encounter, father and son had reached a lopsided compromise. Carl would not go back to school, but would work instead for a minimum of two years. Thomas would select his placement. Every day absent from his job would result in a deduction of five hundred dollars levied against his bursary.

Dismissal from his position would result in the unconditional halt to his allowance. He knew his father would be unrelenting. He had grown far too accustomed to the condominium, wild nights, and overall lifestyle his allowance afforded him. He wasn't about to give it all up.

Reluctantly, Carl had agreed to the conditions.

"So where am I going to be working, *Dad*?

"Leave that to me, son. I'll be calling in a favor or two. Nevertheless, I trust you will be relocating to Washington D.C."

"NO WAY! I'm not moving to Washington. It's freezing up there!" he blurted.

Grinning, Thomas merely said, "You'll get used to it."

Carl had grudgingly packed his belongings four months ago, and moved to D.C. He set up house on New Hampshire Ave, renting a modern two-bedroom condo in downtown Washington.

He didn't mind his job as a courier delivering the correspondence that came and went from the Capitol. Actually he loved it. Being outdoors, running "Top Secret" and "Confidential" files from office to office was intriguing. Occasionally he would go out to the suburbs to a high-ranking government official's home. It had its benefits. He'd met Sarah delivering documents to Congressman Monroe's house one cold blustery day a few months ago.

*****

The big, empty house felt cool. Sarah wasn't sure if it was her loneliness, boredom or actually the brisk wind whistling around the cherry trees outside. But there was no doubt, she felt chilled. The overcast day brought with it a melancholy veil, draping her like a cold, wet blanket. She sat in the family room and pulled a couch throw up over her knees. There were people moving and talking on the large-screened television, but Sarah didn't really see or hear anything. She still couldn't shake the chill. Looking around the stately room, it felt like her life, empty and hollow. She decided on a glass of red Bordeaux. Standing against the bar in the sitting room, she easily opened the wine. She was becoming quite an expert with a corkscrew. Not a drop lost as she filled the wine glass on the granite-topped bar. *This will warm me. A couple of these will probably cheer me up too*, she mused.

After a few drinks, she was still cold.

“Brrrr. I need a nice hot bath,” she murmured. Once the chill had hit her bones, Sarah often resorted to a relaxing bath and a cocktail.

About the same time as the warmth of the tub seeped into her entire body, the wine was taking affect. She lay lounging in the elegant marble tub until the glass was empty. Stepping out of the stylish bathtub, she leisurely toweled off and slipped into her cashmere robe, its soft invisible fingers stroking her skin, making her body tingle.

"HMMMM I love this robe," she said, fixing the sash.

Staring into mirror, she gently applied a rejuvenating facial cream. When she was finished, she stood for a moment surveying the chic bathroom. The granite countertops and marble tiles didn’t mean much anymore, but nonetheless she did feel quite refreshed and even a bit happier, thanks to the Bordeaux. “Yep, I should fill you up again,” she joked aloud, talking directly to the empty glass.

Just as she reached the bottom of the long winding staircase, the door chime rang out.

Sarah peaked out of the spy hole in the door. Shuffling from foot to foot stood a tall, handsome young man. He didn’t appear to be dressed warmly enough, given the cold wind blowing today. With a customary flip of her hair, she set the empty glass down on the front-door accent table.

"Yes may I help you?" she said, opening the heavy door.

"Ma'am I have a delivery for Congressman Monroe,” he said, simultaneously producing his identification. “I’m just going to need a signature please."

She reached out and took his ID card. Below the picture was his name—**Carl Phoenix.** *What a good-looking kid,* she thought staring at the photo just a second too long.

"Come in, come in, please," she said as a blast of cold air blew into the foyer.

Once inside the house, she confirmed what a handsome young guy he really was and without thinking about it, she offered him a warm beverage.

"Ahhh, well thanks, Ma'am, I think I'll take you up on that."

"Please, call me Sarah."

"Hi Sarah, Carl Phoenix," he said, extending his hand.

"YOUR HANDS ARE FREEZING!" she blurted out. "Just come with me, Carl Phoenix," she said, retreating to the modern kitchen. He obediently followed and a few minutes later, Sarah had prepared two cups of hot cocoa.

Sitting at the kitchen table, they chatted about the weather. Carl complimented her on the beautiful home, and asked her about the hustle and bustle of a political wife. She asked about his work delivering dispatches around Washington. Surprisingly, for strangers, they chitchatted quite comfortably.

Sarah had been reading men's faces her whole life. She couldn't help but notice how he looked at her. She'd felt chemistry between them minutes after he'd arrived. It was intoxicating, and unlike an hour prior, she was feeling a bit overheated.

After talking with this wind-blown stranger for the last half hour, she noticed his appreciative gaze had fallen from her eyes to her chest. Glancing down, Sarah saw her robe had slipped open, exposing more than half of her left breast. She unhurriedly pulled the robe together, looking slowly back at the wide-eyed man. Her pulse quickened as their eyes locked and she saw the combined look of awe, panic, and confusion in his face.

Carl looked like a deer caught in fast-approaching headlights. She smirked as he sat motionless, not knowing which way to run. Sarah thought it might be maternal instinct, or perhaps it was just pure lust, but she felt she should rescue him from the moment. Just then he flinched. Looking toward his half-emptied cup, he awkwardly announced, "Well Sarah, I should, um, really should get going. Thanks for the hot chocolate and the chat," he said, rising to his feet.

God, Edward hasn't looked at me like that in years, she thought. Unknowingly, Sarah had decided that she actually *needed* the young man's amorous stare. She was flushed, her body fully alive, she stood as her robe fell open seductively. Impulsively she pulled him toward her. Their lips ground in a frenzied passionate kiss. It all felt so right to her.

*****

Luridly recounting their first time two months prior, Sarah felt her heart begin to race as the charismatic man-child rested on her chest. Sensing her quickened breathing, Carl looked up into her eyes. Passionately, he kissed his way down her body.

"Carl, please stay with me tonight," she cooed, after they made love.

Without pause, he said, "Sure, babe I'll stay. I'm going out on the balcony for another cigarette."

"You can smoke in here if you like," she offered coyly.

"Thanks gorgeous, but I need the fresh air."

That was another thing she loved about Carl. He was so confident, almost cocky for such a young guy, but never offensive or arrogant. His long, windblown hair and the three-day-beard all served to epitomize his youthful, cavalier demeanor.

As he walked out on the balcony, she found his lean body, rippled with muscles, exciting. *I'm really falling for him,* she thought staring. *Who am I kidding, it's too late.* Acknowledging the truth, Sarah accepted that she'd already fallen hopelessly in love with him.

Chapter 24

Carl glanced at the morning paper as he sipped his coffee. The headline boldly challenged the reader,

Could she be the First Woman President?

Below the brazen caption was a photo. Not a very flattering picture of a woman with a raised arm, clenched fist, and a rather pinched looked on her face. Her mouth was half-open, the top lip peeled back, in what appeared to be a menacing sneer.

He frowned at the photo. Squinting with one eye, he held the paper in hand while taking a swallow of his coffee. He'd spotted President Jonathan Cantrell's daughter in the Capitol building on several occasions. Emily Cantrell was far more pleasant looking in person than the photo suggested.

The article listed a string of achievements. It began with a Harvard law degree earned twenty-six years earlier. Two years after graduating, she'd become a partner in a large law firm in Atlanta. Three years later, she‘d abruptly exited her practice. Emily Cantrell traveled Europe and Indonesia for a year, then returned to school. At Oxford University she achieved a master's degree in psychology. Shortly after her return to the U.S. she entered politics. The article also mentioned that she spent five years at the mayoral helm of New York, the largest city in the United States. The accolades went on. They were randomly rehashed every couple of weeks in the media. She was an accomplished woman at forty-nine years of age. Her husband, Jason, had been mentioned in one sentence, her three children not at all. The article simply stated what most people knew. Emily Cantrell, eldest child of the reigning president of the United States, was leading the polls by eleven points. In addition to leading the pack in the race for the White House, the gap was steadily growing. Americans loved her. Her father was a very well respected and competent leader. Despite unpopular tax increases and making what he referred to as the "tough decisions," the people admired him. His second term, had been rather uneventful. He'd kept the deficit down, employment rose consistently, and the average American could feel the country prospering. Americans wanted more of the same.

Emily was following in her father's footsteps. When Carl had been at one of her Washington rallies, relaying dispatches as necessary, he recalled her primary platform.

"Running the country is like running a business. More dollars can't go out than are coming in, folks. The business would simply go broke. Americans cannot starve, living in the streets, while we fall deeper into debt by sending foreign aid to over eighty other countries." After a round of applause, she continued. "Taxes cannot be cut to the point where Americans are unable to receive basic, essential care. Furthermore, tax dollars cannot be spent frivolously. Monies must be used for housing, medical care, and development of our industries. As president, I will make your dollars count!" Her address was followed by continuous applause as she suggested practical strategies. The people believed her, and so did Carl. In the past he had had no political preferences, but found that he liked her. She was bold and straightforward, saying the things that most politicians avoided. The novel approach worked for her, and was more evident every day in the polls. Unless there were dramatic changes, it looked like she was a shoe-in. Emily Cantrell was destined to be the first female president in the history of the United States of America.

Yawning from lack of sleep, Carl stretched, and letting out a bear-like grunt, he threw the newspaper on the table.

His night with Sarah had been magnificent, like all their nights together, but he felt that she was getting too close. Carl enjoyed the time they spent together, but knew this would nothing more than a wonderful affair for him. The last thing he needed were the tabloids plastering his face with Sarah's on the front pages. He shuddered as he imagined the headlines.

"Congressman's wife has affair with Senator's young son"

The old man would surely love that, he thought chuckling.

Forty minutes later he arrived at the Capitol parking lot. The first security measure was a biometric thumb scan. That allowed him to enter the parking lot. Once his vehicle was parked, he proceeded to an armed Marine who checked his identification. Before finally entering the building, he stopped in front of the heavily fortified door. Carefully pressing his forehead against the pad, he lifted his left eyebrow. Within seconds the quiet whirring sound was replaced by the loud noise of the automatic door lock disengaging. Carl's iris had been scanned, his identity verified, allowing him entrance into the Capitol.

He was ready for another day of deliveries, pick-ups and inter-office memos. Cynthia's scan was the final security check.

"Good morning, sugar," she cooed, as she moved the hand-held device over his body.

"Hey, Cynthia, you're looking fine today!"

"Oh, Carl, you're just the sweetest thing," the thick, black woman gushed. "You have a good day now, you hear?"

Cynthia's security-guard uniform was stretched to the limit, straining to contain all two hundred thirty pounds of her.

"You too, take care," he said as he recovered his keys from the bowl.

He walked into the inner sanctions of the building. Strolling past the armed Secret Service members, he said his good mornings. Outside, the agents had small headset wires dangling from their ears. Inside the building they simply carried two-way radios. Some of them he knew by name, others he just greeted with a friendly nod and a courteous 'good morning'.

Carl arrived at what the messengers jokingly referred to as the 'belly of the beast.' He was in the basement of the Capitol. Like most large operations, it was just one of many 'behind the scenes' components of the big machine. This section was devoted to the paper communications of the government in Washington and the rest of the country. Because telecommunications did not involve physical handling of information, it was located off site.

This was where all the paper trails began. Every delivery required a confirmatory signature. Some careers ended with the fingerprints left on those pieces of paper, some began. This was the division that determined who would take what, where.

Patrizio Salvatorie, Carl's immediate supervisor, was in charge of assigning routes and ensuring that the *'whatever'* actually got to the *'wherever'*. Everyone simply called him Sal, a nickname he'd carried since he was a kid.

"Morning Sal, so, what do we have today?" Carl asked.

"Hey," he responded raising a bushy eyebrow, "How are you this morning?"

"Good, a little tired but ready to go," Carl said, looking at the sixty-something manager.

Sal was a second generation Italian who'd inherited his father's receding hairline and short, barrel-chested frame. Carl liked him. He watched as the old man chucked the mail into its respective slots. Sal just barely glanced down at the name before hurling in the next piece. Finishing the bundle in his hand, he passed an electronic register over to Carl.

"Here you go. Your pile's over there," he said, motioning with his head.

"Thanks Sal. So how's the wife? You two go out dancing last night?" Carl joked. Both men chuckled at the thought.

With a dismissive wave of his hand, Sal started down a long corridor. "Just move your ass, funny boy. You have work to do," he said, still smiling.

Carl grabbed the secure cell phone that all couriers were issued. The phone was for direct communication between the mailroom and the drivers. Occasionally they would get calls informing them of unscheduled pick-ups.

With his protected satchel of mail, Carl left, weaving his way back out of the building. Exiting through security, he spotted Cynthia's bright, wide smile and waved.

Zigzagging through the streets of Washington, the morning passed quickly as he jumped in and out of his unmarked government vehicle. He liked exchanging pleasantries with the secretaries and receptionists while working his route. After a couple of hours it was time to return to the Capitol and get a new lot of dispatches.

Casually driving through the light morning traffic, he'd thought about his father. He had no idea why he was so hard on the old man. He loved him immensely and respected his ability as a leader, a father and a man. But still, he rebelled. For a moment, he considered calling his dad to tell him he was really enjoying this job. Almost instantly he changed his mind, recalling how his father had pressured him into the position. The memory, a grim reminder of just how powerful the senator was…

"Carl, PLEASE, I'm on the phone." Thomas's voice was laced with agitation as he shot a stern look in his direction.

"Yes…my son, Carl Phoenix, correct. You can? Wonderful, Phyllis, I owe you one. Right, I'll have it faxed over immediately, thanks again Phyllis, yes you too."

He sat glaring at his father, as Thomas replaced the receiver. "Dad, I told you, I didn't want any special treatment. I wanted to do this on my own," he snapped. Thomas's iron jaw was set with a smug expression.

"Carl, you don't seriously think just anyone walks in off the street and is hired to work at the Capitol Building, do you? You'll be handling sensitive, government documents daily. It's very tight security there son, very tight."

"I don't think every employee there has a father who's a senator, pulling strings, bypassing the process, DO YOU?" he roared back, his face contorted with frustration.

The Senator leaned forward, slowly locking his fingers together on the desk. He had a look of sincere concern stretched across his face. Carl rolled his eyes. He recognized the deportment. *Great,* he thought. *This is his, 'I'm thinking of something clever that will win them over,'* stance. Thomas always gave public speeches from behind his desk, never the podium. The effect was disarming. Carl braced for defeat. Whatever his father was about to say would leave little room for rebuttal.

Thomas, always the politician, responded calmly, "No son, I don't think they all have someone pulling for them, but you, my boy DO. Because I'm a Senator, you've had the opportunity to bypass the usual bullshit, and move to the front of the line. So instead of getting yourself in a knot about it, perhaps you should be packing. A 'Thank-You dad,' is not necessary. Glad to be of help." He said matter-of-factly. Thomas concluded the interaction with a smile. His son assumed he was gloating.

Carl had wanted to delay his departure for as long as he could. He was counting on the very process of security checks and bureaucratic red tape to give him another couple of months in

Dallas. He had no argument with his father's logic and he should have been grateful for the time and effort Thomas saved him. He was not. Without a word, he left the large office with its high solid oak ceilings. His father sat behind the luxurious desk with a victorious, self-satisfied look on his face. Carl went home to pack. He was determined to hate this posting, arranged by his father. That, too, hadn't worked out as planned.

A blaring horn from behind startled him out of his daydream. The light had turned green.

Spotting the illuminated time on the dash of his car, Carl unconsciously sped up. He wanted to be a bit early today for his standing lunch date. Twice a week he met a homeless character that he'd taken a shine to a couple of months before. He smiled as he thought of *Beau Jangles* and how agitated he would be if Carl were late. It was 11:02 in the morning as he sped down Albert Street and back toward the Capitol building.

*****

Earlier that morning, across the city in front of the small diner the bedraggled man known as Beau Jangles pushed his shopping cart and ranted.

"Where is he, he's late. Shoulda been here by now. Where the hell is he? Bugger isn't going to show anyway. Bastard. The universe is full of 'em. They're all liars. Say they're gonna do something, then don't do it," Beau fumed.

He'd walked back and forth mumbling incessantly in front of "Reggie's," a small hole-in-the-wall lunch stop. The homeless wretch occasionally stopped, ducking, as if an unseen object had fallen in his general direction. Then, looking wildly at the empty space surrounding him, he would begin again. He paced, swore and carried on full conversations with himself about the liars. Beau Jangles had no way of telling the time, or he would have known it was only 9:45. After about twenty minutes had passed, the decrepit man of about sixty pushed his cart back to the place he called home. Today he lived in an alley beside a dumpster used by the Publix Supermarket.

"Good place," he'd said when he first discovered it. "Lot of good food going in here, yes sir-ee. Can't hang around during the day or they'll kick my ass out for sure," he mumbled to no one.

During the daylight hours he'd wander the streets with his cart, gathering all the treasures he could. By dark, it would be brimming with other people's unwanted items.

With his fingers wrapped firmly around the handle of the buggy, he decided that today he needed to hide it by the dumpster. "Can't leave you outside of Reggie's, someone'll steal you for sure," he said loudly, addressing the inanimate object. Grabbing a handful of boxes, he began ripping them apart. A few minutes later he'd created what appeared to be an overflow of cardboard from the dumpster. The cart with all it riches was now completely camouflaged. Stepping back, he surveyed his handy work and smiled.

"Bastards won't get my stuff now, they'll never see it. Gotta go back to Reggie's, see if that lyin' kid's gonna show up there," he said aloud.

Kicking at the ground, Beau walked back toward the small restaurant, then stopped dead. "Dammit! Damn!" he said punching at the still morning air. He turned and headed south on Jefferson, mumbling. "Get cleaned up, get cleaned up,' he mimicked. "Need to take me a shower—Jesus—." It had been the only condition he was given for a free hot lunch. *"Take a shower before you come,"* the kid told him.

"Damn, yep, that's why he didn't show. Gotta take a shower and clean up," he muttered. Grabbing a handful of his shoulder-length, dirty hair, he smelled it. Wrinkling his nose, he quickly made his way to the shelter on 32nd street. He was always able to get a hot shower there. No one ever turned him away, probably because he never asked for anything else. Other than showering occasionally, he stayed clear of the shelters. He feared that someone might recognize him. No one would.

When he arrived at the safe haven, he entered through the kitchen. Pushing open the heavy door, the smell of food greeted his growling stomach.

"Well, Mr. Beau Jangles, how are *you* doing? We haven't seen you here for a while," the chunky woman said, ladling soup into a container. Waiting in line were about a hundred men, women, and children, all shuffling with bowls in outstretched hands.

"Yeah, hi Mabel," he replied, his eyes turned downward staring at the floor. "Gotta clean up. A shower, can I get a shower?"

"Sure, Beau. Are you hungry? Good chicken soup today with lots of vegetables," she announced proudly.

"No thanks, going out for lunch, just need a shower. Can I go take a shower?" he asked again, shuffling his feet.

"Going out for lunch are you? Mighty high roller today! Go already, big-shot, get yourself that shower," she teased. Her kind, round face was beet red from the heat, as she stood over the huge boiling cauldron.

Beau Jangles was the only name he gave. The volunteers at the shelters were quite used to aliases. In Beau's case, it was the name he gave to everyone he met in the homeless community. People outside his environment couldn't have cared less what name he used. Their only real concern was that he might actually *talk* to them.

Walking to the rear of the old building that served as home for seventy residents, his eyes darted from side to side. Suddenly, there was a big crash. One of the anxious souls dropped an empty bowl and hitting the concrete, it exploded into a hundred tiny shards. Beau Jangles dove to the floor as if a bomb had went off. He was not alone. The streets were a war zone and the homeless, its foot soldiers. Loud, startling sounds usually meant danger in the personal battleground they called home. As a result, many of the down-and-out folk were jittery.

An hour later, he was stationed once again outside Reggie's, clean, with his hair neatly combed into place. His arms flailed wildly as he engaged in animated conversation with himself. So engrossed was he in his tête-à-tête that he didn't see the smiling young man as he approached.

As Carl exited the car, he quietly laughed. He watched as Beau's arms rose and fell to the beat of an invisible drum.

"Beau, you ready for a lunch? I'm starving!" Carl said, as he clapped his shoulder. Beau yelped as if he'd been hit. His hands immediately covered his face. With squinting eyes he gingerly peeked through splayed fingers at his assumed attacker. Seeing it was Carl, he grinned sheepishly.

"You're late," Beau muttered, "Got better things to do than wait here all day for you, ya know."

Carl was ten minutes early. "Yeah, sorry about that, got hung up at work. Let's get in there and grab a table before the lunch rush hits." He'd been meeting with Beau every Tuesday and Friday for weeks. Swatting an invisible fly, Beau smiled as they entered Reggie's and the home-cooked smell flooded his nostrils. Walking over to what had become their usual spot, neither said a word. They sat and Carl opened a menu. Marc mimicked the move. A moment later Sue's voice interrupted the read-through of the days choices.

"Well boys, see anything that catches your eye?"

Before Carl could respond, Beau chirped up.

"Hot turkey sandwich, fries and gravy on the side," he said.

Carl set down the menu and looking from Beau, over to Sue, he shrugged. "Same for me I guess, please and thanks."

She turned on her heel and barked out the order. "Two turks, fries, side gravy."

Through the steam rising from the grill, Reggie simply nodded.

Carl stared at Beau, who in turn stared back. After a few seconds, Beau's brow furrowed.

"What? I got snot in my nose or something?"

Carl laughed, and then replied, "No you don't have anything in your nose. I have a question though."

"Okay, what?" Beau asked guardedly.

"We've been coming in here for a few weeks. Every time we meet, you pick up the menu, go through the whole thing, and then order a hot turkey sandwich."

"Yeah, so what about it?"

"I don't know, I was just wondering why." Carl asked.

Beau dropped his eyes and stared at the table for a minute. Looking up at Carl, he said, "Turkey reminds me of Christmas."

Chapter 25

Washington D.C. was magnetic, attracting a wide variety of sorts. There were the motivated females, long on looks, short on talent that buzzed in from all over the country. These sirens greatest ambition was to find and land a 'suit', the assumption being that a fellow wearing a suit in Washington, well—the possibilities were endless. Then of course there were the legitimately skilled gals. They'd come to the nation's capitol with all kinds of aspirations. Some were happy on the secretarial team while others reached for higher rungs of the ladder. The melting pot of males was just as varied. The over-educated and under-experienced flooded the job pool. The men hoped for anything from lobbyist positions to personal assistants for high-ranking executives. It seemed that everyone was ready to do a little ass-kissing or backstabbing, whatever it took to climb the political ladder. It all seemed very natural on the Hill. Carl found the predatory nature of it all a bit intriguing. He'd also found his first week on the job had been very interesting.

He'd never thought about it before, but the landslide of correspondence coming to and going from the big domed capitol, in itself, was fascinating.

'C,Y,A,' I guess. Cover Your Ass; written memos and records. Wonder how much stuff goes on here that there is NO trace of?' he'd thought idly while in training.

During his first week on the job, he'd casually asked his supervisor, "Sal, where is there a good spot to eat around here?"

"Well, the *best* place to eat would be my house. The Missus cooks better than any restaurant in the city," the big-bellied man stated proudly. He then slapped his stomach to emphasize the point. "I'm not sure about the eateries around here, Carl, the wife packs my lunch," he said, pointing to a brown paper bag.

Carl had suspected, that like in most cities, there would be some modest *greasy spoons* around. They usually offered little in the form of ambiance or atmosphere, but managed to draw the crowds with good home cooking and huge portions.

The next day, during the inspection ritual, he asked the one person he was sure would know all the great spots.

"Cynthia, where's good place to eat lunch around here? I'm looking for good food, nothing extravagant."

"Well, sugar, I like Reggie's over on Portage Avenue. Now understand, it's not near fancy. But the food is fine and the price is right. Reggie cooks, his wife Sue waits tables. Parking is free on the street," she said, eyeing him as if he were something good to eat. She told Carl on his second day that he reminded her of veal, young and tender. He'd laughed all day.

"Thanks, appreciate the tip. I'll check it out."

Carl quickly became a regular at Reggie's. By the second week he was frequenting the small, friendly spot for his lunch-hour ritual. Around the same time, he spotted a homeless man outside panhandling. One afternoon, he slipped the hobo a few bucks.

He entered the restaurant and moved to the old, arborite table surrounded by two heavy kitchen chairs. He took the same seat every day and it was quickly becoming his '*usual spot.'*

"Hi Carl, what'll it be today?" Sue asked in a friendly tone.

The aroma emanating from behind the long counter easily coaxed Carl's taste buds into overdrive. He suddenly felt famished. Looking between the patrons, he saw Reggie deftly filling the orders that kept this place packed at lunchtime.

"Hey Sue. What's Reggie making that's special today?"

"Well, he's—"" Sue was cut off in mid-sentence. The bum who'd been panhandling outside just minutes before was speaking.

"Sir," he said uneasily as his eyes stared downward, "you put a ten in my cup." He stood there, with a ten-dollar bill in his outstretched hand.

"Beau, I told you never to come in here. I don't want you bothering my customers. Sorry, Carl," she said as she began escorting him back out into the street.

"Whoa, Whoa, hold on a minute, Sue," Carl said confused.

"I'm not sure I understand. Beau? Is that your name?" he said addressing the edgy man.

"Yeah. You put a ten spot in my cup. Nobody puts a ten in on purpose. One dollar is the most. Maybe you thought it was a single. I didn't want you pissed off when you figured it out, so here," Beau said, shoving the ten toward him again.

"Very nice, Beau, just leave it on the table and GO," Sue said, gently pushing him towards the door.

Carl was intrigued by this poor man's sense of integrity.

"Wait, Beau, please sit, have lunch with me," he implored.

Carl saw the panicked look in the bum's eyes and thought he might run, but it faded and Beau looked toward Sue, his eyebrows slightly raised. Carl assumed he was awaiting her approval. Sue must have figured the same thing. Looking at Carl, she simply shrugged her shoulders.

"Sit down, Beau," she said, tolerating his presence in her little joint.

"Sue, give us a minute will ya? Thanks." Not waiting for her response, he turned his attention back to the bum. "No, I gave you the ten. I knew it was ten bucks. You looked like you could use it," Carl explained sincerely.

"I've been panhandling for over twenty-five years. Nobody ever gave me a ten. Not on purpose anyway," he replied, looking directly at the face of the generous young man for the first time.

Carl saw something in those sad, gray eyes, a flash of intelligence or perhaps regret of a life misspent. Whatever it was sparked his curiosity about the man's story.

"Well, let me buy you lunch, Beau. What do you feel like?"

Looking at the menu, he quickly inspected his choices. "I'll have a hot turkey sandwich with fries," Beau said timidly.

Calling Sue over, Carl mimicked the request, asking for two orders. During their first encounter, neither man said much. When the bill came, Carl instinctively went to pay it.

"I can pay for my own lunch, I've got ten bucks," Beau announced meekly.

"Alright, Beau. I'm curious, is there someplace you can go to get a bath or shower?" Carl asked.

Beau's brow knitted at the offensive question. He looked down at his dirty hands, which had spent the morning rummaging through garbage bins. His overgrown fingernails had a clearly visible rim of black dirt, and he instinctively tucked them under the table. "Yeah, I can go to the shelters. They'll let me take a shower there. Why?" he asked defensively.

"I come here at least twice a week. If you're here, I'll buy you lunch on one condition. You need to have a shower and show up clean."

"Now why would you want to buy me lunch twice a week?" Beau's voice was laced with suspicion.

"Because, I'm new in town and I don't like eating alone," Carl replied honestly.

"We'll see, we'll see," the vagrant replied. His eyes started darting wildly as he sought out his escape.

"Gotta go, gotta go now."

He quickly stood, abruptly exiting through the front door. A few seconds later, he re-entered the restaurant, walking directly to the table he had occupied only a minute ago.

"What day?"

Carl smiled, "Friday, twelve o'clock."

"Okay, just don't be late," he said without looking directly at Carl. As he exited the building for the second time, he stopped, looking back at the curious man. "Thanks," he shouted out. Beau Jangles forgot to pay for his lunch that day. Carl suspected there were many things in his life the strange man chose to forget. And that was how Carl Phoenix met the man they called Beau Jangles.

Slowly Beau became more at ease around Carl. Their association eventually developed into an awkward friendship. Beau shared his stories of the streets with him. Some days he talked incessantly and on others, he said very little.

During one of their earliest lunch dates, Carl's ongoing curiosity set the tone of conversation. "Beau, so what did you do for a living before, did you have a job?" His eyes were wide with childlike anticipation as he awaited the bedraggled recluse's response.

His strange lunch companion froze at the question. Staring intently at Carl, his mouth turned into a twisted snarl of teeth. "Hey pal, a free lunch doesn't give you the right to poke your nose into my business," he barked. Throwing down his fork, he stood up and stomped toward the door.

Stunned at his hostile response, Carl, too, rose, following Beau as he stormed out of the establishment.

"Hey, Beau, look I'm sorry. I was just curious, I didn't mean to pry," he called after him, as the man darted away.

Beau stopped dead in his tracks. With the agility of a panther, he had spun around and closed the distance between them in the blink of an eye. Carl's heart rate had instinctively bumped up to racing speed, as the adrenaline rushed in, sharpening his senses.

Poking an extended finger in Carl's chest, spittle flew from Beau's mouth as he snapped, "I appreciate the company and the food, but I'm no freak show. My life is my own damn business Ivy League. GOT IT?"

"Beau, look I'm sorry." Carl said shakily, but the hobo was gone.

Carl moved back into the restaurant, but was surprised at how unsteady he was. His appetite lost, he looked at the uneaten meal that had been Beau's. He was shook up by the sudden surge of anger that had swelled in the harmless bum. Suddenly, he felt guilty for his morbid curiosity, never considering Beau's story would most likely be an unpleasant rehashing of a heartbreaking fall from grace. Carl felt like one of those people who gathered around an accident scene, standing on tiptoes to look over the crowd, straining to get a glimpse of the carnage. He felt like hell. For the rest of the day he was down in the dumps, as he glumly went about his duties.

The recluse was a no-show for the next two weeks. Just when Carl had given up on seeing him again, there he was, standing at the table, clean as a whistle.

"Uhhmm…sorry Carl, about freaking out the other day. You still want some company?" he said weakly, staring at his well-worn sneakers. Carl looked up from his meal and a smile crossed his face.

"Sure, Beau, sit down. I'm the one who's sorry. You were right. It's none of my business. I shouldn't have pried."

Beau nodded in agreement, his eyes fixed on the table. He sat quietly, waiting for Sue to bring his hot turkey sandwich. By the end of the hour, a level of comfort had returned. As the two walked out of the diner, Beau stopped in front and turned toward Carl. "I don't like talking about the past. Didn't mean to be yelling at you, man. You're a good kid. Sorry. Just don't ask stuff about my old life, okay?" With the hatchet buried, the weekly lunch rendezvous resumed.

*****

Today, Beau's conversation went in a different direction.

"I didn't have to come for lunch ya know. Mabel over at the shelter wanted me to stay for soup when I went for my shower. They were having good soup today, verrry good CHICKEN soup."

Carl had become accustomed to Beau's ramblings. Often in the middle of a story about what he'd found in the garbage, or the location of his newest home, he became very coherent. He would use a word or a phrase that didn't seem to fit his vocabulary, or make an astute comment on current affairs.

"So why did you come?" Carl asked innocently enough.

Looking up from his plate, the etched lines on Beau's forehead deepened slightly.

"Having lunch with you makes me feel normal, like before," he said solemnly.

Carl looked up cautiously; after the last outburst he'd experienced with Beau over his "old life," he treaded lightly.

"Normal? What do you mean by '*normal*', Beau?"

"I used to have a normal life, shit head. I wasn't always a street bum. I had a car, an apartment and girlfriends, just like normal people..." he trailed off staring down at the table, his hand suspended in midair. As he summoned up his guarded memories his fork stopped moving, his meal ignored.

Carl, too, had stopped eating as he hung on, waiting for some revelation about his unique luncheon companion.

"I wasn't always like this. I had a job once, a real job, and a real bright future. I would have been rich too. Bastards. They took it all away. Took it all away, just like that," he said, snapping his fingers loudly. "BOOM! All gone." Beau's moist eyes were fixed on an invisible spot on the small square table as he spoke. "I was like you once. Young, good looking, nice place, money, everything."

An observer might have confused Beau's sadness for regret. Carl guessed regret played no role in his ill-fated friend's circumstance.

He also knew from previous experience that a question could end explosively, but still Carl dared to ask. This time it was Beau who had traveled down that road. "Beau, what happened in your other life?"

The question snapped Beau back to the moment, his trance broken by the sound of Carl's voice.

"Shit happened. Shit happens every day and some shit happened to me, that's all."

Carl was intrigued and wanted to know more about what had brought the jittery, old man to this point. He wondered how a person regressed from a life of work, home, people and situations to this? What catastrophic event could lead someone from a regular life to living on the street? Eating in restaurants to eating out of dumpsters and begging for change? He decided to drop it.

"Well, Beau, sorry to hear that. Must have been pretty bad shit. So do you feel like a piece of pie?" he asked casually.

"Carl, I feel relaxed around you. I have no idea why, but I trust you. Maybe I just need to tell someone a bit about the real person I am, or at least, used to be."

Wrestling with what he had just put out there, Beau spoke up again. "Yeah I'll have that piece of pie, and the name's Marc, Marc Andrews."

Carl sat staring, his mouth agape. Even though the name had no meaning for him, it was a real person's name, not a fabricated name of a song character. Snapping his mouth shut, he reached over, gripping his hand and said, "It's very nice to meet you, Marc Andrews."

Chapter 26

Minneapolis was a great town for Emily. For that matter, she seemed to have all the cities in the Midwest pretty much sewn up. A recent article, which appeared in the Chicago Herald, stated, "Miss Cantrell gets down and talks to her constituents on their level. No fast-talk, no double-talk, and we Midwesterners just love that."

Unaware of the pounding rain outside, Emily Cantrell casually walked toward the elevator. The secret service detachment was already positioned at the back of the glass-walled transporter. She'd just finished giving a campaign speech to two thousand supporters. As she proceeded down the hallway, the muffled applause emanating from the Residence Inn banquet room faded. Smiling as she waved, Emily embarked on the clear cylindrical tube that would whisk her to the seventeenth storey. The throng of press shadowing her since the beginning of the campaign disappeared as the elevator doors came together at a snail's pace. The instant the two halves became one, the mechanical device began its upward journey. Emily's hand immediately went to her right temple, her smile contorted to a pained grimace.

Spencer, the head of her secret service detail, caught the sudden change in Emily's expression in the reflective stainless steel doors. If a casting director were searching out the perfect look for a secret service agent, Spencer's would have been it. He was forty-seven years old and a former navy seal. Tall and well muscled, with a crop-top haircut, he was pleasant-looking in a vague and nondescript way. Other than the slight graying in his temples and a jagged scar over his left eyebrow, there was nothing terribly distinctive about him. Spencer blended into the background perfectly. "Are you feeling alright Miss Cantrell?" he asked dutifully.

"Yes, Spence, thanks, just a migraine," she responded. Emily's eyes closed as she massaged her temple with a circular motion.

The doors automatically opened as the elevator stopped at the seventeenth floor. She stared as each half mysteriously disappeared into its secret abyss. Momentarily fascinated by the doors and the pockets into which they slid, she hadn't noticed Jason standing there.

"Hi, honey, how did it—"" he said, stopping mid-sentence. He stiffened as he caught sight of her face. Her color was terrible. With a mix of concern and annoyance, he said "Another migraine?"

"No, Jason," Emily replied, weakly, "just a bit tired." From behind her, Spencer nodded once, confirming the assumption.

All four walked down the well-lit corridor, stopping at suite seventeen forty-four. Spencer swept the key card through the electronic lock. Jason then escorted his wife into the oversized foyer of the luxury suite. Spencer and the junior secret service man dutifully took up their stations at the small desk, just inside the door of the outer room. The couple continued into the main section of the temporary lodging. Closing the sound proof doors, Jason chastised her as she slowly lowered herself to the bed.

"Emily, I want you to cancel next week's appearances. You need to have some tests run," he said, annoyed.

"Jason, we've been through all this," she said. "I can't afford to lose the momentum we have going."

"Emily, I don't CARE about the momentum, or this campaign for that matter. What I do care about is your health," Jason replied firmly.

She opened her eyes and looked at her thin, fragile husband. His shiny head sported the few wispy strands of white hair that had not yet abandoned him. His cloudy, brown eyes had a look of worry in them, a concern which she was secretly beginning to share. Jason was a weak man. He had mothered the children more than she had. He'd been the family's caregiver and nurturer. She had been the career-driven provider. Emily's eyes watered as she looked through the haze of pain at her weak, wonderful Jason. She loved him for fretting over her. As long as he was alive, she'd never feel alone. Summoning her reserve of strength, she sat upright.

"Jason, you're a considerate, thoughtful man and I love you for it, but I'm fine, sweetheart. Headache's all gone. I feel much better." The pain wasn't gone and she did not feel well at all. Standing, she went to him, kissing him affectionately on the cheek. "No worries, Dear. When we get back to D.C., I'll have a complete physical. It'll be good for the campaign. My supporters will see what a picture of health I am," she teased.

Beaten, Jason conceded. "Alright, Emily, on your word, you will have a thorough check-up, blood tests, cat scan, the works. I mean it. I won't be taking 'no' for an answer when we get home," he said firmly.

She stood at attention and gave a mock salute. Placing her right hand over her heart, she raised her left and said, "Yes, sir, Scouts honor!"

Both did their best to make light of it. Emily managed a fake laugh as her head continued pounding, a millisecond after each heartbeat. Jason forced a counterfeit smile, not quite trusting her mock *scouts' honor.*

Looking over the rim of his glasses, he reaffirmed, "I mean it, young Missus."

They hugged with a familiarity, a comfort, which came from many years of friendship, sprinkled with genuine love.

"Gottcha," Emily agreed, once more. "Jason, I'm going to take a nap. Could you please pick me up the *Minneapolis Tribune and a Post,* from the lobby?"

"Okay, Hun, anything else?"

"No thanks. I just need to snooze a while, give me about an hour, okay?"

"Sure. I'm going to grab the kids a few souvenirs. You just get some rest. I'll see you later."

Jason vacated the sprawling suite just as Emily entered the powder room. She briefly heard the muffled voices as Jason spoke to the secret service detail on his way out. When the second door banged shut, it confirmed he'd left the apartment. Emily began frantically searching the medicine cabinet, pulling several pill bottles onto the vanity. The tears streaming down her face were not generated by feelings of love or appreciation. They were the result of the excruciating pain emanating from behind her eyes. She found them, the migraine tablets her doctor had prescribed before they left D.C. Unsteadily, she spilled several into her hand,

and then popped them into her mouth. Wrapping her lips around the sink's waterspout she took a shallow drink then threw her head back.

The headaches had become more frequent lately. Emily had tried to rationalize their increasing occurrence. *It's likely the stress, menopause, or lack of sleep,* she'd thought. Any or all of these conditions singularly or combined could have been the culprit. Over the next half hour, Emily felt the headache slowly ebb.

St. Paul's tomorrow, Duluth Tuesday, and then the Dakotas. I'll be home in a week, she thought, lying there. Resolving to stay true to her word, she'd have a few tests run when they got home to Washington D.C. She *would* take advantage of the clean bill of health. Assuming that it was a clean bill.

As Emily drifted off to sleep, she hoped the constant throbbing pain was the result of her hectic schedule. In the midst of a short prayer she succumbed to her catnap.

*****

Carl sat. He'd been stuck in the same spot for fifteen minutes. A traffic jam had brought work to a screeching halt. Congestion was not uncommon for this time of day in Washington, but a total standstill was. As he waited, his patience thinned. Seeing drivers ahead of him standing beside their cars, he jumped out to investigate. He approached two young guys who were sitting on the hood of their car. "Hey, fella's. Any idea what the hold-up is?" he asked.

"Yeah, trucker up there said it's an accident. Says we're going to be bottlenecked here for at least an hour."

"Thanks, guys," Carl said, walking back to his vehicle. He killed the engine, turning the key to auxiliary power. Carl turned up the radio that was preset to a g*olden oldies* station. Growing up, his father had been a patron of the upbeat 50's and 60's music. He too had become a fan of the lively tunes and just then the Righteous Brothers were churning out their ballad, "Unchained Melody." Suddenly remembering a half-read paper, Carl scoured the car. After a brief search in the front and back seats, he gave up. *Ah, guess I took it out. Can't remember doing it.* He scratched his head trying to recall when he removed the paper.

He was bored after ten minutes of sitting, doing nothing but waiting. Not able to back up or go forward, he looked at the bundle of dispatches on the seat beside him.

What the hell, let's see what's so damned important anyway, he thought, mischievously.

He grabbed up the manila envelope sitting on the top of the pile. A sticker boldly proclaimed, **'TOP SECRET'** in red letters. He casually untwisted the small string, tightly wrapped around the fastener.

"Hmmm let's just see what's so top secret. T**O: J.R. Wright.** Don't know him... **FROM: Calvin Warren**." He mumbled in the empty car. *That* name he did recognize. Calvin Warren was a lobbyist for gas and oil and was a very powerful person on Capitol Hill.

Carefully pulling the contents from the envelope, he saw several blank pages. *So what's this, invisible ink?* He thought, grinning.

Flipping through the blank pages, he came across one with a hand written note on it. He fished it out carefully, noting its exact position in the pile. Looking straight ahead, then side to side, he was satisfied that no one could be spying on him. Realizing his actions were an indictable offence, he felt a twinge of fear...or was it excitement? Casually glancing over the note, it occurred to him that Calvin Warren's handwriting was horrible. Carefully examining the memo, he could barely make out the words: "*Chelsea, can't meet you tonight. Betty's been checking up on me. Will have to make it next week, Tuesday 3 P.M., usual room. Sorry, miss you."* A fanciful 'C' was the only signature. "Oh My God! I'm delivering *love notes,*" Carl breathed out.

It took a couple of seconds for the initial surprise to wear off. Carl was under the impression that everything he took back and forth was imperative to national security. He just assumed that all correspondence somehow related to the running of the government. It had never occurred to him that officials would use this secure, private, specialized service for personal reasons. He grinned as a wave of embarrassment flooded over him at his own naivety.

Carl spent the next twenty minutes looking at other documents. All but two were of an official nature. One was a request for a secretary to pick up a gift for some technician's nine year-old son (the memo mentioned this was *his* weekend with the boy). The other asked for the name of a good caterer for a house party. Carl read each memo and file, carefully placing everything back as it had been. He was halfway through the pile when a car horn blasted, surprising him back to the moment. *"Shit,"* he blurted loudly, startled by the sudden racket.

He instinctively looked in his rearview at the annoyed guy who was blowing his horn. Dropping his eyes he saw that the vehicles ahead had begun moving. Flustered, he started his car. It lurched forward as he engaged it into drive. The last file was strewn carelessly beside him. At the first red light, he gingerly put the papers back in their manila envelope and wrapped the string around the button that held the contents in place.

Twenty minutes later, he was standing in front of a busty, gum-chewing young woman. He saw the name plaque on her desk. It read *Chelsea*. Smiling, he handed her the folder with its 'TOP SECRET' warning clearly indicating the delicacy of the enclosed message. "Here you go, ma'am. I need a signature right here, please." Carl said, grinning as he helpfully indicated where to sign.

She shot him a warm and friendly look as she made her mark on the electronic tablet.

"Chelsea, you have yourself a wonderful day!" he said. Leaving the front office, he chuckled, knowing the secret about to be unveiled to the young tart. For a moment he wondered if she would be disappointed or relieved about the rescheduled, adulterous rendezvous.

Remembering his own tryst with Sarah, he casually looked down at his Rolex, a gift from the senator on his twenty-first birthday. *Dammit, nothing I can do about it. I'm going to be late. Friggin' accident.* Suddenly feeling rushed he picked up his pace.

*****

Across town in the open foyer of his home, Congressman Monroe was also noticing the time. "Sarah, where are you?" Edward shouted through the vast expanse of the house.

"I'm up here, Ed," she called back, stepping out of the bath.

"I'm getting ready to leave," Edward hollered. "Could you please come downstairs?"

Her hair wrapped in a towel, Sarah reached for her husband's housecoat. Edward watched her as she came down the stairs, donning his oversized bathrobe.

Looking at him, looking at her, Sarah was taken aback. The expression he wore had clearly changed over the years. She sensed his lack of desire and was oddly offended by it. Ten years ago, he would have yanked the robe open and taken her right in the foyer. His disinterested glare made the ritualistic departure a mockery. '*Kiss-kiss, hug-hug, have fun and fuck you very much...*' She smirked at the silent witticism. The hushed giggle from the unshared quip was short-lived as she remembered; tonight he would have his mistress.

"Just wanted to say bye, sweetie. I did mention that I was flying off to George's for golf, right?" he reaffirmed.

Golf my ass, Sarah thought, annoyed that he would even bother to lie. "Yes, Ed, I recall. Do say hi to George for me." *Might as well join in the charade,* she thought indifferently.

"Will do. If you need me, just call my cell. My phone will be off, but I'll be checking messages. The damn thing is so annoying when I'm trying to hit my balls," he said, grinning at the unintentional quip.

I'll hit your balls all right, she thought, sarcastically. The disenchanted look on his face made it obvious to her he hated this part almost as much as she did. *We're both drowning in all this bullshit.*

It wasn't as if she were jealous, she just felt that Edward's feeble attempts to deceive her were, well…insulting. Had she really cared about the marriage, his lies would have been as transparent as freshly-cleaned glass.

"Okay, if I need you, I'll leave a message," she said indifferently.

With a small overnight bag in hand, Edward pecked her cheek, and topped it off with "cheers" as he disappeared out the front door.

*****

She listened for the fading sound of his car engine before entering the garage. Sarah gingerly opened the storage closet where Edward kept his stuff. There they were, staring mockingly back at her, Ed's golf clubs. Smiling weakly, she recalled how they'd both laughed when he had come home with the silly knitted head covers. Each one was a different animated animal. There was the horse, a cow, the ostrich (that was her favorite), and more. Edward had picked them up while on a business trip and when he had unveiled them, they'd both roared with laughter. He'd bounced the clubs around and with a silly voice, imitated each animal represented. They had been happy then. Sadly, she closed the door as the round, plastic eyes witnessed Sarah's final acceptance of the withered union. He was off to meet his mistress, and she was anticipating a night with her young lover.

In the empty garage, she accepted the fact that the marriage was over. Dead and buried, now all that remained was to write the obituary. She would give Edward's career one more year, before publicly severing their ties. Twenty years ago, neither of them had much. No prenuptial agreements or marriage contracts existed. A divorce would be very cut-and-dried. They would split the assets down the middle and Sarah suspected she would receive monthly support payments. Financially, she would be fine.

A little surprised at how indifferent she felt by her expired partnership, Sarah proficiently applied her eyeliner. Glancing at the mother-of-pearl clock face on her make-up vanity, she saw that Carl would arrive within the hour. She unexpectedly shivered as a lewd smiled crossed her lips.

Chapter 27

It was a beautiful evening for a walk, as Carl began the trek to Sarah's. He'd parked his car inconspicuously on a side street two blocks away. As Edward's out of town trips had become more frequent lately, the Monroe home seemed to be the safest place for their encounters. Initially, Carl had been uneasy about such bold recklessness. He had succumbed to Sarah's reassurances about her spouse's lack of enthusiasm regarding the marriage. That, and the fact that Edward never cut short his trips abroad alleviated Carl's misgivings about the affair being exposed. He didn't notice the dark sedan slowly crawling behind him as he approached the congressman's house, nor earlier, that a man reading an open newspaper at Reggie's never once looked down at the page. He also missed the flickering light of the video recording device in the dark shadows beside the Monroe home, as he drew near. Someone was watching.

Today, as he casually strolled, all he thought about was the pleasures that would soon be his.

*****

Two hours later, Sarah was soaked with sweat. It was not entirely the product of the intense lovemaking, some of that, but mostly, nervous tension. *This is a good time to tell him. He needs to know how I feel,* she concluded, as he slowly slipped off her body.

"Carl," she began, her voice laced with trepidation, "we need to talk." She sat upright, pulling her knees to her naked breasts, her arms wrapped around them.

"Sure, what do you want to talk about?" he asked unsuspectingly.

"Carl, do you have any idea how I feel about you?"

"I don't know," he responded uneasily. "I guess the same way I feel about you."

"And how do you feel about me?"

The sudden look of bewilderment on his face confirmed her hunch. She'd ambushed him. Some part of her wanted that. Without preparation she was certain that the truth would surface.

“Well, ummm, I enjoy the time we spend together.” There was a pause, and Sarah saw he was already reaching, scrambling.

“I like your company. I like being with you. Actually, it's the best part of my life, lately,” he answered carefully.

She felt hope. *What if he's just saying what I want him to say, but not really feeling what I want him to feel*?

“Are you saying you love me?” Sarah watched Carl's face for a sign, wishing...

“NO. I'm not saying that I love you, Sarah. I have very strong feelings for you. Honestly, I’m not sure I even know what love is,” he said, shocked at the sudden cross-examination.

Her annoyance surfaced without warning, surprising even her. “You mean you enjoy *fucking* me,” she snapped.

His face contorted at the assault, and she saw the startled look in his eyes. “Carl, I didn’t mean that,” she said trying to recover. It was, of course, too late to unsay the words that were already out there.

“What do you want me to say Sarah?" Carl finally responded. His voice was strained. "Yes, of course I like the sex. It is, after all, the foundation of this relationship,” he lashed back.

“Is that what you think? Is that our ‘foundation,’ our touchstone? So, what we have is sex, nothing else?” she retaliated. His response had stung.

“That’s not what I meant.”

Stop! You're going to lose him, STOP! Her heart screamed. But her mouth kept moving, somehow producing the words before she could form the thought. Again she heard herself speak, and with each syllable, she felt him pull away.

“Carl, I've decided to leave Edward. I need to know where this is going." Summoning up the last of her courage, she continued, putting it all on the table. "I want to know if we have a future.” The play was made and her lover’s look of panic told her she'd rolled snake eyes.

“Sarah, I…I don’t know what to say.”

"Carl, I need to know." *I already know. I've lost,* she silently acknowledged.

"Don't cry, Sarah, c'mon." As he spoke he reached out in an effort to comfort her. She recoiled from his touch.

"You just popped this on me. I really need to think about everything. When did you leave Edward? Are you sure it's what you want?" he asked, the alarm evident in his voice.

"Carl, if you felt the way I do about you, you wouldn't need time to think, you'd already know. I think you do know," she said as the hot tears streamed down her beautiful white skin. *I've lost. What did I expect? I should have kept quiet. Now it's over. Why? Why did I have to push?*

"I should go," was all he managed to say. Her face reflected the agony of the abrupt shift in the relationship.

Like Adam in the Garden of Eden, Carl became aware of his nakedness. He covered himself in what had become an uncomfortable awkwardness and reached for his clothes.

"I'm not really sure what to say, but I don't want to lie to you, Sarah. I have a lot to think about. There's my father's career, our age difference, and the fact that I'm not ready to make a commitment."

There it is, the age difference. What was I thinking! I'm the older woman, she thought mortified. *I'm his Mrs. Robinson. I SEDUCED HIM! God, I was driving a car before he was born. I'm so stupid.* She chastised herself. Regaining her composure, she too noticed her nudity. Pulling up the sheet, she covered her breasts and calmly responded, "Yes, Carl, perhaps you should go. I'm sorry I made you uncomfortable. I'm very sorry to have put you on the spot. You don't have to answer my questions. Not out loud. I do understand."

"I'm really sorry. I didn't mean to hurt you. Are you going to be alright?" he implored sincerely.

"You didn't, Carl. I've done this to myself. Just go. I'll be fine." *I should have left well enough alone, stupid, stupid, stupid.*

"I'm sorry, Sarah."

*****

As he drove to the apartment, the glow of the dash lights painted a ghost-like mask over his face as he rehashed the evening.

What else could I have done? I can't say I love her. I don't even know what love really is. I'm such an ass. I should have never started this affair. What an idiot. Where was it supposed to go? Damn, I do like her. I do want to be with her, but she's so much older than me. What would people say? What would dad say? Jesus what would the papers say? NO. I have enough problems.

*****

The crickets chirped, singing their familiar chant outside the open window. Sarah lay alone on the bed in the pitch-black. With her tears now dried, the noisy insects and heartache were her only companions. *Why did I push it? What did I expect him to do? Marry me? But I love him. I really do love him.*

As she stood, the satin sheet effortlessly floated over her body and fell silently to the floor. Walking to the full-length mirror, her hands slowly slid down over her breasts, to her stomach, hips, and stopped at her thighs. She stared at what attracted men. *This is what they see, what they want, all that they seem to want,* she decided. Without blinking she gazed at her reflection.

W*hat happens when it's gone, old, withered? What's left? What will they want then?* She thought morosely.

In the murkiness of her mind, she imagined Edward's face looking back at her in the reflective surface of the glass, *Yes I know what they want then, the same, just from someone else.*

Staring at the image in the mirror, her eyes trance-like, Sarah understood. She would never win. Not with Edward, not with Carl, not with anyone, not ever. It would never be right.

*****

As Carl lay in his bed he tried to put the whole uncomfortable evening out of his mind. *What could I have done? I just couldn't lie to her.*

Trying to ease his guilty feelings, he told himself that it was for the best. Carl had decided that if he wasn't around to distract Sarah, she could focus on her marriage with Edward. Maybe then the congressman would have a better chance at fixing what was wrong in their relationship. He knew he was grasping at straws. He rationalized as best he could, that everything would work out just fine. Sure that sleep would be elusive, Carl drifted into a dreamless slumber.

*****

The only sound was the ice crackling as Sarah filled the large glass for a second time. With the scotch bottle in one hand, her glass in the other, she slowly climbed the long winding staircase. Moments later, steam rose from the tub.

This feels so good, so hot, I want to feel good, clean, she thought, as her entire body lay submerged under the water. After a while the hot water had turned tepid and the full scotch glass had become empty. She stepped out of the marble tub. Casually drying herself, she dropped the damp towel into the bin. A few minutes later she again stood at the bar. For the third time that evening she carefully balanced the scotch bottle over the goblet. Methodically, Sarah again refilled the empty glass and then moved listlessly to Edwards's office. She sank comfortably into the overstuffed chair and mused, *I don't think I've ever sat here before. No wonder Ed spends so much time in here.*

The cool, soft leather caressed her naked body as she opened the top desk drawer.

Sarah smiled as she thought of Carl. She easily recalled how he had desired her earlier that evening. Her smile slowly evaporated as she reminisced about the days when Edward's hands and body had desired her too.

It will never be right, never ever, she thought wrapping her fingers around the cool smooth object.

The sound of the explosion didn't reached Sarah's ears. The hammer succinctly, instantly connecting with the .45 shell propelled the bullet through the roof of her mouth, leaving in its wake a large gaping hole at the back of her head. Bits and pieces of what had been a functioning, thinking brain just a millisecond before, were splattered on the wall behind the soft leather chair. Sarah didn't feel the neck-breaking snap as her head flew back, then slowly fell forward on the rich mahogany desk.

Perhaps it was her intention to let the handful of sleeping pills that she had washed down with the scotch eventually take effect. Or maybe Sarah had decided in those last seconds on ultimate shock value. Most probably it was the combination of her inebriated state and a hair trigger that resulted in the gun discharging. No one would ever know why she took a lethal dose of pills and then put a loaded gun in her mouth. Sarah never felt the single tear run down her cheek as it fell, converging, with the newly formed puddle of blood. Her lifeless emerald-green eyes, instantly dilated, stared peacefully at nothing.

*****

Carl lay in a different darkness, glaring up at a ceiling he couldn't see. The peaceful sleep had abandoned him as he re-thought the evening. *I can't leave it like this. I'll call her in the morning and talk. It shouldn't have ended like this. I'll call.*

Chapter 28

Eric Brunner tapped the pen on his appointment book. He was waiting for the scheduled meeting with his top soldier. Eric stared at the door, his eyes glazed as he recalled their first mission together. It had been over a dozen years before, but the images were locked securely in his memory. He opened the vault where they lay hidden, remembering his first glimpse of Kenichi Nakamura's sadistic blood lust.

It was a warm summer evening and the sun had dropped below the horizon just an hour before. Eric discreetly parked his car outside the abandoned warehouse in the west end of town. It was the *Dallas, Texas* version of Chicago's south side, rough, with lots of dilapidated abandoned buildings. He quietly weaved through the corridors and then down to the murky basement. It wasn't the first time this building had been used for such work. The assignment was a simple one. Exterminate a recognized terrorist organizer named Emil Jazard. It was confirmed that he had orchestrated at least eight bombings in Europe. Responsible for hundreds of deaths and many injured, he'd been on Interpol's most-wanted list for six years. The Patronums couldn't have cared less, that was, not until Jazard stepped foot on American soil. Their Intel confirmed that he was here to organize a terrorist attack within the United States.

"Should have stayed home Emil," Eric said under his breath as he proceeded down the last of the steps.

Soundlessly, he'd pushed open the large, steel door as he walked in on Kenichi Nakamura. He was in the final stages of the mission.

"My god in heaven! WHAT IN THE HELL, ARE YOU DOING?" Eric exclaimed, trying to make sense of the carnage.

Nakamura slowly looked up from the bloody mass. Lying in a pool of blood was the terrorist. The man was unrecognizable. His nose, ears, and both hands, were neatly arranged on a bench beside Nakamura. There was also a lump of bloodied flesh that Eric assumed was the man's tongue. His eyelids were closed, slightly sunken, and a trail of blood flowed from were his eyes should have been. Eric shivered, realizing the eyeballs where not in the inventory of bloodied tissue. Jazard suddenly stirred and emitted a gargled moan.

"You TWISTED FREAK," Eric screamed, pushing past Nakamura. Pulling his revolver, he pumped three rounds into what was left of the terrorist's head. Eric was the senior man, and had sent Nakamura on to see if he could extract any information before terminating the mark. The tall, lean Asian warily stood up. In his right hand the bloodied knife still clung to small pieces of fleshy matter. As he fixed his stare on Eric, the hand holding the knife flinched ever so slightly.

"Don't even think about it," Eric said firmly, as he swung the smoking gun around, shoving it in the Asian's face.

"I'm sorry you are displeased, sir," Nakamura responded calmly, as he bowed.

"JUST CLEAN THIS GODDAM MESS UP," Eric hollered.

He needed air. The stench from Nakamura's sadistic license made him queasy. The incident had taken place just weeks before Bruce Vargo had died.

Eric Brunner never completely understood his mentor's choice. Two years after his own induction into the Patronums, Bruce had recruited Kenichi Nakamura. Eric had an uneasy feeling then, about the Asian American. Although his mentor had been dead for over ten years, their last conversation regarding Nakamura was vivid.

"Bruce this guy's a butcher. Why is he here?" Eric asked.

"Because he's dependable. He gets the job done, no matter what. Sometimes we need that sort of unfaltering commitment."

"Are you losing confidence in my ability, Bruce?"

It was then that Bruce finally confirmed what Eric had guessed for years. "I've always had faith in you. You've been like a son to me. You will be my replacement on the committee. I know that you don't care for Nakamura, but you'll need a second in command and I think he's it. Son, I too find his methods sometimes distasteful, but always effective. Our position sometimes requires that kind of brutality. And if there is chink in your armor, my boy, that's it. You need a second who can be ferocious."

He loathed Nakamura and his methods, but knew that his mentor was right. Eric did not have the stomach or viciousness for some of the assignments.

It was to be one of their last conversations, as time had finally caught up to the mighty oak. Less than a week later Bruce Vargo was gone. The Patronums head of the intelligence and security division had died peacefully in his sleep. He'd been eighty-one years old. Having cared about no one else, he had left all worldly possessions to his replacement and surrogate son. Eric was only forty-five years old when Bruce died, making him the youngest member to ever be assigned a committee seat.

Still staring ahead, the sharp rap on the door broke his gaze, ending the unpleasant reminiscence.

"Come in," he barked out.

The door whisked open and now, over a decade later, Kenichi Nakamura stood in the modest downtown office of the intelligence and security chief. Eric still detested the callous assassin that his old mentor had saddled him with. After a brief review of the file he'd given Nakamura, Eric reaffirmed, "Ken, I need you to stay focused on the job at hand. Please don't deviate. Do the job as outlined in the file. Do you understand?"

Nakamura bowed from the waist, never taking his eyes off Eric.

"Yes, I understand Sensei," he replied.

As his number one stood smiling, Eric felt a shiver run down his spine. He swore he could feel the hatred emanating off the man.

*****

Nakamura despised all pure, white bloods and referred to them with the Japanese slang, Gai-jin. The vernacular translated to *foreigner*. Being half-white didn't seem to dilute the extreme loathing he felt for Caucasians. Clinically he was a sociopath. Nakamura was exceptionally dangerous and like the most infamous serial killers of all time, he *fit in*. He had a special hatred for Eric, often imagining how he would kill him.

He coveted the position of strength and leadership and felt that Brunner was weak and had no stomach for killing. What he detested most about Eric was the fact he, too, would choose his successor some day, just like Vargo had. Nakamura had assumed that *he* would be the chosen one when Vargo died. He alone possessed the iron will necessary for the position. It was the only reason he had *'helped'* Vargo into nirvana, or where ever it was that dead, old assassins went. Against his better judgment, he'd granted the old man a peaceful, painless death. If he'd suspected for a second that the old fool was going to bypass him, his death would have been very different. Nakamura knew that Brunner would not pass the torch to him either. He wanted nothing more than to be the master of life and death, for the Patronums.

"Sensei, is there anything else?"

"No, Ken, thank-you. That is all."

Nakamura bowed again, Eric nodded his head, without rising from behind his desk.

Infidel shows no respect. Some day, you will pay. Nakamura thought venomously, as he backed out of the office.

His blood-lust rose after his exchange with Brunner. One hour later he was on Harry Hines, between Walnut Creek and Route 635. The stretch of road was a mecca for hookers in Dallas. Due to a recent crackdown by law enforcement, they hustled out of their cars. The working girls would drive up alongside a car while *'advertising.'* He'd been trolling for only fifteen minutes when he got a bite. A gray, compact sized car pulled up beside him at a red light. The passenger-side window rolled down as the pretty young blonde yelled out, "Hey, handsome, want a date?"

"Yes, yes, I do," he said, as a disarming smile stretched across his face.

"Follow me, sweetie."

The light changed from red to green. The car quickly accelerated as a puff of blue smoke exited the small exhaust pipe. Nakamura's vehicle fell in behind her instantly. Minutes later the two cars were stopped in an abandoned parking lot.

The twenty-something prostitute, talking to him through his open window asked, "Well, handsome, what'll it be?"

"How much do you charge?" he asked, concluding the sentence in his mind with, *you filthy whore.*

"Well, it depends, stud, what's your pleasure?"

Resting her arms on the car, she leaned in, her face inches from his, candidly admiring his sharp, handsome features.

"The whole works. I want to take you home and do everything. How much will it cost for the entire night?" *I will take my time with you slut. I'll enjoy every inch of your body.*

"The whole night with anything you can think of, stud, will cost you five hundred dollars. Oh, and handsome, the name's Kelly."

"Kelly. That's a beautiful name for very a beautiful girl. Five hundred dollars, done, leave your car here, please." Nakamura pasted a warm, inviting smile on his hard face.

"Uhhh, I don't really want to leave my car here. It'll be stolen or full of condoms by morning," she half joked.

"Kelly, my dear, can we drop it off someplace safe? You know, neighbors, very nosey. I don't want to do any explaining. I'll throw in an extra hundred."

"Sure. Hmmm, we're going to have a wonderful time, handsome. Trust me. I'll make it very special for you tonight."

Leaning into the car, she pressed her lips hard against his. Her tongue darted and swirled as she pushed inside his mouth. Breaking the kiss she began walking toward her car, then turned and said, "I'm right behind you, lover. Don't loose me!"

"Oh, I won't, sweet Kelly, I won't," he replied as he rolled up the window. "You rotting whore. You'll pay for that," he said venomously, as he pulled away. Driving ahead of her Acura, he frantically wiped her salvia from his lips.

Thirty minutes later, as he inserted the key into the door lock, Kelly rubbed her body against his back. He could feel the bile in his throat rise.

"Wait, sweet Kelly. There'll be plenty of time for that. Tonight will feel like… *forever* for you, I promise."

"What's your name, stud?"

"Ken, actually Kenichi Nakamura."

"AWESOME name. Are you Chinese?" she said excitedly.

He felt the hair on the back of his neck bristle. W*e all look the same, don't we, you stupid whore.* "No, I'm half Japanese, half American," he replied.

She slowly traced her fingers from the outside corner of his eye down to his lips. In a soft voice, she said, "Ken, we should take care of the business end of things right now. All together, it'll be seven hundred and fifty dollars, please." She extended her tiny hand, palm up.

His head tilted slightly as he raised an eyebrow. *Slut, five hundred and a hundred extra makes six. What's the difference? I'll start by cutting her pretty little fingers off one at a time.* Staring at her small-outstretched hand, he smiled at the prospect.

As the fantasy unraveled in his mind's eye, he pulled the wallet from his hip pocket. Counting out a thousand dollars, he handed her the ten crisp, one hundred dollar bills.

"I've added your tip, my pretty Kelly. I'm sure you'll provide just what I need tonight."

With her mouth agape, she took the cash.

"Ken, you're so generous. I PROMISE, I'll make this a night you'll never, ever forget. Baby, can you get me drink, please? Anything with alcohol will do."

"Certainly, young Kelly, How about a whiskey on the rocks?"

"That would be great, thanks."

Exiting the small living room, Nakamura rounded a corner and went into the kitchen to mix drinks. *This won't help the pain, sweet girl, but it will thin the blood,* he thought smiling. He made the drinks as he schemed. *I'll cut off her fingers first, the lips next, yes, and the foul tongue. Then her firm young breasts, I will... what the...* With her drink in hand, he ran into the next room, just in time to see Kelly re-entering the house through the front door.

"What the hell! WERE YOU TRYING TO RUN OUT ON ME?" Nakamura shouted angrily, as he banged the glass down.

"Oh, no, baby, NO, of course not. I just gave the cash to my driver." Kelly rushed to him. With the skill of a seasoned professional, she seductively palmed his chest while opening his shirt. The stern set of his jaw made it clear he was furious.

"Baby, I'm sorry, I should've mentioned my driver. He followed us, and he collects for me. That way, he knows where to pick me up in the morning. Don't be mad, baby, I want you," she said, trying desperately to reassure him of her intentions.

Nakamura firmly took hold of her wrists, squeezing as he pulled her hands off his chest.

"You had someone follow us HERE?" he asked incredulously.

"OUCH, owwww, THAT HURTS, Ken, easy will you?" she said, yanking her wrists free from his iron grip. "Yeah, I had my driver follow us. It's the procedure, man. Do you think I get in cars with strangers and nobody knows where I am? Are you NUTS?"

"Who's your driver?" he demanded through clenched teeth. *Show restraint, control yourself, tonight can still be special* he thought.

"It doesn't matter who he is, Ken. We'll still have a good time, I promise."

"WHO IS HE?" he shouted.

"Okay, but it doesn't matter, Hun. His name's Jimmy, he's my husband. But Jimmy's cool with everything, don't worry, he loves my job. He doesn't have a jealous bone in his body. As a matter of fact, when I went out to take him the money, he told me that, for three grand, you could keep me for a week. He insisted that I do everything I could to please you. So you see, everything is cool, believe me," she said reassuringly.

He glared at her with a chilling gaze that made goose bumps jump to her arms. The sight of the raised skin caught his eye, and in that, he got a small thrill.

He weighed the risks. He knew that a random driver with one thousand dollars might not report a missing hooker to the police. A spouse was too risky. *Men pimping their wives out! This country needs help, MY HELP.*

"Get out whore...leave, leave, LEAVE NOW!" he hissed.

Without a word, Kelly scrambled for her purse, never taking her eyes off Nakamura. She escaped the house backward, turning the doorknob with her shoulders pressed tightly against the door. Clumsily she opened it, backing into the cool, night air.

*****

Jesus, that prick was going to beat the hell out of me, Kelly thought, running down the short sidewalk to the street.

"That's it, I'm getting into an escort gig first thing tomorrow. I've had it with these freaks and freezing my ass off. In-calls are a lot goddamn safer too," Kelly, babbled, as she quickly distanced herself from the house. Every few steps she looked back over her shoulder, praying he wasn't following her.

Several blocks later, she pulled out her cell. On the first ring, her husband's voice rang out, "You got Jimmy, SPEAK."

"Baby, it's me. I need a pick-up. I'm on Fifth and Elm. You are *not* going to believe what just happened. I'll tell you when you pick me up. Love you too, bye." Snapping her phone closed, she thought about Nakamura. *Slant-eyed bastard would've hurt me.* She shivered, unsure if it was the cool night air, or the thought of his cold, black eyes boring into her as she escaped.

*****

At the same moment that Kelly was rambling to Jimmy about what she thought would be a beating, Kenichi Nakamura lay in bed masturbating. With his eyes closed, he vividly imagined the pleasures that had almost been his. The slut Kelly, her dead, blue eyes glazed over, staring at him as her breast-less chest bled. Her teeth are a perpetual grin without the camouflage of lips to conceal them. He shuddered as he erupted.

A short while later he was sleeping, and he dreamt of Brunner. In the dream, Eric sat on the floor in a dark, cold place. His mouth agape, his remaining eye bulged, staring, as Nakamura fastidiously pulled out his intestines. A smile spread across Kenichi Nakamura's sleeping face. He looked at peace.

Chapter 29

Somehow, the sounds outside just weren't as distinct as they'd been a few days before. The sun, too, had lost some of its luster. The air seemed thicker and a little less breathable today. An incessant horn-blast on the street barely caught Carl's attention as he jerked opened the wood-framed screen door of the diner. He wandered toward his usual spot and then dropped into the chair with a thump. An old-timer who was hunkered over a coffee had just finished ordering. Sue moved toward Carl's table as she belted out the soup and sandwich request to Reggie.

"Got it," Reggie confirmed. The hash-slinger moved like a master, seldom looking up from the sizzling grill.

"Hey, Carl, how are you today?" she asked cheerfully.

Glancing up from her pad she looked at him. Her brow crinkled as the smile slid off her face. "You look terrible. Are you okay?" she asked, a little concerned.

He stared blankly at her, as if her words hadn't quite registered. Carl's hair was a mess and his clothes looked wrinkled. He had dark circles under his eyes. All were telltale signs of a rough night.

"Ahhh, just didn't get much sleep, Sue, but I'm fine, a bit tired is all," he answered feigning a grin.

"Okay, Hun, what'll ya have?"

"I don't know. How about some liver and onions? I could use the iron," he said with a shrug.

"Sure, sweetie."

Turning, she shouted out, "Liver and onions, Reg."

Through the steam, she heard him respond, "Got it!"

Sue's maternal look evaporated and was replaced by a shrewd smirk. Carl caught it out of the corner of his eye. It was a mischievous look that said, '*I know* what YOU did last night.' A smirk crossed his face as he fleetingly thought how far off the mark she was, if she was thinking '*sex*'.

A minute later Sue was back with a cold glass of water. Setting it down in front of him, she dashed off to the next table. He gazed intently at the growing puddle forming at the base as beads of sweat ran down the outside of the glass.

A sudden voice startled him out of his self-induced spell. "Hey, man, you're early!" Marc commented.

"Oh, yeah, hi there."

Carl had forgotten the regular Tuesday lunch meeting and he really wasn't in the mood for 'crazy'.

Marc sat, taking his place across from his young friend. It took him a minute to see that Carl wasn't himself.

"What's wrong, kid?" Marc asked, his voice sandwiched somewhere between concern and fear.

Marc's head instinctively turned side to side, apparently checking for signs of possible danger.

Firmly clasping down on his forearm he repeated, "Carl, what's the matter?"

"I just didn't get much sleep last night, is all."

"Yeah, no kidding. I know you didn't get any sleep. You look like shit. So what's up?" Marc repeated.

After a momentary pause Carl answered. "A friend of mine died. I just found out yesterday."

"Oh, I'm sorry, was he a good buddy?"

"Actually, it was a woman. We were kind of seeing each other."

"Wow, that *really* sucks," Marc, offered in condolence.

"Yes. Yes it does. She was a great woman."

"What happened?"

Carl suspected that he asked more because it was the polite thing to do, rather than out of any real interest or concern.

"She committed suicide," he replied, surprised that he was sharing details of the tragedy with his homeless lunch partner.

"Hey, like I said before, Carl, shit happens. It's not your fault."

The look on Carl's face made it obvious; the furrowed brow and hard-set expression indicated that he *did* feel it was somehow his fault.

*****

Rumors of Sarah Monroe's death were floating all over the Capitol first thing Monday.

When he had arrived at work early that morning, he suffered the first taste of the gossip from his supervisor.

"Good morning, Carl."

"Hey, Sal, how's it going?"

Carl had been tired yesterday morning. He wasn't able to reach Sarah over the weekend, and he'd slept poorly as a result. He was still upset about the way things had ended Friday night.

"Shame about Congressman Monroe's wife, don't you think?" Sal said in a hushed voice. Carl stopped dead in his tracks. Goose bumps leapt to his bare arms as a feeling of dread swept over him. He tried to maintain a neutral tone.

"Ahhh…what about her?"

Sal, like most people who have a secret, kept his voice low as he began to repeat the hearsay.

"Poor woman's dead. Nobody's saying much. I heard the congressman's secretary had been blabbing about how Mrs. Monroe blew her brains out. Apparently her husband had been away for the weekend. When he came home, he found her dead in his office, naked. Yep, said the gun was still in her hand."

Not noticing the color had drained from Carl's face, Sal continued the gruesome account. "I heard that they figured she'd been dead for a couple of days. Her head was actually stuck to the desk with dried blood." Sal seemed to shiver as he wiggled his shoulders. "Poor woman, shame, darn shame. She was such a beautiful girl. I used to make deliveries there myself years ago. Hey, didn't you take some files to the Monroe home a while back? What could make someone like her do something like that?"

The old fellow was talking more to himself, than Carl at this point. Carl's legs had gone weak as he reached out to steady himself. Sal lifted his eyes, and noticed the young man's pallor.

"Are you alright? Boy, you don't look good. Did you know her?" he asked.

"No, I just have a queasy stomach," he answered, trying to recover. "I'm sorry, but I didn't feel well this morning when I got up. The story just put me over the edge. I gotta go home."

"Yeah, sure, Carl. I'll call in Smitty. You just head home and go to bed, maybe you've got a touch of the flu. It's been biting everyone around here, and boy, you look like hell."

Leaving the Capitol, he drove home. He replayed the story during the drive, and realized why his calls went unanswered. Sarah wasn't ignoring him. She'd been there all along, sitting beside the ringing phone in a puddle of her own blood. He didn't feel well. He pulled the car over, opened the door and threw-up.

*****

"HEY Man… did you hear me?"

Marc's voice snapped him out of the reminiscence.

"No, sorry, what did you say?"

"It's not your fault man. People do things. You can't control shit sometimes. Sometimes it controls you."

Carl found that he wanted to talk about Sarah. He'd not spoken to anyone about the affair.

"Marc, I told her we had no future the same night she killed herself. *I think I'm responsible.* The woman was married to someone important. She was older than me, a lot older," he continued, the image of her face hauntingly vivid as he spoke. "She blind-sided me, asking me how I felt about her, wanting to know where it was all going. I… I wasn't ready, I panicked."

Just as he finished his sentence, Sue arrived with his order. "Here ya go, Hun." She looked at Marc. "Hot turkey sandwich, slaw on the side?" He just nodded.

It was Marc's turn to look sickly, digging into his own memory as he watched Carl wrestle with his guilt.

"You panicked? Man, you don't know what panic is."

Wallowing in his own regret and private hell, Carl didn't catch the meaning of Marc's last comment.

"What? What are you talking about?" Carl asked confused.

"Panic. I've experienced real panic, real fear, real TERROR. Don't sit there feeling sorry for yourself because some middle-aged woman had a menopausal meltdown. So the young dude she was screwing told her the truth and she couldn't handle it. She made the choice to end it all. Not everyone has a choice."

Carl stared blankly at Marc, trying to figure out why he was telling this recluse about Sarah. Did he seriously expect him to understand? He needed to get home.

"I've got to get going, Marc. I'm not in the mood today for company, or food," he said, pushing his untouched plate away.

Just then, Sue re-appeared with Marc's lunch order.

"Here you go." Looking over she asked with a small frown, "Carl, is the liver O.K.?" seeing the ignored dish.

"Yeah, just waiting for my appetite to show up," he said, trying to make light of the moment.

"You let me know if it's not good. If you like, Reggie can warm it up," she offered.

"No, it's all good, Sue, thanks."

With a shrug, she moved on, clearing the dishes from an empty table.

"Like I said, Marc, I'm going to get moving." As he began to rise, a look of disdain etched Marc's face.

"Sit down, Ivy League," he commanded, "I'm not always in the mood for your company either. But I don't make you eat alone."

*****

He hadn't felt like a regular person in years. The lunch times he spent with Carl brought him a sense of routine, of normalcy. He wanted to tell him his story. He needed to tell his story. The telling might take Carl's mind off the grief and guilt he felt, if only for a while.

"Fine, I'll stay for a bit, I guess. I really don't want to be by myself anyway." All day yesterday, Carl had been alone in his condo, alone with his guilt.

"I told you I had a real life once, remember?" Marc asked quietly.

Carl would have normally found this opening statement quite intriguing. Today he just didn't care and nodded as he shrugged. "Yeah, not only did I have a real job, I went to college, and graduated—with a doctorate."

"Doctorate? In what?" Carl asked doubtfully.

"Biochemistry." Marc stopped for a moment, letting the word sink in. "Yeah, that's right BI-O-CHEMISTRY. I was a research scientist. I was educated at Stanford, top of my class, 1969. After I graduated, I bought a ticket and made my way to Woodstock, in August. Free love and drugs, I was all for that, man."

Bullshit, Carl thought. A smile, more of a smirk, found its way onto his face. For the moment, he managed to put the 'Sarah tragedy' out of his mind.

"Yeah, that's right, funny boy, laugh it up. But I *did* go to Stanford and I was a scientist. I just wish I'd never left Woodstock," Marc sneered defensively.

Over the next hour, neither touched his food. There were times when Marc's voice lowered to scarcely a whisper. In hushed tones, he carefully unraveled the far-fetched tale of his days at Novatek Pharmaceutical and the laboratory.

Carl half-heartedly listened assuming it was a fabrication. He found himself drifting in and out of the story as renewed guilt over Sarah clouded his mind. He did catch the part about Woodstock and a youth plastered with recreational drugs, LSD and heroin. He had no problem accepting *that* part of the story as true.

He listened as Marc jabbered on, sharing his feelings of dread and rattling off a collection of unlikely conspiracy theories.

Coming to the end of his unbelievable fantasy, he told Carl about 'stepping out' for a hit of LSD.

"I drifted off. The champagne was drugged I guess, laced with a tranquilizer or something to make us all fall asleep. When I woke up a few hours later, the whole building was an inferno. They were dead, all of 'em, Edwards, Rose and my girlfriend, Vanessa. The pricks killed them, killed 'em all. They missed me. The bastards didn't figure it out until they did a body count. I knew I had to run," he said, his eyes glazed and staring.

The strained look on his weathered face convinced Carl of one thing for sure. In his tormented, lonely mind, he knew Marc believed every word he was sputtering.

"I went back to my apartment, got what I could, grabbed all the cash I had lying around and bought a bus ticket. I knew Washington had a large, homeless community. Whiny Liberal bastards were always writing about how so many were homeless in the country's capitol. I decided that here was a good place to get lost. I knew they wouldn't look under every rock in the country for me, at least I'd hoped not."

After a brief pause he looked directly into Carl's eyes and said, "Look kid, I've never told that story to anyone, not ever."

Carl could see the hope in his eyes as Marc watched for his reaction.

"Wow, that's incredible," Carl stammered. Staring at Marc he felt a new sadness, realizing how delusional he really was.

Marc had his moments of complete clarity and this was one of them, as he eyed the young cynic.

"You don't believe me, do you?"

"Well, you have to admit, it's quite a tale. It's a lot to digest. Let me get this straight. You're telling me that some mystery killers murdered a group of scientists for no reason? I realize that you're convinced this all happened, but you know…" he looked almost apologetic. Marc glared with such intensity that Carl squirmed a bit.

"I didn't say they murdered them for no reason. I just never *mentioned* the reason, kid," he spit bitterly.

Carl found himself drifting, mentally preparing a list of excuses to leave the diner. He'd had it with Marc's wild tale.

Marc looked nervously once again from side to side, obviously checking to see who might be listening. Sue was busying herself clearing tables left by the lunch rush. The diner was all but empty. No one but Carl was paying attention.

"Edwards told us, no he actually showed us the proof, his notes, his research—everything, man. I can tell you that what he showed us, convinced us all," Marc revealed in a hushed tone.

"Convinced you all of what?" Carl asked, mildly interested.

Marc let a moment of silence pass, before exposing the secret he had kept for over a quarter century.

Then, with great reverence he announced in a whispered voice, "A man named Dr. Blake Edwards discovered the cure for cancer and the sons-of-bitches killed him for it!"

Carl barely suppressed a smirk. "Wow, a cure for cancer. Well, if that were true, tell me, why are people dying every day from cancer, Marc?" *At least it's not little green men,* he thought tiredly. *Poor fool's lost it, and he really believes all this crap.* Carl was running out of patience, trying to humor him.

"I've asked myself the same question a million times. I don't know the answer, but I'm pretty sure it's the Nazi's. They don't want us to have the cure," Marc replied with conviction.

"Well, that's a very interesting theory, but I don't really believe something that big could have stayed secret for very long," Carl said definitively.

Marc quickly turned defensive and Carl suspected that he probably regretted sharing his wild story with him.

"Yeah, well, I guess you don't know everything asshole. But if you get bored, check it out. Marc Andrews, Stanford University 1969, check out the yearbook and the fire at Novatek, July 1981. I gotta go, I have an appointment."

Carl was surprised at how much his reaction, or lack of it to his personal life story seemed to bother the recluse.

Marc sat another moment glaring at him, as if staring would elicit a deeper response. It didn't, and in a heartbeat, he was gone.

Carl waited for ten minutes, enough time for Marc to disappear back to the gutter. He was relieved that lunch and the senseless rambling were over.

Bullshit quota, met and exceeded for one month, he thought dismally as he walked out of the diner.

The story faded quickly as despair over Sarah's suicide prevailed.

*****

In another part of the country, Thomas Phoenix sat in his luxurious office reading a periodical. The sound of his secretary's crisp voice brought the wireless intercom to life.

"Senator, you have a call from Congressman Edward Monroe. Would you like me to put him through?"

Thomas frowned. He'd heard about Monroe's wife. He and the congressman weren't exactly pals and wondered why he would be phoning him.

"Yes, put the call through, Paula, thank you."

"Hello, Congressman, Phoenix here. Ed, I'm so sorry for your loss," he offered in the most sincere tone he could muster.

"Thank you, Thomas, thank you very much—yes, Sarah was a wonderful woman, but the reason I'm actually calling is in regard to your son, Carl."

"Oh, you know Carl?" he asked, surprised Monroe would even be familiar with fact that he had a son.

"No, not exactly, Senator, I don't know Carl personally. I am however, aware that he was *banging* my wife. I also know your son was the last person to see her alive."

Thomas stiffened at the dual accusation. "I'm flying out, Monroe. We'll discuss this in person," he responded coolly.

Edward sat momentarily silent. He'd hoped for a more shocked response. He'd just delivered his message to the hardened politician, Senator Thomas Phoenix. Tomorrow he would be seated across from the father, Mr. Phoenix. He was curious to see if there would be a difference between the two roles, played by the same man. Grinning into the receiver, Edward replied, "Have a safe flight Senator, I look forward to seeing you."

Thomas hung up without responding.

Chapter 30

Montana was facing the fourth straight year of drought. The *Big sky country* looked like it had returned to the Dust Bowl days of the 1930's. The lack of precipitation held its own set of problems for the local residents. With less than a million people in the entire state, there were those in Emily's camp who considered the visit a waste of time. Miss Cantrell disagreed.

The turnout was massive despite the stifling weather. The media gobbled up the fact that Emily Cantrell had even bothered with a town as small as Butte Montana. With a population of less than thirty-five thousand, there were not a lot of votes to be garnered there.

She'd held an outdoor address in Palosa Square Park. Shops closed all over town. There was a record 9,478, supporters in attendance. Cantrell's true victory wasn't winning the whole state that day. It was the message sent to every small community across the country. Their campaign momentum was unstoppable.

Bored and overheated, Jason had already begun organizing while Emily finished up with the press. He was neatly placing the contents of the hotel dresser into a suitcase when she arrived back at the suite.

"Hey, dear, before I forget, I've booked you an appointment with Dr. Worthington tomorrow morning at nine," he said casually, as he packed their clothes.

"Dammit, Jason! I said I would see to it myself," Emily replied with a tinge of indignation.

The migraines were getting worse, and lately she had a hard time keeping anything down. Another week on the road, and she suspected that her weight loss would become evident to everyone.

She was actually relieved that Jason had made the appointment, but worried that the doctors might find something serious. *What if I need surgery or something*? *I don't have time to be sick right now,* she thought angrily.

"He's set up tests for first thing tomorrow, blood, MRI, cat scan, the works. You're getting completely checked out."

"Good god, Jason," she snapped crossly. "I'm not a child. I think if I'm qualified to run a country, I can manage my own damn doctor's appointments," she concluded resentfully.

"Emily. *I didn't* set up those tests," he replied. "Dr. Worthington asked me what seemed to be the trouble. When I mentioned you've been getting a lot of headaches lately, those were the tests *HE recommended*,"

The wounded look he wore resulting from the criticism didn't soften her. During this leg of the campaign tour she'd become easily irritated. Secretly Emily was worried over the cause of her migraines. Lately worry had turned to fear.

"Look, you can't have anything to eat or drink after midnight tonight as per *the doctor's* instructions. That was the only reason I even brought it up," Jason said defensively.

Emily might have smiled under different circumstances. It was obvious that her adoring husband hadn't noticed that she'd not eaten after midnight in years. And it was a pretty sure bet that he didn't notice she'd hardly eaten at all these past few weeks. She prayed that it was just a case of nerves and the hectic schedule.

The stress of the last few days was evident. She knew that Jason was becoming even more concerned at her erratic behavior. Twice, she had abruptly stopped speaking during an address to supporters. It appeared that she'd forgotten what she was about to say next. Jason had also caught her several times and called her on it. He quizzed her and mentioned that she seemed to be staring at nothing with a bleak, empty look on her face.

Emily knew he was worried about her. As he stuffed the last of their belongings into the suitcase, she could see that her reaction had silenced him. A couple of minutes later, he closed the snaps and locked the combination on their luggage.

Looking over in his wife's direction he gingerly asked, "Emily, are you ready, dear?"

Staring out the window of their suite, she heard Jason's voice but didn't understand what he was mumbling.

"Pardon me, Jason? I'm sorry...just daydreaming."

Emily did that a lot lately. Not long ago she adopted a phrase from a movie she'd seen. Ed Norton played the main character, Aaron, who had a multiple personality disorder.

When his dual personality emerged, he'd claim to have no memory of the events during that period. *Aaron* referred to the memory loss as 'losing time'. That's exactly how Emily felt. Not like she was *daydreaming*, but that she'd actually *lost time.*

"Ready, dear?" Jason repeated.

"Yes, I guess so."

She walked toward the restroom, trying to recollect if she'd packed her toiletries. The flight was leaving in one hour. In approximately five more hours, she would be in her D.C. home.

She stood in front of the mirror. The reflection looked drawn and haggard. Her puzzled face stared back as she tried to recall why she'd come into the powder room. *I really do need some rest*, she decided, suddenly remembering the toiletries.

*****

Seven hours later Jason turned the key in the lock. As the door swung open, he sang out, "Home, Sweet Home!"

Spencer moved toward the front entrance with Emily's suitcases, almost bumping into her. She was frozen to the spot. A shooting pain in her head had immobilized her. She didn't dare move. Spencer stopped short and waited. Jason was already in the house and turned toward her as he set down a briefcase.

"Well, honey, are you coming inside? Emily, Em, are you alright?" he asked, spotting the vacant gaze. No response.

"Miss Cantrell?" Spence asked from behind.

She could hear them but she couldn't see them. *I can't SEE!*' her mind shouted out.

What seemed like only a moment later, she was looking up at the bright lights. Aware that she was no longer standing in the doorway, she tried to sit up.

"Where am I?" she inquired groggily.

Suddenly, Jason's face appeared. He was hovering over her. His furrowed brow emphasized the look of concern. Although her vision was slightly blurred, she recognized her physician, Dr. Franklin Worthington, as he too came into view.

"Sweetheart, you're in George Washington Hospital. You passed out at the front door when we got home," Jason said.

Lifting her hand, a look of confusion crossed her face as she saw the tubes protruding from her arm. As her mind cleared, worry once again began to invade it.

"I fainted? I must have really banged my head good. I have a terrible headache."

"No, honey, you didn't bang your head. Spencer caught you just as you were going down."

With a weak smile she said, "Thank him for me."

"You're welcome, Ma'am," he answered from his post just inside the private hospital room.

"Emily, I've bumped up your evaluation. I've given you something that will help you relax. I'll personally be conducting the tests and you'll probably just sleep through them. I plan on staying the night to review the results."

"I'm just tired Doctor. I'm sure all I really need is a few good nights' sleep."

"Well, we're just going to make sure everything is normal. You're right, though, it may be a simple case of exhaustion," he said, not believing it for a moment.

Shortly after Miss Cantrell's admittance, he'd placed a secure call to his mentor in the White House, Nancy Saunders. Not only was she Chief of Staff to the president, she was also a revered committee member and head of the governmental arm of the Patronums.

Once he'd reached her, he followed protocol. He explained the situation regarding Emily Cantrell's collapse outside her Washington residence. He proceeded to inform her of Cantrell's admittance to the hospital for tests and observation. Nothing to report yet, but even so, he wanted to make the committee aware of his special guest.

Miss Saunders spent the next ten minutes giving the doctor very specific orders. The instructions were simple. Worthington was to do all testing personally. He was not to share significant findings or prognosis with the press, the family or colleagues. All test results were to be sent directly to her via White House dispatch. He would be provided with a prewritten press release at the appropriate time.

"Franklin, do you think it could be anything more than stress or exhaustion? Emily Cantrell runs a very hectic schedule, particularly these last few months," Saunders queried.

With the diplomacy of a seasoned medical professional Franklin responded, "Miss Saunders, I don't know. I'm going to perform a CAT scan and an MRI, as well as a full blood work-up. But given her symptoms, it could be anything."

First rule of medicine, cover-your-ass, he thought as a bead of sweat rolled down his cheek.

"Thank you, Doctor, please keep me apprised."

Worthington was aware that personally performing the tests might raise a question or two from the lab techs. Given who his patient was, he was sure he could easily skate past any queries. *Skating past the Cantrells will be another story,* he thought.

*****

"She's in good hands here, Jason," Franklin said reassuringly. "I'd like you to go home and get some rest before I have to admit you too."

"I think I'll just spend the night, if you don't mind. Just in case there's something serious."

"Jason, really, I insist. I won't even have the results until tomorrow, possibly as late as noon. There's nothing I can even tell you at this point. Please, go home, get a decent night's sleep. Emily is heavily sedated. She's not going to even wake up until sometime tomorrow afternoon."

Jason decided Worthington was right; if it was serious he needed to be alert.

"Okay, Franklin, you win. I am tired. I'll go home. I will come back at around eight?"

"Certainly, and if I have anything for you, we'll talk then. I'll have maintenance set something up for them in the hallway," the doctor said, indicating Emily's Secret Service detail.

"Thank you, Franklin. Take good care of her for me," he said. Overwrought with emotion, tears filled his tired eyes.

Franklin clapped him on the back. "Just get some rest Jason, I'm sure everything will be fine."

Later that evening, the hospital was unusually quiet. Worthington had no long waits for any of the necessary equipment. Spencer was the only member of the Secret Service detail who accompanied them, as Emily was wheeled to the MRI machine.

"I'll personally be conducting this scan," he said to the pretty technician who was dutifully attending the desk. "Take a break young lady. I should be finished here in an hour."

"Are you sure, Doctor? I could help, if you like," she offered politely.

"No, thank you, I have it covered."

She quickly disappeared. He grinned, knowing she was probably grateful for the breather. He was quite familiar at how a night shift could drag out if there wasn't much action. Tonight had been very slow. Emily was oblivious of the four vials of blood expertly drawn from her left arm while she slept. She was equally unaware of the hands gently lifting her off the gurney. She was then positioned on the surface that would transport her into the MRI chamber.

*****

In her unconscious state, Emily is in the grips of a fitful and vivid dream. In her nocturnal illusion, she stares intently at her reflection in the mirror. Her head is itchy, so itchy that she feels her scalp is alive. Hypnotically staring, she parts her hair, closely examining the skin covering the dome of her skull in the mirror. The reflected image is strange, making no sense to her dreaming mind. She looks closer; *is that a worm*? Squinting, she looks again, this time even closer. Hundreds, no thousands of worms appear, not on the surface her head, but burrowing out of it. Emily screams silently, screaming as the MRI machine sends her brain's image to the film.

*****

Dr. Worthington glanced at the clock on his desk. The illuminated numbers read 6:09 a.m. He had run all the tests, cross-referenced his journals, and had then run a second set of tests on Emily Cantrell's blood. Exhausted and disturbed at the findings, he began the fateful report. It would find its way to Nancy Saunders' desk before the end of the day. For now, all he could do was ensure that Emily Cantrell was comfortable—and await further instructions.

The challenge would be to keep the Cantrells at bay, to answer questions without answering them. As he planned his strategy, he thought of what he would say. Declarations like, "Inconclusive, nothing alarming, run a few more tests, relax. Everything seems to be normal."

In the meantime, there was the task of creating a clear report for his mentor, Nancy Saunders. Sitting in front of the computer on his desk, his fingers skillfully sped over the keyboard as the words began forming on the screen.

"EMILY CANTRELL: Female; Aged 49.

Diagnosis: Gliobastoma mutiforme-Brain Cancer.

Gliobastoma mutiforme or GBM. Glioblastoma multiforme (GBM) is the most aggressive form of the primary brain tumors known collectively as gliomas. The patient has an advanced Grade IV (GBM). Grade IV GBMS grow rapidly, invading, eventually altering brain function. Miss Cantrell's tumor is in the advanced stages. It is untreatable and terminal."

He spent the next hour assembling the report as well as a detailed inclusion of the supporting test results. Carefully placing the contents in an envelope marked '*Confidential, Medical*', he dialed Chief of Staff, Nancy Saunders' direct line. After the third ring, he recognized her voice.

"*I'm sorry I was unable to receive your call. Please leave a message.*" He did not leave his name, and just simply said, "The report is ready for pick-up."

Yawning, he sat back in his chair as he thought about the media frenzy that would be unleashed in the next few days.

Gonna be a shit storm around here. Damn shame, good woman. She had my vote. She'd have been a helluva great president, he reflected.

Stretching himself out, he yawned again as he slowly rose to his feet, mentally preparing for his 'face off' with Jason.

*****

Carl stared at the red light on Higgins and Main when the secure cell phone rang. "Hi, Carl, Sal here. You have a pick-up at the front desk of George Washington Hospital. Can you be sure to bring it back before quittin' time?"

"Sure, Sal. George Washington Hospital. Got it, see you later." He double-checked the address of his next delivery. Just as he'd figured, take seventeenth and make the hospital pick-up on his way to Reggie's. He'd have time to spare.

Wondering who had gotten whom pregnant, he'd decided that checking out that little tidbit would help the kill the half hour before lunch. He wheeled the car into the turning lane on Jefferson and then headed toward George Washington.

A short while later Carl was parked in the back lane beside Reggie's, busily snooping through the hospital dispatch he had picked up. It had nothing to do with office indiscretions. He was blinking in disbelief as he read Worthington's report. A lot of the terminology was familiar. He recognized it from his days in med school. Without thinking, he began snapping pictures of each page of the report with his cell phone. When he returned home he would download them onto his computer. *I just need to look up a few things, not exactly sure what GBM is... God, what the hell am I doing?* He kept taking the photos.

He carefully replaced the contents of the envelope. Suddenly a feeling of intense sadness, mingled with embarrassment, overcame him. *I shouldn't have read the file. It's just so...so personal,* his mind stammered. Carl felt like someone who had peered into an open window, then watched a woman undress. He knew he had violated Miss Cantrell.

That poor woman, I really liked her. As the thought slipped through his mind, he realized he was already thinking about 'presidential hopeful' in the past tense. His mood sank even further.

Just then, he felt too lousy to deal with Marc over lunch. He figured that he'd finish the rest of his deliveries and head back to the Capitol. The glimpse of Cantrell's future was too much for him, first Sarah, now her. He needed a break.

Arriving home at days end he went straight to his desk. He spent almost an hour on the computer downloading the images of the report and researching GBM, Cantrell's type of cancer. Sadly, he read how swiftly it claimed its victims.

Hours later thoughts of the 'almost president' swarmed his mind as he lay in bed, staring into the darkness. He wondered why life was so unfair.

Over thirteen hundred miles away in Dallas, Texas, the Patronums called an emergency meeting, just as Carl dozed off.

Chapter 31

Not only were the faces different, but the number of them had changed as well. No longer was the committee made up of the revered fifteen. As with many American corporations of the new millennium, the Patronum executives had been downsized. Personal computer screens sat faithfully at each of the nine seats. Satellite uplinks, equipped with the most advanced electronic information-gathering capabilities, were at each committee-member's fingertips.

The Patronums' meeting place had a definite air of nostalgia. Other than communication modernization, almost everything was identical to an era long since passed. Personal meetings were now only a rarity. All information could be easily exchanged in the modern age of technology. Emails, telephone and video conferencing, even text messaging had long since replaced the necessity of *in the flesh* encounters.

One very distinct difference from days gone by was the admission of women. Today, three women sat on the council, something unheard of in the earliest days of the committee. Survival of the Patronums, and indeed the country was now based on the best *person* for the job as opposed to the *best man.*

Eric Brunner studied the faces of those seated. In his almost-eleven-year tenure, he'd only seen them gathered at the round table a total of four times.

Almost all gatherings were now conducted via 'web conferencing.' Only the most crucial issues prompted a face-to-face convergence. The emergency meeting had been called less than twenty hours earlier by the head of government, Chief of Staff Nancy Saunders.

As she stood, the room was blanketed in an inquisitive silence. No one was ever made privy to the subject of an emergency meeting in advance. The only person who'd know the content was the committee member who'd called it.

"Thank you, fellow Patronums for attending this conference on such short notice," she said, out of courtesy; attendance to an emergency meeting of the committee was never an option. Every individual's presence was mandatory.

"Please refer to your screens," Saunders directed.

Suddenly the blank, flat screens leapt to life. There in front of each member was an attractive picture of Emily Cantrell. Her hair and make-up were complimentary, her outfit fashionable yet reasonably modest.

"On your screens is a photograph of Emily Cantrell, daughter of President Jonathan Cantrell. It's common knowledge that she's currently leading the race for the upcoming presidential elections."

The screen suddenly changed. The latest polling numbers were revealed.

"Miss Cantrell is in front by eighteen percent. As you are all aware, we carefully analyzed the overall impact of each different candidate on the country. This model, of course, was based on the assumption that they would be elected. Our respective cells thoroughly compared each individual's abilities. The focus was on terrorist suppression, foreign affair policies, and overall economic growth. As demonstrated by Miss Cantrell's lead in the polls, the country stands behind her. You will all recall that based on our research, so do we."

Nancy Saunders chose not to rehash the points that had brought the Patronums to lend their support to Miss Cantrell fourteen months earlier. That endorsement was in the form of large anonymous campaign contributions as well as some of the most powerful members getting firmly behind the candidate.

The screen with the polling results suddenly faded, as page one of Dr. Worthington's report appeared.

"Ladies and gentlemen, it seems our champion has come up lame. Please take a moment to review Dr. Worthington's initial diagnosis of Miss Cantrell."

The same hush that had hung over the round table since the meeting began, intensified. The room was deadly silent as members read and digested the contents of the ill-fated report.

All eyes were focused on Miss Saunders, and before they could begin, she redirected the questions.

"All questions regarding the report may now be addressed to Dr. Earnest Ashton," she invited.

Helen Sharp, head of the legal department, was the only one to speak. "Dr. Ashton, given the diagnosis, are we to understand Miss Cantrell's tumor is inoperable? That she is, in fact, going to die?" The words hung painfully in the air.

"That's correct, Mrs. Sharp. This type of cancer spreads rapidly and is always terminal. As indicated in the report, Miss Cantrell's tumor is in the advanced stages, at a Grade IV. The cells, which will eventually destroy her brain function, are multiplying even as we speak. I might add, it's a testament to her strength that she did not succumb earlier."

The chamber fell silent once again.

Nancy Saunders momentarily returned to the floor.

"We do have an alternative to Miss Cantrell's pending fate. The purpose of this gathering is to determine whether we exercise that option in light of her unfortunate circumstance."

The solution had occurred to some of the committee members as early as the first reading of Worthington's findings. Others were not as familiar with all the hidden arsenals the Patronums controlled. Certain classified secrets were restricted to even the committee members and carried a '*need to know*' status.

"Dr. Ashton will explain what we can do."

Ashton slowly rose again and addressed the executive. "Thank you, Miss Saunders. Ladies and Gentlemen, as some of you are probably aware, we have in our possession a cure for Miss Cantrell's invasive tumor. It is called *Elixir*." A few surprised members, as well as those who could maintain a poker face, hung on every word. "Based on research conducted over a quarter of a century ago, our country would have suffered irreversible financial and social damage had this 'wonder drug' been made freely available. I'm afraid that position has only intensified since the discovery of *Elixir*. Unfortunately, this medicine, were it to be made public now, would irreparably weaken our fragile, socio-economic system."

The elderly doctor stopped for a second as he reflected on the information that the Patronums had kept secret for the past twenty-five years. Like his predecessor, he too thought of the countless lives that could have been spared and shook his head.

"So in conclusion, it quite simply comes down to whether we use Elixir to spare Emily Cantrell or not," he concluded.

There were murmurs within the group, speaking in low voices to one another. Only Eric Brunner remained silent, staring vacantly at a spot on the wall directly in front of him, but it wasn't the wall he was seeing. The picture was that of his beloved Monique. Her beautiful face, drawn, devastated by the radiation treatments. Her long, silky hair had first dried, becoming listless like the rest of her body. Eventually her locks had succumbed to the chemotherapy as they fell out, a clump at a time.

For the second time in his life he'd fallen in love and had married his sweetheart. She'd had the heart of a lioness and the soul of an angel. He remembered talking to Vargo when she'd been initially diagnosed with the incurable cancer.

"Bruce, I'm begging you, please appeal to the committee for my sake. I want one vial, that's all I am asking for, Bruce, one vial of Elixir for Monique."

"Eric, you know I want to. I would give my life for you and Monique. But I'm sworn to the Patronum decree, and the welfare of the country, not to any one individual. My moral obligation will not allow me to ask for the committee's vote on something like this." He hung his head as he spoke. "Eric, they'd deny the request anyway. I'm sorry, son."

"Jesus, Bruce, I've served you, the committee, and this country with undying loyalty. I've asked for nothing in return, ever. Now I'm asking, get me Elixir. I don't see what THE BIG FUCKING DEAL IS," he'd screamed. His mentor had sat there helplessly, unable to offer solace.

In Eric's heart, he knew what 'the big deal' was. First it would be Monique, then a committee member's son, daughter, grandson. Eventually it would lead to downstream Patronums, and the secret would not be safe. *But I love her, oh, god, I want the Elixir*, he'd thought gravely.

For more than a year he'd watched as his one true love withered, her vitality gradually drained. Eventually, her vivacious spirit slowly ebbed.

Monique had been strong, strong for *him.* In her final week on earth, she had done her best to lessen his pain.

"My Darling, I'll never be far from you. You have to live your life for us both. I want you to marry and have beautiful, wonderful, children. Remember that I'll be waiting for you all when you come to join me." They'd both sobbed.

The plea to release one vial of Elixir to spare Monique had never been presented to the committee.

Eric could not remember how many times he'd felt the cold steel of his revolver resting on his lips in the weeks following her death. He was afraid to pull the trigger. Afraid that God would not grant him entrance to the place where Monique now lived in the after-life.

His memories did not serve him well this evening. He was clouded. He felt intensely resentful that the life-saving miracle, Elixir, might be used to save a life. That it had not been used to save Monique's seemed so unfair.

A voice rang out, disrupting his recollection. Reality yanked him back to the moment as the Chief of Staff spoke again.

"If there are no further questions, I move that we take a vote immediately," Nancy Saunders announced.

All the modern technology had not changed the traditional procedure for secret ballot voting. The cylinder was somberly passed from member to member.

Eric gazed hypnotically at the ballot. The two words came into view, with a small line appearing on the right of each, YES___. NO____.

Eric moved his pen to the ballot, then with a sense of intense gratification, he checked off the word NO. As long as he was alive, his biggest desire was that *no one* would ever reap the benefits of the magic, life-giving Elixir.

After everyone had placed his or her ballot in the box, it was again in front of Nancy Saunders. She opened it, calling out the results. Helen Sharp recounted the ballots, to confirm. The Chief of Staff leaned down and Sharp whispered in her ear.

Saunders waited momentarily, and then made the announcement. "Ladies and Gentlemen, six for, three against. Miss Cantrell will receive the cure. Dr. Ashton, how long before we can have a sufficient dose of Elixir produced?" she asked.

"I'll have a vial prepared before you leave in the morning, Miss Saunders. If you like, you can transport it back to Washington personally."

"Thank you Doctor. If there are no further questions, I suggest we retire to the lounge. For those of you who have to take their leave, on behalf of the United States of America I would like to thank you for your patronage," she said dutifully.

Eric quickly left the committee of the Patronums. *These 'protectors of the moral majority' couldn't be there for Monique, could they?* He thought bitterly. Even though he knew better, the memories conjured up by the unexpected meeting were still painful. It had been twenty years and he had just learned to manage weeks at a time without missing her.

In fact, like most of the voting constituents, he too, had admired Emily Cantrell and felt childish for his negative vote.

Walking down the busy street, he decided that a quiet drink or two were in order. He slipped into a small, Irish pub. The neon outline of a four-leaf clover flickered and appeared to mysteriously float above the sign: *McClenahan's*.

As Eric entered the establishment, a black sedan slowly stopped at the corner. The heavily tinted windows concealed the identity of the driver. The only clue that someone sat inside the car was a swirl of cigarette smoke snaking out of the window as it quickly dissipated into the cool darkness.

Once inside the pub, the rhythm of Eric's heart increased as adrenaline flooded his veins. He knew he'd been followed.

Scouring the place for a back exit, he took little notice of the sights and sounds of the energetic nightspot. The lively music did nothing to distract him. He quickly navigated his way to the heavily dented rear door. Opening it, he was once again in the fresh night air.

Eric's sense of danger was on high alert as he carefully traversed the small, back alley. He came out just south of the black sedan. Moments later, a couple walked by him heading toward the intersection. Casually, he fell into step with the young pair. He moved toward the sedan, his stride matching theirs. The couple looked perturbed as he strolled side-by-side with them.

"Beautiful night, isn't it folks?" he asked nonchalantly.

"Ahhh, yeah, I guess," the male answered warily.

Cleverly using the unsuspecting couple to conceal his approach, he broke off from them. Crouching to avoid detection in the rearview mirror, he rounded the back of the car. Coming up to the open window with his gun drawn, he pressed the muzzle into the cheek of the surreptitious driver.

If Kenichi Nakamura was startled, he didn't show it as he slowly turned his head toward the cold gun barrel.

"Sir, I am here to give you a report," he said evenly.

"What the—" he began, realizing his tail had been Nakamura. "Slide over NOW!"

With his gun still raised, he carefully watched as the Asian slid over to the passenger seat. In one fluid movement he was in, seated behind the driver's wheel. "What in hell's name do you think you're doing, Nakamura?" he asked in amazement.

"Sir, I've been trying to call you all day on your cell phone. I wanted to report my findings on the current mission. When I couldn't reach you, I became concerned that you might be in danger"

Eric suddenly remembered turning off his phone hours before the meeting. He had been so lost in his memories of Monique that he'd forgotten to reactivate it. He found Nakamura's explanation weak. The mission he was working on was not urgent, nor was the report. *Worried I was in danger, that's crap too,* he thought guardedly.

"That doesn't explain why you didn't pull over while I was walking. Do you think that with thirty years of training, I wouldn't spot a tail?"

"Of course, sir, I wasn't sure if this was the right time to approach. Once I saw with my own eyes that you were safe, I thought I'd wait. After you had socialized, I wanted to be at your disposal for a ride home. I would have given you my report then."

His explanation sounded pathetic, and Eric knew he'd caught him off guard with his stealthy approach.

"Nakamura, if I ever catch you following me again, I WILL kill you, do you understand me?" he said warningly.

Bowing his head slightly, eyes averting Eric's as if ashamed, he replied, "Again, sir, I am sorry I have disappointed you. I meant no disrespect and only feared for your safety."

"Protocol, use regular procedure. Do I make myself clear?"

"Yes, Sensei. I am your humble servant. I apologize once more."

"Yeah, whatever. Get you ass home. Report tomorrow. Use regular channels."

A second later he was gone. Between the committee meeting and Nakamura's questionable appearance, his night was shot to hell.

He'd hailed a cab and one hour later, was sliding between the cool sheets of his queen-sized bed.

Eric slept poorly. His dreams were filled with haunting images of Monique. In them, she was gaunt, her head wrapped with the colorful bandana she wore in her final months. Without warning the dream turned into a nightmare as Nakamura appeared. In one hand, a bloodied knife, in the other he held something bright. Maniacally staring at Eric, he smiled as he slowly wiped the blood from the blade with Monique's bright bandana. In the dream, Eric froze.

*****

As Eric wrestled with his nightmare, Nakamura lead the unsuspecting prostitute to the basement. By dawn, she was barely alive and begging him to kill her. For a long time, he didn't.

Chapter 32

"Good afternoon ladies and gentlemen, this is your captain speaking. We are experiencing a bit of turbulence this afternoon. I would ask all passengers to please secure your tray in the upright position and fasten your seat belts. The current weather conditions in Washington are seventy-one degrees Fahrenheit, overcast, with steady showers."

A unified groan emanated from the passenger compartment.

"We'll be arriving in approximately thirty minutes, folks. That puts us about twelve minutes ahead of schedule, thanks to a very co-operative tail wind. On behalf of the crew and myself, I'd like to take this opportunity to thank you for flying *American Jet Liners*. We hope you enjoy your flight."

Just as the captain's voice faded, there was a shimmer in the plane's fuselage. With the steadiness of a veteran sailor, the flight attendant walked down the aisle ensuring that trays were in the upright position and seat belts were secured.

"Wow, these wind shears are bad," the co-pilot, said.

"Yeah, and with the weather in D.C. they aren't going to get any better," Captain Murdock confirmed as he looked at the bleeping radar.

Washington was in the midst of a torrential rainstorm with gale force winds. Murdock had considered requesting permission to divert and land at an alternate airport. Then he'd reconsidered. He had Chief of Staff Nancy Saunders and the senator out of Texas aboard. Diverting unnecessarily would not bode well for the airline, or for him. He decided to tough it out. This was not the worst storm he'd ever encountered, but it was bad enough.

"Let's just give 'em a smooth ride boys and put this puppy down gently," he said to the flight deck crew.

*****

"Hey, Thomas, are you alright?" Saunders asked her longtime friend and seating companion.

Reluctantly peeling his eyes open, the senator slowly released the white-knuckled grip he'd had on the armrests. Wearily, Thomas Phoenix shifted his gaze toward her.

"Yes, I'm fine, Nancy, just not what you'd call *a relaxed flyer*. Frankly, traveling is the only part of the job I hate," he said. He took several deep breaths to control the nauseous feeling rising in his stomach. He left in such a rush that he'd forgotten to pack some Dramamine to control the queasiness.

"Relax, Thomas. This flight will end like they all do. A few bumps and grinds, and then we'll be on the ground before you know it." Nancy was an excellent flyer, never a worry. However, today was a bit different for her. Given the precious cargo she carried, her nerves had also jumped to life. Earlier, she'd said a small prayer.

"So I didn't realize that you and Congressman Monroe were such good friends," she said. Thomas thought he detected an overtone of muted sarcasm in her comment. Before take off he revealed the reason for his trip to Washington. It was common knowledge that he and Monroe didn't click.

"Yes, well we're not real close, but I wanted to personally convey my condolences to Edward for his tragic loss." He forced a look of concern as he spoke. Thomas was aware that Edward Monroe thought he had him over a barrel with this thing. He didn't.

The fact was Thomas and the good congressman had locked horns on many issues over the years. They couldn't be in the same room without sparring. Basically, they hated each other.

"Well, Thomas, you're very considerate."

"Yes, uh, thank you, Nancy," he replied. Wanting to change the subject, he added, "All went well with the meeting, I trust."

"Uh ha, yes, it did." Now it was her turn to try and change the subject.

"How's your boy, Carl, doing?" she asked.

Dammit, will this plane ever land? He squirmed.

"Fine, Nancy, just fine. He's—"

Suddenly there was a thump and the plane pitched abruptly to the left as it lurched forward. This time, the flight attendant was unable to regain her footing. Lunging forward, she landed in the lap of a surprised first-class passenger. Overhead compartments sprung open, spewing out some of their contents. There were a few surprised yelps. One woman's scream pierced the pressurized cabin, adding to everyone's uneasiness. The skies darkened as the aircraft approached Washington.

The radio abruptly crackled to life. "Sorry about that one folks. We're experiencing some crosswinds on our final approach this afternoon. Please check that your chair back is straight and your seat belts securely fastened. Everything is fine and we should be on the ground in a couple of minutes. Sorry about the bumpy ride, but we look forward to serving you again real soon. Thank you." Moments later the plane taxied to a complete stop as the rain battered the thin skin of the jet.

"That was one rocky landing," Captain Murdock said as he wiped the sweat from his brow.

"Fellas, first round's on me," he announced. The flight crew let out a small cheer as they gathered their bags from the storage compartment.

*****

After deplaning, the senator and Chief of Staff walked toward the baggage carousel in silence, each engrossed in their own thoughts as they measured the tasks ahead.

Reclaiming her luggage, Miss Saunders made her departure.

"Well Thomas, you have a wonderful visit with the Congressman. I'll be in touch," she said, tongue-in-cheek.

"Thank you, Nancy, I will," he replied. Relieved that the burden of small talk was over, the sardonic remark eluded him completely.

He didn't want his family laundry out on the line. *God, what were the odds I'd grab the same flight as Saunders?* He'd wanted to slip in and out of D.C. without having to explain anything to anyone. With a trench coat draped over his arm, he approached security. *I should have said I was just going to surprise my son. He'll be surprised all right. Damn you, Carl.*

*****

Dr. Franklin Worthington's nerves had begun to frazzle hours earlier when John McNamara, the Hospital Administrator, cornered him. Nancy Saunders had instructed Franklin to stall. Dodge any direct questions, if he was pressed.

"Worthington, how's Emily Cantrell?" McNamara asked.

"Well, she's fine sir," Worthington offered uneasily.

"I know that she's your patient, but I want to see her chart before day's end. What tests have you ordered?"

"An M.R.I., and a CAT scan, along with a full blood work-up." Franklin didn't like McNamara. He was a short, stocky Scotsman with reddish-blonde hair and a ruddy complexion. Not only did he fit the stereotypical physical make-up of a Scot, but he also had the infamous temper. He was long on questions, short on patience.

"Does the hospital have anything serious on our hands here? This could be a great P.R. opportunity as long as we have nothing to worry about. Worthington—do we?" he grilled.

Stall, how do I stall? It's the President's daughter we're talking about for crissake! Worthington thought frantically.

"I don't think so, sir. Once I've reviewed the test results, I'll add any pertinent information to the chart," Franklin replied. He could feel himself overheating.

He'd omitted two important facts. The first was that he had personally conducted all the tests; the second was the results were confirmed. Emily Cantrell was as good as dead.

*****

Nancy Saunders decided to have Elixir couriered over to George Washington Hospital immediately upon her arrival. Raising the privacy window in the limo she dialed Franklin's direct line. He answered on the first ring.

"Yes, this is Worthington," he said haltingly.

"Good morning doctor, Nancy Saunders here. Please—" He cut her off mid sentence.

"Thank God it's you. I'm under tremendous pressure here. Everyone wants answers. I've got a hospital administrator breathing down my neck, wanting to see the Cantrell test results, whom I've been dodging all day. Her husband has been hounding me for answers as well. What am I supposed to tell them?" he asked almost hysterically.

"Sir, get a hold of yourself," she said in a cool, even tone. "In less than an hour you will have an entirely new set of charts, tests, and records. You will also be receiving a vial of serum for injection. You are to immediately administer the medicine to Miss Cantrell. Tell her husband everything will be fine, that there's nothing to worry about. Now, Doctor, listen very carefully…"

Over the course of the next few minutes she'd mimicked the instructions precisely as given to her by Dr. Ashton.

"Are you clear on everything?" she'd asked, after relying the detailed instructions.

"Yes. Yes, I am. But how is an injection going to—" He was not given the opportunity to finish.

"Dr. Worthington that is the one aspect of this conversation you need not concern yourself with. Just follow your directions, and remember your decree. The Committee and the United States thank you for your loyalty, as well as your discretion." Pausing a moment, she added, "I trust we *can* count on both, correct, Doctor?"

The fleeting flash of pride was quickly replaced with concern, as Worthington noted the apprehension in Saunders' voice.

"Absolutely, Ma'am. You can definitely count on me." He stiffened momentarily as he wondered what he was thinking. Asking questions? *There are no questions. I'm a Patronum* he thought staunchly, regaining his full composure.

Making his way down the disinfected corridor, he proceeded to Emily Cantrell's ward. There were two new Secret Service agents posted outside the private room. After showing his hospital I.D., he went in, his face looked a bit pasty.

"Emily, how are you feeling?"

"Better Doctor, much better, when am I getting out of here?" she asked impatiently.

"In answer to your question, the tests are almost complete. I should have an answer for you in just a few more hours." He had the bedside manner of a friendly, country doctor.

"I don't think it's anything serious," he lied. The fake smile plastered on his face would have been comical under different circumstances. His jaw ached as he pressed his teeth together, holding the fragile mask in place.

He imagined his decline in Technicolor. He would be totally disgraced, full feature headlines and worldwide newscasts. CNN, FOX and the BBC, even the Canadians wouldn't be able to resist. He expected newspapers would read something like; ***President's daughter dies. Personal physician misdiagnosed obvious brain cancer. License to practice REVOKED INDEFINITELY!***

"Jason, your bride should be right as rain just as soon as I get a complete work-up done," he lied again convincingly.

"Thank you, Doctor, thank you." An indescribable look of relief was etched on Jason's face.

"Emily, I'll let your father know. He was going to have security make arrangements to visit, but we should be home soon, right Doctor?"

"Absolutely, Jason, let me finish my rounds. I'll be back in an hour or two with some answers for you both. Ohhh, one other thing Emily, when I return I'll be giving you a flu shot," he said non-chalantly. "You're a little more susceptible right now because of your weakened state, so we're going to vaccinate you so you don't end up as our guest again."

Once more, he pressed into service the confident smile of a television doctor. *God help me. Saunders thinks a serum is going to make the tumor just disappear? I'm ruined,* he thought, beaten.

After making a few scribbles on her chart, he nodded as he shuffled past the security detail. He proceeded directly to his office. Once inside, he desperately clawed at the knot in his tie. He couldn't breathe. Everything was closing in. Although he'd diagnosed many panic and anxiety attacks, he'd never experienced one. Franklin thought this could be the first of many. Arriving at his office, he quickly shut and locked the door. Dropping in his seat he closed his eyes, rubbing his face.

He pulled a half bottle of scotch from his bottom drawer. His hands trembled unsteadily. He poured a generous shot into an empty coffee cup. As the mug touched his lips, he threw his head back, emptying the contents. Shakily setting down the mug, he poured again.

*****

"Hi Carl, This is Sal here."

Why does he always say that? He's the only one who can CALL this number, Carl reflected, teetering between amusement and annoyance.

"Yes, Sal?"

"Where are you, right now?"

"Hmmm, let's see, I am heading south on 19th street."

"Perfect, turn around and get back here. I have a package for George Washington Hospital. I need it there, A.S.A.P."

Carl felt a chill run through him. He was sure the dispatch concerned the Cantrell file he'd read yesterday.

"Sure Sal, I'll be there in fifteen minutes."

On the drive back to the hill, his thoughts flipped between Emily Cantrell's death sentence and Sarah. He assumed Sarah's suicide made him more emotional about Cantrell. The stories were so different, but the outcome was going to be the same.

Carl rushed into the building and a few moments later, was standing in front of his supervisor. "Get this over to the hospital, post haste, Carl. Leave it at the front desk," he said, as he gingerly handed over the large manila envelope.

"Not a problem, Sal," he said, accepting the packet just as carefully. "I'll get it there as fast as I can," he confirmed soberly.

"That's why I got you on it, kid. Thanks. Now get your skinny, little ass going." Sal smiled as he waved him off.

As Carl turned off Pennsylvania Avenue, he looked at the thick envelope beside him on the front seat. He was guessing it would be the press release. He knew how government worked from a life surrounded by it. First there would be an outline of what everyone should and shouldn't say. It would be clearly specified in the press release. Then there would be some suit that was a public relations guru. He'd be the one who would actually stand in front of the cameras answering all the delicate questions. Carl was just surprised there wasn't a trail of officials delivering this personally. All principals would be thoroughly coached before any public announcement was made.

How do you tell an entire country that the person they wanted to lead them is about to die? He thought morosely.

As he drove, he looked at the package repeatedly. Fifteen minutes later, Carl was parked in an alley, the contents of the envelope carefully arranged on his lap.

It was addressed to a Dr. Franklin Worthington. The instruction was simple. 'Read it word for word,' no signature.

"Emily Cantrell has been diagnosed with a case of extreme fatigue as a result of a hectic campaign schedule. Miss Cantrell is expected to make a quick recovery and will be back to rejoin her campaign after a week of well-deserved rest."

What the hell?

He continued flipping through the rest of the file.

Patient: Emily Cantrell

Sex: Female, Age 49

He read the hospital chart, puzzled as to why a George Washington chart would be *going to* the hospital *from* the Capitol. Glancing at his watch, Carl decided that he didn't have time to figure it out just then. He had to get the package there. He fumbled in his glove box. A moment later he pulled out his Nikon. It was a powerful digital camera with a multitude of minute settings. After yesterday's discovery, he had purposely brought the camera, just in case. He began taking pictures of the report. When he could sit and think clearly, he would compare these with the ones he'd snapped yesterday. *I must be missing something*, he thought, frowning.

As he carefully replaced the pages back in the envelope, something fell out and rolled to the floor. Straining to find it, he groped under the front seat until he touched a small, cylindrical glass vial. Holding it up, he read the label on the front. Only one word appeared. **ELIXIR.**

*****

Thomas opened his umbrella as he exited the cab. The rain had lightened up only slightly since the touch-down of his bumpy flight. As the yellow taxi pulled away, Thomas took a moment to revere the majestic sight. He so loved the Capitol building. More than the building, he loved what it represented. After a moment, he proceeded to the door. Before being granted entry, he had to undergo the full security procedure. Fifteen minutes later he was seated in the corridor outside the offices of Congressman Monroe.

"Senator, the congressman will see you now," the attractive receptionist announced. He repressed a smirk as he noticed her nametag; *Susan*. She held the door open as Thomas stood. With his damp *London Fog* trench coat folded neatly over his forearm, he entered. There seated were several support staff, all busily doing whatever it was they did to keep their jobs. Standing with a correspondence in his hand was Edward Monroe. He looked slowly up from the letter and waited for Thomas to speak first. For an instant, an awkward silence hung in air, as the men squared off.

"Edward, I am truly sorry for your loss," Thomas said, extending his hand. The smug look on Edward's face delivered a very clear message. It said; '*not as sorry as you're going to be.*'

Monroe clasped the extended hand firmly. "Thank you, Thomas. This is a very difficult time. That you've come means so much. Please come in," he said with feigned sincerity.

Once the two men were comfortably seated in Monroe's office, the act played out for the prying eyes of the staff was quickly dropped. With an unpleasant smirk, Edward tossed a pile of eight by tens across the desk. The photographs floated on a cushion of air, as they spun directly to Thomas. With a forceful slap of his hand he stopped the spiraling snapshots. His eyes never left Monroe.

Looking down, he instantly recognized his only son.

The first image was of his naked son standing on a balcony, staring up at the night sky, puffing on a cigarette. Oddly, his initial observance wasn't the nudity, but the cigarette. He had no idea that Carl smoked. In the next photo his head was resting on Sarah Monroe's bare bosom. Thomas couldn't help thinking what a beautiful woman she'd been. He caught himself in mid-thought. Given her tragic end, he stopped before impure scenarios formed.

"All right, Monroe, so you were spying on your wife, what of it?" he asked casually.

"I wasn't spying on her, Senator. I was preparing to divorce her. Which seemed appropriate considering that Sarah was screwing your son."

"Okay, so Carl was seeing your wife. Why did you call me and why am I here? Obviously you're no longer concerned about a divorce."

The words' impact was obvious. The resentful look on Edward's face confirmed that they'd hit their mark and stung. Monroe tried to regain his footing with the wily Senator. Thomas knew why he was there. Monroe was looking for some political advantage. He must have thought he had something to bargain with. The congressman was way out of his league. This was the Hill, and Thomas was a gladiator here.

"Yes, Senator, your son wasn't exactly *seeing* my wife, he was regularly *fucking* her. He was also the last person to see her alive," he retorted angrily. Thomas read him like a book. Monroe still assumed he had the advantage.

"Ed, I generally find vulgarity offensive, but somehow, it seems natural coming from you."

Edward had hoped to shock Thomas Phoenix with the crudeness of his words and the gravity of the act. It did not have the desired effect.

Thomas picked up the collection of explicit photos. Holding them, he glanced down. Without warning, he forcefully flung them at Monroe. Startled by the suddenness, he caught a few of them against his chest. The rest fell on the floor by his feet.

Thomas leaned over the desk and glared at his surprised opponent. "Congressman, if you believe that my son murdered your wife, then I suggest you call the D.C. Homicide Squad. On the other hand, if the careless tactics you exercise in congress seeped into your marriage…" He paused, letting his words take a moment to register. "And drove your wife into the arms of another man, then I suggest a therapist or perhaps a priest."

This was not the reaction Edward Monroe had anticipated when he'd cooked up this little scheme.

"Well, Phoenix, how do you think this would affect your re-election chances if it was plastered all over the front page of a tabloid?" he retorted defiantly.

Thomas smiled. He'd expected this type of tactless assault and was well prepared.

"Monroe, you ever heard of Patti Davis, daughter of President Ronald Reagan? She posed nude for Playboy in 1994. How about Roger Clinton. He's former President Bill Clinton's brother. He was convicted of selling cocaine and sentenced to one year. The most successful political family of the twentieth century, the Kennedy's …numerous scandals. Most happened while these men were in office. Do you think that my son having an affair with your wife is going to cause *ME* embarrassment or votes? I'm curious to know what skeletons the reporters will find in *your* closet, Edward. Affairs, infidelities, and the betrayals Mrs. Monroe must have suffered before she blew her brains out."

He stopped, letting the words sink in. A comical look of panic crossed the Congressman's face. It was apparent he hadn't considered the possible ramifications.

Observing Monroe's reaction, Thomas smiled mischievously. He knew he'd kick his ass at this cat-and-mouse game.

"That's right, Edward. I suggest you get every copy of those photographs from your private investigator. You'd better pay him a nice, big bonus to keep *his* mouth shut. You know the Hill is a dog-eat-dog world. Earning a reputation as the cheating bastard who drove his wife to suicide, well, in all probability, not many votes there. But on the other hand, it would be a hell of well-earned epitaph, I'm sure."

It took Thomas less than seven hours to gather all the details regarding the congressman's mistress and affair. After all, he'd met her on the way in. She sat not thirty feet outside the entrance of Monroe's office. *'Never shit where you eat,'* was a crude axiom. Most politicians considered it the eleventh commandment. From the breast pocket of his trench coat, he produced a small manila envelope of his own.

"I don't think your supporters would be nearly as enamored with 'Susan' as you appear to be here," he said, tapping the package. Slowly he pushed it toward Monroe who snatched it and ripped it open. He stared at the lewd photographs of himself standing behind his naked young assistant. The color drained from his face, while the senator grinned. Raising his voice to a small thunder Thomas roared, "DO *YOU*?"

"No, no I guess not," he replied awkwardly.

"Now, Edward, I trust that when I need a favor on the Hill I can count on your full support, correct?"

Edward Monroe simply nodded his affirmation.

Without another word, Senator Phoenix took his leave, quietly closing the door as he exited the State office.

Edward stared at the gray sky as the rain pelted the oversized window. His mind raced, trying to figure out how he was going to be sure that his investigator had surrendered all photos that he been hired to take. Then there was the senator's manila envelope to worry about…

Son-of-a-bitch, how am I going to get those negatives?

*****

Carl was in the process of downloading his own pictures from the Nikon as the crisp knock broke his concentration. Looking over at the security monitor, he was shocked to see his father standing outside the door. Even the grainy black and white image of his face indicated that he was upset.

"Dad, what are you doing here?" Carl said, opening the door.

"For crissake, CARL! Sarah MONROE? GOD—DAMN YOU! Are you trying to RUIN ME?" he yelled as he stormed past him.

Carl stumbled backward, shocked that his father knew anything about Sarah Monroe.

"What were you thinking? BANGING a CONGRESSMAN'S wife? Not to mention the WIFE of a BITTER opponent?" he continued shouting.

"Then she turns up dead, AFTER you finished screwing her!" Thomas's unrelenting outburst lasted for ten minutes.

During the onslaught, Carl decided there was no way he could tell his father about Cantrell. He couldn't remember ever seeing him so upset.

I can't tell him what I think, not now, not ever, he thought guardedly.

The rain continued to pound relentlessly on the windows of the condo. An ominous feeling overcame Carl; he felt the storm had just begun.

Chapter 33

Carl was surprised at how restful his sleep had been. Thomas Phoenix had ripped through him last night like a tornado. His father had paced while he'd ranted about responsibility and growing up. It had been a long and repetitious thirty minutes. Nonetheless, Carl had found his dad's parting comment somewhat comical. With the door to the apartment half open he'd spun around, delivering the final reprimand, "and another thing. When the hell did you start smoking? You quit that damn filthy habit dammit-it-all-to hell!" And like a puff of smoke himself, the exasperated senator from Texas was gone.

Carl sat stunned. Ten minutes later, with the rain still pelting down, he went out on the balcony. Sheltered from the overhang of the balcony above, he'd lit up a Marlboro. Somehow the cigarette didn't produce the same relaxing effect it usually did. He'd only taken a few drags when somewhere deep in his subconscious a switch flipped. He looked at the half-spent smoke and knew he'd be quitting soon. He flicked it off his thumb with his middle finger and retreated into the suite.

Perhaps it was seeing his father so outraged. Maybe it was the emotional drain of the last few days. He wasn't sure why, but he slept like a baby that night.

Carl was out of bed the second his eyes opened. He barely finished peeing and was at the apartment door. Yanking it inward, he saw the morning paper had arrived and was there in carpeted corridor. He sat in his briefs at the small kitchenette and hastily flipped through it.

He found what he was looking for on page two. The headline read; **Emily Cantrell takes week off.**

The article went into very little detail. It simply stated that Miss Cantrell had been admitted to George Washington Hospital for an apparent fainting spell. The piece went on to confirm that a variety of tests had led to the conclusion that she was suffering from fatigue. A spokesman for Cantrell said she would be back in action within the week. *"She can handle the mental stress, but the rigors of the campaign trail can be physically taxing."*

He walked over to his computer, once again reviewing the original chart he'd copied. He just didn't get it. Why weren't they telling the public the truth about her condition?

What do they hope to gain? he wondered.

He imagined the party might be scrambling for a new candidate. But that plan didn't seem to make sense either. He assumed they would gain a larger sympathetic vote if they publicized Cantrell's *real* condition. Staring at the screen displaying the details of Emily's original diagnosis, two questions went through his mind. *Why the phony chart?* And *who at the Capitol could produce it?*

He wanted to talk to his dad. He cringed at the thought. *If the ole' man ever found out, he'd probably have me arrested himself,* Carl thought nervously. He wasn't even sure how many laws he'd broken by going through the highly confidential dispatches. Noticing the time, Carl finished his morning coffee. Setting down the empty mug, he quickly left the condo and began making his way to work.

The streets of Washington were clean from the heavy rains of the previous day. The rushing water had carried the accumulation of debris to the covered drain grates. Approaching Capitol Hill, he noticed a growing army of city workers clearing the rubbish from the covers. The Capitol was always the first address attended to, boasting the look of a well manicured estate. From the outside, it had the appearance of perfection, pure and fresh. Carl was beginning to see more than the visual façade.

He decided to let the whole Cantrell episode go. It was none of his business. He concluded that anything related to it could be dangerous to his father's career. Maybe even more.

As the morning slipped by, he found himself recalling the events of the previous night. He couldn't remember ever hearing his father swear so much as the words replayed in his mind…

"Do you realize that BASTARD tried to blackmail me? Did you have any *idea* you were under *surveillance*? That Monroe had hired a *private investigator*? He had you *photographed* with Sarah, for crissake! I'LL bet you *didn't know that!*

His father had continued in a similar vein the entire time, asking a barrage of rhetorical questions. Carl was grateful that his father hadn't expected answers to the questions he was asking. He would come up short. He had no answers as to why he was seeing the congressman's wife, none that would have satisfied Thomas Phoenix, anyway.

Y*ep, better let sleeping dogs lie,* Carl thought cautiously. He did not want another episode like that one. The morning passed, as it should have, uneventfully.

Three hours later, he was eyeing the perfect spot right outside of Reggie's. Tucking the car neatly into it, he parked, and a moment later entered the restaurant. Carl was a bit surprised to see Marc at their table. It was barely 11:40.

"Hey, Marc, you're early today."

"Yeah, I wanted to see if you were going to show. What, did you forget the other day?" he asked.

"I just got busy at work, Marc. I'm sorry about not showing. Did you stay for lunch anyway?"

Carl had set up a credit with Sue in the event that Marc ever came in hungry. Even though Marc was aware of the free ride here, he'd never taken advantage of it.

"No, waited here for 'bout an hour. Sue brought me coffee on the house. After a while, I took off. Glad to see you're not still sulking about the broad," he added tactlessly.

Carl had managed to keep Sarah out of his thoughts all morning. *Thanks a lot dickhead,* he thought sarcastically.

Just then, Sue took their orders, two turkey sandwiches, fries and a side of slaw. As she disappeared, Marc began chatting about the downpour of the previous day.

"That was some pisser we had yesterday. I really got soaked. All my stuff is wrecked, too," he said pitifully.

Carl, recalling his father's blow-up, concurred, "Yes, sir, it was a bad storm, seemed to get even worse last night." He smirked at his own private joke.

Marc became quiet, gazing downward toward the table. After a moment, he looked solemnly at Carl.

"I thought maybe you weren't coming back anymore. Ya know, after everything I told you the other day," he said.

With all that had happened over the last four days, Carl had pretty much forgotten the conversation.

"Marc, to tell the truth, with almost no sleep and the mood I was in the other day…." His voice trailed off as he desperately tried to recall the conversation. "I hardly remember what we talked about."

Then it came, a few shards of the exchange. *Oh right... Marc thinks he's a scientist. The people he supposedly worked with were murdered...while he was having a hit of LSD... some crap like that.*

"Good, just as well anyway," Marc mumbled.

"Here you go, boys," Sue said, setting down their plates.

As Marc jammed several fries into his mouth, he spoke past them in a barely audible voice.

"Bet you never even checked, did you?"

"Sorry, didn't catch that. What did you say?"

"I said, I bet you never even checked," he answered, as a few small pieces of french fry escaped his mouth.

Raising his brow, Carl tried to recall what he was supposed to 'check', but drew a blank. He'd seen Marc like this before. *Oh great, he's on the verge of a fit.*

Proceeding cautiously, he responded. "Marc, I'm sorry, I don't remember what I was supposed to check out. Believe me, I've had a couple of very horrific days."

Marc was on the threshold of rattling off a string of obscenities. His expression suddenly changed as he broke out into a strange, nearly hysterical laughter.

An almost embarrassed grin appeared on Carl's face as he tried to get what the joke was.

"What?" he asked sheepishly.

"Boy, let me tell you, you have no idea what horrific is. When your friends get murdered and you go from a nice home to living under bridges—that's horrific. You try being on the run for twenty-five years, afraid to even say your own name out loud. Let me tell you buddy, that's *goddamn horrific*."

Focusing on Marc's words, Carl felt a wave of compassion for the crazy old man society had tossed aside.

"Look, I'm really sorry. Refresh my memory, I promise I'll check out whatever you like."

"Forget it, man, nobody gives a shit anymore, especially me," he responded miserably.

After a bit of coaxing and a piece of Reggie's apple pie, Marc grudgingly repeated the name of the school and year he'd graduated. He then added the details of the Novatek lab fire in 1981.

Carl made a mental note of the information, silently promising himself to do some surfing on the computer. He'd be happy to take his mind off the Emily Cantrell puzzle.

*****

As Carl completed his deliveries later in the afternoon, his mind kept pulling him back to the same nagging question, trying to understand the 'why'. He just didn't get it. *Why would the Capitol release a press statement like that? What are they going to say when she dies?* It just didn't make sense.

Arriving at his empty condo, Carl changed into a pair of track pants, neatly hanging his slacks in the closet. He was fastidious about his surroundings, an idiosyncrasy passed down from his father. Switching the fifty-inch plasma TV to the news, he leisurely walked into the kitchen. Scouring the well-stocked freezer, he pulled out a frozen pork chop. Reaching for a fry pan from the rack, he abruptly stopped as the newscaster spoke.

"*Emily Cantrell, daughter of President Jonathan Cantrell, is resting comfortably at George Washington Hospital where she is recovering from what has been described as 'extreme fatigue'. Recent polls indicate that Miss Cantrell has gained another half point even while hospitalized. It seems that the campaign trail will have no time to cool for the ever popular Cantrell.*" The announcer's voice trailed off as he began another 'news breaking story.'

Jesus, I have to stop thinking about this thing.

He switched the TV to the music channel, on the way to his desk. Seated in front of his computer his dinner was soon forgotten. He did a global search and punched in Stanford University past graduates. The list was inclusive up to 1990, but not prior. A 'classmate search engine' popped up on the right side of the browser. Carl began the search. After entering his credit card number twice for the services offered, he got lucky. For $24.95 he had access to a printable version of a complete listing of graduates. The listing also included yearbook photos. He scrolled to Stanford, 1969. In amazement, Carl stared at the screen.

Department of **Biochemistry** and Molecular Biology

Graduates 1969:

Top honors this year go to Marc Andrews with a grade point average of 3.96.

There in black and white was a photo. It was a very recognizable version of younger Marc, with long ruffled hair, wearing an impish grin. Now older and a bit grizzled, but definitely him. The caption next to his picture, under the heading; 'Aspirations' read: **'Make a ton of cash, listen to great music, and save the world.'**

It's him. This guy is Marc Andrews! Alias Mr. Beau freaking Jangles. He immediately pushed the 'print' button.

Carl had read stories of people like him. Regular folks, who for one reason or another had fallen into the impoverished life of homelessness.

After the shock of discovering who his lunch-mate had been all this time, he began tracking down any evidence of the fire.

Carl hit the sheets well after midnight but sleep eluded him. After staring at the ceiling for an hour, the title of a movie he'd recently seen popped into his head. *Sleepless in Seattle my ass, how about sleepless in D.C.*, he quipped.

He played over the newspaper account in his restless mind. He'd easily found it on the computer. The archived headline read: **Explosion at Novatek Pharmaceutical tragically kills four.** The article continued, saying that three bodies had been '*unearthed in the aftermath.*' The recovered bodies were listed as Dr. Blake

Edwards, Dr. Rose Frechette, and Miss Vanessa Hargrave. The remains of Dr. Marc Andrews were never found. With temperatures exceeding 2000 degrees Fahrenheit, it was believed that Andrew's body was incinerated in the intense heat. The ages of each of the victims was listed. Marc had been thirty-four when he was assumed to have died. A quick calculation confirmed that he was fifty-nine years old. Carl thought he was younger and guessed that Marc had quickly adapted to life on the streets. His teeth were white and his face, although leathered, was still roguishly handsome.

He felt an urge to talk to Marc, wishing he knew how to find him. *At least I owe him an apology for not buying his wild story,* Carl thought as he finally started to doze.

Somewhere between the fine line of sleep and consciousness, Carl sat bolt upright. Eyes bulging, he glared into the blackness. He replayed the last cognizant thought he had as slipped into that state between consciousness and sleep. Marc had said, *"Edwards discovered the cure for cancer, and the bastards killed him for it."*

Carl jumped out of bed, almost running to his desk. The printer whirred momentarily as it spit out the opposing copies of Emily Cantrell's hospital charts. The two questions that had been nagging him since reading the diagnosis were answered. He finally understood the *'why'* as he gawked at the opposing reports. He also grasped '*how*' the powers that be could make such wild statements about the '*fatigue claim*'. A miracle drug did exist, and somehow, Emily Cantrell had gotten it. She was cured.

Chapter 34

The grass sparkled in the early morning sun as the dew clung to its blades. Carl sat on the park bench. A bundle of nervous energy, his knees alternately bounced up and down.

Since before dawn, an unending stream of commuters and joggers' filed past him. There seemed to be a multitude of people, going nowhere fast. He studied each face in vain, trying to spot Marc in the anonymous crowd.

After the revelation of the previous night, he couldn't sleep a wink. The walls of the condo seemed to be closing in on him. The need to speak to Dr. Marc Andrews had escalated from a mere desire to an overwhelming necessity. He'd decided the three days until the scheduled luncheon would be unbearable. Carl had jumped out of bed and pulled on a pair of faded jeans, then a logo tee shirt his father had given him. This was the first time he'd worn it. **"If you don't like America, we'll let you leave"** was boldly etched over the American flag. He'd then called work.

"Hi Sal, this is Carl," he said into the message machine. "I'm still not feeling a hundred percent. Sorry, but I won't be coming in today. I'm going to stay home and unplug the phone. I hope to shake this bug by tomorrow. Call you later. Again, I'm sorry about the short notice. Have a good day, bye."

After placing the call, he walked out of the condo. It was 5:15 and the cool morning air was invigorating. He didn't know exactly where Marc lived or slept, he didn't want to know. Marc dwelled in the underbelly of the city. *I probably won't find him anyways,* he thought, walking toward his car.

Carl was certain of only two things. He desperately wanted to talk to Marc, and he needed to tell him what he thought he knew, what *he was certain he knew.* After he spoke with him, he wasn't sure what the next move would be.

He drove from one park to another. There weren't many from the down-and-out crowd he was looking for in the cities scenic parks. As the morning waned, it became clear the haphazard approach wasn't working.

Think man, think. All at once, it occurred to him. Reggie's should have been his starting point. His search should have been launched from there and fanned out. It stood to reason that Marc would be within walking distance of Reggie's. He also remembered that he had mentioned a grocery store dumpster. Carl felt he had a direction, regardless of whether it turned out to be the right one. The prospect of *doing* something other than sitting in the park, re-energized him. He had grown frustrated with sifting through nameless faces that he knew couldn't provide answers.

*****

Across town at George Washington Hospital, sleep had eluded someone else that morning. With the overhead light brightly illuminated, Emily Cantrell was sitting upright in bed. Carelessly flipping through magazine pages, with hardly a second between them, she was anxious to get home.

I'm better! Her mind screamed. She hadn't had a migraine in two days. *Worthington and Jason are being ridiculous keeping me in here. I feel fine.* Just then Worthington entered the room.

"Good morning, Emily, how's my patient today?"

"I'm glad you came by, Doctor. I want out of here. This is becoming ridiculous. I'm feeling good. No actually, *I'm feeling great*, except for being cooped up in here."

"I am delighted to hear it," he said, glancing at her chart. "See what a few days of rest can do for the body?"

"Yes, Franklin, but now I'd like to get back to my campaign, if you don't mind. I *need* to get back to work," she said, barely able to conceal her agitation.

*****

His phone had rung at 5:17 earlier that morning. "This is Dr. Worthington."

"Good morning, Doctor. How's Miss Cantrell coming along?"

He immediately recognized Nancy Saunders' voice.

"Oh, good morning. Our patient is apparently doing very well. Her symptoms are certainly gone, no complaints about migraines. She's brighter and seems more energetic. From the outside she appears perfect," he said warily, his *'cover-your-ass'* instinct automatically engaging.

"Wonderful, Franklin. That's very good news. She'll be asking to be discharged soon. You'll be able to arrange that sometime today, I trust?"

Worthington felt warm. He detected a sudden increase in his pulse. His armpits were damp. He spoke slowly, carefully wording his response.

"Well, Ma'am, I think it would be prudent to at least run a few tests. It will help confirm that what was there is getting better." He could not form the words. Just couldn't quite say 'gone,' 'disappeared' or 'cured'. All of his medical training told him the test results would be the same as they had been seventy-two hours before.

"Dr. Worthington, you're right, it would be *wise* to run another MRI. The Cantrell's would expect no less. Please arrange it as soon as possible. I think it advisable to oversee the test, but don't conduct it personally. We don't want to raise suspicion at this point," she stated.

For the first time in days, Franklin Worthington breathed a sigh of relief. *Thank god, this won't be on me.* He now knew he wouldn't be held personally accountable for any negative findings.

"Yes, ma'am, I'll see to it immediately. Then what?"

"When the results come back clean, discharge her."

"What if they don't?" he asked cautiously.

"Relax, Doctor. They will, believe me they will."

As he hung up the phone, he reached into his second drawer. He was sure he'd aged years in the past three days. Wrapping his hand around the neck of the bottle, he anxiously tipped it into his coffee mug. He rarely drank alcohol on the job, but was convinced that he would've never been able to get through the last few days without it.

An hour later Emily Cantrell's wrist was in his hand. Without thinking he was counting off her pulse as he watched the second hand smoothly sweep off fifteen seconds. After taking her vital signs, Franklin smiled down at her. "Emily, I've ordered one more

MRI just to confirm everything is fine. Once I view the film and it checks out, you're free to get back to the grind."

"Good, very good Franklin, when do I have the test?"

Dr. Worthington flashed his TV smile again.

"Well, Emily, the reason I came was to let you know that we're slotted for the MRI at five this evening. You should be sleeping in your own bed tonight."

*****

Carl's car had been parked outside Reggie's for over three hours. He'd asked at least a half dozen of the homeless if they knew Marc Andrews, before he remembered. *Nobody knew Marc Andrews.* He had been dead for the last twenty-five years, or at least the name had been. In his sleepless state, Carl had completely forgotten. The only name that anyone *might* recognize was *Beau Jangles,* Marc's street alias.

Feeling discouraged because of the time he'd wasted, he tried to decide whether to backtrack or just plow ahead. Clutching the envelope that contained Emily Cantrell's two separate and conflicting charts, he trudged on. Fatigue was clouding his judgment. It was becoming difficult to remember which back lanes and alleys he had already traversed.

He'd talked with about twenty homeless men and women. Each one he spoke with had been given cash in hopes of finding out something about Marc, a.k.a. Beau Jangles.

At one point, Carl thought he'd gotten lucky. A young woman he questioned seemed to recognize the name. She was a slim, tall woman who, in better circumstances, might have been a model. Her face, smudged with dirt, could not hide what was beneath. When her huge brown eyes met Carl's, he felt a surge of shock at what he saw. She was simply beautiful. Her high cheekbones, full rich lips and willowy figure could have definitely earned her a spot in the world of high fashion.

"Excuse me, ma'am, do you happen to know a fellow who goes by the name of Beau Jangles?" he asked.

"I'm no ma'am, buster, and who wants to know?" she snarled contemptuously. "Are you a cop or something?"

Carl had learned in his dealings with Marc that the homeless were suspicious of anyone from outside the 'cardboard' community.

"No, I'm not a cop. My name's Carl Phoenix. I'm a friend of Beau's."

Seeing an opportunity to make some easy money, she said coyly, "Maybe I do know him and maybe I don't. What's it worth to you…*Carl Phoenix?*"

He immediately produced a twenty. She subsequently tried to snap it out of his hands but he was quicker, pulling it just beyond her reach. "Not so fast. What's your name?"

"Drop dead, cop. I'm not telling you anything."

Deliberately, he slowly reached into his pocket, producing another twenty. He held up both bills, fanning the two of them out, and again baited her. "I'll give you forty bucks if you have any information about Beau."

She looked longingly at the money, "Ryan. My name's Ryan Klusack and yeah, I know him."

Carl felt the first flash of hope all day.

"Do you know where I can find him? Where he lives?"

Laughing, she swept her hand with her fingers spread as she did a half circle. "He lives here, like the rest of us. But if I wanted to find him, I'd be looking behind a Publix grocery store. He likes the garbage bins in back. There's lots of good food. There's fruits and vegetables everyday. Helps keep a good figure," she replied, as she swayed her hips left, then right in an exaggerated motion.

"For an extra twenty bucks, I can show you a real good time," she offered seductively.

"Ryan," he said, adding another twenty bucks, "go get a room and buy yourself some food. You know, if you took a shower and got yourself cleaned up, I know some people who might be able to help you. Have you ever thought about modeling?"

She laughed cynically. "How do you think I got here, man? Goddamn modeling money, so much of it. Ohhh baby, the money, the parties and the coke, it was all sooo good. I started buying cocaine all the time. After a while I was too stoned to work. This is my home now. I live here," she said. She reached out and grabbed the sixty dollars he held out. "Do you have any rock you want to sell me, stud?"

His naïveté shone through as he shook his head, his mouth gaping open. Ryan shrugged as she turned on her heel and walked to the corner. There, she engaged in a full conversation with a Hispanic youth who was leaning against a wall. Less than a minute later, Carl saw his money change from her hand to the youth's as he slipped a mysterious object into her palm. Ryan skipped down the street like a young schoolgirl, looking for a quiet place to get high. Carl stood dumbfounded for another full minute before starting out to find a Publix grocery store.

Hours later, he finally gave up as night began to fall like a dark, heavy cloak. The growling in his stomach reminded him that he hadn't eaten since yesterday's lunch. It was also the last time he'd seen Marc.

Making his way in the general direction of Reggie's, he decided to weave one last time through the alleyways. It would be a lot safer taking the well-lit streets on the way to his car, but the back lanes would be quicker and, although slim, there was the chance of running across Marc.

Passing the last Publix garbage bin on the way to the small restaurant, he stopped. He saw an accumulation of boxes that had not been there on his first pass. They were neatly piled, sandwiched between the cement wall and the rear of the bin.

Veering to the far side of the lane, he decided to check out the cardboard shanty. He bent over, about to peek in and see if Marc was huddled among the boxes. Just then he felt something press down on his windpipe, yanking him backward. Startled, he began to struggle. Suddenly, it felt like there was sandpaper rubbing the side of his face. His nostrils filled with a putrid stench.

"Are you tryin' to rob me, asshole? I'll cut you open like a fish," a voice quietly whispered in his ear. His unseen assailant pushed something sharp into Carl's back as he spoke. There was no doubt; it *was* a knife.

Startled, he screamed out, "NO, no I am not trying to *rob* you," *Oh god. I'm going to die*. The thought activated his body's involuntary reactions. His stomach knotted, as his heart began to pound. He felt his hands shaking. Not knowing what to do, he thought, *Mention Beau's name. Maybe he knows him.*

"I'm looking for Beau Jangles, *Beau Jangles*. I have money. I can pay you." He felt the tip of the knife press his skin. There was no pain, but the threat was real, very real, as his assailant bore down.

"Oh, I'm gonna take your money white boy, all you got, you can believe that. What do you want with that 'shit for brains', Beau Jangles anyway?" As the attacker asked the question he'd pried the envelope containing the charts from Carl's hand. *I haven't seen his face. He's just going to rob me,* Carl rationalized. *Take the charts, take my wallet, I don't care...*

"Answer me, sweet cheeks."

Again, Carl felt the knife pressing the area protecting his ribs.

"Answer me right, then maybe we'll have us some fun," the hidden attacker hissed.

The arm holding him in the headlock was like steel.

With his ears partially covered by the man's arm, he heard something that sounded like a dull clunk. Simultaneously, he lurched forward. Suddenly he felt the blade cutting. The spot where the knife had pressed was warm, then wet. He heard another 'CLUNK' as the arm slid from around his neck and the man crumpled.

Spinning around, he instinctively looked toward the ground. He saw his assailant for the first time. There on the asphalt, lay a large black man. His face was covered with a scraggly beard. The long dirty hair clumped in a pile of matted dreadlocks. Beside him was the envelope. Carl bent down and snatched it. As he turned he saw his savior weaving back and forth, like someone caught in a strong wind, body swaying, feet firmly planted on the ground.

"Ryan? Is that you? My God, it is you! Thank you, this bastard had a knife in my back. He was going to kill me!"

He moved closer and looked into her face. The faded streetlight barely illuminated her features. The glow was bright enough to show her glassy eyes. She murmured something; no, she was singing under her breath. In her hands, she held a two-foot length of two-by-four wood.

"Naw, he wasn't going to kill you. Clive doesn't usually kill people. What he likes to do is *rape* you, and then *steals* all your *coke*. Don't you, you black *bastard*." He stirred, and she kicked him, viciously hitting him again with the board.

As Clive lay on the ground unconscious, Carl felt a chill as the blood began to cool near his open wound. He reached back, feeling the spot. His fingers were wet. Holding them up he could make out the blood. "Ryan, I'm cut. I need you to take a look and see if it's serious."

She leaned in closer as he turned, lifting his shirt. "No man, barely a scratch, it's nothing," she slurred.

He relaxed a bit, but still not entirely trusting her opinion of how bad it really was. Feeling an enormous debt of gratitude, he was compelled to offer her some sort of help.

"Ryan, do you want to come home with me? I have an extra room in a very nice place. I'll make you something to eat. You can take a hot bath and then a warm, clean bed to sleep in. I don't want anything from you in return. You can stay as long as you like. C'mon, what do you say?" he implored anxiously.

Her eyes cleared a bit, as she tried to make out the words he was saying. She stared earnestly at Carl. "Do you have any crack at your house?"

His brow wrinkled, as he answered, "No, Ryan, just food and a safe, warm bed."

Looking almost disgusted, she flung back, "Yeah, thanks for nothing, kid." Then as if a light had pierced the haze of her clouded mind she softened. "Do you think I could have some more money?" she asked innocently.

He reached into the wallet he still owned, thanks to Ryan. Pulling out a bunch of twenties, he clasped her hand as he pushed them into her palm.

"Ryan, please get a room. Eat something, please. Don't spend it all on drugs, okay?" She quickly pulled her hand out of his with the money, as if he might change his mind. Staring intently she squinted her eyes, as if trying to etch him into her now, unstable memory.

"You're alright, man. What did you say your name was again?"

Recalling what had brought him there in the first place, he repeated, "Carl, my name is Carl. Please remember it if you see Beau, tell him *Carl* is looking for him. I'll be in Royal Creek Park tomorrow. Ryan, can you remember that?" He doubted that she could.

"Oh yeah, no problem, Carl. Royal Creek Park, I'll tell him when I see him," she said, still swaying, unable to focus her eyes.

The whole run-in with Clive had taken less than five minutes. Carl was concerned that his wound might be serious. Right then all he wanted was to get back to his car. He would go to the emergency ward at Washington General. He figured he'd probably need stitches, or a tetanus shot at the very least.

Thanking Ryan again for rescuing him, he added, "Are you sure you are going to be alright?"

"Right as rain, man. Right as rain."

He said a final farewell and began walking back to Reggie's and his waiting car.

Twenty minutes later as his car came into view, he saw something. A shadowy figure was moving in the darkness. There, between the old brick building that housed Reggie's and a television repair shop, was a man. Carl's nerves were raw after the dangerous encounter just minutes before. Speeding up, he kept moving in the direction of his vehicle. He anxiously reached into his pocket and began feeling for his keys until he'd found the one with the plastic end. Out of the corner of his eye, he saw the figure rise from the shadows. It was moving toward the sidewalk. It was now directly across from his parked car. In the dim light all he could make out was that the man was wearing a hooded poncho. The hood was pulled over his head. The oversized material concealed the man's arms and hands. He wondered why he'd allowed himself to be wandering these streets and neighborhoods after dark. He silently cursed his foolishness as his heart began to pound for the second time that night.

He tried to guess the distance between himself and the driver's door. Suddenly the walking poncho made its way in the same general direction. Carl began to sweat. If he broke into a sprint he might make it to the door first. On the other hand, if the menace approaching ran as well, he could easily beat him to the car.

Why is this guy following me? Does he think he's going to rob me, or take my car, or—worse?

Carl decided in that moment it wasn't going to happen twice in one evening. He would not be victimized a second time, in less than an hour. He would stand his ground. Pulling the key ring from his pocket, he bunched all but one in his palm. That, he slipped between his fingers. Closing his fist around the bundle it protruded from his white knuckles like a spike, and he quickened his stride.

Abruptly changing direction, he began walking toward the ominous figure. Carl couldn't be sure if it was the adrenaline or just the best line of defense. With dusk quickly turning to night, the stalker was unidentifiable. Nothing more than the hulking shadow of a faceless man, cloaked in his cape-like poncho. They changed direction in unison and the man now bore down upon him. Less than thirty yards away, Carl quickened his tempo. The quick walk became a slow jog toward his new nemesis. The man increased his pace as well. In the dim light of the street lamp, they looked like two gladiators preparing to clash in battle. With the distance closing between them, Carl broke into a full run, shouting incoherently. The man stopped in his tracks, taking a step backward. Carl launched his attack, howling like a crazed lunatic. With less than ten feet between them, the man raised an arm to ward off the first blow as he screamed out. Carl came face to face with the man. The hunted had become the hunter.

Chapter 35

The huge, cylindrical chamber hummed quietly. A pretty, young nurse carefully explained the procedure to Emily.

"Miss Cantrell, you should use these," she said, handing over a set of earplugs. "Please try to relax. The test will take approximately forty-five minutes. You'll be laying on the padded table and will be able to speak to the staff through the intercom at any time during the procedure."

Emily looked apprehensively at the tube-like machine and with a nervous smile said, "I'm not crazy about small spaces."

When she was just sixteen years old, she'd been stuck on an elevator between floors during a blackout. She had been alone and frightened, trapped in the darkness for almost four hours. It had been the most terrifying time in her young life. The scar left from the ordeal was a fear of confined areas. She considered this to be her Achilles heel and worked bravely to overcome it.

"Miss Cantrell, if you need help, we'll be right here for you. The machine makes loud banging sounds during the test, so please don't be alarmed. It's quite normal. If you would like, we can give you a headset with music instead of the ear plugs." The nurse then hesitated for a moment. She was barely able to mask her excitement. "Miss Cantrell, I'm so honored to meet you, ma'am. I just know you're going to be our next president! You're our hero—I mean to all the girls on night shift here," she giggled nervously.

Spying the nurse's nametag, the constant campaigner replied, "Well, thank you, Jo-Anne. I appreciate the vote of confidence. I'll look forward to your other vote too. As for the music, I think these earplugs will be fine. I'll be okay. Let's just get this over with, Dear," she said uneasily.

Damn you Worthington, you and your tests, she thought as the table slowly transported her into the chamber.

*****

"*JESUS CHRIST, CARL!*" Marc screamed raising his arm to ward off the attack, "Have you gone *FUCKIN' CRAZY*?"

Carl tried to stop, but his forward momentum was so forceful that he had to side-step Marc to avoid the head on collision. Marc pulled the hood of his poncho down as he spun around.

"YOU ASSHOLE! *What the hell is your problem*?" he shouted at him.

A look of stunned disbelief crossed Carl's' face.

"Marc, oh my God! It's you. I'm so glad to see YOU!"

"Well, I wouldn't have guessed, running at me like a goddamn madman," he blurted out, obviously shaken.

"What are you doing here?" Carl asked, still trying to compose himself.

"When a couple of my friends told me some preppy kid was looking for me, what do you think I thought?" he said. "I came here and saw your ride. I figured, rather than trying to find you, I would hang around here until you came back. Son-of-a- bitch, what the hell were you doing? Trying to kill me, man?"

Carl anxiously recounted his run-in with Clive. He then described how Ryan had intervened on his behalf.

"Yeah, that Clive can be a real bastard. He wouldn't have killed you, might have kept carving on you though. Ryan's okay, when she's not high. You're lucky kid. He'd have robbed you, and probably raped you if he could've held you down. Too many years in the slammer, he likes young guys. Let me see that cut."

Carl turned, lifting his shirt to expose the wound.

"Jesus Marc, I'm really sorry, I was scared. When I saw someone hanging around in the alley, well, I decided I wouldn't go through *that* twice in one day. I never thought for a second that it was you. Sorry. I'm just too freaked out. I didn't get a wink of sleep last night," Carl rambled apologetically.

"Yeah, yeah, okay, kid. Don't worry about it. Well, this cut's not so bad, but it looks like you're going to need a few stitches. So what are you doing here anyway?"

Recalling his initial mission and everything he wanted to tell Marc, he became reanimated. He quickly put the sordid events of the day behind him.

"Marc, I checked out what you asked me to, I mean, *Dr. Andrews.*"

In the still, cool night, even the soft light of the street lamp caught the tears rolling down Marc's cheek.

"I haven't heard that articulation in many years, *'Dr. Andrews'*. Never really cared for it when I was a punk like you, but after this," he said with the wave of his hand, "it's a bit uplifting."

"I also checked into the fire at Novatek. Everything you said was true."

"No-shit-Sherlock," he replied mockingly.

"I have to talk to you about something else. I need you to come to my place. I have to show you some stuff."

"What kind of stuff, kid?" he answered warily.

"You thought that the fire at the lab had something to do with Dr. Edwards' discovery, his *cure for cancer*. You were right. Not only do I believe Edwards had found a cure, I have proof," he said, and remembering the medical-charts, he lifted his empty hands.

"Damn, I brought it with me—I must have dropped…" Turning, he looked over his shoulder and could make out the envelope on the street some twenty feet behind him. He ran and retrieved it. In seconds he was back, standing directly in front of the defunct Dr. Andrews.

Without warning, Marc took two handfuls of his tee shirt, pulling Carl's face to within inches of his own. His eyes bore into Carl's and in a quiet shaken voice he said, "I don't want to see it, kid, and you don't want to know it. The last time someone showed me proof, they got dead. DO you understand me? *THREE PEOPLE DIED*. I almost died, *AND THEY DID!*"

He tried to recoil from the hot, bittersweet breath that flooded his nostrils.

"You can forget it, I don't know what you've got there and I DON'T want to know. *Go home*, burn it, shred it, do whatever you have to do to get rid of it. Get this out of your head now. You get back to your golden life boy, and forget all about this bullshit. *Do you hear me?*" Marc sputtered desperately.

Maybe it was exhaustion. It could have been that Carl had been pushed around enough that night. Or perhaps he was imagining his father screaming in his face, telling him what to do. Whatever it was, he snapped.

"Screw you, Marc," he said as he pulled himself away from the former research genius.

"Why should some benefit from this cure while thousands die everyday? There's a cover-up going on here and it's gone on since the day of the fire. There are two of us. We can tell someone. They have to believe it when we show them the proof. You can tell them your story. *God Marc*, don't you want some justice for your friends?" he implored desperately.

Carl was exasperated. He had truly expected Marc to be overjoyed, thrilled even, at finding someone who believed his story. He had figured Marc would want to prove his case and avenge the murders of his colleagues. Naively, Carl had assumed he would be an undeniable witness. The only survivor of the Novatek fire *had* to be the most reliable source to help him expose a conspiracy that had cheated so many out of life.

"Marc *they're using the cure*, but only for some. The president's daughter had—"

Pressing his palms flat against his ears, he shouted, "I DON'T WANT TO HEAR IT! You're not listening to me. I don't want to know anything about it!"

Carl stared at the frightened man. He looked more like a child having a tantrum as he tried to block out his voice. Gently, he reached up to pull Marc's hands away from his ears.

"Listen, my father is a senator. He can protect you. He can protect both of us. We can get someone to listen," Carl said gently.

"Don't be an idiot. You tell your father anything about it, not only are you dead, so is he. You can't talk to anyone about this ever again. *Don't* ever mention my name to ANYONE. I'll disappear, I've done it before and I can do it again."

"I think you underestimate my father. You don't know him. He is a very powerful man with a lot of resources. He has connections at the highest levels of government. He's also very wealthy."

Marc looked at him as though he was a naïve child. His eyes softened as he quietly said, "son, who do you think has kept this secret for so long? Do you think regular people, or John Q. Public? It's been the government and the wealthy that have managed to cover this up for twenty-five years. Think about it. *If* your father *is* one of the good guys, then you'll be signing his death warrant by getting him involved."

"Marc, I can't believe you're so blind. Can't you see what this is?" he pleaded.

"Yes, I can, Carl. This is *dangerous*. I've been through it once, and I won't go through it again. It's been great knowing you kid. Forget you ever knew me, and if you were smart, you'd forget this whole mess." Marc turned and walked into the murky night.

Carl didn't know what to do. Frustrated, he yelled after him, "I'll see you at Reggie's for lunch."

Without responding, Marc vanished.

Carl got into his car feeling despondent and alone.

This is crap. The old man's a loser. Gutless bum, he thought miserably. The idea of actual danger had never really occurred to him. Now, more than ever, he was nervous about involving his father. Then it dawned on him: he knew how to expose the story without becoming directly involved. Grinning, he accelerated his car towards George Washington General.

*****

Worthington studied the pictures from the MRI.

"Amazing, I can't believe it. The tumor's GONE, it should be right here," he muttered aloud, actually touching the film. He looked over at the original MRI pictures and there it was. Skeptically his eyes darted between the two films. *It's a miracle.*

Convinced that Emily Cantrell was out of the woods and out of his hair, he'd resolved to take a week off. After going through the security checkpoint stationed outside her room, Worthington announced, "Emily, the test results are in. Congratulations, you have a clean bill of health."

"Well, I told you I was fine Franklin, just a bit overworked." Looking at Jason who had leapt to his feet when the doctor entered, she added, "Sweetheart, are you satisfied now?"

"Yes, dear, I am," Jason responded as he put the last of her personal effects in the overnight bag.

"All that's left is to discharge you, young lady. I'll be happy to personally wheel you out to the car," Worthington added.

"I am *not* going to be wheeled anywhere, Franklin. I'm not an invalid for God's sake," she protested.

"Sorry, Emily, hospital policy. We can't have you slipping on your way out now, can we?" he said, again flashing the disarming TV doctor's smile.

"Fine, just get me home, Jason," Emily said, irritably.

Spencer dutifully took the handles of the wheelchair as he pushed it towards the bed. "Ma'am, ready to go?"

"More than ready, Spence, thank you," she said plopping herself into the waiting chair.

Emily, surrounded by her entourage, was at the discharge station signing out, just as Carl came through the emergency room doors of the hospital. He walked to the desk where the nurse asked, without raising her head, "What's the nature of your emergency, sir?'

"I was mugged and the assailant cut my back with a knife. It's not serious, but I'd like to get it looked at. I think I might need a few stitches and a tetanus shot."

The nurse reached into the cupboard behind her back and took out a pair of surgical gloves and a large absorbent gauze bandage. Walking around the counter, she instructed Carl to lift his shirt, as she stopped directly behind him. Snapping the gloves on, she positioned the self-adhesive gauze over the open wound. Ensuring that it was completely covered, she returned to her station without commenting. Discarding the gloves, she robotically scribbled something on a form attached to a clipboard and handed it to Carl.

"Sir, it doesn't look bad, but you probably *will* need a few stitches. Just take a seat and fill out this form. If you've filed a police report, please indicate the incident number here," pointing to a spot on the paper. She handed him the clipboard and a pen.

Carl took a seat in the crowded waiting room as he began filling out the questionnaire. He heard the small commotion before he actually saw her.

"Goodbye, Miss Cantrell, hope you're feeling great," the discharge nurse said as she signed her out.

"Thank you, Carolyn," Emily said, noting the nametag. "I'm good as new."

He looked up and saw the procession. There were Secret Service men, a man he didn't recognize, and someone dressed in a lab coat, no doubt her doctor. They were all walking beside and behind Emily Cantrell as she was wheeled to the exit doors. Just outside, he could see a long, black limousine parked, when a moment before, there had been an ambulance.

*****

Two hours later, sitting at his small kitchen table, Carl dialed the phone. It was well after midnight as the pleasant female voice on the answering machine gave instructions. Following the specific commands he spelled out the first four letters on his dial pad, L O G A. Immediately, a man's voice sprang to life on the other end.

"You have reached the desk of Harry Logan, Investigative Reporter for the *Washington Herald Press*. I'm on the phone or away from my desk just now. At the sound of the tone, please leave a brief message. I'll get back to you as soon as I can. Thanks," the voice said, immediately followed by the message tone.

"Mr. Logan, I have a story for you. At noon tomorrow I will call your desk. If you're not there I will immediately contact another reporter. This is not a hoax. I have the biggest story of the century, and I am prepared to give you an exclusive. Be there at noon."

After hanging up the phone, Carl dragged his exhausted body to bed. One hour later he was still staring into the blackness, recalling Marc's eerie words. "*I almost got dead... and they did.*"

Chapter 36

The newsroom was in a constant state of chaos, with people bustling down aisles, and phones continuously ringing. The short walls separating the desks offered little privacy, and the entire floor was a zoo. The steady buzz served as cover to the actual conversations taking place from desk to desk. The result was an indecipherable drone of mumbles.

Contrary to first impressions, the place ran like a well-oiled machine and was the heart and soul of the Washington Herald Press. Out of the mayhem rose a first-class publication every twenty-four hours.

Harry Logan plunked into his chair just before 7 a.m. Setting down a steaming cup of double-churned mocha coffee, he checked his messages. Wrinkling his brow, he listened as a young male voice reaffirmed promises of grandeur.

Yeah, right, everyone's got the biggest story of the century, Harry thought, listening to the disembodied voice as he tipped the insulated paper cup to his thick lips.

The morning had passed uneventfully and he found himself curiously wondering if there *would* be a call at noon. Staring at the huge clock, he waited for midday. As a seasoned journalist he humored many who had called him over the years with alleged '*great stories*'. He stated to colleagues on numerous occasions that it was all 'just part of the gig'. The majority of the so-called *big stories* were a result of personal vendettas. Many were jilted lovers, a few one-night stands, and the rest came from pissed-off former spouses of the powerful. Years ago, that type of retelling could make the third section. These day's it was nearly an accepted part of political life.

Just as the big clock's smooth, deliberate, second hand approached the number twelve, Harry Logan's phone rang.

"Afternoon, Logan here."

"Good afternoon, Mr. Logan. I'm the guy who—"

"Yeah, yeah, I know. You're the guy with the biggest story of the century—*this week*. Okay, you've got my attention for about sixty seconds. Let's start with your name," Harry said in an attempt to control the conversation.

Carl had slept restlessly the night before, replaying Marc's warning over and over. He'd decided not to disclose his real name. He also thought that it would be wise to use a pay phone. On the corner of Fifth and Regent, he'd stood patiently for a half hour, waiting for his Rolex to strike noon.

"Just call me *Bill,* for now," Carl said guardedly.

"Okay, *Bill,* so tell me what it is you think you know?" Logan said, as he wrote the name *Bill* down on a pad of paper.

Logan loved the guys who tried to think like the infamous *Mike Hammer* from a Mickey Spillane novel. They all had an alias and a wild story. *Probably just another crackpot,* he thought.

"Well I really don't want to discuss this on the phone, Mr. Logan," Carl proceeded cautiously. "I'd like to meet with you."

"Come on *Biiilll*, you've gotta give me something if you want me to find time for a meet," Harry replied, exaggerating the alias. "You do understand *Bill* I'm a busy guy. I get a dozen crank calls every week. Now I'm not saying that *yours is one of those,* but at least I need to know what this is about."

Carl did appreciate his point. Harry Logan was a respected reporter who had a very loud voice on the Hill. Carl was so jumpy recalling Marc's persistent warnings that he wondered if the call was being recorded. Perhaps someone was listening in.

"Sir, I do realize your position, but I can't trust that this call isn't being taped. If the information I have, fell into the wrong hands, it could be very dangerous for all involved," he said solemnly.

"Sorry, I don't believe '*Bill'* is your real name and you're not telling me a thing. You want a meeting based on, well… nothing."

"I realize your time is valuable, Mr. Logan. I guess you'll just have to read about this in the *Post*. The next call I'm making is to Kiefer Nelson."

"Okay…hold up a minute there Bill, just give me a second."

Harry cringed at the thought of Nelson getting a scoop that had been laid at his feet first. It had happened once before.

Two years prior, Harry received what he'd considered an erroneous tip about a powerful politician. The mysterious caller had claimed that a certain cabinet member had ties to kiddy porn. The story was so vague, so preposterous, that Logan had passed on it. He wouldn't meet the caller, who swore he had undeniable proof of the man's guilt. The information had been completely legit. For weeks it had been the biggest, the *only*, story on the Hill. Kiefer Nelson and the Post had gotten the exclusive scoop.

"I'll tell you what, I'll meet with you and even let you buy me a drink. I trust you won't be wasting my time, right?" Harry was sure he would be.

"You'll be happy we met, Mr. Logan, I guarantee it."

The rendezvous was set for seven o'clock in the evening. They would meet at a discrete lounge on the west side. Carl would approach him. He would recognize him, having seen his picture beside articles he'd written. Satisfied that Logan was actually going to show up, Carl thought he'd play it safe. He'd share the vital information only after securing a guarantee that his identity as the source would not be revealed.

Logan hung up the phone, wondering if there might be something of interest here. He tapped his pencil on the tablet of paper, glancing at the few words he had jotted down. *Bill (fake name), male aged 20 to 35, college educated. Information, potentially dangerous.* It wasn't much, but it was all he could extract from the obscure conversation.

Unsure if it was his years of experience, instinct, or just plain old curiosity, but Harry wanted to make the meeting. He was pretty sure it'd be just another wild goose chase.

Grinning, he thought about it. *What the hell, I'll probably need a drink by tonight anyway.*

*****

Carl replaced the receiver on the payphone. With a smug look of satisfaction, he turned and walked toward his building. He felt this was the safest route to go and was confident Logan would expose the truth. That's what investigative reporters did.

Nobody will ever know how I got the information or even my involvement, he thought, re-entering his condo.

Carl spotted the flashing light on his answering machine as he walked toward his desk. Pressing the button, the computer-generated voice announced, "You have, two-new-messages." He pressed play.

"Hi Carl, Sal here. I guess you're still under the weather. Call me and let me know when you'll be back to work. See ya."

Damn, forgot all about work, better give him a shout, he thought as the second voice began.

"Carl, this is dad. Just checking to make sure everything's all right. You've missed the last few days of work. Don't forget our deal about showing up, son. Call me."

Jesus, does he know everything I do? Is he getting reports on me? he thought bitterly as he slumped on the couch. Carl momentarily recalled the night of the storm. Frustration flooded his mind as he thought about the message. He wondered how his dad could be so callous. He sadly accepted the simple truth. His father had become so insensitive over the years, that it hadn't dawned on him that Sarah's death might cause him some regret. *Obviously, it didn't occur to the ole' man that I might feel guilty or even responsible about Sarah,* he thought glumly.

The anger was replaced with despair as he suddenly realized he hadn't even thought about Sarah in the last forty-eight hours. Exhausted and emotionally drained, Carl closed his eyes as he reclined on the couch. His mind swam with images of Sarah, Ryan and Marc, and a dark figure lurking in the shadows.

Within minutes he fell into a fitful slumber, his mind flashing vivid images, laced with faces. Like most dreams, nothing made sense. In one scene Marc was talking to Emily Cantrell. She held a small, prune-like object in her hand.

"Here you go, Dr. Andrews. You can have my tumor now." He took the twisted, shriveled object and stuffed it into his mouth, smiling at her, Marc chewed. As he slowly turned, she faded from the picture. Flames suddenly shot from Marc's empty eye sockets and his lips moved. Then, in a clear, strong voice, he said, "See, Carl, they got dead, and now I got dead, thanks a bunch kid." Marc faded and Ryan appeared, walking hand-in-hand with his father. Her face came within inches of Carl's and she said, "The Senator doesn't want to kill you, he just wants to screw you and

then steal all your coke." Ryan and his father walked off the stage of his dream-mind, laughing hysterically.

The picture changed again. Suddenly, a naked Sarah appeared dancing and laughing. Grinning she looked into his eyes and asked, "Tell me how do you feel about me now, Darling?" The top of her head was gone and blood ran down her forehead, streaming past her emerald green eyes. Her hand reached behind his head. She pulled him toward her open mouth. "Kiss me lover, kiss me."

He awoke sweating. His heart was beating like a drum, arms wildly flailing as his hands push away the empty air in front of him.

"*NO—NO! GET-A-WAY, GET-A-WAY!*" he screamed aloud, frantically looking at his surroundings. Dazed and shaken, the last remnants of sleep fell away. He recognized it was all just a nightmare.

As his mind cleared, he remembered the meeting with Harry Logan. The time 6:37 glowed from the face of a black clock.. Flying off the couch, Carl ran to his bedroom and pulled open a drawer. Without looking, he yanked out the first top his hand touched. Pulling the Tee shirt over his head, he scrambled toward the door of the condo. He didn't think to comb his hair or freshen up for his meeting.

*****

Harry Logan glanced at his watch. 7:07. *A waste of time. Looks like Billy-boy's a no show,* he mused, draining his scotch on the rocks.

The waitress appeared in the corner of his eye as he returned the glass to the lacquered tabletop. "Would you like another?" she asked, the glass vanishing as she swept the table.

Harry glanced at his watch again. 7:09.

Ah, what the hell, I'm here anyway. In his mind he accepted the fact that 'Bill' was a waste of time.

"Sure, why not?"

"Coming right up," the waitress said, turning on her heel.

"Make it a double," Logan called after her.

*****

As Carl sped towards the lounge on the far side of town, he organized his thoughts, deciding what he would and wouldn't tell the reporter. *Where do I start, Cantrell or Marc, the lab, the fire or Edwards?*

Looking toward the passenger seat, he eyed the envelope with the conflicting Cantrell hospital charts. What if he didn't believe him? Should he bring the charts in? What if Logan wanted to show them to other people for verification? *I could go to jail, or worse.* Doubt and fear clouded his mind as he saw the time illuminated on dash; 7:05 o'clock.

Damn, I'm ten minutes away, he thought, speeding up. He focused on the current problem; getting to the bar before Harry Logan left. He ran a yellow-turning-red traffic light.

*****

As he finished his double, Harry's drinking limit had been reached. He looked at his watch for the final time. 7:17. He left five bucks beside the emptied glass for the waitress as he stood to leave. Feeling a little tipsy, he stepped away from the table. A hand firmly gripped his arm. Startled, Harry turned to see whose. There, wearing a wrinkled tee shirt with his arm outstretched was a disheveled looking young man with ruffled hair.

"Bill?"

"Yeah, sorry I'm late Mr. Logan," he replied, trying to catch his breath.

"Have a seat and let's get you a drink," he said beckoning to the waitress. "Well let's hear what you've got, Bill."

Harry instantly shook off the buzz he'd gotten from the scotch. The reporter in him surfaced as soon as they began. After a moment, the waitress left with their drink orders. Harry's was now ice water, and Carl's, a beer.

Carl nervously began the story. He tried to keep it vague, all the while keeping Marc's real name out entirely. Harry made notes in the dimly lit lounge as he listened.

Finally, when Carl had stopped talking, Logan said, "Well Bill, that's quite a story, but I don't get it. So Emily Cantrell gets overworked, goes to the hospital and gets better. Big deal. Some old vagrant named *Beau* says he knows of a national conspiracy, a cover-up about a medical revelation. And Cantrell is a benefactor of this mystery cure. Kid, where's your proof, a homeless bum, your theories? You've got nothing here. You're wasting my time," Harry taunted, still in pursuit of the real scoop.

Carl hadn't told him the heart of the story. Feeling the columnist out, Carl was trying to determine if he *could* be convinced, even with the evidence. He had to take the chance. After all, he had come here to recruit Harry Logan's help in exposing the whole Elixir cover-up.

"Emily Cantrell didn't go to the hospital because of exhaustion Mr. Logan. Overwork wasn't her real diagnosis." Carl took the envelope from the empty chair and slowly positioned it in front of his beer. Both men stared at it.

"No? Then what was her *real diagnosis*, Bill?" Logan asked, eyeing the envelope. Now it was just his journalistic curiosity. He wanted to know what Bill knew.

"Emily Cantrell was diagnosed with an inoperable brain tumor. This type of cancer spreads rapidly and is terminal. She was given less than three months to live."

Raising his eyebrows, Harry's forehead was a mass of wrinkles. "This is your proof?" he asked, indicating the envelope on the table.

"Part of it, yes."

"So, what are you saying? Cantrell had terminal brain cancer, and now she's all better? And this is because… why exactly?"

"What I'm saying, and what I have proof of, is that the government or someone in the private sector has found a cure for cancer. I'm also saying that they've kept it a secret for at least twenty-five years."

Harry smiled cynically as he reached for the envelope.

"Well, Bill, let's have a look at what you *think* you have here. The only thing that I'm sure you have at this point is my attention."

Chapter 37

The clouds had been busy during the night. Searching each other out, they'd grouped together. The accumulative overcast blocked out the sun and the bright blue skies that hid behind them. The morning light revealed the dark, hovering shroud of gray and with it, the imminent threat of rain.

Marc pushed the newspapers from his chest that had served as a blanket during the long cool night. Sitting up, he stretched and let out a groan as he worked the kinks from his back. Slowly getting to his feet, he bent and rubbed his right knee. He stared at the morning sky, looking for confirmation.

"Yep, she's gonna rain cats and dogs," he said aloud, the gloomy skies validating the arthritic ache in his knee.

Removing some debris, which had provided the camouflage for the shopping cart, he took up his station behind it. The day began like they all did, as he walked down the alleyway.

Yesterday, he'd been approached by several of his displaced homeless brethren. The first had been Rudy, who in another life had once been a first class cabinetmaker. "Hey Beau, some guy was looking for you yesterday. Good looking, rich punk forked over twenty bucks. So message delivered." He smiled a mouthful of yellow, rotting teeth. "Well I guess I'm square with *buddy*," he added, cackling as he walked away.

Every time Marc managed to get the naïve idealist out of his head, another one of his neighbors would share a similar story.

"Damn kid. Blake was an optimist and look at what it got him. Save the world, help everyone and make things better. Like they say, nice guys finish last," he mumbled as he pushed the cart to nowhere in particular. The stress of the last few days had reverted Marc back, back to a mumbling, ranting, air-swatting recluse.

"Can't get involved, can't get involved. Mind my own business and stay alive. That's my job, nothing else, just staying alive, staying alive," Marc's mind repeated. Soon he was singing an old Bee Gee's song under his breath.

He was mumbling incessantly when a voice jerked him out of his daze. He jumped back, simultaneously, letting out a yelp.

"Whoa, whoa, you okay, man?"

Focusing on the source of the voice, he saw Ryan leaning against a building that lined the side of the laneway. She was exhaling the spent smoke of a long cigarette butt found on the sidewalk.

"Ryan, damn, girl you scared five years off me," he said, embarrassed, as a childlike smile spread across his lips.

"Oppps, sorry about that Beau," she giggled. "Some young guy was looking for you the other day. Said his name was Carl something. I looked, but I couldn't catch up with you. He was going to wait for you at some park. Sorry, don't remember the name of it. I guess it doesn't matter now anyway, he was going to be there yesterday."

"Thanks for the message, Ryan, I met up with him. We sort of found each other that day," he said recalling the near attack Carl had launched that evening.

Abandoning his cart, he walked up to Ryan. He gently gripped her shoulders and gazed at her, his eyes reflecting the sincerity he felt. "Ryan, you did my friend a solid that night. Clive would have messed him up. I really owe you. You ever need anything, talk to ol' Beau. I'll do whatever I can." Marc had a soft spot for her and wished she'd get off the streets.

"Don't sweat it, Beau. He was a nice kid, even tried to help me out. I offered to do him, but he wouldn't," she said as her eyes darted anxiously. "Gave me some money and tried to get me cleaned up. Too late for all that, ya know. Then I saw Clive messing with him, so I figured he could use a hand."

"Listen, girl, it's not too late for you. You shouldn't be here, Ryan. You're a young woman with a full life ahead of you. Don't let these streets eat you up. In the meantime, you watch your back. Don't tell anyone about helping Carl out or about whacking on Clive's head. That bastard has a real mean streak. He'll try to get even with whoever clobbered him, but only if he can find out who it was," he cautioned.

"Thanks, Beau, I'll be okay. Hey, you don't have some crack do you? You know I could fix you up nice," she said seductively.

"I don't do that shit, Ryan, and you shouldn't either," he said in a fatherly tone. "BE GOOD!" he added, embarrassed by her offer. Standing behind his cart, he hastily walked off.

*****

Ryan took the last drag off the spent smoke as she nervously bit her lower lip. She'd shot her mouth off all day yesterday, bragging about how she'd clipped Clive, got him good. Boasting how she had paid him back for raping her and then stealing her small hit of rock cocaine a while back. *Shouldn't have yapped it up yesterday, Clive's such a jerk. He ain't gonna like a woman getting the drop on him.* Ryan shrugged it off as she made her way to the corner where the Hispanic punk sold cocaine. Maybe she could get a hit in exchange for sex. Smiling at the prospect, her pace quickened.

*****

Marc felt like hell. He cared about Carl, but mostly he liked the way Carl had made him feel these past months. For the first time in years, he'd felt like a normal human being. *Stupid kid, he's gonna get himself hurt, hurt bad.*

He decided to try one more time. Marc felt he owed him that. He was going to make one last effort to get Carl to forget about this whole thing, before it was too late.

Although it was not quite ten o'clock, he headed in the general direction of Reggie's. Just then the rain started, followed by a huge clap of thunder. It was as if God slapped his hands together. Marc jumped at the sound. As the rain began pelting down, he instinctively pulled up the hood of his poncho.

*****

Hours before the rain began falling, Harry Logan scrolled back to the beginning of his article. He had begun writing two hours earlier and was ready for the final proofread. He always read his work aloud before sending it to the presses. In the abandoned office, the title of the article rang out, as Harry began. **The mysteries that elude us—are they really inexplicable?**

Bill had later confessed to being Carl Phoenix. He was the son of the great senator, Thomas Phoenix. Harry had sworn to the young man that he would rot in jail, before giving him up as a source. After spending hours with Carl, he felt *there was* a story here.

Potentially, it *could* be the story of the decade. He wasn't sure if he believed every word of it, but his instincts told him there was definitely something going on. And he was convinced that the government or members of it were involved. The story would be bigger than Watergate. It touched everyone.

He decided to make it a series of articles. It would give him time to do some digging. With a few bucks spread in the right places, verifying the authenticity of the charts would be simple enough. He'd already found out that Cantrell's doctor was Franklin P. Worthington. If he could find a little dirt on him, maybe he could even get the good doctor to bend a bit.

Harry had gathered a short list of names. He had nurses, maintenance men, and even a cafeteria worker at the hospital who, in the past had fed him tips. It was amazing what secrets folks would share for a few bucks.

His first article would be the base. He wanted just enough to spark the interest of his readers. He continued reading.

We all know that there is information that is kept from the American public in the name of national security. There is secret information, which, were it to fall into the hands of our enemies would have a detrimental effect on our nation. We as a people accept that. But what if there were secrets that went beyond our wildest imaginations? Secrets that could personally affect every living American, directly or indirectly? Secrets that were actually a *matter of life and death*?

It has long been known that many secrets are protected under the guise of *'national security'*. Many of them are legitimate, and serve to keep those who wish harm to America, off balance.

But where is the line drawn in protecting *public interest?* And who draws these lines? Who makes those ultimate decisions… as to what is good for us, as Americans. Let's say for example, that *an individual or a group* decided that on April 12, 1955 the public should NOT be informed of the successful discovery of the polio vaccine, and that the vaccine should NOT be made available to the masses? How would that decision have affected Americans, or people of the world?

That particular disease claimed hundreds of thousands of lives, from the youngest infant to the oldest members of society. It struck without warning, leaving in its wake thousands, dead or crippled.

Could there exist a body of individuals today that have stepped over the line? Individuals who have decided for us all that only a select few should benefit from medical discoveries, miraculous discoveries which dwell secretly in the hallowed halls of somewhere and nowhere.

For your deliberation, Dear Reader, we ask, can economics and politics run organized medicine? Can it replace the desire to revolutionize the conditions conducive to human suffering?

These questions will be examined in a special series of ongoing articles. The answers may place into question the very reality of our freedoms. Read about "Who's keeping WHAT SECRET" in this publication soon.

Harry sat back, his full cheeks bunched up as a smile of satisfaction crossed his face. He looked over at the big clock. He still had ten minutes to get it to print. He was going to burn a favor, a big one, by running this without his editor's approval. In the end, he knew this would fly with the big man. He couldn't help but think of how the boldness of a couple of young reporters named Carl Bernstein and Bob Woodward had exposed the Watergate scandal. Today their names were forever etched in the chronicles of history. Harry Logan felt this story could mark his place with theirs and he was willing to take the chance.

He pushed the print button on his computer. The printer instantly sprang to life as he stood with his hand opened to accept the pages being spit out. Within seconds he was waddling to the pressroom.

*****

Carl was starving and had been looking forward to a good, home-cooked meal at Reggie's all morning. He'd hardly eaten a thing the last several days. Driving through the pounding rain the Archies were crooning their hit "Sugar, sugar" as the wipers methodically slapped back and forth.

He doubted that he would see Marc at Reggie's. *Maybe never again,* he thought. He was spooked, and Carl couldn't blame him.

Apparently, there was good reason. *I wish he knew I had Logan involved, he'd feel safer. The media protects everyone. Once what happened is exposed, he can get back to a real life.* He silently vowed to help Marc get back on his feet when this was all over.

Entering Reggie's, he walked toward his table. Sitting there dripping wet was his skittish friend.

"Marc am I ever glad to SEE YOU." Carl said, hardly able to contain his excitement. "I thought I'd never see you again."

"Yeah, well, kid, I almost didn't come. Good thing for you it's raining out and I'm hungry," he said forcing a smirk.

"Howdy, gents, coffee for starters?" Sue asked, as she approached the table.

"Hi, Sue, yeah coffee sounds good. And I'll have a hot beef sandwich today. Could you get Reggie to double up on the fries please? I'm famished."

Nodding, Sue looked over toward Marc.

"Same," he said, without looking up.

Sue glanced over at Carl as she raised an eyebrow. He just shrugged and shook his head.

After she left, Carl grinned. "Marc, we've been in here at least forty times. You've never ordered anything but a hot turkey sandwich. Feeling adventurous, or just sampling the local cuisine?"

Marc's eyes met his friend's as a dark look masked his face. "Kid, it don't feel like Christmas anymore."

"Well, I've got some great news for you," Carl said, suppressing a smile. Not knowing what to expect from Marc, he wanted to enjoy his first hot meal in three days. "I'll tell you everything after we get some grub."

Thirty minutes later Sue picked up the empty plates as she refilled the coffee mugs with the steaming, hot brew. Carl shared his theory about the press, as he described the meeting with Harry Logan.

"We're safe, Marc, and this *will get out.* Nobody can keep a secret like this once the press has it."

"What have you done, Carl?" Marc said softly, his voice trailing off. "I came here today to beg you to forget this whole thing, but now it's too late. You've gotta hide, boy. Come with me, you'll be safe," he pleaded.

Carl looked at him in disbelief. "You have to stop being so paranoid. I'll help you get on you're—"

He cut him off. "Carl, I've never asked you for anything, have I?"

"No."

"Are you going to give this thing up?"

"No"

"Can you give me five hundred dollars?"

"Yes, sure, of course, Marc," he replied.

"When?"

"You can come with me right now, we'll go to the bank and get it," he said, confused by the urgency.

"No. You go to the bank, just bring it back here and leave it with Sue, okay?"

"Sure. I can do that. Can I ask what you need it for?"

"I'm sorry kid, can't tell you."

"No problem, I understand," Carl said. But he didn't.

Both men left the eatery just as the sun broke through the clouds, smiling brightly on the freshly washed world.

Standing outside of Reggie's, Marc grabbed the young man by both shoulders. His eyes began to well with tears as he peered, intently into Carl's.

"Son, be careful, trust NO ONE, I mean NO ONE. I'm gonna miss ya, kid." He turned and ran in the opposite direction.

Carl shook his head. *Poor bugger. He's so paranoid, between the lab fire and living out here for all these years, I guess...* His thoughts trailed off as he made his way to First National Bank, four blocks away. A half hour later he was back on his route, the cash envelope safely with Sue at Reggie's.

*****

Ryan was high. The punk had accepted her offer earlier that morning. She was smart enough to get the fix before completing the deal. Walking, she stared downward, momentarily fascinated by her feet. She watched, captivated as one went in front of the other, propelling her forward. She was singing lightly under her breath, when she walked into something. Still staring at her feet, she slowly became aware of a second pair of shoes, directly in front of her own. Slowly, she looked up.

"Hey, what are you doing here?" she asked with her voice slurring, a smile spreading across her face.

"I've been looking for you, bitch. What am I doing here? Well I'm gutting me some fish."

Ryan's eyes still had a look of confusion even as the knife entered just above her navel. Clive pushed the short blade all the way in, then quickly withdrew it. He repeated the action twice more before he took off running.

She looked down, bewildered, as a red circle grew in the middle of her dress. Although there was no pain, instinctively, she covered the wound with her hands as blood seeped between her fingers. Swaying, she went down on her butt, legs splayed out in front of her. Looking at her stomach, she peeled her bloodied hands from the wound, spreading her fingers out before her eyes. Ryan collected her thoughts as best she could in her drug-induced state and muttered quietly,

"Clive, why'd you stick me, you rotten bastard?"

Chapter 38

After leaving Reggie's, Marc had headed off towards the shelter to grab a shower. The cool, steady rain had soaked him to the bone. He wanted the shower more for its warmth than anything else. As the hot water cascaded down his body, Marc could still feel the chill; he was sure that it was from his knowledge of the dark days that lay ahead.

Two hours after saying goodbye to Carl in front of Reggie's, he was back, talking to Sue. "Yes, Beau, Carl did leave something here for you, give me a second." She went into the back room and a moment later, emerged with an envelope. It was folded over, securely bound with a large elastic band.

"Here you go. Carl also wanted me to mention that you still have free meals here on his account." With genuine concern she asked, "Beau, did you and Carl have a falling out? I got the impression you two won't be lunching here together anymore."

He took the envelope from Sue's outstretched hand, then without looking up he mumbled, "Yeah, well you know, he's busy, I'm busy, and everybody's got things to do. Thanks, Sue." Not wanting to get trapped into a conversation, he turned and was gone. Once outside, he walked to the same spot where he'd been several nights before when Carl had almost attacked him. Slipping the elastic off, he unwrapped the envelope.

Jesus, kid, did you give it to me all in ones?' he thought as he unfolded the thick envelope. Peeling open the sticky flap, he reached in and pulled out a note.

Marc. I understand that you're scared. When I get this all worked out, I'll find you and help you get your life back. This should tide you over until then. Your friend, Carl Phoenix.

He felt a lump in his throat beginning to form as he reached into the envelope. Inside, he found five small bundles and pulled them out. There was a sleeve wrapped around each bunch of twenty-dollar bills. Every sleeve was stamped $1000.00, which made five thousand in total. Tears dropped on the envelope as Marc muttered to himself, *Five hundred, kid, all I needed was five hundred.*

He hid the money between the layers of clothes he wore. He'd have to find a safe spot in the alley, where no one would discover the cash. He had an idea. Looking both ways to make certain no one was following, he began quickly walking to the hiding place. His old friend, paranoia, was back in full force.

As he proceeded down Fife Street, he rounded the corner of the laneway where he intended to stash the money. Looking up, he saw Clive towering directly in front of Ryan, about seventy feet inside the alley. Although Ryan's back was facing him, he recognized the willowy figure. He stopped short and withdrew around the corner, out of sight. He had told her to stay away from Clive. *Damn, that's all I need.* He hesitated only a few seconds. *I owe her for helping out the kid. Gotta make sure he doesn't give her a lickin'.* Just as he entered the lane, Clive turned on his heels and took off running. Relieved that he didn't have to deal with the big man's mean streak, he walked toward Ryan.

With her back to him, she swayed a bit. Marc saw her look down at her hands, which were clamped over her stomach. Seeing her weaving unsteadily, he figured Clive had gut-punched her. Just as he was approaching, Ryan fell square on her behind. He walked around to face her.

Ryan held her open hands out. They were covered in blood. The center of her dress was a bright, ruby red.

"*Ohhh Ryan, no-no-no*," he said, dismayed. He ran to her and quickly applied pressure to the open wound with his hand. Pulling her to the side of the lane, he propped her against the wall of the adjoining building. As he unbuckled his worn leather belt, he ripped the bottom half of her ragged dress. In seconds, he concocted a makeshift bandage of folded material, resulting in a two-inch-thick pad. Finding the wounds, he gently put the pad directly over them to slow the bleeding.

Flopping her forward, he wrapped his belt just above her thin waist and pulled it snugly over the improvised dressing.

"Ryan, you hold on, I'm going to get an ambulance. You'll be fine girl, don't you worry, ol' Beau's here."

She looked up and weakly smiled. "Ain't that what they say when someone's dyin'? They always say it in the movies and then the guy dies." Still smiling, Ryan lost consciousness.

He frantically began looking for a payphone, his mind racing as he ran down the street. *I gotta call an ambulance, but will they come? Will they come here?* He wondered. He frantically considered the homeless shelter over on Third Avenue. *Maybe I should go there, they'd get someone to come.* He didn't know what to do, so he kept running, looking for a phone. *Ryan's in this jam because she helped Carl. I owe that girl, I owe her.*

Suddenly, he heard a voice yell out to him.

"Hey STOP, what's *your* rush, old timer?"

Marc jolted to a stop, recklessly spinning around.

A patrol car had pulled over to the curb and the cop in the passenger seat was talking.

Marc ran up to the cop whose hand had instinctively slid to the butt of his revolver, wary of the bum's rapid approach.

"There's a woman in the alleyway just down the street, she's been stabbed," Marc blurted out. "RYAN, Her name's RYAN! Clive stabbed her! He's a big, black dude with dreadlocks. He lives out here, on the streets," he jabbered breathlessly.

"Whoa, whoa, take it easy, sir, calm down and get in, show us where she is." Marc hesitated for a second. He didn't want to get involved. *I gotta help Ryan. I owe her*, he thought again, as he reluctantly climbed into the police cruiser.

Within minutes the police were hunched over Ryan and the ambulance sirens sounded in the near distance.

"Where will they take her?" Marc asked gingerly, not wanting them to ask *him* any questions.

"Probably GSE on Southern Avenue," the cop said. Then looking at Marc, he added, "Hey, don't go anywhere, sir. We're gonna want to get a statement." He nodded as the ambulance pulled into the back lane. With the commotion and the growing crowd, no one noticed the old homeless man quietly wandering away.

*****

Eric Brunner had not finished pouring his morning coffee when the phone rang.

"Hello."

"Good morning, Eric, Nancy Saunders calling. Have you had an opportunity to read today's paper?"

"No, ma'am," he said. Looking at the kitchen clock, he rolled his eyes. It was only 6:09.

Politicians got nothing better to do but read the paper before six? he thought sarcastically.

"Has your morning paper arrived?"

"Yes, ma'am. I'm just about to have a coffee and read through it.'

"Section B, page one, Eric. Please start there. Read the article by Harry Logan. I'll call back in ten minutes. I would like your take on it."

"I'm on it, Miss Saunders. I'll talk to you soon."

His half-filled coffee mug was left ignored on the counter. When Chief of Staff, Nancy Saunders telephones at six a.m. asking if you've read the morning paper, you don't stop for a coffee fix.

He immediately went to the table and sat as he opened the paper to Section B. He spotted the article instantly and beside it, the photo of the pudgy-faced, smiling author, Harry Logan. He'd barely finished the second reading of the article, when the phone rang again.

"Eric, we think there may be a problem with the article. What was your first impression?"

"Yes, ma'am, I agree. It seems that somebody's been doing some talking, and someone knows more than they should."

"That was our interpretation of the article as well, Eric. We need it to stop. We also need to find out who knows what and the source of the information. Do you think you can take care of that before the next article is printed?"

"I'm on it, ma'am. I'll report back to the committee by next Wednesday."

"Thank you, Eric, I'll be in touch."

Thirty minutes later the phone rang in a small home on West 32nd.

"Speak," a curt voice abruptly instructed.

"Nakamura, Brunner here. I have a case for you. Level one."

Level one cases were always of an urgent nature. They often carried the possibility of some action, interrogation, and possible elimination of the suspect. Nakamura loved it. He considered himself gifted at extracting the truth from those accused of possessing information sought after by the Patronums. By the time he was through with them, they were telling him things they wouldn't tell their priest.

"Yes, sir, when would you like to do the briefing?"

"One hour, you know where."

Nakamura's lips curled into a malicious smile. This would give him the opportunity to look for an opening to deal with Brunner. "Yes Sensei, one hour."

*****

Later that night, after a complete briefing, Kenichi Nakamura waited in the empty parking garage. His mind wandered as he thought about Harry Logan and Eric Brunner. During the briefing he had learned that Logan had collected top-secret information. The Patronums had no doubt about what he had uncovered. Nakamura's job was to find out who had provided it.

The leak came from someone, and that someone needed to be silenced. *When I'm finished, that little piggy will be squealing the name of his informant,* he thought wickedly as he lurked in the shadows. Nakamura continued to fantasize, this time about taking care of Eric Brunner. *With no intelligence leader, would I not be the logical choice? Tonight will be Eric Brunner's last.*

The sound of the bell snapped Nakamura out of his pleasant daydream. His five senses instinctively jumped to life. He was like a panther, about to pounce. The familiar elevator 'DING' reverberated through the deserted underground parking complex. Nakamura took his position behind a large concrete pillar. As the 'click-clack, click-clack' of the heavy footfalls came closer, he doused the cloth he held with chloroform.

Harry Logan passed the column unsuspectingly. Nakamura, with cat-like stealth, stepped out from behind the pillar. Silently, he slipped his arm around the thick neck of the reporter, simultaneously placing the rag over the short man's mouth and nose. Logan thrashed in the iron grip, but every breath he took made him weaker as he inhaled the chloroform. The struggling slowly became less urgent, as he eventually slumped into a heap on the cold concrete floor.

Nakamura effortlessly threw the stocky man over his shoulder. Approaching his car, he pushed a button on the key and the trunk popped open.

Carelessly, he tossed Logan into the trunk. The back end of the sedan sagged slightly as the 240-pound cargo landed with a thud. He drove to a deserted building on the east side of the city. It was one he'd used before, one with a quiet basement. Tonight he would need someplace desolate, without listening ears. His first guest would be the reporter and with any luck, later, Mr. Brunner.

Chapter 39

Earlier that morning, Harry Logan's day had begun much differently than it had ended. It began with visions of grandeur. He was at his desk in his personal jungle.

The columnist gingerly tested the steaming coffee as passing thoughts of stardom slipped through his tired mind. The buzzing telephone broke the daydream.

"Good morning, Harry Logan here," he chirped brightly.

"Logan, what in the hell is this?" Carl shouted into the phone. Pacing like a caged animal, he shook the newspaper at the receiver, as if some technological magic existed allowing the reporter to see through the phone.

"I told you a story, *the real story*, and you pussy foot around with this trash?"

"Carl, you just don't blurt something like this out. I have to nudge it, and then massage it into the climactic revelation that it is. Not to mention, you have brought *some* evidence, the accuracy of which is questionable, at best. Before I make any allegations that I can't retract, I need *hard* proof *and* verification. I need some time to complete my due diligence. I want to talk with Worthington, and see if I can get anything out of him," he offered.

"Proof, what kind of proof do you want? CANTRELL'S TUMOR ON A PLATE?" Carl shrieked.

"Calm down, you're getting wound up for nothing, I'll get this story out. But I have to get a few things in order first, case in point, this *Beau Jangles* character. I know you're holding out on me, Carl. You're not telling me the full truth about him," Harry coaxed.

Carl didn't want to get Marc Andrews' alias *Beau Jangles* involved, not at this point anyway. He was certain that Marc would be very uncooperative. He was sure that if cornered, Dr. Marc Andrews would go into his crazed, homeless routine, so much so that not only would the story be less believable, but Carl, too, would lose all credibility. He was quite sure that Marc's true identity could be verified through fingerprints. Novatek would have taken all employees' prints in case of theft. But Marc had promised that he would disappear. Carl believed him. *Can't use him, not yet,* he thought warily.

"Fine, Logan, but don't sugar-coat this. People are dying. They have a right to know what's going on," he concluded.

Harry leaned forward as he realized that Carl was right. He had to get on the 'Net and see how many died each hour. The information would serve to further sensationalize what *was* shaping up to be the *hottest story of the century*.

"Remember, my boy, that's what I do. I write stories and get people to *believe*. Just sit back and let me do my job."

After he hung up, Carl stared at the phone for several seconds, contemplating what Logan had said. In mid-thought the ringer pierced the silence, starling him.

"Hello."

"Carl, what the hell's going on with you?" his father's voice roared. "I know that you haven't been to work for three bloody days. Jesus, son, what sort of trouble are you in now?"

"Dad, give me a chance to explain, will you?"

"EXPLAIN WHAT? Explain that you're screwing somebody else's wife? I'm just glad that *your mother's not alive to see the mess you're making of your life!*"

Carl felt the full brunt of his father's disappointment in that moment, and his heart sank.

"Son, I'm sorry, I didn't mean that," his voice, laced with regret.

"Dad, I can't explain what I've been doing, but it will all make sense soon. I'm sorry I've been such a big letdown."

"Talk to me, Carl. What *is going on* with you? Just tell me everything's alright, son."

I can't, I just can't take the chance, Carl thought, wishing that he could.

"Yeah, everything's fine, dad. I've just been under the weather, you know. Just give me some time. Bye."

Not waiting for his father's response, Carl hung up the phone. He was physically and emotionally drained. The weight of the last few days and the call were all too much. He pushed his hair back. Leaning forward, he rested his head in his upturned palms and wept.

*****

After receiving his orders from Nancy Saunders, Eric made the fateful call that set the wheels in motion. He'd arranged a meet with Nakamura for later that morning at his downtown office. Nakamura would interrogate the reporter. There was no doubt that he would find out who had been the source of the story. Eric briefly thought it might be a disgruntled Patronum, perhaps someone in the chain that led to the committee. He almost immediately dismissed the notion. Discontent amongst the ranks of the secret society spelled doom. One thing was certain. The leak could not be allowed to get out of control. The promised follow-up to Logan's story could not be written.

At twelve noon, Kenichi Nakamura arrived at the small reception-less downtown office. Eric rented the seven hundred square foot, two-room workplace for meetings like this. Centered in the actual office was a plain steel desk, behind it, a comfortable high-backed leather chair. On the opposite side were two uninviting chairs. A green leather loveseat lined the wall. Next to it was a small corner table littered with unread magazines. On the other side, the file cabinet and water cooler. A few feet from the cooler was a closed door. Tucked behind the door was the larger of the two rooms. In the middle of that room was a Bowflex 2000 exercise machine. Eric would often come here and work out for hours. It was the way he relaxed.

Nakamura's salutation was a formal bow, after which Eric began conveying his orders regarding the assignment.

"Ken, your mission is to interrogate the reporter and find out where the hell he's getting his information. We need the name of his source, plain and simple."

"I understand, sir. Has a retirement order been approved?"

"That's undecided at this point. First see what Logan actually knows, and how much is conjecture."

"Sir, I will need you to come when I have finished, so that you can update me regarding the final order. Sensei, I've written down the directions and when you should come, sir, to make the final decision," he said offering the hand written map.

"Ken, for crissake just phone me. I don't need to be there. And knock off the sensei crap, will you?" Eric said. Unable to mask his irritation he flicked Nakamura's extended hand, turning away from the offered directions.

Nakamura dropped his eyes to the floor and half bowed as he retracted his hand. "I apologize if I have upset you, sir. *'Sensei'* simply means a *'teacher or mentor.'* I have always considered you my teacher *and* mentor."

"Yeah, well whatever. I find it uncomfortable," he said awkwardly. What was more, Eric's instincts told him that something was off-kilter here. He tried to figure out what Nakamura might be up to. He'd felt uneasy about the Asian American ever since the night he'd tailed him. Nakamura had never asked Eric to meet with him on a job before today.

A few more cursory bows and dubious apologies later, Nakamura made his departure. Eric didn't see the bloodthirsty contemptuous look a split second after his exit. Tapping a pencil on the desk, Eric thought about the meeting. He had an idea.

*****

Marc felt responsible for Ryan getting stabbed. *She helped Carl, MY friend. If she'd just kept walking, she wouldn't be in this jam,* he thought as he trudged on. Marc contemplated the cops' involvement. The last thing he needed was the police asking him a bunch of questions. He knew there was no chance they'd accept that his name was *Beau Jangles. The first thing they'll do is run my fingerprints to see if I'm wanted. Dammit! I don't need this right now,* he thought.

Fretting obsessively about what to do, he shuffled along. Cursing and punching at the air, the decision was made. Marc turned left and went south on Lyon's Gate, toward the hospital.

Arriving at the information counter, he kept his head lowered. Speaking in a voice that was barely a whisper, he said, "A woman came in here yesterday, about thirty-five years old. She was stabbed."

The slim, black lady looked up from the stack of papers she was working on. "What's her name, sir?" she asked.

Marc stopped. He didn't know, not really. He knew she *went* by Ryan, but didn't know her last name. If she had told him, he couldn't recall it.

"*Sir, can I have her name, please?*" the woman repeated impatiently. Marc heard her ask God to grant her patience.

The words stumbled out of him. "UH, ummm, I only know her first name, it's Ryan. *Ryan*."

"Address, sir?"

"She lives on the streets like me. We have no addresses."

The frown on the woman's face slid off unexpectedly. It seemed that she'd been granted the patience and tolerance requested for the sad-looking wretch.

"I'm sorry, sir, could you please tell me anything at all you might know. Did you bring her in or was she ambulatory? Sir that means—"

Marc's eyes met the nurse's gentle stare as he raised his head. "I know what that means. I'm homeless, not illiterate, ma'am. No she was unable to walk herself in. She was brought in by ambulance around 3 p.m. yesterday afternoon," he said matter-of-factly. It was one of those moments of pure clarity. They had become more frequent, since Carl had come into his life. Looking at the woman's softened features, he hoped the information might help.

Getting up from her chair, the nurse looked at Marc.

"Give me a moment, sir. I'll try to find her for you. I'm sorry for being impatient before, it's just been a long day. There may be something in yesterday's admitting records."

Looking up, Marc offered a guarded smile and nodded. He couldn't have known if Ryan had given a first or a last name or if she was even conscious when they brought her in. He sat in the waiting room across from the counter. Looking around, it occurred to him he'd never needed medical attention. All those years on the streets and not once did he get sick. It was the first time he'd even been in a hospital in thirty years.

Must have been all that good clean living, he thought, chuckling.

Glancing at the faces, he recognized a few from the streets. Others, he'd seen at the various shelters. A couple of the less jittery said hi to him. In response, Marc offered only a curt nod.

I don't want to get jawing with these ingrates or it'll be all over the streets that I was here,' he thought suspiciously.

Word amongst the vagrants spread quickly. The fact was they didn't have a whole lot to talk about. Within an hour of the ambulance carting Ryan away, he'd heard the cops had picked up Clive. Apparently he'd been charged with aggravated assault and attempted murder. Marc assumed Clive wouldn't be bothering anyone for a long time, no one living on the outside, anyway.

The nurse returned with some papers in hand. "Sir, we had a female stabbing victim, approximate age, thirty to thirty-five years old, came in yesterday. On her admit slip all we got from the officers was a first name, '*Ryan*'. I believe that is—" She stopped abruptly. Looking up from the admittance slip she asked, "Are you related, sir?"

"No, I'm a friend."

"Sir, Ryan just came out of intensive care. Visitors are limited to family only, for twenty-four hours." Leaning over she said in a hushed voice, "You might want to tell them at the nurses' station that you're her uncle, that is, if they ask. She's on the fifth floor, room 504. Good luck," she added, offering him the paper with directions.

"Thank you, ma'am," he replied.

Marc followed the hand-drawn map to the elevator. Once inside, he stood motionless. So many years had passed since he was in one, he'd almost forgotten what to do next. Studying the panel for a moment, he finally pushed the number 5. It jerked him upward, slightly buckling his knees as his arms flailed for a split second.

"Whoa! Damn thing's like rocket ship!" he said aloud. A little embarrassed, he grinned at the scare he'd given himself.

As the doors opened, he walked around the corner. The ladies were busy at the nurses' station answering phones and looking at charts. They were behind the enclosure. Glass surrounded three sides of the long, cluttered desk. He prayed no one would try to talk with him. If cornered and he claimed to be Ryan's uncle, they would surely want to speak to him. At the very least they'd be after her full name and date of birth.

He managed to slip past without being stopped and quizzed with questions that he couldn't answer, and for that he was grateful. *Yep, just a quick howdy, get better soon and I'll be on my way.* Suddenly, remembering the custom, he cursed himself for not bringing flowers or the like.

Marc proceeded down the long corridor looking up at the room numbers as he passed. He was careful to stay to the side. He didn't want to attract attention from attendants or other visitors. It wouldn't be the first time he was kicked out of a public place. People assumed when they saw a street person that they were always looking for a handout. The smell coming from the open doors of patients' rooms as he passed was clean and sterile, but stale somehow. The distinct stench of sickness hung in the air. He wanted to run, to escape the confines of the building and be outside again. The streets were his home.

He walked into an open door, which had the numbers 504 stretched across it. The large, disinfected room was all white. It was a ward with six beds. The first four were empty. The privacy curtains of the other two were closed and were across from each other. Nervously, he proceeded to the end of the first bed and peeked in. There he saw an old woman who looked about eighty. The constant bleep…bleep…bleep of the heart monitor was the only clue that she was still alive. Turning, he pulled the curtain to the adjacent bed. There, sitting upright and alert was a very plump woman in her fifties. Both hands were at her mouth. She was gnawing at a chocolate-bar wrapper. He realized she was digging the rest of the treasure out with her teeth. Loosening her grip on the wrapper she glared at Marc.

"Are you looking for somebody or are you lost?"

"No, I'm looking for my friend. She's supposed to be in this room," he replied meekly.

“Oh, that skinny young thing they brought in here yesterday? The pretty woman who was stabbed?”

“Yeah, that’s right.” Marc looked confused and embarrassed.

Her hands suddenly dropped from her mouth. Off to the side was a line of chocolate smudged across her chin.

“Yeah, sorry to be the one to tell you.“ Looking directly at him, she paused before finishing the sentence. Next to the *Mars Bar,* this was to be the highlight of her day. “She died last night. They took her out of here around three in the morning. There was a bunch of doctors and nurses making a huge racket. But they couldn’t do anything for her. I heard them say her bowel was cut and leaked… or something like that.”

Marc just stood staring at the fat woman. After the *update* she dug back into the wrapper, chasing the few remaining crumbs of chocolate.

His chest suddenly felt like something tremendously heavy was pressing down on him. Walking past the nurses’ station he felt dazed. He was in the elevator. The ride down seemed much slower. As the doors parted he walked toward the information counter where he’d begun ten minutes earlier.

The helpful nurse spotted Marc passing her counter.

“Sir, did you have trouble finding your friend?” she asked, with a touch of concern.

“No, I found her alright. She died last night. Thanks anyway,” he said without slowing his pace, or looking at her.

Out in the open air again, the pressure in his chest seemed to lessen. *I knew it. Kid started talking about Edwards’ shitty Elixir and people die. All the wrong people die.*

Marc’s decision was made in that moment. He knew what he had to do.

Chapter 40

Kenichi Nakamura had been born to an American mother and a Japanese father. His mother, a tall beautiful woman, had spent her youth as a Vegas showgirl. His father was obsessed with her after seeing her perform. Undaunted, he pursued her. She resisted. In the end his wealth and position had won her over.

Nakamura had spent many years and thousands of dollars tracing his Japanese heritage. The family ancestry dated back to the year 1250 A.D. with the birth of Hojo Tokimunee. His forefather had been a famous samurai general who lived on in the historic archives. The Asian American fancied himself a modern day samurai, but like his predecessor he felt he wasn't merely a warrior, but a general.

His time had come. He would take his place as head of security and intelligence for the Patronums. *Today shall be the day I kill Eric Brunner.* But first came the mission.

*****

With all the abandoned buildings in the neighborhood, the local squatters did not consider the damp, chilly basement desirable shelter. The dilapidated house had served him well in the past; it would again tonight. The shabby bungalow sat hidden in a clove of whispering willows, and it was all but soundproof.

He was pleased that the knife had taken so well to the stone. Smiling sadistically, he ran his thumb across its breadth. The blade was as sharp as a scalpel. Balancing the knife between his forefinger and thumb, he tapped it on the hard surface of the table. It produced a pleasing musical note with each strike. Ting…Ting…Ting Ting…Ting…Ting. Barely touching the reporter's fat face, he watched with sick fascination as the skin spilt open like a ripe peach. Nakamura stared as he squirmed. Logan was not the first to be '*one with the chair*'.

*****

"Mr. Logan. Who gave you the information for the column in this morning's paper?" Nakamura asked, his voice calm and even.

Harry, gripped in fear, could barely comprehend the question. "*Please, don't hurt me*," he begged. Suddenly he remembered the blindfold. "I haven't seen your face, I won't tell anybody! Please, please don't hurt me," he whimpered.

Harry, sitting in a puddle of his own urine felt the blindfold slowly being removed. He stiffened. Tears squeezed from the corners of his tightly shut eyes. Running down his cheeks, they mixed with mucus and blood, dropping silently onto his briefs. Terrified at the prospect of seeing his tormentor's face, he began trembling uncontrollably.

"PLEASE NO! I'll TELL YOU ANYTHING. JUST DON'T HURT ME!" he screamed, all promises about protecting his source abandoned.

"Open your eyes." Nakamura said evenly.

Harry violently shook his head from side to side. He was like a man possessed.

"NO, NO, I DON'T WANT TO SEE YOUR FACE! PLEASE NO!"

"Mr. Logan, open your eyes now or I will cut away your eyelids. Trust me. I am very good at it. Open them NOW," he commanded menacingly.

He slowly opened his eyes, blinking to clear the blurriness and tears. Looking up, he spotted a table in the harsh glow of the bulb hanging precariously from a threadbare wire. On the surface, which was higher than his vantage point, were the edges of unrecognizable objects.

"WHAT'S ON THAT TABLE? WHAT ARE YOU GOING TO DO TO ME?" he cried as spittle flew from his bloodied face. The sheer terror of seeing the hacksaw, plastic bags, and small propane blowtorch would have, and later did, challenge his very sanity.

In the shadows, Harry saw the dark, well-dressed man. The figure before him was clearly over six feet tall with jet-black hair and dark skin. Nakamura's height and fine features were genetic gifts from his mother. His father's lineage provided the cunning and lack of emotion.

What am I gonna do? I'll tell, I'll tell him everything about Carl, Harry's mind raced.

He first assumed that the kidnapper was black. As his vision cleared, his eyes adjusted to the dim lighting. He could now see clearly. His ambusher was Asian.

Harry's mind racing irrationally, suddenly recalled a horrifying experience he'd had three years before. It involved a story he'd written about the infamous Japanese crime syndicate, the 'Yak Uzi'.

An oriental man named, 'Kiyoshi Yamamoto' had arranged to meet him at the Washington Herald Press. Requesting a private place to talk, Harry had directed him to an interview room.

"Logan-San, you mentioned my name in your article," he had said as he carefully unfolded a white handkerchief on the table.

"I have lost face with members of my organization." As he spoke, he'd pressed the palm of his hand in the middle of the white linen. Yamamoto pulled out another handkerchief, setting it beside the first. As if, out of nowhere, a knife suddenly appeared in his other hand, as his haunting eyes burrowed into Harry's. Thrusting the knifepoint into the table one inch from his pinky, he quickly cut down, separating the small appendage at the first knuckle. Yamamoto had barely winced. Harry recoiled as he cried out.

"Logan-San, I shall leave this as a reminder of the things that can happen to *you* if my organization or a name is *ever* mentioned in an article again," he said, indicating the finger on the table. Carefully wrapping the stump of what remained of his pinky with the second handkerchief, he glared at the reporter as he exited the interview room.

He left Harry gawking in total disbelief at the finger he had severed. It looked so odd sitting there, contrasting unnaturally to the bloodstained white cloth in the middle of the table. They'd been in the interview room for only a moment. Recalling the experience in the millisecond it took him to identify the assailant as Asian, he screamed out again.

"I DIDN'T WRITE ABOUT YOU. I DIDN'T SAY ANYTHING! PLEASE, PLEASE DON'T HURT ME. I SWEAR I'LL NEVER DO IT AGAIN!!" he blathered.

Nakamura smiled sardonically. Fear was his aphrodisiac. He moved toward him. Slowly leaning forward, he closed the distance separating their faces. Logan could not help but notice that this larger-than-life Asian had very distinctive features. The sharp, well-defined nose, slightly protruding brow and prominent jaw line were not common features among Asians. He intuitively deduced that he was of mixed blood. Mixed blood was not accepted in the 'Yak Uzi.'

All observations were instinctive and made in a split second. The insight did not serve to alleviate the moment. As the enemy approached, his face was less than a foot away. His cold, black eyes tunneled into Harry's, and again he asked the question. "Mr. Logan. Where did you get the material for the column you wrote in this morning's paper?"

"SOMEONE CALLED... SAID THEY HAD PROOF OF A MEDICAL COVER-UP TWENTY-FIVE YEARS AGO. *PLEASE DON'T KILL ME,*" he sobbed.

"Names, Mr. Logan. First I want the name of the person or persons who initially contacted you. Then, anyone you spoke with concerning this information and everything they told you"

Harry held nothing back. Within minutes he'd told him everything. Nakamura was satisfied that the reporter had given up the one and only person involved. The useless information that followed kept him from his work. Mr. Logan was rapidly becoming expendable. The Asian leered. His time was near.

"You are absolutely certain that no one else knows anything about what you have told me?"

"NO, *no... I swear it, on my mother's grave, I swear it."* Harry sniveled.

Although his captor had not touched him since sliding the knife down his face, the terror was overwhelming. Knowing he'd answered all questions truthfully, the delusion of freedom besieged him. Foolishly, Harry believed he would be released.

"Mr. Logan is your mother deceased?" Nakamura responded with a sad, concerned voice.

"What? WHAT DID YOU SAY? *I SWEAR I WON'T TELL ANYONE, PLEASE LET ME GO!*"

"I said, is your mother dead?" he repeated calmly.

Confused, wailing, Harry responded, "MY MOTHER... WHY? WHA...YES, *YES SHE'S DEAD*."

The ominous, twelve-inch blade that he'd used earlier was suddenly in his hand again. Shards of light reflected, scattering on the damp, cold walls as he slowly turned it over.

Smiling peacefully, he said, "You'll be together soon, Mr. Logan, very soon."

The fog lifted in Harry's mind, as he comprehended the meaning. The cool dank basement reverberated with renewed screams of terror. Harry Logan lost control of all bodily fluids. The putrid odor pleased Nakamura. The reporter was stripped of all dignity. It was time to begin his work.

Later, Nakamura resorted to waving smelling salts under the tortured reporter's nose when he'd lose consciousness. Each time he was brought back to unrelenting torment. When Nakamura pulled out the hacksaw, Harry's mind snapped.

*****

Eric had sat patiently outside Nakamura's home earlier that evening. *Let's just see what you're up to*, he thought, sitting in the dark rental car. Aware of Nakamura's skill level, tailing him without detection would be tricky. The fact that they were assassins demanded extreme caution, even when it seemed unwarranted.

Nakamura was driving in the general direction of the *Washington Herald*. Once Eric established that fact, he turned off and took an alternate route to the paper giant. He'd decided it was much too early in the game to give Nakamura reason to think that he had a tail.

After waiting down the block for almost an hour, he saw the Asian's black sedan leave the parking structure.

Carefully pulling in four cars back, Eric began the chase. Nakamura's vigilance was obvious as he drove, taking quick lefts and rights, never signaling his intentions. He headed away from the busy downtown area. Approaching the east side of town, the traffic thinned noticeably. Three times Eric turned off, and resumed the pursuit several blocks away. Each time, he caught sight of the black sedan and inconspicuously rejoined the light stream of vehicles, keeping well out of sight. The closer Nakamura's car came to its final destination, the less traffic was in the area to cover Eric's approach.

I know where he's going. I have a good idea anyway, Eric assumed, as he sat three stoplights back. *Damn, if I get any closer, he'll spot me for sure.*

Eric was familiar with the abandoned buildings that were in this section of east Washington. He'd mentioned to Nakamura that he'd used them years ago to conduct interrogations.

Then it happened. Eric lost sight of the sedan. Taking a left, he went about ten blocks east and came out on a dark, deserted street. There was no sign of Nakamura's car.

It was just a matter of scouring the area. He thought about the directions that Nakamura had offered, but realized had he taken them, he would have lost the element of surprise. Eric did not want to approach while Logan was being brought into the building. The delay meant that Nakamura would already be inside.

Finding the vehicle proved more difficult than Eric had first anticipated. He spent more than an hour driving the different streets, searching out the sedan. On his second pass of a dark street, he spotted something. For an instant, he thought he saw a twinkle in the glare of the headlights. Pulling his car adjacent to the curb, he saw it. Beneath an overgrown willow was the shadowy outline of the black car. It sat fifty yards from a run-down house with boarded windows and a rotted, sagging porch. *Clever, Nakamura, very clever.*

There was less chance of squatters there than one of the apartment buildings. Eric turned off his headlights and wheeled his rental around the corner. Carefully, he made his way back to the house. As he approached, he contemplated how he would enter the broken-down shack without making a sound. Standing at the back door, he saw the doorknob was gone. Looking for a way in, he heard a soft moaning, followed by an anguished scream.

Nakamura was so engrossed in his work that he didn't hear his mentor descending the steps. Logan's previous pleas for freedom had changed. His hoarse voice now begged for death.

Eric's drawn gun was fitted with a silencer. The scene before him was eerily similar to the last time he had surprised Nakamura at work. Beside the Asian, two dismembered feet and hands lay on plastic bags. The stumps cauterized with a blow- torch. The reporter's face was a road map of gashes and slices. His eyelids had been cut away.

"*You miserable piece of trash,*" Brunner said in a small disbelieving tone.

*****

Nakamura realized the time was now. This was the showdown he'd been hoping for. He'd lured Brunner to the cellar. Sealing his fate would be easy. He cursed himself for being so consumed by pleasure that he had not been more alert. Standing to his full height, he slowly turned. He could not talk his way out of this, but hoped that Brunner wanted the information he had before making a move. Stalling, his mind raced to plan an attack. He needed Eric to hesitate, just for a second. He bowed.

"Sensei, I am sorry you do not approve of my methods. I have information vital to the Patronums." He took a step toward Eric, the knife at his side. "Sir, the source of the information…" He lunged at Eric with the speed of a Jaguar. His arm rose so quickly, it was scarcely a blur. The wet bloodied knife flashed in the dim light. The muted sound of air came an instant later.

The bullet struck Nakamura, spinning him to the right, burrowing into his chest, but the knife had already begun its downward trajectory. Missing the fatal mark intended, it instead sliced Eric's left arm. Nakamura fell to the dirt floor.

Eric's wound was deep. Blood dripped from his raised arm. Shaken, he managed to keep his gun trained on the deadly Asian. Nakamura turned and sat upright. He pressed his back against the cold, concrete wall. Looking down at the hole in his chest, he saw the blood running freely with each beat of his heart. Nakamura accepted his inevitable fate. He'd be dead in minutes. He looked at Eric. "Brunner, allow me to die with honor."

Aware of Nakamura's obsession with Japanese tradition, Eric suspected he was referring to seppuku, the ancient samurai ritual of suicide by self-disembowelment. Westerners knew it as *hari-kari*.

"Yes, if it causes you pain, do it," he said maliciously.

"Brunner, it should be you down here in the dirt. I was the right choice when Vargo died. Your *mentor*—your *surrogate father* , HE died by MY hand. Nirvana had not called him yet. He might have lived on another ten years. Had I known *you* were his replacement, *you* would have passed to the next life with your beloved teacher. Both of you would have met the same end as this abomination," he said venomously, indicating what was left of Harry Logan.

Applying pressure to the wound with one hand, Nakamura struggled to his knees. With the other, he managed to rip open his bloodied shirt. His eyes locked with Eric's as he gripped the handle of the dagger, the same knife he'd used so many times to impose unspeakable torture. Positioning it over his left side, he quickly plunged it in and slowly began to pull it to the right.

Eric looked at the dying reporter, his nerves still raw and alert. A millionth of a second after the first small clap, the slug broke through the bone of Nakamura's forearm. His eyes bugged out incredulously, as his hand fell uselessly from the knife handle. Again, the muffled clap from the silencer resulted in bone splintering. This time it was Nakamura's shoulder. He weakly yelped. Pain was now *his* world. In a whisper barely audible he said, "Brunner, you promised I could die with honor. You are not a warrior."

Taking a step toward the assassin, Eric said in a quiet voice, "You would've had to live with honor, to die with it."

A PSSST was the only sound as the silencer did its job. Nakamura's dead eyes stared forward, one might say, in disbelief. A slow stream of blood trickled from the small hole in his forehead as gravity pulled him forward and downward. His intestines spilling out, he fell on the dirt floor.

*****

Eric watched for movement from the killer. Some part of him half expected Nakamura to jump up again, like in a cheesy horror flick. Satisfied that the dead Asian was human after all, he walked over to what was left of the reporter.

Logan was bleeding to death, and again, had mercifully fallen unconscious. Suddenly, Eric remembered the mission. Grabbing the smelling salts on the table, he waved it under the reporter's nose. He groaned, and somehow regained a semi-conscious state.

"Kill me, please kill me." His voice was barely a murmur.

"I'll get you help Logan. You'll be all right. WHO talked to you? Where did you get the information for the article?"

Logan couldn't have seen that it was he, Eric who was now speaking. Eric guessed that somehow his tormented mind acknowledged that Nakamura was no longer a threat.

"Kill me, please," he begged. Pathetically he tried to raise the stump where his hand had been just an hour before.

"Logan give me a name, or I keep you alive for days."

Years of fatty food and a disdain for exercise paid off in that very moment. Harry Logan's heart just quit. He went to the same place as his mother.

Eric began the tedious task of cleaning up the mess.

Chapter 41

"You have reached the desk of Harry Logan, Investigative reporter for the Washington Herald Press. I'm on the phone or away from my desk just now. At the sound of the tone, please leave a brief message. I will get back to you as soon as I can. Thanks. Beeeeeep."

Carl flopped back on the tan, leather couch, the telephone pressed against his ear. "Harry, I've been leaving messages for two days. What's going on? I need to talk to you. Have you gotten anything from Worthington? Call me!"

Carl hung up the phone. Leaning forward, he pulled a cigarette from the pack. Out of habit, he walked to the double glass slider and pushed it open. The light wind slid over his bare arms and legs as he drew hard on the Marlboro. Carl stood in his briefs. He hardly noticed the fresh D.C. morning, the rising sun, or the mild temperatures. *Where is he? I'll call his editor. Harry said not to talk to anyone, but where the hell is HE?* Carl pondered. His mouth opened slightly as pushed the cigarette filter between his lips. Minutes later he was on the phone again.

"This is the *Washington Herald Press* general inquiry line. Where may I direct your call please?" a female voice asked.

"Hi, I am calling for Harry Logan."

"One moment please I will conn—"

"Hello? No, I don't want his voice mail. I've left messages for the last few days. May I speak to his supervisor please?"

"One moment, sir, I'll connect you to the chief editor"

A moment later, a voice barked out, "Dave Robinson, how can I help you?"

"Hi Mr. Robinson, I'm trying to reach Harry Logan. Can you tell me if he's in today?"

"Harry hasn't been in for a few of days. Who's speaking?"

"Bill Andrews. Harry was supposed to get back to me yesterday about a story he's working on. Do you have any idea how I can reach him?"

"To tell the truth, Mr. Andrews, Harry seems to be m.i.a. His car was left here two nights ago. He hasn't been seen since. The police would like to speak to anyone who had contact with him in the past seventy-two hours. Could you contact Detective Rom—"

He hung up the phone before Dave Robinson finished saying the detective's name. With his hand still holding the receiver, Carl felt he had no choice. For the first time since this all began, he felt the full gravity of the situation. He dialed his father's private number. He felt a wave of relief when he heard his dad's voice.

"Hello, Thomas Phoenix here."

"Dad, thank god you're alright."

"Carl, is that you?" Thomas said. He walked around his massive desk, dropping into the large leather chair.

"Yeah, it's me dad, is everything okay there?"

"Yes, yes of course, why wouldn't it be?" Thomas said. There was a distinct hint of concern and confusion in his voice.

"Dad, I have to talk with you. It's important, urgent actually."

"Alright, yes, of course, Carl. But, son—about the other night, look I didn't mean—"

"Forget about that, dad. I'm a screw-up and I know it. But this is really important."

The senator closed his eyes, rubbing his brow.

"What now, Carl, what have you done now?"

"DAD! For CRYING out loud, JUST listen to me! I haven't done anything. I've—well, I've found out something that's going to be pretty hard to swallow. Now listen for a minute and I'll explain."

He'd gotten as far as the Emily Cantrell story and the conflicting medical charts, when his father stopped him.

"Carl have you told ANYONE of this?"

"Yes, a reporter named Harry Logan, and now he's missing."

"I want you to take the pictures of the charts and fly back here to Dallas. When can you leave?"

"I'll phone the airport right now. I'll catch the first flight out."

“Carl, can you see those medical charts now?"

"Yes, they're on my desk, I’m looking at them."

"Good. From this point forward, carry the charts with you. Do not, under any circumstances, let them out of your sight until you hand them directly to me. Is that clear? Get out here as soon as you can,” the senator said firmly.

“Okay, dad, I will.” Lost for words, all he could manage to say was, “Thanks dad, I love you.”

“I love you too, son.” Thomas responded.

I should have called him in the first place. What was I thinking? Nobody can touch him, Carl thought replacing the receiver.

He called the airport and the ticket agent informed him that the next flight left in twenty-eight minutes. He’d never make it.

“When is the one after that?”

“Four thirty-five p.m, sir.”

Ten minutes of information exchange and he was booked on the four thirty-five out of Washington to Dallas. He called Sal and fortunately got the answering machine. After a brief message telling him he was off to visit his dad on a personal matter, he showered. All cleaned up and ready to go and he still had six and a half hours to kill. Too restless to sit around the condo, he packed an overnight bag and wandered out.

Standing in the elevator, he watched as each number illuminated. As quickly as they flashed on, they went dark again as the compartment descended to the parking garage. He thought about his dad. So anxious to help and protect his son, he didn’t wait to hear the full story. It was the incredible story of two heroes. Dr. Marc Andrews, alias Beau Jangles, homeless recluse. The other, Dr. Blake Edwards, the father of Elixir, soon to be known as the man who discovered a cure for cancer. As the elevator doors opened, he smiled. There would be plenty of time to fill his father in on all the details soon enough.

For the next hour and a half, he drove aimlessly. Deciding to grab a cup of coffee and read the daily news, he parked his car on the strip. As Carl walked, he spotted a newspaper vending machine. It was pressed up against the stucco wall of the coffee shop. With the envelope containing the Cantrell charts tucked securely under his arm, he reached for his wallet. As he opened it up to take out the quarters for the newspaper, it fell. Bending, Carl reached for his wallet. Suddenly, the stucco above his head exploded. Scattering debris bounced off the newspaper box. Random fragments ricocheting in all directions pelted his face. Carl instinctively ducked. Had the bullet found its mark, the gesture would have been in vain. Dropping to the ground, he looked around frantically. He knew that someone had just tried to shoot him. People gawked at the well dressed young man crouched on the sidewalk with an arm covering his head. Carl did a kind of duck-walk toward the coffee shop door.

*****

"Dammit!" Eric whispered under his breath. It was a difficult shot and angle. Nancy Saunders' instructions had been very clear.

"One head shot, take his wallet, watch, and any jewelry. Secure the envelope he's carrying. Make it look like a robbery. You'll have only one chance, Eric. If you're unsuccessful, call me for further directions."

Eric quickly holstered his firearm and blended into traffic. As he passed, Carl stood upright and, looking wildly in every direction, disappeared into the coffee shop.

*****

Marc retrieved his envelope containing all the cash that Carl had given him. He decided to see if he could pay for a casket for Ryan. He didn't want her stuffed into a cardboard box. Homeless people who had died with no next of kin became the city's problem, their remains cremated and buried with a small marker. Marc suspected that Ryan would not even have a marker. She didn't give a last name before she died. *I don't want the bastards frying her in an oven.* He cringed at the thought.

Walking into the hospital, he stopped at the front counter. He spotted the same helpful nurse who had treated him so kindly a few days before. When she saw his face, she had the puzzled look of one trying to place somebody. The bewildered expression was replaced with a broad smile as she put the pieces together.

Marc reminded the nurse that he had been in a few days prior, looking for his friend. He then said that she had died and he wanted to pay for a casket for her. As he spoke, the confused look once again crossed the nurse's friendly face.

*****

Carl stumbled backward into the coffee shop. Satisfied that the assailant had given up, for the moment anyway, he turned to see all eyes on him. A dozen or so patrons were gawking at him. He'd created quite a ruckus flailing and banging his way into the small diner. Suddenly conscious of his actions and the look that must have been on his face, he pulled himself together. Peering out the window, he waited another full minute. Cautiously, he ventured back out into the street. Holding the envelope tightly in his hand, he quickly moved toward his car. Carl looked at every passerby as a possible threat. As his eyes darted from face to face and car to car, a sad thought dawned on him. *I'm acting just like Marc.* Carl pointed the car to the only place he could think that would be safe. Shaken, he sped toward the airport. On the seat beside him lay the proof that would save his life.

Less than an hour later he pulled his car into long-term parking. Going through the check-in procedure, he quickly made his way through security to the boarding area. Carl sat beside a sleeping woman and tried to rest as the hours slowly dragged by.

On the first announcement of his flight, Carl was on his feet. After proceeding through his gate, he produced the boarding pass. Next was his corresponding identification. Everything was presented to the young man at the desk.

After a customary, *thank you and enjoy your flight sir,* from the ticket taker, Carl walked down the Jetway. He looked cautiously around the telescoping corridor, which extended from the airport terminal to the aircraft. A moment later he arrived at the aircraft doorway. The accordion bellows draped each side of the opening, and once again, he produced his ticket.

"Good evening, sir, could I see your boarding pass please?" the attractive flight attendant asked. "You're in first class row nine, seat F," she said indicating the forward section of the aircraft.

Twenty minutes later he was staring out of the window as the ground whizzed by and the plane lifted off the tarmac. Moments after the aircraft took to the air the radio crackled as the captain welcomed his passengers. Feeling the full weight of the last few days, Carl's shoulders sagged as he finally relaxed. Exhausted, his eyelids slowly fell as he drifted off to sleep.

The flight arrived in Dallas without incident at eight fifty seven in the evening. On touch down he reset his watch, reflecting upon the hour he'd picked due to the change in time zones. With only his overnight bag the porters all but ignored him, scouring the crowds for those with luggage. Carl was on his guard after the attempt in Washington. Producing a twenty-dollar bill, he held it in front of a tall lanky porter.

"YES SIR!" he said, taking the twenty. "Where's your luggage, sir?"

"Right here," he replied,, indicating the small carry-on. "Grab a cab, then come get me at the door will you please?"

The porter shrugged as he took the single bag, and stepping through the sliding glass doors, he hailed a taxi.

The gangly man opened the back door of the cab and was on his way to get Carl when he dashed out and past him. Thanking the porter as he passed, Carl hopped onto the back seat and quickly slammed the door closed.

I'm sure whoever took a shot at me is still in D.C. but I'm not taking any chances, he thought warily. Carl tried to convince himself that maybe it was a drive-by, or possibly a botched robbery attempt at the sight of his fallen wallet. Somehow, he'd prayed that maybe, just maybe it didn't have anything to do with the envelope he was clutching. But Marc's words of warning kept haunting him. *"After Blake told us about Elixir, people died...I almost died."*

"Where to, pal?" the cabbie asked.

His eyes in the rear view mirror, and a Detroit red wings cap were all Carl could make out.

"Thirty-two, oh thirty-four Bennett Boulevard," he instructed the driver. "I'm going to take a little nap."

"Not a problem, chum. I'll wake you when we arrive."

He had no intentions of napping. He simply wanted to lie low in the backseat of the cab to obscure his identity, just in case. The one potshot today had produced more stress than Carl had ever experienced in his young life. Even after the airplane nap, his nerves were still frazzled.

Forty minutes later, the cab arrived in front of his father's sprawling house. He paid the cabbie and added a twenty-dollar tip, asking him to bring the bag to the front door. Carl simply wanted a shield to block his view from anyone looking for a second chance.

Jesus, STOP IT, you're acting exactly like MARC! his mind warned.

He was feeling a lot more sympathetic toward his paranoid friend. Out of the blue, he remembered the age-old cliché about, *'walking a mile in my shoes,'* after his own frightening day.

He unlocked the front door with his key. Once inside, Carl actually let out a huge sigh of relief.

"I'm home, I made it," he whispered under his breath.

"DAD, I'm home, DAD, where are you?" he shouted dropping his bag. He peered into the family room. No sign of Thomas there, or in the kitchen. He proceeded to the dining room singing out, "Hello, helloo…Daaad? I'm home," as he went.

Suddenly afraid for his father's safety, he sprinted toward the study. The door was slightly ajar. He rushed in. The chair facing the window, turned ever so slowly towards him.

"Dad? Thank God. Dad, dad… are you all right? What the—?" Carl shouted.

*****

It was a gloomy, somber day. A writer, creating an impression of the sad event would have written just such a day. The weather accentuated the tone of the tragic end. Only the classic clap of thunder was missing. The swollen clouds emptied as the rain came down in a steady drizzle. It was just enough to warrant the portable nylon shields. The picture from far above the mass of open umbrellas looked like a large black flower.

Everyone was there. Most of the massive crowd had made the journey from Capital Hill to Dallas for the funeral.

Many familiar faces could be found among the mourners. Included were Emily and Jason Cantrell, and Nancy Saunders. Even Edward Monroe was in attendance.

The graveside service had been beautiful. The priest spoke solemnly of the senseless violence surrounding us all. There was talk about guns and the tragedies they brought down on families. He prayed to God to forgive the wicked and bless the righteous. He asked the crowd to pray for the innocent that were sacrificed. Then the talk had moved on to meeting our Heavenly Father. The sermon had rejoiced in the eternity spent in God's care.

The priest said all the right things. Sniffles from the women could be heard during the address. Even some of the men dabbed their eyes. The heavy oak casket lay across straps, skirted with black material to conceal the gaping hole beneath it.

Marking the end of the ceremony the priest said in conclusion, "God be with you all," as he made the sign of the cross.

As people left the gravesite, some shook his hand. Most were not able to speak. Others tried to express the inexpressible, as they offered their condolences. *"I'm so sorry for your loss...Such a tragedy... Please call me,"* they went on.

*****

The drizzle had stopped abruptly. Suddenly the sun seemed to have no trouble making its presence known, breaking through the few remaining clouds.

Finally, he was alone, more alone than he'd ever felt. Everyone was gone, with the exception of one black limousine. The driver got out of the car and opened the rear door. A woman stepped out.

An attendant stood dutifully off to the side of the coffin, waiting patiently for a signal. The woman quietly approached. Looking in the direction of the funeral assistant, he gave a curt nod. Lowering his eyes in respect, the funeral director moved next to the coffin and flicked the concealed switch. Methodically, the flower-covered casket began its slow decent into the ground. The woman arrived, and took her place beside him just as the motor began a quiet, steady whirring sound. She gently placed her hand on his shoulder. Both stood silently as the beautiful oak container dropped out of sight forever to its final resting place. Finally she spoke, her voice cracked with emotion. “Sir, you’ve made the ultimate sacrifice, for your country. God bless you.”

He almost collapsed into Nancy Saunders’ open arms. As she comforted him, Senator Thomas Phoenix wept openly.

Epilogue

Sitting in the overstuffed, high-backed chair, he waited. Eric doubted that this was what his grandmother had meant all those years ago, when she had said to a small boy, *'Someday you may have a chance to do something great for America.'*

He had lost the desire to protect the American way of life. The carnage that he, his mentor Vargo, and his nemesis Nakamura had left in their wake was more than he could bear. He stared intently at his reflected image in the window. For the past thirty years his was not a typical existence. He was *'death and destruction'* under a different guise. In that moment, he decided this would be his last assignment. The end of his life had to be a gentler time.

The slamming of the front door broke his trance. Instinctively his grip tightened on the pistol in his lap, the silencer jutting out menacingly. Moments later, Carl's reflection appeared in the large window behind Thomas Phoenix's desk. Slowly, Eric turned the chair. Suddenly the youth became aware that the man in his father's chair *was not his father*.

Carl raised his voice, demanding to know about what had been done with his father and where he was.

Eric's voice, barely a whisper, simply responded, *"I'm so sorry, Carl."*

With lightening speed, Eric leveled the revolver and squeezed off two rounds. The first *'psssst'* emanating from the barrel of the silencer resulted in a small hole in Carl's forehead. The second bullet plowed through the left ventricle of his heart, immediately stopping the rhythmic beating. Carl never knew what hit him. At least that was what Eric had hoped.

*****

The call placed by Thomas Phoenix earlier that day to Nancy Saunders revealed the source of the leak. The same call set into motion a series of events that would permanently seal Carl's fate. Eric realized that a dedication as tremendous as Thomas Phoenix's was one he no longer possessed, or wished too. Eric stood for a moment over the young man's body. Tears welled in his eyes, then spilled, running down his cheeks.

He knew that everything this boy was, the lives he'd touched and everything he was to become, was gone. Eric, too, was finished. His last duty would be to deliver the envelope, laying beside the lifeless young man, to Nancy Saunders.

Thomas Phoenix had been whisked away earlier that evening. Eric was told that he would be sedated and unconscious during the event. The next time he'd see the senator would be at the funeral. He pressed the redial button on his phone and when the voice at the other end spoke, he simply said, "Now." One hour later the clean-up crew had turned everything into the perfect crime scene.

*****

Months had past since the news of a senseless home invasion in Texas had hit the airwaves and papers. During the break-in, the son of Senator Thomas Phoenix had been murdered, in his sovereign state. Even the homeless had heard the rumors. Most couldn't have cared less; all but a few.

Marc knew that there had been no burglary, just the murder of a kind, young man. An optimist like Dr. Blake Edwards, Carl Phoenix felt responsible. He wanted to make things better.

He thought of Carl often, of his good and generous nature and his idealistic and naive view of how the world worked. Marc had decided that after Carl's death, he would leave D.C. and stop hiding in the underbelly of humanity. If they caught him, so be it.

He'd waited, waited until Ryan mended. The fat, chocolate-eating woman had been only partially correct. Clive's blade had perforated Ryan's bowel and she had been rushed away for emergency surgery. The comment overheard that night by the fat woman was, '*she almost died.*'

When he'd went back the next day to ask about paying for a casket, the kind nurse had informed him that Ryan was recovering nicely. Released four weeks later, she'd spent eight more weeks in a rehab program. Marc had found a reason to go on. Ryan needed him. For the first time in many years, Marc had a renewed sense of purpose. Determined to make a new life, they had taken Carl's five thousand dollar parting gift and boarded a Greyhound to Florida. With his education, Marc soon found work in a clinic for the homeless.

Often, when the skies are clear and he's alone, Marc's moist eyes look toward the heavens. Anyone who cared to listen would hear him whisper two words; 'Thanks, kid.'

THE END

From the Author

I felt that a note from the writer of this novel should be included at the end of this book. The story is in no way meant to diminish the great efforts by all the wonderful people who work day after day in the quest for the elusive cure to this terrible disease. Nor is it intended to minimize the care and labors of those working to make the many who are sick and hospitalized trying, often without hope, to survive, or at the very least to pass on, with a semblance of comfort and dignity. To those people, I salute your endeavors and am truly grateful that such people choose a vocation of offering hope and comfort to the ailing.

Elixir is not meant to persuade, convince, or sanction such a theory. It is intended to engage and entertain. At the end of *Elixir*, maybe some will just say…maybe. Maybe there has been a cover-up, a conspiracy.

Patrick A. Pipoli